SUPERMAGE

RISE TO OMNISCIENCE

BOOK ONE

Aaron
Oster

For my wonderful brother and his wonderful wife, without whom this book would have not have been as great.

Ribbit.

1

Morgan arose to sunlight streaming in through the many cracks of the dilapidated shed he called home. He blinked a few times, shielding his eyes from the bothersome rays and groaning in protest.

Why did the sun have to be so bright? Couldn't it let him sleep for just a few more minutes?

Finally, admitting defeat, he threw off the threadbare blanket and rolled off of the lumpy pile of rags he used as a bed. He shivered, as his bare feet touched the stone floor. Quickly; he made his way to the other side of the small room, where a basin of cold water lay. Steeling himself, he plunged his entire head into the basin; clearing any lingering sleep from his mind.

He quickly dried his hair, then he slipped a tattered shirt over his head and slid his feet into a pair of shoes that had definitely seen better days.

He then moved to stand in front of the cracked mirror, rubbing his slightly bloodshot eyes as he examined his features. He stood at just over five and a half feet tall, which was a bit short for his age. Bright silver eyes peeked out from under a mop of brown hair that hung down to his shoulders. A small scar ran from his lip to his chin, where a city guard had smashed him with the haft of a spear. He had a light complexion and his cheeks were slightly sunken from years of malnourishment.

No one in City Four liked orphans. For some reason, they hated him most of all.

Morgan was only a few weeks away from his sixteenth birthday, but had yet to awaken an ability, which was almost unheard of at his age. By now he should already have joined the awoken, by developing either a super or mage ability. There were of course late bloomers, but those were rare, and none of them developed an ability past the age of sixteen.

He might just have to resign himself to being an even bigger freak than everyone already thought he was and stop dreaming of becoming something more.

Morgan snorted and walked away from the mirror.

He was meeting Sarah soon, which meant he would eat well today. Just the thought of eating fresh food, as opposed to the half-rotting garbage he was used to eating, made his sour mood evaporate instantly. He headed to the door, then turned to look around his hovel, making sure that he hadn't forgotten anything. Then, peering through a crack in the door, he quickly let himself out into the muddy alley.

He closed the door behind him and hung a dirt covered cloth in front of it; effectively camouflaging the door. He double-checked to make sure that none of the door was visible.

He'd kept this place a secret for over a year and didn't want to risk being found out by another beggar, or worse- the city guard.

Nodding to himself, he quickly made his way out of the alley and into the bustling crowd. He walked with slumped shoulders and made sure not to jostle anyone as he moved. Attracting any attention was the last thing he wanted.

Staying with the crowd, he moved through the wide streets of City Four and made his way toward the center of the city.

He took a chance and looked up at the sky so he could get a better idea of what time it was. It was nearly noon, and he was supposed to meet Sarah nearly twenty minutes ago.

He could feel a cold sweat break out on his back as he thought of how angry she likely already was. He'd better hurry.

Sarah was a mage, and a prodigy by all accounts. The last time he'd been late she'd encased his legs in ice and doused him with freezing water until he'd promised never to be late again. That thought alone was enough to make him speed up his pace. He accidentally jostled a few people, but luckily for him, no one seemed to take notice. He breathed a sigh of relief as the city lord's manor came into view.

He was only a little late, and he hoped Sarah wouldn't blame him too much.

Morgan quickly ducked into a side street and cautiously approached the open courtyard surrounding the manor walls.

Here goes nothing, he thought to himself. This was always the tricky part.

Sarah was the only daughter of Lord Simon, the lord in charge of City Four; and it was known that Simon despised him. In fact, he'd ordered his guards to kill Morgan if he was spotted near the manor.

Morgan wasn't worried about dying; as the guards couldn't legally kill him for just walking near the manor, no matter what Lord Simon said. But he wasn't overly fond of beatings either, and he had gotten several of those when he'd been caught in the past.

He moved to the end of the alley and crouched in the shadows as he watched a group of patrolling guards pass, then began to count under his breath. When he reached twenty, another group of guards came into view. He waited for them to pass out of sight, then made a mad dash for the wall, counting down in his head.

Fifteen, sixteen, seventeen...

Morgan began panicking, because he knew that he was nearly out of time. The clump of bushes he was running toward were still a good twenty feet away. He chanced a quick peek over his shoulder and saw the tops of spears coming around the wall. Heart pounding, he made a wild dive and just made it into the bushes as the guards were coming around the bend.

He held his breath, despite his pounding heart, as the guards marched passed. He let out an explosive breath once they were out of sight, relieved to have not been caught. He turned to the wall and began trying to loosen one of the stone blocks there, pausing every time a guard patrol passed. After about a minute, he had the block free and quickly slipped through the hole, moving the block back into place as he did so.

He looked around the grounds, thankful that guard patrols were less frequent here and ran toward the small cluster of trees near the far side of the wall.

Sarah was already there when he arrived a few moments later. Her arms were folded over her chest and a scowl was planted on her face as Morgan slipped into the secret spot that they'd cleared out years ago.

"What took you so long? I've been waiting for almost an hour!" She exclaimed.

She glared at him as he bent over, wheezing, as he tried to catch his breath.

"Overslept... Increased patrols... Almost caught..." He panted, each word caught in between breaths as he worked to slow his heartrate.

Sarah's expression softened slightly at this and she went over to the small stump to get him a glass of water.

He took it gratefully and downed it in one quick gulp. A minute or so later, he had his breathing down to a normal level and straightened up to look at her.

"Sorry I was late. I overslept and only noticed the time once I left," he said sheepishly.

"You know that excuse is getting old, right?" She asked with a mock scowl. "I don't think you've been on time once!"

"It's not my fault that it's so hard to get in here. If your father didn't hate me so much, I wouldn't have to sneak past so many guards just to visit," he replied.

He walked past her and sat down on one of the tree stumps. He grabbed a loaf of bread and ate hungrily, cramming huge chunks into his mouth. He barely chewed before taking the next bite.

Sarah watched him eat with a mixture of disgust and fascination.

"You shouldn't eat like that in front of a lady. It's very rude."

"I don't see any lady here," Morgan said.

His mouth was still full of food, so the words came out garbled and he accidentally sprayed her with breadcrumbs.

"Oh, you wound me, sir," Sarah said, as she moved her hand up to cover her mouth.

"No, I'm just getting rid of your delusions. The sooner you accept it, the better off you'll be."

Sarah pretended to swoon, and then fell dramatically to the ground. Morgan snorted a laugh, spraying the contents of his mouth everywhere.

"Fine, you win. I don't want to waste any more good food," Morgan said, as he wiped the mess away from his mouth.

He took a drink of water. He stood up, then gave her an exaggerated bow.

"Please do excuse my rudeness, Lady Sarah. You are the epitome of lady-ness. May I please kiss your feet?"

Sarah tried to keep a straight face, but her resolve lasted all of five seconds. She burst out laughing and began rolling on the ground, in a very un-ladylike manner. Morgan found himself smiling as well.

Let her laugh, he thought.

He knew it would give him more time to eat uninterrupted.

When she'd finally calmed down, Morgan held out a hand to help her to her feet. She brushed off her dress as Morgan continued stuffing his face.

"So, do you like the way I look today?" Sarah asked with a coy smile.

Morgan shrugged. She always asked him this question for some reason, though he couldn't figure out why. He glanced up at her.

She had a pale slim face with light green eyes and high cheekbones. Her long red hair was bright and lustrous, falling in waves down her back. Her lips were painted a light pink color and she wore a dark green dress that showed off her figure, without revealing too much.

Yup, same as always, he thought to himself.

"I don't know why I even bother asking!" She huffed, slumping down in her seat.

Normally, Morgan would ask her why she was mad and receive a vague answer; but today he was too distracted by his upcoming birthday and his seemingly lack of an ability.

She noticed this and the annoyed expression slipped from her face, replaced by one of concern.

"What's wrong?" She asked, as he began picking at the plate of chicken in front of him.

"I'll be sixteen in just three weeks," he said sourly, taking a piece of chicken and popping it in his mouth. "My chances of developing an ability are shrinking by the day."

Sarah leaned back in her seat and let out a long sigh. Morgan's lack of an ability had become a sore subject over their last few visits, so she had to approach this carefully.

"You still have time," she said, trying to force false cheer into her voice. "There are plenty of people who don't awaken until well into their fifteenth year."

"But no one has developed one this close to their birthday," Morgan said forlornly.

Sarah sighed, unsure of what to say. She felt sorry for Morgan. After all, they'd been friends for years and it hurt her to see him so distraught.

"Tell me again how it felt," Morgan said, breaking her out of her thoughts.

Sarah knew what he meant by that. Ever since she'd awoken her ability three years ago, Morgan had asked her about it every time they met. She'd started becoming annoyed after the fifth time he'd asked her to recount it, but eventually realized that it gave him hope. Once again, she recounted her tale.

"I was getting ready for bed on the night of my thirteenth birthday. The lights had already been turned down when I suddenly began to feel very nauseous. At first, I thought it was just a passing thing and it would wear off in a moment or two, but the nausea soon turned to pain. It wasn't long after that when I lost consciousness. When I awoke, I felt better, sharper, as though I'd been living my life in a fog and suddenly, I could see clearly. It was the most amazing feeling and the feeling only intensified when I was able to open my status for the first time."

Sarah finished her story with a wistful smile on her face and looked over to Morgan, who was pulling a chicken bone out of his mouth.

"Weren't you listening?" Sarah shouted, "After all, you were the one who asked to hear the story!"

"Keep your skirt on princess, I was listening," Morgan said, as he popped another piece of the chicken into his mouth and chewed slowly. "I can listen and eat at the same time."

Morgan reached out for the pitcher of water, but he froze when the entire contents rose out of it and began floating towards him.

"Sarah?" he asked slowly, eyeing the floating orb of water nervously.

"Yes, Morgan?" She replied, in a sickly-sweet tone as the water floated over his head.

"What are you planning to do with that water?"

Sarah pretended to think for a moment, watching him squirm as the ball of water undulated over his head.

"You know, Morgan, you are a bit stinky. I thought you could use a bath."

"Thank you for the kind offer, but I really don't think…"

Morgan was cut off as the water fell over his head. He didn't know how, but the contents of one pitcher somehow managed to soak him completely.

"Thank you for the bath," he said between clenched teeth, as he glared at her.

"You're quite welcome," she answered.

Morgan opened his mouth to retort when they heard voices nearby calling out for Sarah.

"Shit! I wasn't expecting them to come looking for me so soon," Sarah said, standing up. She moved toward the wall of foliage to peek out. She then turned back to look at Morgan, who was looking at her with a raised eyebrow.

"What? Just because I'm a Lady doesn't mean I can't curse."

"Your words, not mine," Morgan said, hiding a grin.

She made a rude gesture at him, then peeked out from between the trees once more.

"I have to go. Wait for a few minutes to sneak out. It was good to see you again, Morgan. I'll send a messenger to schedule our next meeting."

Morgan waved as Sarah pushed her way out of the clearing and disappeared. He sighed and sank back down on his tree stump.

He likely wouldn't be able to see her for at least another month and even then it would be a risk to come.

He did as he was told and waited a few minutes, taking the time to finish his chicken and pack away the rest for later. He smiled to himself as he did this. Sarah always brought extra, because she knew how hard living on the streets was for him.

Slinging the small bundle of food over his shoulder, Morgan made his way out of the clearing and ran to the spot with the loose brick. Looking up the sky, he was astounded to see that at least three hours had passed since he'd made his way in.

Had it really been that long? he wondered to himself.

It certainly hadn't felt that long.

He worked the brick out of the wall,. Then, slipping out into the bushes, he slid the block back into place. He waited for the first round of guards to pass, then started counting.

Once the second patrol passed, he made a quick dash across the open courtyard toward the safety of the alley ahead; but he'd misjudged how quickly he could run with a full stomach. He was only halfway to the alley when he began to cramp up and his speed began to flag.

Just then, a troop of guards came around the bend in the wall and immediately spotted him.

"Stop right there, Morgan!" One of them shouted.

Morgan groaned inwardly, knowing that he'd been recognized, but didn't slow down.

He wasn't stupid enough to do that.

He could hear the guards giving chase and pumped his legs even harder, shooting into the alley and taking a sharp turn.

He could hear the clanking of armor as the guards packed into the alley behind him, but he was pretty confident he could lose them. Taking a few turns, Morgan was soon back on the main road. He was having a hard time breathing again, and his head had begun pounding. He stopped running immediately, slowing to walking pace and losing himself in the crowd.

He heard the guards crash into the main road, shoving people out of the way as they looked frantically around for him. Morgan smiled to himself, despite a mounting headache, as he ducked out of the crowd and into another alley, heading towards his home.

He grimaced as a sharp pain lanced through his chest and he stumbled, nearly falling to the ground.

He must have eaten more than he thought.

He wobbled sloppily towards his home as the pain in his chest intensified. It wasn't only his chest that hurt either; his entire body felt like it was on fire and he felt like he couldn't breathe. He had to find somewhere to rest for a few minutes so he could catch his breath.

He entered the first deserted alleyway he could find and collapsed on the ground in a heap. He lay there writhing in agony as he tried to inhale, to get even a drop of air into his starving lungs. Then he blacked out.

2

Morgan came to in complete darkness. With a start, he sat bolt upright and he felt as his heart began pounding in his chest, in an unfamiliar rhythm. His head whipped from side to side as his mind tried to process what was going on. After a few panicked seconds, he slowly relaxed, leaning against the alley wall as he tried to piece together his last few hours.

He'd gone to visit Sarah… Then he'd been chased by the guards and escaped. There was that burning pain in his chest and then nothing. He didn't feel any pain now though. In fact, he felt better than ever.

Something wasn't quite right, however; he'd never felt this good before. His mind was clear, his body felt strong and he wasn't even the slightest bit hungry.

Then Sarah's recounting of her awakening flashed through his mind.

It couldn't be! Could it? He was suddenly very much aware of his surroundings.

Concentrating inward, Morgan soon felt what he'd been hoping for. A small circular mass of red energy sitting on the left side of his chest, which he instinctively knew to be chi. He realized that wasn't all he felt. There was something else; a blue sphere of energy in the same spot on his right side, which he knew to be mana.

But that was impossible- he couldn't have both chi and mana. Could he?

Even that wasn't the most shocking thing to him. The biggest surprise was that he no longer seemed to have a heart! Instead, the red sphere of chi seemed to be acting in it's place.

No wonder the process of awakening his power had been so painful!

He was now glad that he'd passed out, shuddering at the thought of staying awake through the process of having his heart replaced.

He could feel the two masses of power calling out to him and instinctively, he knew what to do next. Concentrating inward, he manipulated a tendril of both chi and mana. They fused together in his body and a light purple screen flickered into view.

Name: Morgan
Super: Rank - 0
Energy to next rank - 0/100
Mage: Rank - 0
Energy to next rank - 0/100
Super ability - Gravity
Mage ability - Air
CP - 90/90 (Regen - 0.8 per second)
MP - 90/90 (Regen - 0.8 per Second)
Strength - 8
Agility - 11
Constitution - 7
Intelligence - 9
Wisdom - 8
Super skills - Fly, Heavy handed
Mage skills - Wind blade, Tailwind

Morgan could hardly contain his excitement.

He'd been so afraid that he'd never awaken at all and now he not only did he have an ability, he had two.

Tamping down on his excitement, he focused back in on his status and began opening each tab to figure out what each stat meant.

Super/Mage: Rank - 0

The world is divided between supers and mages, who each have unique abilities and skills. Supers generally have more direct melee based abilities, while mages tend to have more ranged abilities. There are of course, a wide variety of abilities, and not all are combat oriented.

All supers/mages begin at rank 0 and can increase in rank all the way to 50. By collecting energy from the world around them, supers/mages can increase their rank.

Morgan blinked. He was very interested in ranking up and gaining more power, but how was he supposed to collect energy from the world around him?

He sighed when no further information was forthcoming and focused in on the next tab.

Super ability: Gravity
Harness the power of gravity and bend it to your will.

Mage ability: Air
Harness the wind and bend it to your will.

He groaned in frustration. What was up with these vague explanations?

He took a deep breath to calm himself and moved further down the list.

CP/MP: While mages use mana to power their skills, supers use chi (pronounced KEE) to power theirs. CP, or chi points, determine how many times you can use super skills. MP, or mana points, determine how many times you can use mage skills.

Well, at least that explanation made sense. Morgan moved further down his status page.

Strength: Determines physical strength and power of super based skills. Supers develop this attribute at twice the rate of mages.

Agility: Determines both speed and dexterity. Supers develop this attribute at twice the rate of mages.

Constitution: Determines health, endurance and how much damage can be absorbed. Both supers and mages develop this attribute at the same rate.

Intelligence: Determines intellect, how much chi/mana can be used; as well as power of mage basked skills. Mages develop this attribute at twice the rate of supers.

Wisdom: Determines learning speed, memory retention and how quickly chi/mana regenerates. Mages develop this attribute at twice the rate supers.

This all made sense to Morgan.

Supers, who were more physically inclined, would be quicker to develop strength and agility, as they helped with hand to hand combat. Mages on the other hand, mostly dealt with spells and ranged attacks, so their strength and agility wasn't as important as intelligence and wisdom.

Finally, Morgan focused on the last tab on his status.

Skills: These determine what aspects of your super/mage ability can be used.

Fly: Manipulate gravity to make yourself lighter and move through the air.
Cost - 1 CP per second
Max. height - 30 Ft
Max. speed - 20 Ft per second
Max. carry weight - 50 pounds (carrying any more weight will decrease speed by 0.1 feet per second for every additional pound)

Heavy handed: Manipulate gravity to make your blows land harder (currently X2)
Cost - 20 CP
Duration - 10 seconds

Wind blade: Manipulate the air around you to create whirling blades sharper than steel
Cost - 40 MP
Duration - Until dismissed

Tailwind: Manipulate the air around you to increase speed (Currently X2)
Cost - 20 MP
Duration - 10 seconds

Morgan closed his status as his thoughts began to race.
Those were some pretty amazing abilities!
Fly would let him, well, fly. Heavy handed would allow him to hit twice as hard, effectively doubling his strength for a full ten seconds.

Tailwind was also pretty straightforward. Just like his heavy handed ability, this would double his agility for a full ten seconds. He wasn't entirely sure what the wind blade skill could do though.

"Well, only one way to find out," he muttered to himself.

At the cost of *40 MP,* Morgan activated his *wind blade skill.* There was a sound of rushing air and Morgan's arm shot out to the side. A two foot cone of wind extended out from his arm, swirling at high speed and forming a wicked point. He swished his arm through the air a few times, but the wind didn't disperse.

It looked more like a lance than a blade and it seemed to be almost insubstantial.

Taking a step forward, Morgan stabbed the point of the blade towards the alley wall, not expecting much. Instead of dissipating, as he'd been expecting, the tip of the blade easily punched through the wall. The spinning, condensed air tore apart the brick and mortar as the blade sunk further in. Quickly dismissing the blade, he stared in awe at the gaping hole he'd just created.

So, that was what wind blade did, he thought.

He shuddered at the thought of what that would do to a human body.

He would have to experiment more later. For now, he knew that he should probably head home and get some sleep.

Morgan took a single step towards the mouth of the alley, when two figures moved in front of it; silhouetted from behind by the moonlight streaming in.

Morgan cursed silently as he recognized two of the city guards, Gimple and Sqwee. They were recent additions to the guard. They made an extremely nasty pair and were the absolute last people he'd wanted to run into in a dark alley.

3

"Well, well, well. Would you look what we've got here?" Gimple asked rhetorically, as he took a step into the alley, while sneering down at Morgan.

Gimple was a very heavy man. So heavy, in fact, that Morgan was surprised he was even allowed in the guard.

The only reason he'd be allowed in, was if he had an ability-which he was pretty sure he did.

"We've been looking all over for you, isn't that right Sqwee?" The guard asked, turning to his companion.

Sqwee was the exact opposite of Gimple. He was tall and lanky, with shallow cheeks that gave him an almost skeletal appearance.

"Well, you found me. What can I help you with?" Morgan asked,while taking a step back.

There was only one reason they were here. They were here to punish him for being seen near the manor today.

"Well you see," Sqwee began. "Lord Simon has had enough of you hanging around his daughter."

"We're here to make sure that you don't ever do that again." Gimple said, pulling a knife from his belt.

Morgan felt his blood run cold, as he saw the moonlight reflect off the blade.

"Wait, you can't kill me! It's against the law for a city guard to kill someone for no reason!"

It was only then that he realized they were both out of uniform.

This was planned!

Lord Simon had been trying to have him killed for some time and finally two men were willing to do so.

Morgan clenched his teeth as they continued to move towards him.

He knew he had an advantage. They were expecting to kill an unarmed and defenseless teenager. They had no idea that he had an ability and were approaching carelessly.

He took a moment to size up their threat level.

Judging by his appearance, Sqwee was a mage, while Gimple was most likely a super. That meant that Sqwee was the biggest threat at the moment as he would have range.

"Don't make this harder than it has to be, Morgan," Gimple said as his expression hardened. "Just stand there, and don't move. It'll be over before you know it!"

He launched toward Morgan, knife poised to strike, but Morgan had already begun to move.

Activating *tailwind,* he deftly dodged the knife strike and ran toward Sqwee. He felt light as a feather as the air swirled around him and massively increased his speed. He didn't have time to activate another ability, so he used his forward momentum and threw a heavy punch into the man's stomach.

There was a sound of crunching bones and Sqwee howled in pain as his ribs were shattered. Morgan followed up his attack by grabbing the back of Sqwee's head and bringing his knee up. With a loud crunching sound, his skull caved in and the guard went silent.

Morgan felt a rush of power enter him as Sqwee's lifeless body hit the ground with an audible squelch. Then he turned to face Gimple, who was staring at Sqwee's body in dumbfounded shock.

"How did you…?"

Gimple was cut off as Morgan's fist crashed into his face, but the devastating attack that had just killed Sqwee didn't have nearly the same effect on Gimple.

He stumbled back a few steps, rubbing his cheek as an angry bruise began spreading from the point of impact.

"So, you went ahead and got yourself an ability," Gimple said, taking a step forward and flexing his fingers. "It's too bad for you that you're so weak!"

His voice picked up in volume as the air around his fists began to glow red.

"What are you? *Rank 0*? 1 at most," he laughed maniacally, as he took a step towards the stunned Morgan. "Well, guess what you little bastard? I'm at *rank 4*, and my *constitution* is much higher than your pitiful *strength* can hope to match!"

He lunged forward, throwing a wild punch, which Morgan barely managed to avoid. Gimple's fist connected with the alley wall and Morgan gulped as the solid stone shattered under the blow.

Morgan cursed silently as Gimple turned to face him.

This was not good. Supers relied on strength to damage their opponents and if he couldn't hurt Gimple, then it was only a matter of time until he was caught.

He debated using his *wind blade,* but ultimately decided that he didn't yet have the stomach to use it on a human being.

"You can't keep this up forever Morgan," Gimple said, this time approaching slowly.

Morgan took a step backward and felt his back hit the alley wall. He hadn't noticed before, but Gimple had been backing him into a corner. It looked like the fat slob had more brains than he'd given him credit for.

He could always use fly to escape, but then there would be a witness to go back and tell Lord Simon; and when he sent men after him the next time, he wouldn't stand a chance.

A nasty smile curled Gimple's lips, as he pulled his fist back to deliver the finishing blow.

It was then that Morgan made his move. Activating his *heavy handed* skill, Morgan felt strength flood his body in a rush. The air around him warped slightly as gravity distorted and a countdown began in his head.

Morgan snapped his left arm up, wincing in pain as he deflected the incoming blow. Then his right arm snapped forward, catching the overconfident Gimple with a stiff punch to the ribs. This time however, Gimple couldn't simply shrug it off. There was a loud crack as Morgan's fist connected and the pudgy guard stumbled back with a gasp of pain, clutching at his side.

Gimple whimpered as Morgan walked slowly towards him, a hard expression on his face. That was when the begging began.

"Morgan, buddy, we never really meant to kill you, we were just joking," Gimple tried, as Morgan continued moving toward him.

Morgan stopped just three feet before the man and raised an eyebrow. "Is that so?" He asked in a flat voice. "You weren't just trying to kill me?"

"No, not at all!" Gimple said, straightening to his full height. "We were just gonna rough you up a little, but we were gonna let you go. Honest."

Morgan could see the guard subtly shifting his stance, likely in preparation of some sort of attack.

It was then that the timer on Morgan's *heavy handed* skill ran out and the distorted air around him vanished. Gimple's arms shot out and grabbed Morgan by his shoulders, a nasty smile on his face.

"You stupid boy. Of course we meant to kill you! It looks like your little skill has run out. You should have run when you had the chance!"

Morgan's expression didn't change at all as he activated *heavy handed* once more. Then he twisted smoothly in Gimple's grip and punched a hole straight through the man's chest.

The guard stared down in horror as Morgan ripped his arm free, leaving a gaping hole where his chi-heart used to be. He took a step forward, reaching a hand out toward Morgan, then he collapsed face-first in a pool of spreading blood.

A rush of power entered Morgan as the guard died. He felt a tingling sensation run through his entire body, washing away his fatigue.

He felt stronger and healthier than before, and he was sure he'd just ranked up.

Opening his status, he couldn't help but grin.

Name: Morgan
Super: Rank - 1
Energy to next rank - 149/300
Mage: Rank - 1
Energy to next rank - 77/300
Super ability - Gravity
Mage ability - Air
CP - 110/110 (Regen - 1.1 per second)
MP - 110/110 (Regen - 1.1 per Second)
Strength - 10
Agility - 13
Constitution - 9
Intelligence - 11
Wisdom - 10
Super skills - Fly, Heavy handed
Mage skills - Wind blade, Tailwind

Well, at least he now knew one way to rank *up*.

He did notice that more energy had gone towards his super ability than his mage ability.

This could be for one of three reasons: either Gimple was higher ranked than Sqwee, he'd used one ability more than the other, or destroying the chi-heart had somehow given him more.

He closed his status and looked around at the now blood drenched alley.

He'd just killed two men, but strangely enough, he didn't feel anything. Even when he'd shoved his arm through Gimple's chest, he'd been more fascinated with his strength, than the man dying before him. Maybe he would use his wind blade ability next time.

Morgan shook himself out of his musings.

This was no time to be standing around. Even if no one had heard the fight, he was clearly no longer safe in the city if Lord Simon had sent these men to kill him. He had to leave.

He quickly bent down near Gimple's body. After a moment of searching, he came away with a slightly bloody coin pouch. Moving on to Sqwee, he found a similar pouch. Taking a quick peek inside, he was delighted to see the glittering of gold, and not the dull copper or bronze.

Morgan couldn't help but notice that they were both uncommonly heavy for mere guards.

Likely a bribe from that bastard Simon, he thought.

A grim smile touched his lips as he thought about the smug city lord, sitting in his fancy manor and waiting for news of his death. He stood, dusted off his pants, and wrinkled his nose at the putrid stench the two bodies were already giving off.

He would need to find a change of clothes. His were covered in blood and gore.

Taking one last look at the two guards, he turned and ran from the alley.

4

Morgan tore through the darkened streets of City Four, the wind whistling around him as he ran.

He'd tried activating *fly* together with *tailwind,* but nothing happened.

He assumed that he couldn't use mana and chi at the same time. He was sure he'd be able to in the future, as he used both when opening his status. It also didn't escape his notice that his status page was purple, a mix of red chi and blue mana.

For now, it would probably be safer to move on foot. It was a clear night and he didn't want any guards to spot a flying boy.

He did have to slow down whenever his timer ran out, though, as his regen wasn't high enough to keep up with the *CP* cost.

Just a few more ranks and he'd be able to keep his skills going indefinitely.

At first, Morgan wanted to leave the city right away, not even taking the time to stop by his hovel to collect his few belongings. After a few minutes of running, he decided to say goodbye to Sarah. After all, she was his only friend and deserved a proper farewell.

As he approached the square where the Lord's manor was located, Morgan slowed down, allowing his skill to run out.

He then waited five seconds, the minimum amount of time he'd found was required when switching between mana and chi, then activated *fly.*

A feeling of weightlessness overtook him as Morgan rose slowly into the air. He felt the drain on his chi immediately after activating the skill, but his regen kicked in just a second later and refilled his chi bar.

He floated up to the maximum height that his skill would allow, then moved slowly forward. He could see the city sprawled out before him, illuminated by moonlight. He felt giddy as he glided smoothly over the empty courtyard. His clothes flapped lightly in the wind and he took a deep breath, enjoying the feeling of freedom the skill gave him.

He was tempted to increase his speed- to fly as quickly as he could and feel the rush of wind on his face; but he held himself back.

He had to be careful not to attract attention while still in the city.

He passed over the manor wall and flew around to the side, where he knew Sarah's room was located. After a few seconds of looking, he finally spotted the correct window and was pleased to see the light of a flickering lantern coming through the shutters.

Good, he thought. *She's still awake.*

Gliding up to the window, Morgan knocked on the wooden slats covering the glass. When no one answered, he knocked again; this time louder

The shutters banged open so suddenly that Morgan reeled back in shock. Sarah stood there, dressed in a nightgown. A massive spear made of ice poised in the air above her.

"Sarah, wait! It's me," Morgan said quickly, as she pulled her arm back to send the spike through him.

"Morgan?" Her voice was soft and it sounded as though she'd been crying.

Flying forward, Morgan could see that her eyes were indeed puffy and red.

"What happened?" He asked, hovering right in front of the open window.

She lunged forward, wrapping her arms around him and sobbed into his shoulder.

"This entire night has been a nightmare! Father said that he'd had enough of you, and sent out guards to get rid of you for good!"

Morgan floated there, awkwardly patting her back as she cried.

He really wasn't good with emotions.

Deciding that it was best to talk inside, he slowly floated into her room and landed on the floor. After another minute of crying, Sarah finally pulled back and wiped her eyes. Holding him at arm's length, her eyes widened as she got a good look at him.

"You're covered in blood."

"Well, your father did send two of his cronies to kill me. I wasn't about to let them," Morgan said with a shrug. "They weren't expecting me to put up a fight though."

Sarah laughed. "I can see that. You finally got an ability?"

"Two, actually," Morgan said, trying to sound nonchalant about it.

"Two?! Wow, that's really rare! So do you have a super or mage ability? And which two do you have?"

Sarah's excitement bubbled over, and Morgan could hardly believe she'd been crying just a minute ago.

"I have… Um, both. I guess," Morgan said.

Sarah's expression changed from excitement to annoyance. "Yes, you already told me you have two abilities. Which two do you have, though?"

Morgan shrank slightly under her withering stare. It was never good to get on her bad side.

"I meant that I have both a mage ability, and a super ability," Morgan said.

Sarah's mouth dropped open. She stared at him, and he began to squirm in discomfort.

"You're a supermage!" She exclaimed.

"A what?"

"A supermage," she said, annunciating each syllable as if he hadn't heard her. "You know, someone who has both a super and mage ability; wielders of tremendous power and only heard of in myths?"

"No," Morgan said, confused.

He had no idea what she was talking about. He'd never even heard of this supermage ability.

"Of course you wouldn't know," She said, rubbing her temples for a few seconds.

She then turned her back to him and moved towards her dresser, pulling the drawers open as she began to pack her things into a bag.

"Um, Sarah?" Morgan asked, now very confused as to what was happening. "What are you doing?"

She turned to look at him as she shoved a pair of leggings into her bag.

"Isn't it obvious? I'm packing," she said, bending down and piling a few books onto her bed.

"Yes, I can see that," he said, "but *why* are you packing?"

She didn't even bother looking at him this time.

"I'm coming with you. Isn't it obvious?" She asked, stuffing the last of her belongings into the bag. "There, that should be everything. Now just give me a moment to change, and we'll be on our way."

"I just came to say goodbye. I didn't want you to come with me!" Morgan exclaimed.

"So what you're saying is that you don't want me along?" Sarah asked, turning to look at him, with a hurt expression.

"No, that's not what I mean at all!"

"Great," she said, the smile returning to her face. "Just give me a minute and we'll be on our way."

Sarah walked behind a partition to change, and Morgan sank down onto her bed, not knowing exactly what had just happened.

He did know one thing: she'd just played him, but he wasn't sure how.

Five minutes later, Sarah emerged. She was dressed in a long sleeved top, tight fitting pants and thick leather boots, with her long red hair tied back in a braid. She hoisted her pack over her shoulder.

Morgan had never seen her wearing anything but a dress, but this somehow seemed to suit her better than any dress ever could.

"You ready to go?" she asked, giving him a victorious smile.

Morgan didn't smile back. "Tell me why."

"Why what?" she asked, trying to evade the question.

He just stared at her, folding his arms and waiting. She stared back at him for a few long seconds. Morgan was beginning to wonder if they'd be here all night, when she let out a long sigh and dropped her pack to the ground.

"My parents never cared much for me. Ever since I got my ability, I've wanted to train and hone my skills; but all they want is a proper lady."

Her expression turned bitter and she let out a snort of derision.

"My father is planning to ship me off to the capital, where he's hoping to marry me off to one of the king's sons."

She looked up at him with a steely expression.

"There's no way in hell that I'm going along with that. So, you either take me with you, or I'll leave on my own!"

Morgan was taken aback at her vehemence, but he understood her well enough. His life had been made miserable by Simon as well, and if he could ruin his plans while helping his friend… Well, this worked just fine for him.

"Fine, I'll take you with me; but tell me about this supermage thing you mentioned before we go."

Sarah bent down to retrieve her bag and slung it over her shoulder once more.

"It's a very long topic, so I'll give you the abbreviated version. Otherwise, we'll be here all night. Supermages are supposed to be a myth, but I know that there are a few scattered throughout the kingdoms. I also know that you need to keep your abilities a secret, otherwise you'll be hunted down and killed. Kings don't like threats to their power. As a supermage, you pose a very significant one."

Morgan scowled.

Of course things couldn't be easy. On the bright side, he had a rare ability. He couldn't use his super and mage skills at the same time, so he wasn't really sure about this whole supermage thing. For now, they had to leave.

"Is there anywhere safe we can go?" he asked.

"There's nowhere that is truly safe, but our best bet is the Central Kingdom. They are the only neutral spot in all the Five Kingdoms. There is a school there for mages and supers, and it's likely the best spot you can go to learn more about your abilities. I've always wanted to go, but my parents refused to send me."

Morgan felt his heart skip a beat.

A school where he could learn about his abilities? He hadn't even known one existed.

A frown creased the corners of his mouth.

"I don't think I have enough money for a school like that."

"The king of the Central Kingdom, Herald, sponsors plenty of people. Even if he didn't, I have plenty of money," she said, as she pulled a coin pouch from her bag and jangled it at him.

A smile spread across his face. He felt his excitement grow at the prospect of learning more about his abilities.

"Alright. I just have one more question before we go."

"Oh, and what might that be?" Sarah asked, as Morgan placed one foot on the windowsill.

"How much do you weigh?"

5

Morgan winced at the throbbing pain in his cheek. Sarah had not responded well to the question about her weight, and the explanation about needing to know for his *fly* skill didn't seem to mollify her.

Sarah was riding on his back, her arms wrapped around his neck and her legs draped down either side of him. He'd been a little nervous when they'd cleared the city walls, but the guards appeared to be half asleep and hadn't noticed them.

Once they were outside of the city, Sarah began questioning him about his abilities; what his stats were, what skills he had and how he could use them in a fight. Morgan answered all of her questions, not wanting to be hit again for saying the wrong thing.

"Your stats are much higher than they should be," she said, when Morgan finished speaking. "But then again, you do have two abilities. Maybe that's normal."

"That makes sense," Morgan replied.

If supers had a bonus to strength and agility, mages had one for intelligence and wisdom; he'd have all four.

They flew on in silence as the night wore on. Morgan began to grow bored. They weren't moving that fast. According to Morgan's *fly* skill, they were moving at just about 12.5 feet per second. Morgan did some quick math in his head.

If Sarah's pack weighed about ten pounds, he thought, *that would mean that she weighed around one hundred and fifteen pounds.*

Morgan had no idea why she didn't just tell him. He was about to open his mouth to say something, when he thought better of it. Thinking back to the terrifying look on her face when he'd asked the first time was enough to convince him to keep his mouth shut.

They flew until the sun began peeking over the horizon. Morgan was so tired at this point that he could barely keep his eyes open. In fact, he'd nearly fallen out of the sky. Twice. Sarah, on the other hand, had managed to fall asleep at some point. Morgan thought longingly of his bed back in City Four.

It was too dark to see much when he'd been flying during the night, but Morgan could now make out a long, winding road some twenty feet below. Scraggly bushes grew in clumps on the side of the road and all he could see in any direction were wide open rocky plains.

The North Kingdom truly is a desolate place, he mused.

Yawning, he began scanning the plains for a place to rest. He finally spotted a good place to make camp about half and hour later. There was small outcropping of rock, with a clump of bushes growing around it, set some forty feet back from the road. He could see a small stream flowing nearby and the thought of a cool drink consumed him.

As his feet touched the ground, Sarah stirred and woke up.

"Is it morning already?" She mumbled.

Morgan set her down on the ground and walked over to drink from the stream.

"Yes and after I get a drink, I'm going to sleep."

"Okay," Sarah mumbled, stumbling over to a mossy section of ground near the outcropping and lying down.

Morgan stooped near the stream, cupping his hands and dipping them in. It was only then that he noticed his arm was still covered in blood. It had dried since his fight in the alley and was now a dark brownish color.

Sighing at the inconvenience, Morgan quickly stripped out of his shirt. Shivering in the cool morning air, he proceeded to wash himself as best he could. He then dunked the shirt in as well. He watched as the water became cloudy with the accumulated filth.

He wrung his shirt out while he waited for the stream to carry all the filth away, then leaned down to take a drink. The cool water felt amazing flowing down his throat. He drank deeply until his thirst was quenched.

He picked his shirt up when he finished. Still wet, he decided to leave it off and let it dry. Then, walking back to the outcropping, he lay down with a groan of pleasure, stretching out on the soft moss. Within a few seconds, he was fast asleep.

***

Lord Simon stared at the guard standing nervously before him. Despite the dire situation at hand, it still gave him pleasure to see the lowly peasant quaking in fear.

This was undoubtedly a shit storm, he thought.

Both of the guards he'd sent after Morgan were found dead this morning. From the reports coming in, their deaths hadn't been pleasant, either. One's skull was caved in, and the other had a gaping hole through his chest. There was also a massive hole in the wall of the alley that their bodies had been found in. Furthermore, his daughter was missing and the sniveling bastard was nowhere to be seen.

Simon felt the pleasure of the guard's discomfort quickly turn to anger.

There was only one explanation for this, he thought. *Sarah had somehow gotten out last night to go warn that little mongrel. When the guards showed up, she must have killed them to protect him. Then he'd somehow convinced her to leave the city with him.*

He slammed his fist down on his desk. He heard a cracking sound and knew it would have to be replaced.

I'd finally found two people willing to kill that little shit and Sara just had to get in the way! That stupid boy had been corrupting her for years, ruining all of my plans for her and now she'd left with him. Maybe Morgan had killed them, then come to the manor to get her?

Simon shook his head, dismissing the possibility.

Morgan had no abilities that he knew of. Even if he had awakened since the last time he'd checked, there was no way he could kill a rank 4 super and a rank 3 mage on his own.

Sarah, despite how much he despised the idea, was more than capable of such a feat. The more he thought about it, the more sense it made.

She must have crushed Sqwee's head in a chunk of ice, then speared Gimple through the chest and created that hole in the alley wall.

Simon nodded to himself.

That explanation made the most sense.

He looked up in surprise as someone cleared their throat. The guard was still standing there, looking decidedly more nervous than before.

He'd completely forgotten that he was still there.

"Do you know in which direction they were headed?"

The guard nodded. "There was no trail to follow, but we found someone in the city who can track someone by their clothes. It isn't exact, but we do know the general direction in which they're heading."

Finally, some good news, he thought.

"We believe that they are heading south, toward City Six."

Simon leaned back in his chair, his mind whirling with possibilities.

City Six was at least two hundred miles away. If they were on foot, then he knew they couldn't have gotten far.

"I want you to send a squad after them, with at least two *rank* 6 mages. I want my daughter back unharmed. Make sure to bring Morgan back alive."

"As you wish, my Lord"

The guard saluted, then scurried out of the room to pass along his orders.

Simon felt a smile tugging at the corners of his mouth.

They would be brought back, and this time, he would kill Morgan himself.

6

Morgan groaned as he felt something hard prod him in the ribs. He waved his arm at the offending object, trying to shove it away.

He felt the object poke him again, harder this time. "Morgan, wake up!"

"Just lemme sleep a little more," he groaned, turning away from the insistent prodding.

"Wake up, you moron," the voice hissed, prodding him much harder the third time.

Morgan cracked his eyes open, blinking at the bright sunlight overhead. He turned and glared blearily up at Sarah, who was preparing to kick him again.

"I'm up! What's the big idea?" he groaned.

Judging by the sun's position, it was just past noon. Meaning that he'd only gotten around five hours of sleep.

"Quiet you idiot," she said in a hushed tone, moving towards the tip of the outcropping and peering out over it.

That got Morgan's attention, instantly clearing the fog of sleep from his mind. Now that he listened, he could vaguely make out the sound of hoof beats echoing over the rocky plains.

Morgan got carefully to his feet, wincing as his cramped muscles screamed in protest. He grabbed his now dry shirt, pulling it on before coming to crouch near her.

"How far away do you think they are?" he asked quietly.

He could make out the road from where they were crouched, but as far as he could see, it was completely empty. Sound carried for long distances out here, so they could still be miles away.

"I'm not sure," she said, biting her lower lip.

She looked worried- and for good reason. Neither of them had expected a pursuit to catch them this quickly.

"How did they find us?" Morgan asked. "We didn't leave a trail or anything like that."

"There are other ways of tracking people, aside from following a trail," Sarah sighed. "I should have thought of that and kept us moving."

"I don't think I could have kept us moving, even if you wanted me to," Morgan said, yawning again.

He rubbed at his eyes.

"Yeah, you're probably right," she agreed.

Sarah started moving to her pack. She began to rummage through it.

"So what should we do?" Morgan asked, not taking his eyes off the road.

The clatter of hoof beats were growing louder by the second.

"It's no use running," she said, as she pulled a small loaf of bread from her pack and tossed it over to him.

"If they have a tracker, there's no way we'll lose them. Plus, they can move much faster on horseback than you can through the air."

Morgan caught the loaf, nodding his thanks as he took a bite out of it. It was a bit stale, but still way better than what he was used to.

"So do we fight?" He asked, barely audible through a mouthful of bread.

"We have no choice," Sarah answered, "though it won't be an easy one. Knowing my father, he likely sent out people strong enough to bring me back. Meaning that we'll be facing people at least the same rank as me."

"And what exactly is your rank?" Morgan asked, swallowing a chunk of bread.

Sarah debated for a moment before letting out a sigh.

"I may as well tell you, seeing as you told me about yours. It's only right. I'm a *rank 6* mage and my ability is called *freezing water*. I have three skills, *icicle spear, condense water* and *frostbite*. *Icicle spear* allows me to launch spears made of ice, *condense water* allows me to control water and gives me the ability to freeze it; and *frostbite* allows me to freeze the water in the air around a specific target to reduce their speed by 30 percent. I also have my mage shield, so I can take quite a bit of punishment."

Morgan was shocked to hear that.

He'd known Sarah was powerful, but rank 6 at her age? Gimple and Sqwee were at least in their twenties, and they had had lower ranks than her.

"What's a mage shield?" Morgan asked.

He could now clearly make out the sound of hoof beats and even distant voices. They had a few more minutes at most.

In response, a blue glow suddenly emanated from Sarah, completely coating her skin.

"What exactly are the benefits of this thing?" He asked, walking over and prodding her arm.

It felt slippery and springy.

She swatted his hand away and allowed the shield to fade.

"A mage shield is an additional layer of defense that mages can conjure by manipulating their mana. Despite our *constitution* growing at the same rate as supers, a mage's skin just isn't as durable, so we have a shield to make up for it."

"How can I conjure one of my own?" Morgan asked, excitedly.

If he could use a mage shield, then his defense would be twice as strong!

"I'll explain later. It'll take some time and we don't exactly have any right now," Sarah said, pointing out toward the road.

Morgan turned and saw a small line of black specs growing larger by the second.

They were here a lot sooner than he'd thought they would be.

"What's the best way to break through a mage shield?"

"Either hit it hard enough, or use a skill that has a lot of penetrating power. I would recommend using your *wind blade* in this fight. If any of them are at *rank 6* or above, their *constitution* will likely be high enough to counter your *heavy handed* skill."

He nodded and turned back to watch the approaching force. He could now make them out clearly. There were six men dressed in uniform of the city guard and a seventh wearing regular clothes.

That must be the tracker, he realized.

As he watched, the man's head swiveled in their direction and he pointed towards their hiding spot.

"Looks like they've found us," Morgan said, turning to Sarah. "So what's the plan?"

Sarah, looking noticeably more pale now, swallowed nervously.

"We let them approach and wait for them to dismount. They likely have orders to bring us both back alive and they may not yet know of your abilities. Once they start talking, I'll single out the strongest person in the group. Take him out first and we'll go from there."

Morgan grunted as the riders turned their horses off the road and approached at a trot.

"Not much of a plan."

"It's the best we've got," she responded.

Morgan watched as the group of soldiers approached their hiding spot, but stopped about twenty feet from the outcropping.

"We know you're in there," the man in the lead called out. "Come on out Lady Sarah, your father sent us to fetch you."

Sarah walked past him and out into the open, her hands raised in front of her. Morgan followed behind, hands raised as well, as he took in the soldiers before him.

As they dismounted, Morgan could see the telltale blue glow of a mage shield surrounding four of the men.

It looked like they weren't taking any chances.

The other two had no shield, meaning they were likely supers. It didn't escape his notice that the seventh man in the group did not dismount. He, in fact, had stayed on the road, a good forty feet away from them and looked ready to bolt at the first sign of a fight.

Sarah stopped a few feet away from the lead soldier. Morgan stopped beside her.

"Lady Sarah," the man started, taking a step forward and holding his arms out to the side. He had a cocky smile on his face and a blue mage shield surrounding his body. "It's so good to see you. Your father is most worried about you."

The man was squat and bulky, with black hair and beady eyes. He looked every bit like a person who got what he wanted by bullying those weaker than him.

"Hicks, you lowlife piece of shit," Sarah responded in a flat tone, "of course my father would send you."

She turned slowly and examined the mage standing right behind him. "And it would appear he's sent Malcom as well."

"Lady Sarah! Such vulgar language is unbecoming of a Lady of nobility." Hicks feigned a shocked expression. "Clearly being around this filth has corrupted you, but do not fear. We have explicit orders to bring him back alive, so your father can give him the punishment he deserves."

Morgan saw Sarah tip her head ever so slightly towards the two people she'd named.

So they must be the biggest threats at the moment.

"I'm sure he will," Sarah said, as a half smile formed on her lips. "But tell me something, you, pompous turd, how many of you will die before you can subdue me?"

At those words, all the soldiers tensed and the few that were carrying weapons reached for them. Hicks didn't look worried at all.

"I would prefer it if you'd just come quietly, my Lady," he said. He looked at his fingernails as if bored. "After all, it's six against one and we have orders not to hurt you."

That was when Morgan acted. In his mind, the idiot was asking for it by dropping his guard that much in a hostile environment.

He activated *wind blade* and *tailwind* simultaneously, then dashed forward. He covered the few feet between them in an instant and thrust the blade toward Hicks. The whirling blade impacted the mage shield with a loud shriek and was halted in place.

Hicks sneered down at him as the attack was seemingly repelled.

"Did you really think that such weak attack…" he started.

There was a sound like shattering glass and the spinning blade punched a hole straight through the shield. The whirling lance of air tore into his chest, tearing it to bloody chunks before emerging out of his back.

7

Everyone stared in shock as Hicks' body hit the ground. Everyone - except for Morgan - who took the opportunity to dart forward and bury the spinning cone of air into another mage's chest.

This one was much weaker and there was almost no resistance. He spun quickly and activated *wind blade* again, sweeping his other arm in an arc toward a third mage.

The new blade destroyed the man's head in a shower of gore. His body fell to the ground as well. He knew surprise would only get him so far and Morgan was forced to jump back, barely avoiding a sword strike aimed for his neck.

He felt his *tailwind* skill run out and took a moment to take stock of their situation.

Three mages were down, including the most dangerous one and Sarah was fighting against Malcom.

That left him with the unpleasant task of taking on two supers alone.

He felt a tingling sensation throughout his body. As the two men approached, he tried his best to ignore the pleasant sensation of ranking up. They were moving cautiously; now well aware of the danger he posed.

Good.

He knew that they would now think twice about rushing in to overwhelm him.

The one with a sword came in and swung at his head, attempting to decapitate him. Morgan dodged back, while activating *tailwind.* He then darted forward and attempted to skewer the man the same way as the mages, but they were apparently waiting for this. One of them stomped his foot and a shockwave went through the ground.

Morgan felt his speed drastically slow down as the solid stone turned to mud under his feet. The other guard lunged forward with his sword once more and this time, Morgan wasn't quick enough to dodge.

He hissed in pain as the icy steel ripped into his shoulder, leaving a bloody gash. The other soldier swung then and Morgan just managed to twist his body to avoid a fatal blow. The guard's fist, which had been aimed for his head, connected with his left arm instead. He heard the sound of crunching bone and cried out in pain, as he was sent flying a good ten feet; his arm completely shattered.

He hit the ground hard and rolled a few times to try and lessen the impact. Grimacing in pain, he forced himself back onto his feet as the two supers approached him. They now looked a whole lot more confident.

He'd lost control of his *wind blade* when his arm had been shattered and his *tailwind* had just run out again. Morgan gritted his teeth as pain, more horrible than any he'd felt before now, radiated from his arm. He didn't look at it, instead trying to focus on the two men swimming in and out of his vision.

"Well, looks like the brat is just about finished," the guard holding the sword said. "Do you think we should bring him back alive like Lord Simon said?"

"Nah, it's too risky. Better kill him now and explain to Lord Simon when we get back."

Morgan gritted his teeth as a plan formed in his mind.

It would be risky, but if it succeeded he would have a chance of winning this fight.

Morgan rushed forward, his arm banging painfully against his side.

The unarmed guard just sneered and stomped his foot, turning the ground to mud once more. As man with the sword stepped forward, Morgan used *fly* and shot toward him. The guard, not expecting this move, panicked and thrust his sword at Morgan in a desperate bid to end him. Morgan again managed to avoid a fatal blow, catching the sword through his already damaged left shoulder.

He yelled in agony as he continued forward, the blade going clean through him as he closed with the guard. He activated *heavy handed* and swung mightily, crushing the stunned guard's skull. As the man dropped, he tried to continue on toward the next guard, but the pain in his shoulder made him lose control of his chi and he hit the ground just a few feet away from him.

His vision flickered as the guard stepped forward and tore the blade from his shoulder. He stared down at Morgan with hatred in his eyes, then raised the blade over his head to finish him off.

Morgan closed his eyes, waiting for the blow that would end him. Nothing happened. After a few seconds, he opened his eyes and saw the man staring down at his chest, where a massive chunk of ice had impaled him from behind.

The guard stared down at Morgan for a few moments, incomprehension in his eyes. Then he toppled backwards, the sword slipping from his grasp and clattering against the ground.

Morgan saw Sarah running towards him. He could vaguely make out a body lying a few feet behind her.

Good, she'd managed to kill the other mage.

He could feel a tingling sensation running through him, and wondered if this was what dying felt like. Then darkness claimed him and he passed out.

***

He awoke some time later. It was dark out and there was a small fire burning off to his left. Morgan groaned as he began to push himself up, expecting at any moment, to be wracked by pain. When no pain was forthcoming, he steeled himself and peered down at his left arm. What he saw was a whole and unblemished limb.

He rotated his shoulder, not feeling even an ounce of discomfort. As he got to his feet, he heard someone call out to him.

"Oh good. You're awake," said an unfamiliar voice.

Morgan's head whipped around and saw a man seated near Sarah by the fire. He had a kindly face, with light blue eyes. His brown hair fell just below his shoulders.

He looked to Sarah next. She looked tired, but had a wide smile on her face as she rose to greet him.

"What happened?" Morgan asked.

Sarah hugged him, then took his hand and led him to the fire.

He sat down and the man handed him a bowl of something, along with a wooden spoon. Morgan nodded to the man in thanks, then dug right in. He hadn't realized how hungry he'd been until he took his first bite of the savory broth.

It was warm and delicious, and Morgan was quick to take another bite. As he ate, Sarah explained what had happened.

"I had just finished off Malcom when I saw that guard about to finish you. I managed to kill him before he got the chance, but by the time I got to you, you had already passed out. You were losing blood quickly and your arm was a total wreck.," she paused for a moment, shuddering at the memory of the bloody mess.

"I thought you were going to die. Then Samuel came along." Sarah gestured to the man who was still smiling kindly at Morgan.

"He has powerful healing magic and fixed you up good as new. You slept for a few hours, but Samuel said that healing can take a lot out of a person."

Morgan put down the bowl and slowly turned toward the man, eyes narrowing in suspicion.

"You just happened to be out here? Out in the middle of nowhere?"

He might owe this man his life, but he'd be a fool to trust him.

"Morgan," Sarah hissed, glaring at him. "This man just saved your life! The least you can do is be courteous!"

Samuel, however, raised his hand in a placating gesture.

"There's no need, miss," he said. "Your friend is correct of course; it is quite suspicious of me to be out here."

He turned to look at Morgan, his smile never faltering. "I won't tell you what I'm doing here, but I will give you one piece of advice. Be more careful while using your power, or else you'll never advance enough to awaken your supermage ability."

Morgan felt his heart skip a beat as the man rose to his feet and dusted himself off.

"How did you…?" Morgan began.

"Know?" Samuel smiled, and his eyes flashed in the firelight. "I know many things; but I think I'll keep that particular piece of information to myself."

He turned to look at Sarah, who looked just as shocked as Morgan.

"Take care of yourself young miss."

Then he turned and began walking away.

"Wait," Morgan shouted, getting quickly to his feet. "Who are you?"

Samuel turned one last time, the kindly smile still on his face. "I'm only a wanderer, young Morgan."

Morgan opened his mouth to ask what he meant, but the man simply vanished, disappearing into thin air.

Morgan stared at the empty space for a few seconds before turning to look at Sarah.

"I'm not going crazy, am I?"

Sarah shook her head dumbly. "No, I also just saw a man disappear into thin air."

Morgan walked back to the fire and sat down with a grunt; his mind racing.

This man had somehow recognized him for what he was. Did that mean that others could, as well? He was also able to heal him completely and then had vanished into thin air.

This entire situation was just plain bizarre.

The two of them sat in silence as the fire cracked and popped before them. The silence was suddenly broken by a horse's nickering. Morgan was on his feet in an instant, a *wind blade* already forming on his arm as he readied himself for an attack.

"Morgan. Calm down. We're not under attack. I kept two of the horses, because I know we'll have need of them in the coming weeks."

Morgan dismissed his *wind blade* and sat back down. He could feel his heart racing, which he found quite odd.

Wouldn't this new chi-heart react differently than the old one? Then again, it did function in its place, so maybe this was to be expected, he reasoned to himself.

"I know that we killed all the soldiers. Shouldn't we be safe for at least a few more days?" Morgan asked.

"You're forgetting about the tracker," Sarah said, with a regretful sigh. "The moment he saw that the guards were losing, he took off back to City Four. My father likely already knows about you having an ability. When he sends people after us this time, they will be much too strong for us to kill."

"So what do we do now?" Morgan asked.

"Well, for starters, I would recommend looking at your status," Sarah said, with a weary smile.

"I moved up an entire rank from that fight, and it's taken me years just to get where I am now. It would appear that killing others with abilities is a fast way to rank up."

She shivered a little, her face going pale at the memory of the lives she'd taken. She felt suddenly ill.

"You had no choice. Either it was us, or them. Don't let it bother you," Morgan said, patting her on the back.

She smiled at him and Morgan could tell it was forced. He decided that a change of topic would probably be best.

"Are we still heading for the school in the Central Kingdom?"

"Yes," Sarah said, getting to her feet. "I think I'll get some sleep now. You should too. We have a hard few days of riding ahead of us."

Morgan nodded, assuring Sarah he would be going to sleep soon. He leaned back against a rock and stretched mightily.

It felt good to have all his limbs intact.

He then manipulated a tendril of his mana and chi to open his status and see what he'd gotten from his near death experience.

Name: Morgan
Super: Rank - 3
Energy to next rank - 466/1,300
Mage: Rank - 3
Energy to next rank - 1,042/1,300
Super ability - Gravity
Mage ability - Air
CP - 150/150 (Regen - 1.6 per second)
MP - 150/150 (Regen - 1.6 per Second)
Strength - 14
Agility - 18
Constitution - 14
Intelligence - 15
Wisdom - 16
Super skills - Fly, Heavy handed
Mage skills - Wind blade, Tailwind

Morgan was more than a little surprised.

He'd moved up a full two ranks in both abilities. Those last people he'd fought must have been much stronger than the two guards he'd killed back in City Four. He was also fairly certain by now that destroying the chi, or mana-heart would give him more towards his next rank.

It would also appear that what Sarah had said was true. If the cost to rank up kept increasing at the rate that it was going now, it could very well take years to rank up at higher levels.

He decided to check on his skills next to see if they'd changed at all.

Fly: Manipulate gravity to make yourself lighter and move through the air.
Cost - 1 CP per second
Maximum height - 33 Ft
Maximum speed - 20.3 Ft per second
Maximum carry weight - 53 pounds (carrying any more weight will decrease speed by 0.1 feet per second for every additional pound)

Heavy handed: Manipulate gravity to make your blows land harder (currently X2.03)
Cost - 20 CP
Duration - 13 seconds

Wind blade: Manipulate the air around you to create whirling blades sharper than steel
Cost - 40 MP
Duration - Until dismissed

Tailwind: Manipulate the air around you to increase speed (Currently X2.03)
Cost - 20 MP
Duration - 13 seconds

So his skills had gotten more powerful.

Morgan was almost ecstatic.

Not only had he ranked up twice, and gotten a nice increase to his attributes- his skills had also improved!

Closing his status, Morgan yawned widely. The fire was beginning to die down. Only small bursts of flame peeked out of the burned wood. He found this oddly relaxing. Turning his back to the fire, Morgan closed his eyes and was soon fast asleep.

***

Lord Simon paced back and forth in his study. His mind was whirling with the news of his guards' deaths.

It would appear that Morgan had somehow gotten an ability - a super ability judging by what the tracker had told him - and he had then somehow killed three men in a matter of seconds.

Simon was understandably furious when the tracker had come back bearing the bad news. His cooling corpse now lay in a pool of blood on his study floor.

There was a knock at the door. His pacing immediately stopped.

"Come in," he called, walking back to his desk and taking a seat.

A man walked into the room. He was tall; well over six feet, with cropped black hair and dark brown eyes. His mouth was turned down in a perpetual frown and a neat black beard covered his chin. He was dressed in black painted plate mail and the hilt of a massive sword peeked over one shoulder.

The door bumped the corpse of the tracker and the man made a sound of disgust as he stepped over the body.

"Couldn't you have had that cleaned up before calling me?" the man asked.

He walked over to the desk and took a seat in one of the chairs.

"I'm glad you came so quickly, Arnold," Simon said, ignoring the man's previous question.

"Of course. With how much you pay me, why wouldn't I?" the man asked, reclining back in his chair.

"I'm sure you've already heard what's happened to my daughter."

It was a statement, not a question. If Arnold didn't already know why he was here, then he wouldn't be working for him.

"I take it you want me to go fetch her?" Arnold asked lazily. "I heard your guards were all killed by a couple of kids. Pretty sloppy on their part."

"Yes. I also want a bounty put out for Sarah's safe return and Morgan's head. As for my sloppy guards; that man on the ground told me that the boy, Morgan, launched a surprise attack and managed to kill half of them before they could even react."

"And you want to kill him?" Arnold asked, raising an eyebrow. "It would be a shame to kill someone with potential like that."

"Yes! I want him dead!" Simon declared, slamming his fist down and destroying his second desk in as many days.

"Fine, I'll kill him," Arnold said, rising from his seat.

He made his way towards the door.

"Make sure to get this done quickly, Arnold," Simon called to the man's retreating back. "The King will have need of our services soon."

Arnold just waved his hand in confirmation, before closing the door behind him.

Simon stared at the door for a few moments once it had closed.

He was aggravated that he'd needed to call Arnold for this job, but it couldn't be helped. He needed to get his daughter back and no one got results like he did.

He looked back to the corpse lying on the ground and wrinkled his nose.

Arnold was likely right; he really should get someone to clean this mess up.

8

Morgan stared up at the approaching walls of City Six. It was well into the evening and the sun had painted purple streaks across the sky as it sunk toward the horizon.

They had been riding hard over the last two weeks to stay ahead of whatever pursuit Lord Simon had undoubtedly sent after them. Morgan was tired and hungry. Above all, he was extremely saddle sore. It wasn't nearly as bad now as it had been on his first few days of riding, but it was still painful enough to cause him discomfort.

Sarah was even worse off than he was. Being the daughter of a city lord, she'd never really felt true discomfort. Their food supply had run out two days ago and although Morgan was used to not having much to eat, even he was feeling the constant pangs of hunger by now.

That was why, despite the risks involved, they were heading towards the gates of City Six.

At first, Morgan had protested the idea, saying that they were likely being watched for. After Sarah had threatened to go in alone, he finally caved in to her demands.

They pulled their horses off the road and into a clump of trees about a mile from the city walls. Sarah dismounted gracefully and led her horse over to an area, where they would be well hidden. Morgan, on the other hand, more fell than dismounted. He hit the ground in an undignified heap. He heard Sarah's laughter as he righted himself and grabbed the four-legged devil's reins.

He glowered at her as he led the horse forward, hearing the hell spawn snorting behind his back.

Mocking him, no doubt.

Before this journey's over, I'm going to kill this monster, he resolved.

Morgan grimaced as his legs flared in pain.

He didn't understand why his constitution did nothing to prevent soreness. Maybe it just wasn't high enough yet; or maybe this hell spawn had a special skill to induce pain.

"I don't see what's so funny," Morgan grumbled, stopping next to Sarah, who had just finished tethering her horse to a nearby tree.

Sarah didn't rise to the bait. Instead, she waited patiently for him to finish tying his horse to a nearby tree.

"You ready?" She asked, once he was done.

He nodded, then turned his back to her and crouched. Sarah wrapped her arms around his shoulders and Morgan placed his hands under her knees. He then used *fly,* not even bothering to straighten from his crouched position.

He flew straight up until they cleared the tops of the trees. Then he headed in the direction of the city. He could feel Sarah's stomach growling against his back and felt his earlier annoyance abate.

If she could stay positive when she was this hungry, he didn't have a right to be this annoyed.

It took another few minutes for them to make it over the city walls and there was a moment of panic when one of the guards looked in their direction. Thankfully, the uncertain light was enough to cloak them and the guard soon turned away.

They touched down on the ground in a darkened alley and were soon walking through the streets of City Six.

"Where do you think we should go first?" Morgan asked, as they made their way into the city proper.

"We should go first to find somewhere for you to buy clothes. Then a supplies shop and an inn where we can spend the night."

"That wasn't part of the plan," he reminded her, his brow creasing in aggravation. "We decided it would be too risky to spend the night in a city until we reached the Central Kingdom."

"Yeah," Sarah said distractedly, as she looked into the windows of the shops they were passing. "But I changed my mind. I need a bath, and there is no way that I'm sleeping on the hard ground when I could be sleeping in a bed instead. Oh, this place looks promising!"

Morgan groaned as Sarah pushed open the door to a small clothing shop and went in.

He felt a knot in his stomach. He feared it would not end well for them.

Morgan followed her into the shop, despite his misgivings, and resigned to his fate.

Three hours later, the two of them were tucking into steaming bowls of stew at a local inn called The Pigeon. Morgan had thought it was a ridiculous name for an inn, but who was he to judge? He'd never been in one before, as the local tavern owners in City Four had made sure he wasn't allowed in.

He tore off a hunk of the crusty loaf near him and dunked it into the stew, soaking up the juices and shoving it into his mouth.

He couldn't remember the last time a meal had been so good.

Sarah, who was sitting across him, had attempted some sense of decorum when a waitress had brought out the steaming bowls. After she'd taken her first bite, she completely gave up and shoveled the stew down her throat like a woman possessed.

Morgan finished his bowl and motioned to the waitress.

"What can I help you with, sir?" she asked, a professional smile plastered on her face.

He found it odd how the people in this place had started calling him 'sir' as soon as he'd walked in.

Looking down at his nice shirt, clean pants, and new leather boots, he could see where the confusion had come from.

They'd checked into the inn and paid for two rooms and a bath. After cleaning up, which took Sarah an inordinate amount of time, they'd headed down to the dining room where they'd ordered a massive meal.

"Yes, I would like a refill on the stew," Morgan said, holding out the empty bowl. "And can you bring me another mug of that dark cider?"

"Of course, sir," the waitress said, taking both the bowl and the empty mug. "That will be four copper for everything."

Morgan fished around in the coin pouch he'd stolen from the guards back in City Four and handed over the money. The waitress left with a smile and he surreptitiously checked on how much he had left.

When he'd left City Four, he'd had a total of 38 gold, 6 silver, 8 copper and 15 bronze. After his shopping spree, along with the fee for the inn and bath, he now had 35 gold, 2 silver and 6 bronze left.

He winced at how much he'd spent over the last few hours.

The currency in the Five Kingdoms was fairly simple. There were 5 bronze to a copper, 10 copper to a sliver, 100 silver to a gold and 1000 gold to a platinum.

With the average person making about 10 silver a week; he had just spent the equivalent of eight month's wages in a single night.

Sarah of course, had just scoffed when Morgan had complained about prices; and when he saw how much money she had he could see why.

While his pilfered purse was mostly full of gold, hers was full of platinum.

She'd of course refused to pay when he'd asked her to, saying that he had his own money and that a real man wouldn't ask a Lady to pay.

Morgan didn't have the faintest idea of what so called 'real men' did, but from his experience growing up on the streets, it was every man; or woman, for themselves.

Morgan closed his coin purse and tucked it inside the pocket of his new pants. Looking around the room, he was suddenly aware of a man, who was sitting in the back corner and throwing them furtive glances every few minutes.

Morgan resisted the urge to bolt up from his seat and run. Instead, he pretended not to notice the man, but made sure to keep an eye on him.

"Don't look now, but there's someone watching us," Morgan said, keeping his eyes straight ahead.

Sarah stopped with a spoon halfway to her lips.

"Where?" She asked, immediately beginning to look around.

"I told you not to look," he hissed.

Sarah nodded, going back to her stew and continuing to eat.

The man had stiffened slightly when Sarah had begun looking around, but he relaxed in his seat when she went back to eating.

"What do you think he wants?" she asked, taking another bite of her stew.

"If I had to guess, we've been recognized," Morgan said, as the waitress came back with his stew and drink.

They waited for her to leave before continuing their conversation.

"What do we do?"

"We finish eating, then head up to our rooms. If the man leaves as soon as we do, we'll have to make a run for it."

Sarah groaned in frustration. "And just when I was going to get a good night's sleep!"

"You can always stay and be caught," Morgan replied, shrugging. "I'm sure nothing bad will happen to you and you can even go back to your handsome prince."

She made another rude hand gesture at him and Morgan laughed.

They finished their meal quickly after that and headed up to their rooms. Sure enough, as soon as they rose from their seats, the man rose as well.

Morgan sighed when he did, and knew they wouldn't be getting any sleep that night.

9

They rushed up to their rooms, and quickly packed up everything they'd bought while in the city. They had bought enough food to last them for a month, a few changes of clothes and Morgan had even bought a leather breastplate. Sarah had bought one as well, but hers was nicer and had some metal worked into it.

After packing their things, Morgan opened a window and used *fly*. He moved sluggishly through the air, weighed down by all their supplies.

"Hurry! Fly faster," Sarah said urgently, clinging tightly to his shoulders.

"This is as fast as I can go with all this stuff weighing me down," Morgan answered, gritting his teeth with the effort it took to keep them moving.

They were flying at a quarter of his normal speed, and with the looming threat, they seemed to be moving even more slowly.

A alarm rang out, startling the two of them, and Morgan almost fell out of the air. Sarah's grip tightened so much that he began choking.

He wondered how high her strength stat was.

"Sarah, I can't breathe!" he croaked.

He began to feel lightheaded.

"Sorry!" she said, loosening her grip, allowing him to take in a lungful of air.

Morgan could feel his heart pounding once again as they made their way safely over the wall and out to the open area outside the city.

"I think it would be faster to land and run for the horses," Morgan said, shouting over the alarm blaring out behind them.

Sarah agreed and he landed quickly. The two of them made a run for the trees. It only took about a minute to reach the horses and the two of them set about tying their packs to the saddles and untethered them. In just a few minute's time, they were racing down the road away from City Six.

They had only made it a few hundred yards when the city gates started to open. Morgan chanced a glance back over his shoulder and felt his blood freeze in his veins. There were at least thirty guard waiting behind the door as it slowly creaked open.

"Sarah!" Morgan called out, his voice taking on a frantic edge. "There are a ton of guards behind those gates and there's no way we can outrun them!"

He saw Sarah look over her shoulder and her face went pale, then set in a determined expression as she pulled her horse to a stop.

Morgan scrambled to do the same, but Sarah waved him on. "Keep moving! I have an idea that might buy us some time."

Kicking the horse on its sides, Morgan took off down the road; his rear end bouncing painfully in the saddle.

Sarah stared at the slowly opening gates and took a deep breath. Then she activated her *condense water* skill and sent a stream of water toward them, freezing the gates on contact. When she felt that the ice was sufficiently thick enough, she cut off the skill and sagged in her saddle.

She tiredly turned her horse back toward Morgan and groaned, seeing that he hadn't made it nearly as far as she'd hoped.

She knew that the ice would only hold them back for a few minutes at most, so their best option right now was to find a place to hide.

She kicked her horse's flanks and took off toward Morgan.

Morgan heard the pounding of hooves and quickly swiveled in the saddle. His racing heart calmed somewhat as he saw Sarah coming up behind him. It didn't take long for her to catch up.

"I've bought us a few minutes," she called over as they rode. "But we need to find somewhere to hide."

"It's no good," Morgan called back. "If we could hide, don't you think I'd have just suggested that we stay back in the woods and wait? There is no way they don't have a tracker, so we need to do something to throw them off our trail."

They rode on in silence for a moment as they furiously thought of what they could do. It was Morgan who finally came up with a solution.

"When I was in the air earlier, I thought I saw the forest come to an end. Do you think there's a cliff there?"

Sarah opened her mouth to answer, when a loud splintering boom echoed out across the night.

"Only one way to find out," Sarah yelled, pulling her horse's reins hard and turning into the woods.

It would be a lot more dangerous going though the woods on horseback than the road had been. The moon was bright and full and with no trees in the way, the road was quite visible. The woods, on the other hand, not so much.

Morgan followed Sarah as they made their way desperately through the woods. He could barely see two feet in front of his face, so when Sarah's horse suddenly loomed out of the dark, he had to jerk his horse to the side to avoid colliding with her.

The sudden tug caused the horse to trip. Its foot caught a tree root, and the horse threw Morgan from the saddle as it hit the ground with a panicked whinny.

Morgan was so shocked that he didn't even think to activate *fly*. He hit the ground with a thud and rolled to try and absorb the impact.

He finally came to a stop, groaning in pain as he tried to force himself from the hard ground. He winced, getting slowly to his feet and checking to make sure nothing was broken. Surprisingly enough, he was completely unharmed.

He heard the sound of approaching hooves and Sarah emerged out of the darkness, leading her horse by the reins.

"Are you alright?" she asked, squinting down at him.

"Fine," Morgan said, looking around for his horse. "Why did you stop so suddenly? I had to pull my horse out of the way and it caused us to fall."

He spotted it a few feet away, lying on its side and letting out pained whinnies.

"You should be thanking me for not letting you run straight off a cliff!" Sarah said, dismounting.

"There really is a cliff here?" Morgan asked, as he headed over to the downed horse.

"Yes, you moron! Right there!"

Squinting through the darkness, Morgan could indeed make out where the tree line came to an abrupt end.

He was lucky he hadn't kept going.

Another few feet and he knew that they'd have been goners.

Morgan crouched near the horse and removed its saddlebags, then activated *wind blade* and put the beast out of its misery.

Sarah gasped as he did this, but she was even more shocked when he walked over to her horse and speared it clean through the chest; killing it instantly.

"What the hell are you doing, Morgan?" Sarah exclaimed.

The horse dropped to the ground.

"I'm making our deaths look convincing," Morgan said, while dismissing his *wind blade* and removing the saddlebags.

He didn't even feel the slightest bit of remorse when killing the horses and he silently swore that he would never ride one of these monsters again.

"And what did killing our only means of escape accomplish?!" Sarah yelled.

"First of all, you need to calm down," Morgan said, shoving the saddlebags into her arms and striding past her. "The only way we lose those guards is by making them think we ran off this cliff."

He walked over to Sarah's horse once more.

"Now; if the guards find two horses with their saddlebags missing, there's no way they won't be suspicious. So I figured that the best course of action would be to kill the horses, then escape using my *fly* skill."

Morgan stopped in front of the horse and activated *heavy handed*; then brought his foot back and kicked the horse as hard as he could. There was the sound of cracking bone and the horse's corpse went flying, breaking through the trees and sailing over the edge of the cliff.

Sarah glared at him for a few seconds, before conceding that he was probably right.

This was their best chance at escape and if the horses needed to die, then so be it.

Morgan walked over to the tree line and peered out over the vast canyon below. Even illuminated by the full moon overhead, he couldn't see the bottom.

Perfect, he thought, pleased.

Sarah walked up next to him. She'd tied the saddlebags around her shoulders and looked ready to go.

Good. He'd always known her to be the sensible type.

"Wait here while I move the other horse. Then we'll get going."

She nodded once as he walked back into the cover of the trees. After a few moments, she heard a loud crashing sound and a dead horse went sailing passed her. The sight was so funny that she actually began to laugh.

Morgan emerged from the woods and when he saw her laughing, smiled as well.

He'd hated those monsters, but he hadn't known she had as well.

***

The two soldiers sat astride their horses as they peered down into the seemingly bottomless chasm.

"What do you think? Can you tell if they fell down there?"

This question came from the man wearing the telltale stripes of a captain.

"Something definitely fell, but I can't be sure it was them," the other man answered. "Though if I were to wager a guess as to what happened to a couple of kids, running through the woods on horseback at night…" The man shrugged.

The captain sighed, pinching the bridge of his nose at the amount of trouble he was likely going to be in.

Lord Simon would not be happy to hear of his daughter's death.

10

Morgan landed with a tired groan as sunlight peeked over the horizon. As soon as Sarah was on his back, he'd flown out over the cliff's edge and sank several feet down. They'd followed alongside it for the remainder of the night, neither of them making so much as a peep out of fear of being caught.

Only once the sky had begun to lighten had he flown back up. The landscape hadn't changed much. The only difference was that the cliff edge now extended a good distance from the tree line.

He yawned, rubbing his eyes as he looked for a comfortable place to sleep. Sarah had already found herself a spot; she hadn't slept at all either, and was now curled up by the base of a tree. Morgan stumbled over to a tree of his own and collapsed onto his back.

They had traveled a good distance, about thirty or so miles from where they'd faked their deaths. Hopefully this would throw off their pursuers and he'd finally have some peace.

***

Arnold stared up at the imposing walls of City Six as he and his companion approached on horseback. As they passed through the front gates, he couldn't help but notice that they had been quite heavily damaged; and recently so.

"You getting anything yet, Weasel?" he asked the man riding next to him.

Weasel shook his head. "Too many people."

Arnold sighed, pinching the bridge of his nose.

Even if he was the best tracker in the North Kingdom, Weasel still had his limits.

"Alright, I guess we do this the old fashioned way," he said, turning his horse toward the speedier part of the city.

If information was to be had, this would be the best place to find it.

***

Morgan woke up suddenly. Something was very wrong.

He stayed absolutely still as he tried to figure out what had woken him. It was quiet. Too quiet. The birds and insects had gone silent and the only sound he could hear was the soft rustling of leaves overhead.

Ever so slowly, he cracked his eyes open and peered around. Sunlight was streaming in through the leaves directly overhead, meaning he'd been asleep for several hours. Sarah was off to his left, but unlike him, she was still sound asleep.

There could only be one reason why it was so quiet.

Morgan got slowly to his feet, eyes sweeping the surrounding forest for any sign of movement. He made his way quickly over to Sarah and shook her awake.

"What's going on?" she asked sleepily.

"There's something in the forest and it's likely stalking us as we speak," Morgan said quietly, his eyes never stopping their scan of the surrounding forest.

"How can you tell?" she asked, getting up on her feet and picking up their bags.

"Listen- the forest is too quiet. No birds or insects are making any noise."

It was then, that Morgan spotted it out of the corner of his eye. Something massive and covered in fur.

Morgan reacted without a second thought. Activating *tailwind*, he threw Sarah over his shoulder and ran toward the tree line. He heard an angry growl, then the sound of snapping branches, as whatever it was gave chase.

He burst out of the trees and out into the open space between the trees and the cliff edge. He ran another few feet before setting Sarah down and taking up a fighting stance.

Sarah was visibly shaken, but activated her mage shield and a blue light flickered across her skin.

"Did you see what that thing was?" Morgan asked, as he used *wind blade* twice, encasing both arms in the whirling lances of air.

"Only flashes," she answered, keeping her eyes on the tree line. "Whatever it is, it's very big."

They didn't have to wait very long to find out. There was a low rumbling growl that shook them to their cores and a massive shaggy bear emerged from the trees.

It was terrifying. The beast was at least eight feet at the shoulder and over fifteen feet long. Its head was the size of Morgan's torso, and had a mouth full of wicked looking teeth. Its fur was a mix of browns and dark greens, making it perfect for camouflaging in the forest.

The bear padded silently toward them, its eyes fixed on Morgan.

How on earth did a creature that big make so little noise?

He was forced back to reality as a massive spear of ice flew directly at the creature, burying itself a few inches into its hide. The bear roared in pain, then charged directly at them.

They'd both been too tired to remove their armor before going to sleep and Morgan was now glad they hadn't.

He would likely need every advantage he could get in this fight.

Morgan used *tailwind* once more and rushed the charging animal. Two more *icicle spears* hit the creature as he closed in, barely doing anything other than further enraging the bear.

He barely managed to dodge a swipe from its massive paw, nearly losing his balance in the process. Only his high *agility* kept him on his feet. Darting forward, he attempted to skewer the bear with his *wind blade*, but instead of sinking into the bear as he'd been expecting, the lance merely bounced off; not even leaving so much as a scratch.

Just what kind of monster was this?

Morgan jumped back from the creature and dismissed his *wind blades*.

They weren't going to do him any good against a creature like this.

While he'd been attacking, Sarah had readied her next skill. As soon as Morgan moved back from the bear, she used *frostbite* and the temperature around the bear plummeted as the skill took effect.

When the bear next moved, it was noticeably slower than it had been.

Morgan kept his eyes on the bear as it turned its attention toward Sarah.

"Any ideas on how to take it down?" he shouted over to her. "My *wind blade* barely left a scratch and your *icicle spear* doesn't seem to be doing much either!"

He felt the timer on his *tailwind* run out then, but since the bear was slowed, he was confident he'd still be able to avoid its attacks.

"Try using your super skills instead," Sarah shouted, as she used her *condense water* skill. A block of ice formed around the bear's head and for a moment, Morgan though it might go down. Then with an enraged roar, the ice block shattered and the air around it seemed to shimmer with heat.

Holy crap, Morgan thought to himself.

The bear had an ability.

Morgan was fascinated as he watched the bear's fur take on a reddish tint as it slowly stalked towards them. Small gouts of flame escaped its nostrils, then it roared and the temperature rose by a noticeable degree.

Sarah threw another *icicle spear* but this one didn't even make it halfway before melting. The creature snarled one last time, then lunged toward Sarah, teeth bared and tiny eyes glittering with hatred.

It was then that Morgan hit it from the side. Hard. He'd activated his *heavy handed* skill and punched the bear as hard as he could. He could feel the bones in his hand grinding together as the bear's ribs gave way under the attack.

The bear was thrown off course with a pained roar, but it was quick to recover and turned back toward Morgan; charging at him without a second of hesitation.

This time, it was Sarah who attacked, launching an *icicle spear* directly into the spot Morgan had just damaged. This time, the spear sunk a good foot into the bear, tearing up its insides. The beast roared in pain and rage, but didn't slow its charge.

Morgan planted his feet and roared back, screaming as he brought his foot around in a massive roundhouse kick. His foot snapped into the side of the bear's head with such force that it was thrown a good two feet to the side. The bear, expecting to meet resistance, plowed face first into the ground; its momentum forcing it forward a good few feet before it came to a halt.

Sarah came up next to him, her body shaking with adrenaline and fear as the two of them stared at the motionless bear.

"Do you think it's dead?" Sarah asked, in a low voice.

"I don't know, but I'm pretty sure I broke its spine with that last attack," he answered, wincing as he felt his leg throbbing in pain.

He hoped he hadn't hurt himself too badly.

"Should we go over and check?" Sarah asked, taking a step forward.

Morgan placed an arm on her shoulder and shook his head.

When she looked back, the bear was rising once again.

Its head was crooked at an odd angle, its jaw seemed to be dislocated and it was bleeding heavily from where Sarah's *icicle spear* was still embedded; but it was undoubtedly still alive.

"What do we do?" Sarah asked, panicked.

"We finish what we started," Morgan answered.

He took a step forward, wincing as he felt another shooting pain in his leg. He gave up on walking altogether, using *fly* to hover a foot up off the ground.

"I'll distract it, you try and finish it off," he said, floating toward the malformed bear.

Sarah nodded, then used *frostbite* once more. The bear snorted in anger, but didn't activate its ability. Either it couldn't use it again, or was too hurt to.

Morgan flew closer toward the bear and used *heavy handed.* The bear swiped out at him and despite it being slowed, he barely managed to avoid the attack. He flew in and threw a few punches into its face- not enough to do any real damage, but enough to distract it.

Sarah watched as Morgan darted around the enraged bear and readied her skill. Then taking a moment to aim, she used *icicle spear* four times in a row.

Morgan flew high into the air as he tried to avoid another attack, but the bear reared up on its hind legs and took another swipe at him.

The monster was nearly twenty feet tall standing up.

He winced as he felt a line of hot pain shoot up his injured leg. The bear had finally managed to score a hit, opening a line of gashes on his leg. But the bear had made a mistake and was now wide open for a counter-attack.

Morgan spun in the air, using the momentum of the turn, as well as his skill, and drove his good leg into the bear's head in retaliation. There was a loud crunching sound as the side of the beast's skull caved in.

Somehow, it still wasn't dead.

"You have got to be kidding me," Morgan exclaimed, as the bear landed back on all fours. "What the hell are you made of?"

The bear took a step forward as four *icicle spears* slammed into its skull in rapid succession, burying themselves deep into the beast's already damaged skull.

The bear took one more staggering step toward him, then finally toppled to the ground. Dead.

11

Morgan stared at the bear for a few seconds, skeptical that it was really dead. Then he let out a whoop of joy as he flew over to Sarah.

"You did it! It's finally down!"

Sarah smiled tiredly at him before slumping to the ground herself.

Now that the excitement was over, Morgan could feel the pain of his injuries beginning to set in. He let his *fly* skill run out, allowing himself to drop down near Sarah and winced as he looked down at his leg.

His new pants were torn where the bear's claws had slashed him and this aggravated him more than any injury the beast inflicted. Rolling up his pant leg, he could see a small trickle of blood flowing from each cut. However, he could see that they were already beginning to scab over.

He sighed in relief. It wasn't nearly as bad as he'd feared.

Finally, he looked up at Sarah. She looked shaken, but was otherwise unhurt.

"What the hell was that thing?" he asked her.

"I've never seen one of those before, but I'm pretty sure that that was a dire-flame bear," she answered in a quiet voice. "I can't believe we killed it."

"Neither can I," he answered truthfully. "Did that bear have some sort of ability?"

She nodded, looking over to where the bear lay in a slowly spreading pool of blood. "It has an innate resistance to magic, as well as a chi charged ability called *raging flame*."

So there were creatures out there that had abilities and could resist other's abilities? If all he had to rely on were his mage skills, the two of them may very well have died.

"Do you think we got any energy from that thing?"

Sarah actually smiled at this. "We likely didn't get anything from killing it, but if you fetch its core, you'll likely get a whole bunch of both."

"It's core?"

He'd heard of cores before, but never really knew where they came from, or what purpose they served.

"Yes, all animals that can use abilities are called beasts and they all have cores. They're located where the heart would be and is the best way to increase in rank."

Morgan was quite excited to hear about that.

There was a better way of ranking up than killing people. That was a relief to Morgan.

He floated up from the ground and drifted over to the bear. Rolling up his sleeve, he plunged his arm into the still warm corpse and dug around for a bit. After a few moments, his hand closed around a hard, spherical object and he removed his arm with some effort.

In his hand was a glowing blue and red sphere, roughly the size of a grapefruit. He shook his arm a few times to try and get rid of some of the gore, then shrugged. He floated back toward Sarah and saw her eyes go wide as he dropped it on the ground before her.

"I've never seen one this big before," her voice, tinged with awe as she stared at the glassy sphere.

Morgan landed next to her and peered down at the core. "How do you get the energy out of it?"

Sarah finally looked up at him and grimaced at his gore covered arm. Morgan gave a surprised shout as icy water drenched his arm, cleaning the filth from it.

"Warn me next time," he yelled, feeling his entire arm go numb with the cold.

"You're welcome," Sarah said with an eye roll. "To answer your earlier question, it's actually quite simple. Just place your hand on the core and the energy will flow into you."

"How much do you think is in there?" Morgan asked, rubbing his hands together to get some feeling back into them.

"The largest I've ever seen was only about a tenth the size of this one and it had just over two hundred."

"So, what you're telling me, is that this core likely has over two thousand points worth of energy?"

She shrugged, non-committedly. "That would depend on the beast's rank."

She placed her hand on the core and motioned him to do so as well. Morgan complied and did the same.

It felt warm and seemed to pulse under his hand, as if it had a life of its own.

"Now close your eyes and do as I say," Sarah said, closing her own eyes.

"Concentrate on your status, but instead of trying to see your stats, try and see the core."

Morgan concentrated on bringing up his status, feeling the two energies combine within his body. Then, as the purple mix of both mana and chi started moving toward his eyes, he concentrated on seeing the core instead of his status.

Morgan blinked as he opened his eyes. A purple status floated in front of him, but instead of seeing his usual stats, he saw the core displayed instead.

Name: Dire-flame bear core
Rank - 8
Total available energy - 3,254/3,254

This core was taken from a dire-flame bear on the cusp of evolution, as such, the amount of energy in the core at the time of its death was greatly increased.

Morgan felt his jaw drop as he read through the description.

The bear had been a rank 8? No wonder it had been so hard to kill.

He looked past his screen to see Sarah staring at what he assumed was a similar screen, with her mouth hanging open.

She finally looked over at him and a wide smile spread across her face.

"I'm guessing you saw how much was available?"

Morgan nodded.

With that much, he could rank both his abilities at once.

He was snapped out of his contemplation as Sarah cleared her throat.

"Since we both killed the bear, I believe we should each get half."

Morgan inwardly cringed at the lost opportunity, but begrudgingly nodded.

After all, if Sarah wasn't there, he likely wouldn't have been able to take it down.

Turning his attention back to the core's stats, he watched as the amount of available energy dropped to *1,627*.

It was still a massive amount of energy, but he wished he could have had all of it.

Concentrating on the core, he willed the remaining energy into his body as Sarah had told him. A message popped up in front of him.

Would you like to absorb 1,627 energy from the dire-flame bear core?

Yes/No

Morgan, surprised to see this message, mentally selected *yes*. Another message appeared.

You have 1,627 available energy, where would you like to assign it?

Super - 466/1,300
Mage - 1,042/1,300

So he actually had a choice where the energy went? He could see the appeal of hunting these beasts for energy even more now.

He stopped for a moment, thinking.

Could he assign energy to each?

Excited by this new idea, he focused on assigning *200 energy* to his mage ability.

He felt the tingling sensation of ranking up and felt the boost in power as his attributes increased. He quickly checked the available energy once more, and was relieved to see that *1,427* remained.

He quickly assigned the remaining energy toward his *super ability* and felt himself rank up once more. He heard a sound like cracking glass and closing the status, he could see that the core had shattered into thousands of tiny fragments.

"What happened to the core?" he asked, surprised that it had shattered.

"When all the available energy in a core is used up, it breaks," Sarah said with a shrug. "Not really sure why, though."

"Did you rank up?" he asked her, getting slowly to his feet and testing his injured leg. He winced as he did so, feeling a sharp pain from his ankle.

It was definitely sprained.

Sarah sighed sadly and shook her head. "Like I said before; it becomes significantly harder to rank up as you go. How about you?"

She got to her feet as well, dusting off her pants, checking for tears.

"Yup, ranked up in both of my abilities," he said with a grin.

"So you're what now; rank 4 in both?" she said, incredulously.

Morgan nodded, feeling his good mood dissipate slightly. "I only wish I could rank up faster. This is taking forever."

"You've moved up a total of 8 ranks in a few weeks and you're *complaining* about it? It took me three *years* to get where I am today! Years, Morgan!"

Morgan had the good grace to look sheepish at that. He held his hands up in surrender as she stalked over to him. "Alright, alright! I'm sorry!"

"You should be!"

She prodded him in the chest with one of her fingers, her bright green eyes flashing in the sunlight.

She glared up at him for so long that he began to fear another dousing of icy cold water, when Sarah snorted out a laugh.

Morgan blinked in surprise as she backed away from him, her head thrown back as peals of laughter echoed out.

"You should have seen your face!" she said, doubling over as Morgan began to realize that he'd been duped somehow.

"That wasn't very funny," he mumbled, but she ignored him; instead, walking over to pick up their discarded packs as she continued laughing.

He tried to walk, but winced as his leg flared up in pain once more. So instead of walking, he used *fly* and floated over to her. He folded his arms, glaring at her as she finally seemed to calm down.

"What?" she asked, the smile still on her face. "You deserved much more than that for almost getting us killed."

Morgan raised an eyebrow at her. "Last I checked, it was the bear trying to kill us; not me."

She walked over and patted him on the cheek, as though comforting an especially dense dog.

"I'm not the one who could literally have *flown* us away when the bear attacked."

Morgan stared at her retreating back, feeling like he'd just been punched in the stomach.

12

Despite what she'd said, Sarah didn't actually seem upset with him. They sat together, back in the shade of the trees, eating lunch and talking as they always did.

He had fashioned himself a splint from two branches and bound them together with strips of the pants he'd ruined while fighting. There was one thing still bothering him about what he'd seen on the core's stat screen, so he decided to ask Sarah.

"What did it mean, that the bear was on the cusp of evolution?"

Sarah leaned back against a tree, her eyes drooping sleepily.

They had been up all night and had only gotten a few hour's sleep before the bear attack. Now that the adrenaline of the fight had worn off, she was likely ready to drop.

"All beasts will evolve as they grow. Every time they reach a certain rank, they gather up a massive amount of energy and evolve into something new."

"So what you're telling me is that somewhere out there, there is a *max ranked* beast with a core just like this one?"

Sarah yawned once more, her eyes beginning to drift shut. "What you're talking about are called *pinnacle beasts.* They are very rare, but every once in a while, one will show up. When they do, a massive hunt is called; usually sponsored by the kingdom. Aside from the threat that such beasts pose, their cores have so much energy that they can push someone from *rank 0* to *rank 30* all at once. To someone who is already at the point where ranking up is measured in decades, finding a beast like that would be priceless."

Morgan's mind was already racing with possibilities.

If he could somehow find one of these beasts and kill it, he would be able to avoid years of effort. And once he was strong enough, he wouldn't have to be afraid of people like Simon. He would no longer need to run.

He looked up as he heard a loud snore and saw Sarah sprawled out on her back, with her mouth wide open; sound asleep. He debated going over and waking her up, but decided it was best to let her be.

They would be traveling in just a few hours and he should likely get some sleep himself. He wanted to take a peek at his status first, however.

Concentrating for a moment, the purple screen flickered into his vision.

Name: Morgan
Super: Rank - 4
Energy to next rank - 593/2,300
Mage: Rank - 4
Energy to next rank - 42/2,300
Super ability - Gravity
Mage ability - Air
CP - 170/170 (Regen - 1.8 per second)
MP - 170/170 (Regen - 1.8 per Second)
Strength - 16
Agility - 21
Constitution - 16
Intelligence - 17
Wisdom - 18
Super skills - Fly, Heavy handed
Mage skills - Wind blade, Tailwind

Morgan closed his status and leaned back against a tree. He placed his hands behind his head and closed his eyes, letting his mind wander.

His agility seemed to be increasing at a much higher rate than any other attribute. Was there a particular reason? He wondered if there were ways to raise attributes other than through ranking up. Right now, he was lacking in both strength and constitution. He desperately needed to figure out how to increase both.

He was still thinking about different ways to increase in power when he finally drifted off.

***

Arnold scowled as he downed another mug of ale. He was sitting in a tavern in the seedier part of City Six and he was not in a good mood.

Three days, and nothing, he thought bitterly as he downed his fourth mug in as many minutes. He slammed the mug down and motioned to the bartender for a refill.

"I think you've had enough," the man said with a scowl.

Arnold moved so quickly that the bartender didn't even have a chance to blink before he was dangling a good foot off the ground; the front of his shirt bunched up in Arnold's fist.

"Do I look drunk to you, bartender?" Arnold asked, wrenching the trembling man over the counter and glaring at him.

The bar went silent as he did this, everyone's eyes fixing on the spectacle unfolding before them.

"Not at all, sir!" he squeaked.

It was then that he felt a light tap on his shoulder. Not releasing his grip on the bartender, Arnold turned his head to meet the gaze of the two bouncers standing behind him.

"I would recommend letting the man go," one of them said, cracking his knuckles and making a visible display of his bulging muscles.

"Oh? And what if I don't want to?" Arnold asked, as the bartender kicked and struggled in his grip.

"Then I guess we'll have to remove you," the man said, a nasty smile stretched across his lips.

The other patrons began cheering as he pulled a stout wooden club from his belt and took a few practice swings with it. They had seen this done several times before, and it always ended the same way; with the bouncer's victory and the aggressive party laid out flat.

The bouncer gave an exaggerated bow to the crowd. Then, spinning on the spot, swung it at the side of Arnold's head with all his might. The club connected with a sharp crack and a howl of pain echoed through the tavern.

The entire room went silent as they stared at the incomprehensible scene before them.

The bouncer was on his knees, clutching his broken wrist and screaming in agony, while the stranger looked on. His expression hadn't changed and his grip on the bartender hadn't loosened.

Arnold slowly stooped down and lifted the man's club. He took a few practice swings with it, then looked down at the now sobbing bouncer.

"Here, let me show you how it's done."

He pulled his arm back to take the man's head off his shoulders; when the door banged open. Arnold looked up to see his tracker, Weasel, walk in.

"I see you're making friends, as always," he said with his trademark sneer.

Arnold shrugged. "They refused to give a drink when I asked for it."

"Well, you can put him down. I found the man who reported our quarry to the city guard."

"Isn't this your lucky day," Arnold said dryly, finally releasing the bartender; who crashed to the ground, sputtering and coughing as he gasped for air.

The door slammed shut behind the two men and everyone in the tavern breathed a collective sigh of relief.

***

Morgan awoke just as the sun was beginning to set. Seeing that Sarah was already awake, he yawned and stretched, getting slowly to his feet and testing his sprained leg. The brace seemed to be doing its job, so he limped over to where she was sitting and plopped down next to her.

She looked up from a book she'd been reading, and smiled. "Sleep well?"

He nodded and leaned sideways to dig through their packs. Emerging with a piece of flatbread and some dried meat, he leaned back and began eating.

Sarah closed the book with a snap and stowed it away in one of the bags.

"Since we no longer have horses and you can't walk very well, it looks like you'll need to be our mode of transportation."

Morgan shrugged, taking another bite of the tough meat and chewed slowly.

"As far as I can tell," she continued, "it will take us another three and a half weeks to reach the border of the North Kingdom and another week after that to reach the capital of Heraldia, where the academy is located."

Morgan nodded, popping the last piece of meat into his mouth and swallowing.

"I think you're right about flying the rest of the way. It'll let us stay off the roads and we'll be able to take a more direct path. I can carry a few more pounds since I ranked up, but I think we should leave everything that we don't absolutely need."

"You're probably right," Sarah said with a sigh. "I was really hoping to be able to hold onto some of these books, though."

"I'm sure you can replace them once we reach the academy," Morgan said with a grin. "You're rich, after all."

She laughed at that and punched him playfully in the arm. The two of them then set to emptying their bags of all non-essential items. Books, extra clothes and even food that they thought might not be needed was left. By the time they were done, the bags were a good deal lighter and Morgan was fairly confident that they'd be able to make good time.

He held out his hand to Sarah and hid a wince as he helped her up. She nodded her thanks and they were soon flying low over the treetops as they headed south toward the Central Kingdom.

***

Arnold stared across the table at the small, greasy man. They were sitting in another tavern, this one even nastier than the last.

"Couldn't you have picked a better meeting place?" Arnold asked, glaring over his shoulder at Weasel, who just shrugged.

He sighed and turned back to the man sitting across from him.

"So, Weasel tells me that you have information about our quarry."

The man leaned forward, placing his elbows on the table. It was covered in so many different stains that Arnold couldn't even begin to guess at what it may have originally looked like.

"Aye, I've got information alright."

The man's accent was so thick that Arnold was having a hard time understanding him.

"But it's gonna cost you. Don't want no bronze or copper either; I want gold."

Arnold could see the glint of greed in his little piggy eyes and shrugged. Pulling a coin pouch from his belt, he dropped it on the table in front of the man.

The pouch made an audible clink as it hit the table and the grubby man quickly snatched it up.

Arnold watched as the man quickly checked the contents of the pouch, before looking up once more.

He recognized that look. It was a real shame, too; he had really been trying to avoid another spectacle.

"I would recommend you think good and hard about the next words you're going to say," Arnold said in a conversational tone. "After all, I just paid you handsomely, so just give me the information and I'll be on my way."

The man seemed to think for a moment, and Arnold could see the battle between greed and common sense going on behind the man's eyes. In the end, greed won out.

"I do agree that you paid me nicely, but this money would just be for my time."

The man leaned forward across the table and Arnold wrinkled his nose at his rank odor.

"If you want the information, it'll cost you a platinum."

"Are you sure that's your final answer?" Arnold asked.

"Yeah, and fork it up quick. I am a busy man, after all."

The next moment, the man was slammed against the wall; his feet dangling a good few feet off the ground as Arnold stared up at him with cold eyes.

"Now I'm going to ask you one more time. What do you know?"

The man struggled and kicked, his eyes bugging out of skull as Arnold's grip tightened around his neck.

"What was that? I couldn't hear you," Arnold said nastily, as he spun and threw the man across the room; where he smashed into the opposite wall with the sound of crunching bones.

One or two people looked up as the man went flying, but soon went back to their drinks. This was not the kind of place where people would interfere in someone else's business.

The man moaned as Arnold hoisted him up from the ground by his hair.

"You ready to talk now?"

The man whimpered and nodded as best he could.

After the man finished speaking, Arnold reached down and took back his coin pouch. Reaching in, he fished out a copper coin and dropped it on the whimpering man.

"Take a bath, you smell like a horse's ass."

Arnold left the tavern with Weasel trailing right behind him.

The information he'd received was quite troubling. If the man was to be believed, then Sarah and her companion had managed to ride themselves off a cliff.

Arnold marched right up to the city gates, forgoing their horse altogether.

It would take too long and, according to the man, the area where they'd last been spotted was only a mile or so from the city walls.

As he got closer, he could see that the gates were closed. Two guards were posted on either side and they moved to block him as he approached.

"Stop right there! No one leaves the city after dark!"

Arnold didn't even slow down. Grabbing both guards by the fronts of their tunics, he hurled them a good twenty feet. When they landed a few seconds later; he didn't hear them cry out.

Marching right up to the gates, he picked his foot up and kicked it open.

There was a sound of splintering wood and shrieking metal as the massive gates were torn from their hinges. He could hear the sound of commotion behind him as guards came running out of the guard house at the base of the wall.

He ignored them and broke out into a run, moving swiftly down the road. He could hear Weasel's light footsteps following behind him and he slowed to allow him to catch up.

"You getting anything yet?"

He shook his head.

"Guess we'll need to get closer."

They ran on for a few minutes before Weasel stopped him.

"That's where they went off the road."

Arnold nodded, letting Weasel take the lead as he moved slowly through the forest.

Weasel had a special skill called *detection*. With this skill, he could pick out even the tiniest of details. That skill, along with another one he refused to disclose, made him the best tracker in all of the kingdom.

He stopped as Weasel held out a hand, and waited. After a few moments he motioned to him and Arnold followed him once more. This went on for the next few minutes, with Weasel crouching and muttering to himself and Arnold following silently along.

He could hear the distant sound of shouting coming from the city and knew that the guards had likely been sent after them.

Now that they were here, he regretted what he'd done. Once the guards arrived, he would have to go back to the city and wait for Lord Simon to get him released. Otherwise, he'd spend his entire trip being harassed by soldiers.

He could see where the ground ended abruptly up ahead, and Weasel was already crouched by the cliff's edge, examining something.

Arnold waited patiently for him to finish, even as the sound of hoof beats grew louder. Finally the man straightened and walked back to him.

"Are they still alive?"

"Something definitely went over that cliff, but it wasn't them." Weasel looked quite happy, an expression he usually never wore. "That boy is quite clever. Are you sure we have to kill him?"

Arnold shrugged. "Lord Simon wants him dead."

Weasel sighed. "What a shame."

"Tell me how they fooled the trackers into thinking they were dead."

As he began to speak, Arnold could feel his respect for the boy growing. By the time he was done talking, he wholeheartedly agreed with the man.

To think, that they had sent their horses over the cliff and faked their own deaths. Then to throw any trackers off, they lowered themselves under the lip and moved along it until it was safe to emerge.

He wasn't really sure how they'd done it, but Weasel said the most likely scenario was that Sarah had created handholds for them. Truly resourceful.

"You're quite right," he said as horsemen burst into view and surrounded them. "It really is a shame."

13

Morgan could feel his heart racing in excitement.

They were finally here. After weeks of travel, they had finally made it to the city of Heraldia.

It had taken them nearly a month to reach the border, but luckily for them, the rest of their journey had gone smoothly. It wasn't hard to get into the Central Kingdom. All Sarah had to do was present her family crest and tell them that she was heading for the academy.

It was a risk showing anyone her seal, but Lord Simon had no power in the Central Kingdom. It was also quite common for the nobility of other countries to send their children to the academy, as the Central Kingdom was the only neutral place in the five kingdoms.

As for not having any guards, Sarah easily explained it away as not wanting to arouse suspicion that she was gone. The guards at the gate had nodded and told her that the tryouts for the academy were already ongoing, and if she wanted to make it in before the term started, she would have to hurry.

So now they ran through the streets of the city, dodging around people as they went. According to Sarah, today was the final day of preliminary tryouts and Morgan didn't want to miss it. Sarah, who was running behind him, grabbed his arm to slow him down.

"Calm down," she said with a laugh. "We still have plenty of time to make it."

He smiled back, deciding that she was probably right and slowed to a walking pace.

"So, what do you think the test will be?" Morgan wondered.

"It shouldn't be too hard. From what I've heard, all they really want to check is whether you have an ability or not."

Morgan was surprised to hear this. "There are people without abilities who try and get in?"

"All the time," she answered. "At least half of the people who try out don't have any ability at all."

"So why bother trying to get in in the first place?" Morgan wondered.

"Beats me." Sarah shrugged.

They walked on in silence for the next few minutes, each enjoying the warmth of the sun as they walked through the wide main street. The weather in the Central Kingdom was always nice, never too hot or too cold; which made it a very attractive spot to live in.

They passed a few stalls selling food and Morgan breathed in deeply, allowing the wonderful aroma of freshly baked pastries to wash over his senses. He could feel his mouth begin to water, and was debating whether to make a small detour; when the crowd around them thinned and he got his first good look at the academy.

They were on a hill overlooking the grounds and he could hardly believe his eyes. A massive section of the city was devoted to the school, and Morgan stared in awe as people streamed through a multitude of gates below. The entire academy was walled off and he could see hundreds of guards patrolling around the perimeter.

"Why are there so many guards?" Morgan asked as they began walking down the hill.

"There are probably several hundred nobles from all over the five kingdoms in there right now. Although this is a neutral kingdom, that wouldn't deter assassins from trying to kill one of them. Those guards up there are some of the strongest in the world. From what I've heard, the minimum rank to join is 24 and most are even above that."

Morgan felt his respect for this King Herald go up a few notches.

Even though they'd thrown off their pursuers when they'd escaped City Six, he was way too paranoid to believe that they weren't still being followed. If King Herald took the security of his school this seriously, they might actually be safe from whoever Simon had sent after them.

It took another half an hour to reach the academy gates and a further fifteen minutes to get in. As they were passing through, a man asked them to stop and ran a flat piece of metal over their bodies before letting them pass.

"What are those for?" Morgan asked the guard, curiously.

The guard looked surprised, as though he wasn't used to people talking to him.

"It's a magical ward detector. Checks to see if you're carrying any dangerous or potentially destructive items."

Morgan thanked the guard for the explanation, and he and Sarah headed toward the main courtyard. There was a raised platform in front of a massive stone building. Several desks stood on the platform and a line of people snaked out from where they were set up.

"Excuse me," Sarah asked the last person standing in line. "Is this line for tryouts?"

The girl turned and gave Sarah a nasty glare. "Yeah, not that you'll ever get in. This school is for talented people, not nobodies like you."

"Friendly crowd," she muttered, eliciting a laugh from Morgan.

This made the girl glare at them once more.

As the line slowly inched forward, Morgan began to grow nervous.

What if he wasn't good enough to get in and the academy kicked him out? He didn't have any doubts as to whether Sarah would get in, but him?

It took nearly two hours for them to reach the front of the line, and Morgan turned to Sarah as the person in front of him went up to one of the tables.

"I'll meet you over there when we're done," he said, pointing to a large fountain in the center of the open courtyard.

Sarah nodded. "Good luck."

"You too," he said, as one of the people motioned him forward.

He walked up to the table, where a young looking woman was taking notes on a piece of paper. She put down her pen and looked up at him with a professional smile.

"Welcome to the Central Academy for Mages and Supers, or CAMS as everyone around here calls it. Here at CAMS, we strive to educate the next generation of talented young individuals, and help them on their paths to success."

The woman stopped here and rifled through a few papers before bringing out a blank sheet.

"I'll need your name, rank and ability type."

Morgan was loathe to divulge this information; but decided that since it was being asked, everyone would be expected to.

"My name is Morgan and I have a *rank 4* super ability."

He had decided to enter the academy as a super, as Sarah was already a mage and he could learn all he needed from her at the end of the day.

The woman scribbled on the paper for a few moments before tearing off a strip and handing it over to him.

"Take this paper to room number eight. Good luck."

Morgan thanked the woman before heading inside the building. The entryway was massive and the ceiling towered at least thirty feet over his head. People were milling about, all holding piece of paper and looking around at the myriad of doors dotting the wall.

Looking straight ahead, he could see a door with the number *4* emblazoned on it in red paint. Looking to one side, he could see the room with the number *8* just a few doors down and headed toward it. Taking a deep breath to calm his nerves, Morgan knocked once and entered.

The room was made of solid stone and light streamed in from above through open slats in the ceiling. A man was sitting behind a stone desk in the corner of the fairly large space and Morgan shuffled awkwardly in as the man didn't seem to notice him.

Even sitting down, he could tell that the man was quite tall. Just over six feet, and he had short blonde hair and dark colored eyes. His face was smooth and had the same sort of ageless quality to it that Morgan had seen on Samuel; the stranger who had healed him. The man finally looked up as he approached and he could see a bored expression on his face.

"Hello, my name is Morgan. I was told to come here," Morgan said, handing over the slip of paper.

The man took it, not even bothering to look and placed it down on his desk.

"My name is Instructor Gold. Let's see what you can do."

"What I can do?" Morgan asked, uncertainly.

"Yes, show me your skills; if you have any," Gold said, waving impatiently.

Morgan stared at the man for a few seconds, then he shrugged. Taking a few steps away from the desk, he used *fly*, instantly feeling a weightless sensation overtake him as he floated up off the ground.

Gold's disinterested look vanished in an instant and he sat up straighter as Morgan did a lap around the room. He landed in front of the man, who was now looking at him in a whole new light.

"I've seen people fly before, but only on very rare occasions," he said excitedly. "Do you have any other skills?"

"Yes, but I'll need to hit something for you to see it. I'll also have to hit it twice so you can see the difference," Morgan answered.

"Excellent!"

Gold pushed away from his desk and walked to the center of the room.

Morgan started at him in astonishment as he motioned him over.

"Go on then, hit me."

"Are you sure? I don't want to accidentally kill you or anything."

To Morgan's dismay, however, the man just laughed.

"Much as I appreciate your concern, I doubt you could cause me any significant harm. Now come on, we don't have all day."

With a mental shrug, Morgan walked over to him and took up a fighting stance. Then he drew his arm back and punched the Gold's abdomen as hard as he could. He didn't budge even an inch. Morgan looked up to see if he'd caused him any discomfort, but the man's face betrayed nothing. He then used his *heavy handed* skill and drew his fist back, slamming it into Gold's abdomen once again.

Instead of hearing the expected crack of bones along with a cry of pain, Gold just smiled.

"Fascinating," he said, smoothing the front of his shirt where Morgan's fist had made contact. "I could definitely feel a difference there, just over twice the power of your first attack." He walked back to his desk as Morgan stared at him in shock.

Just what kind of monster was he?

Gold sat back down behind his desk and looked down at the paper. "So, you're at *rank 4*, and you have a super ability. If you don't mind me asking, just what is your ability called?"

Morgan, still in shock from his complete inability to hurt this man, answered without thinking. "Gravity."

"Ah, that would explain the flight, as well as the increased striking power."

Gold steepled his fingers and stared at Morgan for a few seconds, his eyes appraising him in a new light.

"I can already guess at your *strength* and *agility,* but would you mind telling me about your other attributes?"

Morgan nodded and quickly listed them off to him. He immediately knew he'd made a mistake when Gold's eyebrows shot up in incredulity then narrowed in suspicion. He stared at him for a few seconds and Morgan could feel a cold sweat beginning to break out as he did.

After a few more tense moments, Gold leaned back in his chair and a pleased expression crossed his face. He then waved his hand and a stone chair rose from the ground.

"Have a seat."

Morgan stared at the chair for a moment, then reluctantly sat down.

So this man was most likely a mage, he realized. That was quite troubling, as he hadn't been at all damaged by his heavy handed skill. Worse still, he hadn't even bothered using his mage shield, which meant that this man was on a whole other level of power.

His nerves ratcheted up another notch as Gold appraised him and the silence between them began to stretch.

"I would like to ask you to do something for me."

Morgan almost breathed a sigh of relief when Gold started talking, but he contained himself with an effort of will.

This man was way too perceptive and he wouldn't miss something as obvious as that.

"We normally do our testing in two phases. The first is to determine if the person actually has an ability, and the second is to determine combat readiness, ranking in the class and whether that student is worthy of a scholarship."

"Since King Herald only offers them to the top fifty students of each class per year, we have to be very selective of who we give them to. The second test is also recorded, as the instructors will be choosing which students they would like to teach."

Only the top fifty students of each class?

Morgan was dismayed at this news.

He'd really been hoping to be able to get in on that scholarship, as he hadn't wanted to lean on Sarah for the money.

Gold could see his expression and nodded.

"I can see that the gravity of the situation is sinking in; no pun intended," he said with a light chuckle.

"The reason I'm telling you all this now, is that I'd like you to preform the second part of the test for me now. What do you say?"

"If it'll give me a better chance of getting a scholarship, I'll do it now," Morgan said.

Gold nodded and gestured to the center of the room once more. There was a loud rumbling sound and then a stone golem rose from the ground below. It was roughly man-shaped and stood just a few inches taller than him.

Morgan stepped up to the thing and examined it from all sides. Then it moved; its head slowly following him as he walked around its body.

"You will fight against this golem until you either destroy it, or it renders you incapable of fighting. There is no need to worry about injuries, as we have plenty of healers on hand."

Morgan nodded and stepped up to face the golem. His heart was pounding as adrenaline rushed through his body and he took up a fighting stance.

"Ready?" he heard Gold's voice ask.

Taking one last deep breath, Morgan nodded.

"Then begin!"

14

Morgan tensed as the golem shot towards him with astonishing speed.

He'd been expecting it to be a lot slower, seeing as it was made of stone.

He dodged quickly to the side and used *heavy handed,* feeling his *CP* drop by *20* and the timer begin to count down in his head.

He ducked under a swing from the golem and brought his open palm up, smashing it into its chest as he straightened. The force of his skill, along with his momentum, should easily have shattered a normal piece of stone; but the only discernable damaged he could make out, was a small line of cracks spreading from where his strike had impacted.

He dove to the side as the golem's knee came up, wincing as he wasn't fast enough to completely dodge the attack. He got quickly to his feet and felt at his ribs. Thankfully, they were still intact, though he was sure that a nasty bruise was already spreading under his armor.

He was now quite glad he'd invested in the leather breastplate, as a regular shirt wouldn't have done much to shield him.

He watched the golem warily as it approached once again.

It had barely grazed him and it still hurt like hell. Being hit full on was not an option.

He ran towards the golem as it charged once again. Dodging a swinging fist, he used *heavy handed* once more and slammed an open palm into the same spot he had hit previously. His efforts were rewarded when he heard a loud crack and when the golem turned to him again, he could see that the line of cracks had spread.

One or two more hits should do it, he thought.

The golem charged yet again and Morgan decided to use the same tactic as last time. That was when things went horribly wrong. As Morgan brought his hand up to strike the golem's chest, it pivoted on one foot and slammed its leg into the joint of his knee. Morgan grunted as he felt his leg buckle and just managed to turn enough to avoid having the limb broken.

He stumbled back as the golem began raining down blows and it was all he could do to keep dodging.

Left. Right. Right. Up. Left.

The blows kept on coming from all directions and he was beginning to flag. He tried to use *fly* to get out of range, but as soon as his feet left the ground, the golem leapt into the air and caught him with a particularly nasty blow to his liver. Morgan fell out of the air and landed on the ground with a wheeze.

He couldn't breathe and he felt like he was going to die.

Finally, after a few seconds of panicked gasping, air flooded his lungs and Morgan got shakily to his feet. The golem had landed a few feet away and was now advancing toward him once more.

This thing was way too quick and even with agility being his highest attribute, he could barely manage to keep up; and that was before he'd taken a blow to his leg.

Morgan watched as the golem charged him again, but he wasn't about to wait for it to finish him off. He charged straight in and took a hard blow to his stomach, but he managed to score another hit on the golem hearing a satisfying crack as he did so.

He smiled, despite the pain, as the golem teetered back on one leg. Thinking that this was his chance to finish it, he rushed in for one final attack. Then the golem did something completely unexpected. Instead of falling, it preformed a full three hundred and sixty degree turn; and using the momentum from the spin, slammed its other leg directly into his chest.

Morgan grunted in pain as he was thrown backward and slammed into the opposite wall. He somehow managed to keep his balance and winced as he clutched at his ribs.

He'd heard a snap when the golem's foot had connected and knew that at least two of his ribs were broken.

This was not going well. If this fight kept up for much longer, he would be too injured to continue. As it was, he doubted he could hit the golem anymore. It was hard enough to hit when he'd been at his best; now with two broken ribs and a throbbing leg he didn't stand a chance. Unless…

Morgan stumbled away from the wall and peeked at Gold out of the corner of his eye.

The man was watching the fight with an impassive gaze and he wondered if could get away with what he had planned.

He turned back, just in time to dodge out of the way of an incoming punch from the golem, wincing as his ribs flared up in protest.

There was nothing for it, he had to do this now before it got any worse. He would just need to be careful not to increase his speed too much.

Morgan stopped in the middle of the room and centered his gaze on the golem's chest as it turned to face him once more. The line of cracks was visible and deep; one good blow would shatter it.

The golem shot towards him once more and he knew this was it.

Either he would destroy it and win, or the golem would lay him out flat and any chance of a scholarship would be gone.

As the golem drew near, Morgan crouched and used *tailwind*. He felt instantly lighter, but was careful not to move at his full speed. The golem moved in swiftly and threw a punch that would have undoubtedly cracked his skull.

If he hadn't used tailwind, there was no way he could have dodged it, but now, it seemed almost too easy.

Morgan ducked the blow, careful to allow it to clip the top of his head, but not enough to knock him out. He winced as pain shot through his skull from where the fist had impacted, but he pushed through.

Since the golem had committed everything to this attack, it was now wide open to a counter from him. Morgan rose from the crouch, using both the momentum and extra speed from his skill, and slammed his open palm into the golem's chest.

There was a loud boom, and the golem shattered into a thousand pieces. Morgan winced, shaking his hand as bits of stone rained down around him. Then he fell to the ground, clutching at his chest and gasping in pain.

That last attack must have made his injuries worse.

He heard Gold say something, but he couldn't make out what he was saying through the haze of pain. Then the most wonderful tingling sensation spread throughout his entire body and washed away all his aches and pains.

He blinked, his eyes finally coming into focus and saw a man leaning over him. His hand was on his chest and was glowing lightly. After another moment, the man removed his hand and turned to look at him.

"Any pain or discomfort?"

"No, none at all," Morgan answered, his voice tinged with awe. "Thank you," he was quick to add as he got to his feet.

The man smiled as he dusted off his long white robes. "Just doing my job, but thanks are always appreciated, young man."

He then turned to Gold, who was once again seated behind his desk. "Is there anything else?"

"No, that will be all. Thank you, Eric."

The man nodded to him, then turned and left the room.

"Come have a seat, Morgan," Gold said, motioning again to the stone chair in front of his desk.

Morgan did as he said, noticing that all signs of the fight that had taken place were now gone. The room looked whole and undamaged and there was no sign at all of the golem.

Gold wrote a few more things down on a piece of paper while Morgan sat there.

He wasn't sure what the instructor was writing. He just hoped it wasn't something bad.

"That was well done," Gold said, setting down his pen and giving Morgan his full attention.

"Thank you," Morgan answered, unsure of what else to say.

He nodded. "Yes, quite a feat. It's impressive that you managed to win. Especially seeing as the golem was a full *4 ranks* above you."

He smiled then and leaned back in his seat. "But I guess that shouldn't come as any surprise, seeing as you have a mage ability in addition to the one you told me about."

15

Morgan felt his stomach drop all the way down to his boots when he heard those words. For a moment, he considered fighting; but then remembered how easily Gold had shrugged off his most powerful attack.

There was nothing he could do to hurt him and running away was likely out of the question as well.

Morgan's shoulders slumped in defeat as he began to imagine his impending execution.

"What gave me away?"

"It wasn't anything specific; rather a multitude of separate things that came together for me to come to this conclusion," Gold said with a grin.

Morgan sighed, slumping even further down into the chair.

"Oh, don't look so glum," Gold said with a wave of his hand. "I'm not going to tell anyone."

"You're not?" Moran asked, perking up a bit, but still not trusting that the man was being honest.

He'd learned at a very young age that trust wasn't something to just hand out.

Gold shrugged.

"I'm not a noble, nor do I care for their politics. If I can help another of your kind to unlock the supermage ability, why wouldn't I? I am a teacher, after all."

Morgan felt his spirits rise just a bit more at those words.

The way he'd phrased that last sentence was odd though.

"What do you mean by 'another of my kind'?"

"You caught that did you? Good, that means you've got a brain inside that thick skull of yours."

Morgan wasn't sure if that was a compliment, or an insult, but he didn't really have time to ponder it as Gold continued.

"How old do you think I am?"

This question came so far out of nowhere that Morgan just blurted out the first number that came into his head.

"Thirty?"

A loud bark of laughter emanated from the man when he said this.

"That is very kind of you, but no. Despite my youthful appearance, I am well over three hundred years old and have devoted over two hundred of those years to teaching at this school."

Morgan's eyes widened.

Gold was over three hundred? He'd heard that people with abilities could live that long, but he'd never actually believed it could be true.

"In all the time I've been teaching here, only one other person with abilities like yours came through here and I had the pleasure of being her instructor."

He leaned back even further in his chair and let out a wistful sounding sigh.

"She was just like you. Not attached to any noble family, but wanting to learn all the same. Desperately afraid of being caught and killed for what she was."

"Who was she?" Morgan asked in a quiet voice.

This was the first mention of a supermage other than himself and even if she was dead, maybe he could find out more about her.

"Who is she, you mean," Gold said, still smiling at him. "And sorry, but I swore not to disclose any information about her; and I keep my word."

"How do I know that anything you just told me is true? You could just be making all this up in an attempt to gain my trust," he asked, folding his arms and narrowing his eyes in suspicion.

"You don't," Gold answered, "but what do you have to lose by trusting me?"

He had a good point. If Gold wanted him dead, he could likely do it himself and without any real resistance on his part. That didn't mean that he wouldn't try to get as much out of him as he could before he agreed, however.

"If I'm going to stay, I'll need a few things from you."

"Naturally," Gold said.

"First of all, I have a friend here with me. Her name is Sarah and she's a talented mage. If you're going to take me on as a student, you'll have to take her as well and offer us both a scholarship."

He knew she didn't need it, but if she got one, she wouldn't have to reveal her wealth; which would undoubtedly mark her as a noble.

"That is acceptable," he answered.

"Second, I'll have you give me your word that you won't tell anyone about my secret. If you really keep your word as you say, then that will have to be good enough for now."

"Then you have it. I will not tell anyone of your existence unless you allow me to disclose the information."

Morgan nodded. "And third, I'll need some kind of proof that you really know anything about supermages. You claim to have trained one, so you should know all about it."

This was the real test. If Gold really had trained another supermage, then proving his knowledge should be easy.

"Very well then; an impromptu lesson."

Gold had a smile on his face as he rose from his seat and began pacing excitedly.

"While mages and supers alike each have a different colored stat screen; red for supers and blue for mages; those possessing both mana and chi have purple colored stat screens. To pull up their status, a person possessing both forms of energy must first combine them, otherwise it will not open. The merging of the two energies creates an entirely new source of power called *reiki*; which will become the main energy source once the supermage ability is unlocked.

"The word *reiki* literally means 'universal life energy', meaning that there is no energy source more pure, or more powerful, than that. That is also the reason a supermage is so much more powerful than a regular super or mage; who are only using one half of a greater whole. Now, for someone who has yet to unlock their supermage ability, the manipulation of reiki is limited to pulling up their status. That is all you will be able to use it for until you unlock the supermage ability."

Gold stopped pacing and turned to Morgan, who had an astonished look on his face.

"I can tell by your expression that you're convinced of my knowledge."

Morgan nodded dumbly.

There was no doubt as to whether or not Gold knew what he was talking about, and he would make sure to learn it all.

Gold peered up at the ceiling, where the light was now streaming in from a different direction.

"Well, would you look at the time," he laughed. "I'm sorry to have kept you here for so long."

"No, it's not a problem," Morgan said, rising from his seat.

He still had a few reservations about this man, but most had been put to rest.

"Great," Gold said, placing an arm on Morgan's back and walking him towards the door.

"Term doesn't start for another two days, but I'll take care of any paperwork for you and your friend Sarah."

He handed him a slip of paper with *Q87* written on it, along with a slim iron key.

"This is your dorm and room number. The letter is for the block you'll be in and the number is for the room."

"What about Sarah's room?" he asked.

"No need to worry, you and your friend will be sharing an apartment of sorts with me. It's quite spacious, so no need to worry about room."

"Um, okay," Morgan said.

He was a little overwhelmed by all the new information.

"I just have one more thing to ask before you go. What is the name of your mage ability?"

Morgan thought about lying for a second, before shrugging.

"My mage ability is called *Air.*"

Gold blinked again, then a wide grin spread across his face.

"If luck was an attribute, I'd have to say that it would be your highest one!"

16

Morgan hurried out of the building, and into the open courtyard. Judging by the position of the sun, it was around two hours after noon.

That meant he'd been in there for nearly three hours.

He inwardly cringed, thinking of how mad Sarah was likely to be and broke into a run. It only took a minute for him to spot her sitting by the fountain and sure enough, Sarah did not look happy.

"Hey, sorry it took so long," Morgan called out, as he ran up to her. "A lot happened in there. Have you been waiting long?"

Sarah glared at him for a moment and he saw her eyes flick to the fountain, as if contemplating whether to soak him or not. She let out a long sigh and her hard expression softened.

"I've been waiting for nearly two hours! I was worried that something terrible had happened to you!"

Morgan sighed as well, more in relief at not being given an impromptu bath, and held out a hand to help her up. She took it begrudgingly and he pulled her to her feet.

"I've got a lot to tell you, but before I begin, I've got two good pieces of news."

Sarah quirked an eyebrow at him and Morgan was quick to continue.

"The first bit of good news is that I got in, and on a full scholarship!"

Sarah's face broke into a smile. "Congratulations! I knew you could do it."

"The second piece of good news, is that you also got in on a full scholarship."

The excitement melted from her face, to be replaced by one of concern.

"Explain," she demanded, folding her arms over her chest.

"I will, but not out here," Morgan said, looking around at the bustling crowd. "There's a room waiting for us and once we're there, I'll tell you everything that happened."

She looked like she wanted to argue, but nodded her assent.

It took them a surprisingly long time to make it to the Q section. After getting lost and asking for directions several times, the two of them eventually found themselves at the beginning of a long paved street with the letter Q posted on the side.

The street was lined with small, identical looking houses and several people were moving in and around the block.

"This is not what I expected," Morgan said, as they started down the block.

He had been expecting some sort of large building with a bunch of rooms, not a regular block with actual houses.

They headed down the cobbled street until they reached number *87*. Pulling the key from his pocket, Morgan unlocked the door and held it open for Sarah, who was still carrying their packs.

They walked into a neat room with a few plush looking chairs, a table and a large bookshelf against the back wall. There was a sectioned off area to the side, where Morgan could see several cooking implements as well as a stove. The area was also lined with small wooden cabinets where he assumed food was stored.

So they would be expected to cook for themselves?

"It's not a palace, but I guess it'll have to do," Sarah said, looking around the room.

Morgan agreed that it wasn't a palace, but considering the shack he'd been living in; this house may as well have been.

There were two doors on either side of the room and one had the word *students* painted above it.

"I guess that's where we go?" Sarah asked, walking over as he opened the door.

The room they entered into was almost identical to the last one they were in, with the exception of a large plush sofa against one wall. There were five doors leading off this room and the two of them were quick to explore.

Three of the doors led to identical bedrooms, all of which contained a wooden dresser, a closet and a bed. One was a privy and the last one contained a large bathtub.

After Morgan had put his few possessions away, he and Sarah sat down on the sofa. He explained everything that had happened. By the time he was finished with his story, she looked worried and was biting her lip nervously.

They sat in silence for a few minutes as Sarah mulled over what he'd just said.

"Do you really think we can trust this man?" she finally asked.

"I don't see that we have a choice," Morgan said, reclining into the soft material of the sofa.

He couldn't remember ever being this comfortable in his life!

"I really wish you wouldn't keep getting us into these situations," she said with a sigh, "but, what's done is done I guess."

"So did you find out any information about the school? Where we can buy food or clothes, or where we meet Gold in two days when the term starts?"

"Gold said he'd be living here with us. I'm guessing his room is on the other side of the house and he'll probably explain about the school stuff later. As for clothes and food…" He shrugged, "not really sure about those. Maybe check the kitchen."

"I don't know how to cook, Morgan," Sarah said in an annoyed tone. "I spent my entire life having people do that for me. Do you know how to cook?"

The relaxed expression disappeared from his face and he sat up, becoming a bit worried now.

He'd never been able to afford anything to eat, let alone learn how to cook. The only places he'd gotten food were from garbage bins, or when he visited Sarah.

"Well, school doesn't start for two days; let's go look around and see if we can find a place to eat," he said, rising reluctantly from the sofa.

Sarah agreed wholeheartedly. After they'd both gotten some money from their rooms, they headed out of the house, making sure to lock up behind them.

It was surprisingly easy to find a dining room. Apparently, the way it worked, was that every block had a central dining room. For those enrolled at the school, meals were served three times a day and were free.

Since the two of them were not officially part of the school yet, they were charged six bronze for the both of them; which Morgan had to pay since Sarah didn't have anything smaller than a gold.

They picked up their food at a long counter set against one side of the room, then went to find a table amid the hundreds of students already there. They each had a metal tray with a serving of chicken, vegetables and a mug of some amber colored liquid. The food was surprisingly good and Morgan looked around in wonder at all the people around them.

Was the academy really this big?

"Do the nobles eat here, as well?" Morgan asked.

The only nice noble he'd ever met was sitting next to him; and he somehow doubted that the haughty and self important nobility would stoop so low as to sit amongst commoners.

"From what I've heard, the nobility live in their own block. They have the nicest housing, the finest chefs and the best security," she said, with a shrug.

Morgan felt a little bad when she said that.

"Are you sure you don't want to be transferred to the noble block? After all, this must be uncomfortable for you."

Sarah actually laughed when he said that.

"I appreciate your concern, but I'm actually enjoying myself. Sure, the housing isn't what I'm used to, and the food isn't as lavish; but I've never eaten in a room with so many people before. You're the only friend I've ever had, that wasn't all stuffy, or interested in boring things. like gossip. It'll be a nice change to just be a regular person for once."

He smiled back, completely understanding what she meant by just fitting in.

Back in City Four, he'd have been singled out, beaten by the guards and even been sentenced to death; just for being who he was. But here no one even gave him a second glance and, looking around the packed dining room, he could see why.

People of all the kingdoms were gathered here and some appeared so different, that he couldn't even compare. At least a quarter of the students had the dusky brown skin of the West Kingdom. Over half had strange colored hair; and sitting just a few tables away, were a group of people with yellow eyes!

He'd never felt more at home in his entire life and he was loving every minute of it.

It didn't take too long for them to finish their meal and when they dropped off their trays, they asked one of the serving women where they might buy some clothes.

The woman smiled and bent down to retrieve a folded up piece of paper.

"The CAMS grounds are very large and often confusing to newcomers, so we have maps readily available throughout the campus. I'm surprised you didn't get one of these when you were accepted into the academy. One should have been included in your welcome papers."

Morgan thanked the woman, while inwardly cursing Gold for not even bothering to mention this very important detail.

Sarah was very poorly trying to cover a laugh at his annoyance, as they left the dining room. Morgan, choosing to ignore this, unfolded the map with a huff and began to examine it.

The map showed that the academy was laid out in a sort of grid, each section divided by lines. There was a tiny line at the bottom for scale, and judging by what he could see the academy was over ten miles wide, and fifteen across.

Looking a little closer, he could see their section clearly marked. He could also see where they'd come into the academy, as well as where he'd taken his test.

Searching around for a bit, he soon found an area marked, *Market & Shops*, which was located at the center of the map.

"I think this is where we need to go," Morgan said, pointing the place out on the map.

Sarah nodded and he was about to put the map away, when something caught his attention. There was an area marked *Block A*, and there was clearly a wall or fence around it.

"Hey Sarah, do you think this is where the nobles live?" he asked, pointing to the map.

"Well, seeing as it's in the best location and is fenced off; it's a pretty good bet," she said with a shrug.

Well located didn't even begin to cover it. The two of them were so far out, that they would have to walk miles to get anywhere.

He tucked the map away and they began their two mile walk to the shopping area.

It took them nearly an hour to get there, what with all the people constantly getting in their way.

More than once, Morgan was tempted to just grab Sarah and use *fly,* but he decided against it.

After all, it wouldn't do to draw unnecessary attention to themselves.

Once they arrived at the shopping district, Morgan was glad they'd made the trip. The area was packed with people, but there was so much to see that he feared he might be tempted to spend all his money.

He was immediately drawn to a store that had several sets of armor and weapons on display. Thinking back to his shredded clothes, he decided to stop there first.

Sarah wasn't at all interested, so the two of them decided to meet up after they were done.

A bell tinkled overhead as he walked in and Morgan could feel himself growing excited as he looked around. Oddly enough, the store seemed empty, which surprised him.

Wouldn't a store like this normally be packed?

A friendly looking man entered the shop from a back room and flashed a professional smile. "Welcome, young sir, is there anything I can help you with?"

"Yes. I need a few sets of sturdy clothes that can take some punishment," he said, walking up to the counter.

"The ones I've been using haven't held up well."

He motioned to his pants, which were already showing signs of tearing, despite only being a few weeks old.

A genuine smile touched the man's lips this time and he motioned Morgan to follow him.

"I do, in fact, have what you're looking for. Just got in a new shipment today; follow me around back and I'll show you what I've got."

"I am curious about something, if you don't mind answering," Morgan said, as he followed the man into a room full of clothing and bits of armor.

"Not at all. Ask away."

"Why is your shop so empty? I don't mean to sound rude, but shouldn't your store be packed? People should already know that their regular clothes won't stand up in any sort of combat."

The man laughed, as he took out a long piece of string and began measuring him.

"You must have a least a few *ranks* under your belt already, am I right?"

Morgan nodded as the man continued measuring him.

"Most of the new students are either *rank 0,* or maybe *rank 1*. They've likely never seen any actual combat, so they don't know what to expect. You're lucky you came now; by next week this place will be so packed that you won't be able to move and the selection will be very limited."

He finished his measurements and took a few notes on a piece of paper.

"I have four different options that I think would suit your needs. I have wool, wool with a metal mesh weave, leather, or canvas with a metal mesh weave."

"What would you recommend?" Morgan thought to ask.

The man's smile grew even wider, if at all possible.

"A sensible boy as well," he said with a laugh. "The wool is the cheapest and most popular, and you can't go wrong with leather. But if you have the coin to spare, I would recommend getting the canvas with the mesh weave. It's comfortable, light and can stand up to some serious punishment. It'll also give you more protection than that breastplate you're wearing now without impeding your movement at all."

This sounded perfect to him. A material that could stand up to all that and give him great protection? He was definitely interested.

"How much?" he carefully asked.

"For a full set of the canvas uniform, which include a shirt, pants and a pair of boots, will be two gold."

Morgan winced at the price.

His leather breastplate had only cost forty silver and it had hurt to pay even that much. But if these clothes were as good as the man said, then it would be worth the investment.

"Would you mind if I looked at a set before I make my decision? And can you recommend anything else I might find useful?"

"Of course. Just give me a moment and I'll be right back."

The man left the room and came back a minute later, with a set of clothes over one arm. He handed them over and Morgan fingered the material, amazed at the quality along with how durable it felt.

The shirt was a dark blue and had long sleeves that buttoned at the wrists with slim metal rivet. There were no other buttons;

instead the shirt would slide over his head and he could tighten it with a series of straps that ran along each side.

The pants were much the same, but were black instead of blue. Inspecting them, he could see that there was no need for a belt and that there were several pockets running down each pant leg.

The boots were also made of the same black material, but they felt somewhat different.

Probably some sort of treatment against water and dirt, Morgan guessed.

Finally looking up, he smiled at the man.

"Would you happen to have three such outfits in my size?"

"Of course," the shopkeeper said with a grin, hurrying out to fetch them while Morgan changed into the new clothes.

They felt just as amazing as he'd imagined.

The smooth material hugged his body in all the right places, allowing for the most comfortable and flexible movement possible. He couldn't even feel the steel mesh that was threaded throughout and was glad he'd decided on this purchase.

The boots were snug and light and he moved around a bit, getting a feeling for the outfit.

The shopkeeper came back with the other two sets he'd asked for, as well as another bundle tucked under one arm.

"How do you like them?" he asked, setting the clothes on the ground.

"They feel amazing! Thank you," Morgan said, pulling six gold from his pouch and handing it over.

The man smiled, accepting the gold and pocketing it.

"From the way you mentioned combat and armor, I'm guessing you have a super ability?" the man asked.

Morgan nodded as the man presented the other items he'd brought along.

There were two gloves, but they were missing part of the fingers and seemed to be lightly padded. There were also two long pieces of hardened leather with straps running around them.

"These gloves are for extra protection in case you need to hit something. They're great for training when your *constitution* isn't yet high enough for you to hit things with your bare fists."

Morgan nodded in appreciation.

Those gloves would have come in handy when fighting the stone golem earlier. He'd been forced to hit open handed, or risk breaking the bones in his hands. He could hit people without gloves, but he was still risking a painful injury.

"And what are those?" he asked, pointing to the two pieces of leather.

The shopkeeper became a little more excited as he explained.

"These are a new invention thought up by an armorer in the East. They are extra protection for your shins and ankles, and differ quite a bit from traditional steel shin guards. They're also much lighter and a whole lot more affordable. You simply slide them on under your pants and slip these top ends into your boots."

Morgan could have cheered at his good fortune.

He'd injured himself quite badly against the bear when they'd fought against it and once again when he fought the golem. Until he got his constitution high enough that he wouldn't injure himself, these would be invaluable.

"I'll take them both," he said with a smile.

He paid the seventy-five silver required after the shopkeeper explained that the gloves were made of the same material as his clothes. He inwardly groaned at the price, but told himself that it wasn't too high a price to pay to avoid broken bones.

"If you need anything else, come on by. My name is James. Just ask for me and I'll be more than happy to help."

Morgan thanked the man and left his shop. Taking a peek into his purse, he could see that a little over twenty eight gold remained.

He just hoped that this was the most expensive purchase he would have to make.

He looked around for a few moments and after not spotting Sarah by their meet up point, he walked over to a nearby bench and sat down to wait.

17

The sun was already beginning to set when the two of them finally made it back to their house. After Sarah saw his new clothes and Morgan explained what they were for, she had insisted on going back inside and buying a few sets of her own.

The shopkeeper, James, was so delighted that he'd brought in another good paying customer, that he'd offered him a ten percent discount on all future purchases.

After they were done shopping, they stopped in at the house to drop off their things, then Sarah had paid for their dinner. She'd gotten some smaller currency while they'd been out and the two of them enjoyed the delicious meal of venison and fried onions.

Now thoroughly exhausted and ready for bed, Morgan unlocked the front door.

"Oh, good. You've got perfect timing."

Morgan looked up to see Gold, sitting by the table and eating dinner. The room was well lit by several lamps and the smell of roast meat was thick in the air.

Sarah stepped nervously up next to him and Gold's eyes turned to settle on her. He appraised her for a minute, before smiling and gesturing them to take a seat.

"It's nice to finally meet you, Sarah. I read your paper and was thoroughly impressed. The highest ranking mage of the new students and ranked at the top of the first year mages."

Sarah's cheeks colored slightly at the praise.

"It's nice to meet you too, Sir. What do you mean by 'ranked at the top of my class?'"

"I was going to get to that in a few days, but since you're both here, I'll get the explanation of how the school works and what your lessons will entail out of the way now. I'll also be happy to answer any questions you may have."

They both nodded and Gold continued.

"At the beginning of the year, all students are given a ranking of where they stand in the class. This ranking is very important, as only the top fifty supers and mages will receive a scholarship. Right now, Sarah holds the number one rank in the mage class and Morgan holds the number nine rank in the super class. Any questions so far?"

"Are these rankings fixed? If not, is there any way to move up or down in them?" Morgan asked.

"The rankings are not fixed," Gold answered.

"Every week, students wishing to keep their ranking, must fight in at least one official match. You must fight someone within nine ranks of your own for the match to count. If you beat someone at a higher rank, you will move up by two, while the other person moves down by the same amount. The same is true if you lose."

"What happens if you don't compete?" Sarah asked.

"For every week you don't compete, you will suffer a loss in rank. The first week it'll be one, the second two, the third three and so on. So if you decide not to compete for six weeks in a row, you'll be in danger of losing your scholarship."

"What exactly does the scholarship cover?" Morgan asked.

"The scholarship covers your meals, all lessons that you may want to take, your living expenses and a small budget for clothing. Speaking of which, I can see you were smart and got ahead of the crowds for some quality uniforms. I know they're expensive, but the school will reimburse you for the full cost once you've been approved."

This particular bit of news cheered Morgan up immensely.

"The scholarship will last the duration of one term, which is three months, after which it will expire unless you're still holding a spot in the top fifty. If you fall below fifty in your class, there's no need to panic, as there will be one last fight before the end each term. This gives other students a chance to distinguish themselves and move up quickly in the rankings. This fight is normally followed by a tournament, but we'll get into that later on in the term."

"What's the point of trying to get a higher rank if staying in the top fifty is enough to keep the scholarship?" Morgan asked.

"A good question," Gold said, with a smile. "Those ranked at the top of their class at the end of the semester will automatically gain a spot in the tournament, without needing to fight in the end of term ranking matches. They will also keep their scholarship for the next term."

"So if I manage to keep the top spot, I get automatic entry into this tournament?" Sarah asked.

He nodded, taking a sip from his mug.

"Why exactly would I want to fight in the tournament?"

"Let's just say that the prize is well worth it," he said, with a mysterious smile.

"The day after tomorrow will be the official start of term. The two of you are to be in front of the testing building at eight o'clock sharp. All of the new students will be there, as well as the instructors who will officially choose their students then."

"So, we're not your students yet?" Sarah asked. "What if another teacher wants us? Won't that be an issue?"

"Not at all," Gold said waving his hand dismissively. "When I make my choice, no one will argue with me. Once all the students are chosen, Headmistress Loquin will announce those who have earned a scholarship. This is done to light a fire under the other students and give them a goal to work towards."

"It sounds like this will draw a lot of attention to us," Morgan said, frowning a bit. "That's something I'd like to avoid."

"Well, unless you'd like to pay the three hundred gold tuition fee, you'll just have to bear it," Gold answered.

Three hundred gold a semester?

"If the school is so expensive, how can so many people afford to be here? The nobles I understand, but common people can't have that kind of money."

"Oh, they can't. They are sponsored by their individual kingdoms. They come here to learn, then have to serve a year in their countries' military for each term spent here."

Morgan nodded.

That was a sensible way to become stronger. After all, what were ten or twenty years of military service if you could live for hundreds of years? There were still the obvious risks, but apparently plenty of people were willing to take it.

"Now as I was saying," Gold continued. "Once the Headmistress is done with her speech, we will head off to our first lesson of the day. You'll have a total of three lessons with me, Morgan, and Sarah will have two."

Sarah opened her mouth to ask why, but Gold held up his hand to forestall her.

"The first lesson of the day will be physical training. That class will last for two hours, after which you will go eat breakfast."

"Wait, we won't be eating breakfast until ten?"

Sarah looked shocked.

"You can eat breakfast before that, but I wouldn't recommend it. Not unless you'd like to lose it once we start our training."

Sarah visibly paled, but nodded all the same.

"After breakfast, which should last no more than thirty minutes, Morgan will meet me for a lesson. Sarah will have free time to do whatever she wishes. There are a few lecture classes for *mages* that you would benefit from taking; I would recommend you check them out."

"Why am I getting a separate lesson with you?" Morgan asked, though he thought he already knew.

"I will be teaching you all there is to know about the supermage ability. This class will also be about two hours, after which we will break for lunch. You will have two hours for that and I would recommend you use that time to unwind and relax. Your next class is with me at half past two. This class will be four hours long and will be dedicated to increasing your respective *ranks.*"

"That is a very long class," Sarah said, with an uncertain look on her face.

"How will we be increasing in *rank*?" Morgan asked excitedly.

"Yes, it is a long class; but there is a reason for that. Have either of you two heard of a special kind of animal called a beast?"

Both of them nodded emphatically.

"We killed a dire-flame bear on the way here. It was not an easy fight," Morgan supplied.

Gold's eyes widened a touch. "A dire-flame bear, you say? That's quite impressive, considering that it only takes a quarter of all damage from mage abilities."

Morgan inwardly cringed when he heard that.

They were more lucky to have survived that encounter than he had previously thought.

"Anyway, we will be going to special areas that the academy keeps for training students. There are special portals set up to take us to places called *Beast Zones.* In those areas, beasts are quite common, though we won't be going to areas where their *ranks* are too high. The cores we collect will go towards raising your respective *ranks.* When we get back, you're free for the night. Supper is served until eleven, so you can go whenever you like."

"When are we supposed to fight in ranked matches?" Sarah asked. "The day is kind of full."

"Ranked matches are held from seven in the evening until nine for first years, so you should have plenty of time. Remember, you only need to fight in a ranked match once a week, so making time for it shouldn't be too hard. Now do you have any other questions?"

They thought for a minute, then both shook their heads.

"Then I'll wish you both a good night," Gold said, rising from his seat. "Oh, and one more thing. Sarah, I'm sure I don't need to tell you this; but Morgan, I expect you take at least one bath a day. We'll be working hard and you'll really start to stink if you don't bathe. Someone will collect and clean your dirty clothes each day if you leave them in that bin."

He pointed to a white bin, with a covered top near the front door.

The two of them wished him a good night and he walked into his side of the house. They heard the distinct click of a lock as the door closed behind him.

"That is a lot to take in," Sarah said as the two of them headed into their section of the house.

"Tell me about it!" Morgan said excitedly.

He could hardly wait the extra day for the term to begin. Just the thought of going into those Beast Zones Gold had mentioned made his fingers twitch in anticipation.

Sarah wished him a good night, reminding him to take a bath and closed her door behind her.

Morgan was less thrilled about this, but agreed that it was necessary.

He didn't want to stink up his new clothes right when he put them on.

After a surprisingly refreshing few minutes in the bath, Morgan was curled up under the fluffiest blanket he had ever felt.

The bed was soft and warm and despite his excitement for the coming days, he was sound asleep within minutes.

18

Arnold ground his teeth in frustration, debating breaking out of the small cell where he was confined.

Three weeks. He'd been stuck in this damn cell for three weeks.

As soon as they'd caught up with him, the guards of City Six had arrested him and Weasel. When they returned to the city, they'd been thrown into cells and had had no contact with anyone for two whole days.

After that, it had taken him an entire week just to convince them to send a message to Lord Simon. He was still waiting for an answer.

He had decided to be patient, but he had his limits. If they didn't let him out in the next two days, he'd be releasing himself and anyone who tried to stop him would meet an early grave.

There was the sound of a door slamming up above and soon the face of the guard captain came into view, lit by flickering torchlight.

"Here to mock me some more, Captain?" Arnold asked in a flat tone.

The Captain was understandably unhappy with him for killing two of his guards. But it wasn't his fault those men were so weak. All he'd done was throw them, even someone at rank 8 should have survived that.

"I'm here to let you out," the man said, through gritted teeth. "For some reason, I've been ordered to release you; though I argued with the city lord for a week about it."

So he'd been stuck here an extra week because of this asshole. Arnold felt his fists tighten at his sides.

He would return once this job was over, and kill him for it.

There was a rattling of keys as the captain opened the cell for him and Arnold made sure to thank the man as he passed, giving him his widest smile.

He blinked a few times, shading his eyes as he emerged into bight sunlight. Weasel was waiting there for him with their horses already saddled and ready to go.

He nodded at the man and swung up into the saddle. The two of them rode in silence until they were well outside the city gates.

"So which way are we headed?" Arnold asked.

"South, toward the Central Kingdom. That is their most likely destination."

Arnold grunted in reply and turned his gaze back to the road ahead.

He couldn't wait to get this job over with.

***

Morgan rushed around his room, desperately trying to tug on his second boot while still pulling up his pants.

Of course he'd overslept. The one morning where he had to be on time and they were going to be late because of him.

"Are you ready yet?"

The shout came from Sarah, who was pacing impatiently outside his door.

"Just give me another minute!" he yelled back, finally getting his pants up and cinching them with the straps at his waist.

"We have to be in the main square in ten minutes and it's at least a twenty minute walk!"

Morgan slammed the door open to see a very angry looking Sarah waiting there for him. She was dressed in her own canvas uniform and had her long red hair tied back in a braid.

"We can make it in ten if we run," Morgan said.

"Oh, hell no! I am not running! If we have to run, then you're going to carry me," she said, placing her hands on her hips and daring him to fight back.

"Alright, fine. My *agility* is probably higher than yours, so you'd just slow me down anyway," Morgan said, as he opened the front door.

Sarah was about to reply indignantly, when Morgan bent down and scooped her over his shoulder eliciting a loud shriek of protest.

"Put me down!" she yelled, attracting the attention of several of their neighbors.

"Didn't you want me carry you?" Morgan asked, setting her down on the ground.

"I meant on your back, not like a sack of flour, dumbass!"

"Oh yeah, that would make more sense," he said sheepishly, turning his back and crouching to allow her to climb on.

She really did need to watch her language. He wasn't really sure where a noblewoman would pick up such a bad habit.

He heard her huff in annoyance as she climbed onto his back and felt her arms wrap around his shoulders. He made sure he had a good grip under her thighs before straightening and took a few seconds to become accustomed to her weight; then took off running towards the main building.

They pair made quite the odd sight and they got more than a few strange looks as Morgan sprinted by, but no one said anything. As he ran, he became very aware of her pressed up against him. Her soft body rubbing up against his and the feeling of his hands cupped under her thighs.

She'd definitely put on some weight in the last few weeks, he thought as he readjusted his grip.

Just under five pounds if his guess was correct, though it was likely more from muscle gain instead of fat.

He didn't think mentioning this to her would be a good idea, so he wisely kept it to himself.

They made it into the square just as the bell began tolling and Morgan breathed a sigh of relief as he saw they'd made it in time.

Luckily for Sarah, all of the other students were facing the stage and she was able to slide off Morgan's back before anyone noticed.

He looked over at her as they joined the crowd of new students and made their way to the front.

Her face was all red and flushed, though he wasn't sure why. After all, he'd been the one running; not her.

They stopped near the front of the crowd and he was about to ask her is she was feeling ill, when someone on the stage began speaking.

All the students quieted immediately and Morgan turned his attention upward, where a woman in an official looking uniform was looking down at them.

He could see several dozen men and women standing behind her, all looking out at the crowd. After a moment of searching, he spotted Gold among them and felt his nerves settle somewhat.

"Welcome, one and all, to the Central Academy for Mages and Supers. My name is Loquin and I am your Headmistress."

Her voice boomed out over the open courtyard and Morgan wondered what kind of skill she was using to get this effect.

"As you know, this school is dedicated to helping those with abilities hone their skills and work for the betterment of their countries."

Here she nodded at a group of well dressed individuals standing off to one side and surrounded by guards.

Most likely the nobles, Morgan thought as he looked over.

"You were all given tests when you applied and seeing as you're still here; you all obviously passed."

She stopped here and everyone gave her a polite laugh. To Morgan, it sounded more like sounds of discomfort than actual humor.

He had no idea why they were faking laughter at a time like this.

"However, only fifty students from each class earned a scholarship this semester. I will be reading out the names. When your name is called, please step forward."

A low murmuring went through the crowd as Headmistress Loquin pulled a folded sheet of paper out of her pocket and began reading off names.

One by one, students began moving through the crowd until they stood out in front. Finally, Sarah's name was called and she gave him a nervous glance before stepping forward.

"These are the top fifty students in the mage class for your year," Loquin continued. "Remember their names and faces. They are the one's to beat if you want a scholarship during your next semester."

She then took out another piece of paper and Morgan felt his heart rate increase. When he finally heard his name called, he moved forward in a daze; feeling the eyes of hundreds on him as he did.

When the last name was called out, Loquin said the same thing about them being the best in their class.

She then turned to the men and women standing behind her.

"Which students would you like to choose?"

Several of them stepped forward and Morgan felt his heart skip a beat as he heard Sarah's name mentioned by several of them.

He looked over to where she stood at the front of the crowd of mages; she looked nervous as well.

"I will be taking Sarah on as a student."

The entire crowd on the stage quieted instantly as Gold stepped forward with a half smile.

"I'll also be taking Morgan from the super class."

Morgan didn't move as all the people around him turned to stare.

Why was Gold's declaration getting so much attention?

After a moment of shocked silence Loquin finally spoke up.

"Are you sure?"

She sounded surprised, though Morgan didn't know why a teacher offering to do his job would garner that sort of reaction.

"Quite sure," he answered, in a calm tone.

"Very well," Loquin said, turning back to the crowd.

"Sarah from the mage class and Morgan from the super class; please walk around the side of the stage and wait for your new instructor."

Morgan walked forward quickly, seeing Sarah do the same.

He felt very uncomfortable with every eye in attendance staring at him and he wanted to get out of sight as soon as he could.

They quickly made their way around the stage and soon lost sight of the crowd.

"I did not like that," Morgan said, as the two of them came to a stop. "I've never felt so uncomfortable in my life!"

Sarah nodded in agreement.

"If I don't have to do that for another hundred years, it'll be too soon!"

"Glad you survived that," Gold said, walking around the corner with a smile. "Ready to begin your training?"

Morgan folded his arms and glared at him.

"After you tell us why everyone reacted the way they did when you said you'd teach us."

"You noticed that, huh?" Gold said, rubbing the back of his head in embarrassment.

Sarah and Morgan both nodded, the former even glaring at him.

"Well, I may have understated my importance at the school a bit," he began evasively.

"What do you mean, 'a bit'?" Sarah asked.

Gold sighed and let his shoulders slump a bit.

"Fine. If you must know, I am the highest *ranked* mage at the academy. I am also the deputy Headmaster and I haven't taken on a student in the last eighty or so years."

19

"And you didn't think it was important to mention any of this beforehand?" Sarah practically yelled.

"No, not really," Gold said with a shrug, not in the least bit apologetic.

"I thought we were trying to keep a low profile," Morgan said. His tone was calm, unlike Sarah's. "Isn't being taught by someone in your position going to do the exact opposite of that?"

"Well… It's not really important right now," he answered. "I doubt we'll have any issues, and besides; the lessons you'll get with me will be far more beneficial to your growth."

"How?" they both asked, at the same time.

"As I've already pointed out, I'm quite knowledgeable when it comes to Morgan. As for you, Sarah; do you really think just anyone will have access to a *Beast Zone,* every day for four hours?"

"Doesn't everyone train in these *Beast Zones*?" Sarah asked, now a little less sure of herself.

"Most first year students would be lucky if they got to go even *once* in their first term! Now, no more wasting time; we have a lot of work to do and only so many hours in a day."

"Where will we be training?" Morgan asked. "And how will we get back for breakfast with so little time between classes?"

While he had his second class at half past ten with Gold, Sarah had signed up for a class that began five minutes before his. That meant that she would only have twenty five minutes for breakfast.

"Not to worry," Gold said as he took off in a brisk walk down the busy road. "There is a dining room right near the training grounds we'll be working in. You can eat there and still make it in plenty of time."

Thankfully, it only took another ten minutes for them to reach the designated area; a large space containing identical stone buildings, each painted with a different number.

The area with the buildings was fenced off and guards walked the perimeter. Gold walked right up to the front gate and one of the guards handed him something before waving them through.

As the two of them caught up to him, he handed them each a small red badge.

"Pin this to your shirts. It will tell the guards that you've been cleared to pass and which building you'll be training in."

They both took the badges and Morgan saw a black number 6 embossed in the center. There was a small pin on the back and after a moment of fiddling, he managed to attach it to his shirt.

They continued heading into the block until the correct building came into view. It was made of solid stone and Morgan wasn't sure how they were going to get in, as no door was visible.

His question was soon answered when Gold pressed his palm to the side and a section of the wall slid into the ground.

"After you," he said, motioning them inside.

The inside of the room looked exactly as Morgan had been expecting. It was a large open space made completely of stone and seemed to be way larger on the inside than the outside.

There were a few training dummies, as well as a large stack of heavy looking iron balls. There was also a large steel chain hanging from one wall, with a small clock perched above it.

"Nice, isn't it?" Gold asked, as they walked in.

"It's bigger in here than it is out there," Sarah said as she looked around as well.

"Right you are, my dear. This building, along with all the others in this block, have been treated with spatial magic."

"What are all those for?" Morgan asked, pointing to the walls.

An evil looking smile touched Gold's lips when he asked this and Morgan had the distinct feeling that he'd be finding that out soon. Gold's next words confirmed his thoughts.

"You'll find out soon enough. Now, start running!" he barked.

The shout was so unexpected that they both jumped.

"What?" Sarah asked.

The smile slipped from Gold's face as she said this and was replaced by a scowl. "I said, start running!"

"How long should we run for?" Morgan asked.

"Until I tell you to stop! Now move!" he roared.

Sarah gave Morgan a look of terror, then took off. Morgan was close on her heels.

Who knew Gold could be so scary?

They ran around the room, with Gold occasionally yelling at them to run faster.

Judging from how long it took him to make a full circuit of the room, Morgan guessed it to be around a quarter mile. The outside of the building hadn't looked to be more than fifteen square feet! Whoever had enchanted this building must be pretty powerful.

After they'd been running for about ten minutes, Sarah was visibly flagging and her breathing was coming in ragged gasps. Morgan was a lot better off and in fact, barely felt any strain at all.

Must be from his increased agility and constitution.

This didn't escape Gold's notice, however, and he was quick to rectify that.

"I can see that while Sarah is working hard, you don't seem to mind running."

Morgan shrugged. "It's not like it's difficult."

"That is unacceptable!" he roared.

Why did he need to be so close to him when he yelled like that?

"From now on, I expect you to run twice as fast as Sarah, and while carrying this!" Gold wrapped a steel chain around his shoulders in an *X,* then locked the loose ends together.

Morgan could feel his legs shaking as the weight settled on him and he almost buckled under it.

"What's this thing made of?" he managed to gasp out.

"Compressed steel. There's a super out there who managed to find a way to condense steel to an unbelievable degree."

"How much does this thing weigh?!"

Gold pretended to think for a moment. "Oh, I'd say somewhere around two hundred pounds."

Two hundred pounds of dead weight?

He could barely move. How was he expected to do twice the amount of laps as Sarah?

"Well, off you go," Gold said with a smile and a wave.

He's the devil! Morgan thought as he began running once again. With the addition of the chain, his pace was now drastically slowed. Within minutes he was drenched in a heavy sweat as his muscles strained against the weight and he was breathing just as raggedly as Sarah.

There was no way it was only two hundred pounds. Sarah weighed just over half that and he hadn't had any trouble sprinting with her on his back.

He wheezed in pain as he passed a much slower moving Sarah. His muscles were shrieking in protest and his lungs were on fire, but still he ran on. This went on for what felt like hours, and when finally he heard Gold's voice break through the haze of pain and sweat, he thought he was dreaming.

"Alright, you can stop."

Morgan took a few more stumbling steps before the words reached his brain. He looked over his shoulder to see Sarah collapsed on the ground, in a sweaty heap and panting for air.

He then felt his legs buckle as well and slid down the wall to slump tiredly on the ground. He looked up as a shadow fell across him and Gold leaned down, handing him a cup of water.

"Drink slowly," he advised, before moving over to Sarah.

Morgan took his advice, slowly sipping from the clay cup as he felt his heart rate slowly decrease. He had almost managed to catch his breath when Gold's voice barked out once again.

"On your feet!"

Morgan groaned, but this time did as he was told. He struggled briefly and almost fell back down as his muscles protested in pain; but he managed to catch himself in time.

He stumbled over to the center of the room, seeing Sarah doing the same. They both came to a stop in front of him and he looked them over for a few seconds.

"On your hands and the balls of your feet!" he barked.

Morgan had never done something like this before, but was quick to follow orders. He got down and Gold came by, adjusting his position. Once his position was correct, he could immediately feel the strain on his arms, shoulders and core.

This was hell. Gold was going to kill them.

"How long should we hold this position?" Morgan heard Sarah's voice from his left.

"Until I tell you to stop!" Gold yelled.

They were forced to hold that position for five whole minutes. By the end of it, Morgan could swear that his arms had turned to jelly and that he'd never be able to use them again.

"On your feet!"

And so it went on for the next hour. Gold ran them through one hellish exercise after the next. All of which Morgan was forced to do with the heavy chain around his shoulders.

"Alright, I think that's enough for the day," Gold said at last.

Morgan and Sarah just stood there, heads bowed and panting for breath.

There was a loud click, and Morgan groaned in relief as the chain was lifted off his shoulders.

"Now I want you to spread your legs out like so."

Gold demonstrated the technique.

"I thought we were done for the day," Sarah groaned.

"Unless you want those muscles to cramp up horribly, I would recommend stretching them out."

So they followed his movements, going from one pose to the next and stretching every muscle that had been worked out.

By the time they were finally finished, Morgan was ready for a nap.

He'd never been so tired in his life.

He was drenched from head to toe in sweat and judging by that way she looked, Sarah wasn't doing much better. Her face was red, her eyes were drooping, and her braid had come partially undone, clinging to her face in sweaty strands.

"How are we supposed to eat, or do any classes when we're this sweaty and gross?" Sarah asked.

Gold quickly glanced to the clock, then motioned towards the back wall. Two slabs of stone slid to the side, revealing two small bathing stalls, and what looked like a change of their clothes.

"I took the liberty of bringing you each a change of clothes. You will be expected to bring your own from now on. Simply place your palm on the wall to close the room for privacy. The water will be lukewarm at best, so I would recommend you bathe quickly. Morgan, I will meet you back here in forty minutes."

He nodded once, then exited the building.

Morgan and Sarah looked at each other as the stone slab closed behind him; then tiredly shuffled over to the open doors.

Morgan closed his door and was quick to strip out of his sodden clothes, wincing in pain whenever he moved. Then walking over to the far wall, he turned the spout and shivered as the icy water washed over him.

"I've never felt this much pain in my entire life! I swear that bastard is trying to kill us!" Morgan heard Sarah say as the sound of running water came from her stall.

Morgan looked around for a moment before spotting a bar of soap and quickly lathered himself up.

"I've felt pain before," Morgan answered, remembering well his hard years on the streets; as well as his recent fights. "But I've never felt pain like this."

This pain was different. He'd never inflicted this kind of punishment on himself. It was somehow worse than when he'd broken his ribs, or taken a sword through the shoulder.

"That man is evil!" Sarah shouted, then groaned in pain. "You think he's this quiet, unassuming person, then he turns into that!"

Morgan definitely agreed with her there.

Gold's transformation had been shocking, to say the least.

He rinsed himself off and turned off the water, looking around for something to dry himself with. He found a rough towel near his clean clothes and quickly dried himself; wincing with every movement.

He got into his fresh clothes and turned to get his sodden ones, but was surprised to see that they'd vanished.

"Sarah, did your dirty clothes disappear?" Morgan asked, looking around for them.

There was a moment of silence, then Sarah emerged from her room, still pulling her shirt over her head. Morgan got a flash of her pale stomach as she managed to pull it down.

"Yeah," she said, straightening her hair and tucking her shirt in. "I think this building has more magic in it than Gold was letting on."

"Would have been nice for Gold to mention that beforehand," Morgan grumbled.

Sarah looked up at him, as though just realizing he was there and let out a squeak, running back into the washroom.

Morgan stared at the closed door for a minute, not sure what had just happened.

"Sarah?" he called out. "Are you okay?"

"I'm fine," she said, emerging from the room a minute later. Her shirt was tucked in and the straps at her waist were cinched shut.

The fabric clung to her body in several places where there were damp patches on her skin; and her hair hung, still damp and unbranded, down her back.

Her face was all flushed again, and Morgan started to wonder if she was feeling well.

"Should we get something to eat?" he asked instead, feeling his stomach growling loudly.

"Definitely!" Sarah said, with a smile.

Morgan grinned back at her, and the two of them shuffled painfully out of the room in pursuit of food.

20

"What do you know about abilities?"

Morgan shrugged. "Not much, aside from what you and Sarah have told me."

He was back in the training room, but it looked very different than when he'd been here before breakfast.

There was a large bookshelf against one wall, a desk behind which Gold was sitting, and a large plush chair; which Morgan had gratefully sunken into.

Sarah had already gone off to her next lesson and the two of them had decided to meet up at the house after Morgan's lesson so they could eat lunch together.

Gold was back to his normal, unassuming self and was teaching him as though the last two hours hadn't happened.

"I figured as much," Gold said, with a smile.

"Before we can begin learning about abilities, skills, attributes, and how they work; we will first have to discuss why they exist in the first place. Have you ever wondered why our abilities function the way they do? Why we need to pull up a status to view our abilities, or why we need to increase in *rank* to become stronger?"

Morgan had begun to drift off, as the soreness in his body and exhaustion of the exercise set in. But his eyes opened wide and he sat up straighter when Gold began on this topic.

He'd been wondering about all those things ever since his abilities had awoken. Was there perhaps a higher being that oversaw the laws of this world?

"I can see that I have your full attention now," Gold said with a grin. "Yes, Morgan, there is indeed a reason why the world is the way it is. This reason also ties in with why there are so few supermages alive today."

He cleared his throat and continued.

"This story takes place over ten thousand years ago. Back then, there was no such thing as having a status. There was no separation between supers and mages, and no one had skills, abilities or attributes. When someone awoke their power, they got it all at once, without the need to rank up. On the other hand, there was no increasing in power either. Whatever they got when the power awoke, was what they had for the rest of their lives."

"In those days, there were only four kingdoms, North, South, East and West. The Central Kingdom had yet to be founded and a different royal family ruled the North. The king wasn't an especially kind man, but despite the way he kept peace, people were still happy with his rule."

"That all changed when a man known only as the Tyrant King awoke his power. It was a power unlike anything the world had even seen and before long, he had declared war on the king; demanding he hand over his throne."

Gold's voice took on a much more serious tone here, as he continued his lesson.

"The war that ensued would be recorded as one of the most brutal in our history. The Tyrant King had soon gathered an army of thousands and marched on the capital. He could have taken the throne peacefully, if not for the king's son; who absolutely refused to back down. In an act of defiance he murdered his own father and took command of the kingdom.

"The battle raged on for months, with tens of thousands in casualties; but in the end, the Tyrant King stood victorious. He butchered the entire royal family, then sat upon the throne, declaring himself king for all to hear. But as it is with all tyrants, just ruling the North wasn't enough for him. Over the next few years, he built his strength up and attacked the neighboring West kingdom.

"And so another bloody war began. The West had powerful fighters of their own, but none who could match the Tyrant King, and soon it looked as though they, too, would fall. The other two kingdoms, fearing that they were next, soon joined the battle in hopes of stopping the Tyrant King. The war raged on for years, and even with the combined might of all three kingdoms, it looked as though the Tyrant King would be victorious."

"Then there came a day when the three allied kingdoms faced him for one last battle. The Tyrant King had raised a massive army and was confident of his victory. The rulers met him at the center of the battlefield before the fight began in hopes of sparing their men. The Tyrant King refused to parlay, demanding surrender and threatening to butcher all of them if they didn't comply. The other kings were proud, but weary of the long war and one by one, began to comply with his demand."

"The last monarch was preparing to surrender, when a figure walked onto the battlefield and approached the gathered rulers. The histories aren't clear as to who this person was, but we do know one thing- they were the most powerful being this world has ever seen. Whether man, woman or god; this being demanded that the rulers place down their weapons and return to their respective kingdoms."

"The Tyrant King laughed at his demands and stepped forward to kill this being."

Gold paused here, and Morgan leaned forward in his seat.

"What happened next?"

He smiled and continued, glad that Morgan was paying attention.

"There was a flash of brilliant light and the Tyrant King fell to his knees. The being turned to the rest of the gathered monarchs and its voice boomed out over the field for all to hear. It said that they had all squandered their gifts on war and death. That they were unworthy of wielding the energy of the world bestowed upon them. Then a ripple of power flowed outward and everyone's abilities were torn from them."

"The being then forbade the kingdoms from waging outright war ever again. It then announced that power would never be given so freely and in such great quantity ever again. But the Tyrant King would not accept this. Even though he'd been stripped of his power, he lifted his sword and ran towards the figure, screaming his hate and rage. The figure raised a hand and with a single motion, wiped him from existence."

"Soon after that, the Central Kingdom was founded and a new king placed in charge. The powerful being did not take the throne, instead naming someone else to keep the balance, then disappeared. Coincidentally, the descendants of that king are still ruling to this very day."

"You mean that King Herald is descended from the first King?" Morgan asked.

"Yes. In fact, King Herald is the only person alive who knows the mysterious being who changed the world on that day. After that battle, no one gained tremendous power overnight anymore. The status screens began to show up, mana and chi were born, and people could only control a very limited amount of their power. The first beasts were soon discovered and people began to learn that power had to be earned, and would no longer be handed to them. However, only a few people could still wield the true power of the world and they became known as the first supermages."

Gold finished speaking and Morgan's mind was awhirl with questions.

"How is it that I've never heard this story before? If this is our history, then shouldn't it be more well known?"

"A good question," Gold said, nodding appreciatively. "This knowledge, like that of supermages, has been very well hidden. There are very few people alive today who know of this history, but it's important for you to know, as it will give you a better understanding of your own abilities."

There was a loud chime then and Gold seemed to start, looking up at the clock in surprise.

"Looks like our time is up for today."

"But I have so many questions," Morgan complained.

"Well, unless you'd like to miss your lunch, I would recommend holding off on those until tomorrow."

Morgan debated skipping lunch, but his rumbling stomach and the promise to meet Sarah, decided him against keeping the lesson going.

"One last thing before you go. I want to hear all about your abilities, attributes and skills. Be exact, as I will need to understand exactly what you can do, in order to best teach you."

Morgan sighed as his stomach growled once again, but he listed out everything Gold wanted to know.

"I have one more question for you," Gold said, as Morgan rose painfully from the plush chair.

"Do you know how to use a mage shield yet?"

"No."

Morgan shook his head. "Sarah showed me hers, though, and I really want to learn how make my own."

"Good. Then that will be the focus of our lesson tomorrow. You are dismissed."

And with that, Morgan turned tiredly towards the door.

He now had a twenty five minute walk back to the house and he wasn't excited about it.

21

Morgan groaned as he sat down on the hard stone bench. His entire body was in pain and it hurt to even move.

Sarah sat down next to him with a similar protest, but she was a lot more vocal about her discomfort.

"I'd like to make that asshole run around a room for an hour," she grumbled, as she stuffed steaming spoons full of chicken pie into her mouth.

Morgan grunted in response, shoveling equally large spoonful's into his mouth as well.

He was too exhausted to talk right now. All he wanted to do was eat and then go take a nap until their next lesson.

"Are you alright?"

Morgan turned to Sarah, who despite her bad mood, looked concerned.

"I'm fine, just really tired. I think I'll go to sleep when I'm done eating."

"That sounds so nice right now!" Sarah exclaimed. "My last lesson wasn't exactly taxing, but I still feel like I could sleep for week!"

The two of them were quick to finish up their meal and headed back to the house.

Checking the clock on the wall, Morgan could see that he had a little over an hour before their next lesson.

Sarah was already taking off her boots and threw them unceremoniously on the ground, before entering the room and closing her door.

Morgan debated going into his room, but decided to nap on the couch instead. He sighed in contentment as he sank into the soft material and within a few seconds, was out cold.

***

A light tapping on his forehead brought Morgan out of a deep sleep. He blinked a few times and squinted up, at the smiling face of his instructor.

"Oh good. Finally awake, are we? I thought I'd take the liberty of waking you. Our next lesson will be in ten minutes, best get prepared."

With that, he turned and left the room.

Morgan could hear Sarah cursing away through her door, so he knew she was awake. He tried sitting up, then cried out as his entire body throbbed in protest. He fell back against the cushions, feeling as though every muscle in his body had been tied to knots.

He gritted his teeth and forced himself into a sitting position, wincing as his cramped and aching muscles slowly stretched out.

He now very much regretted taking that nap.

Forcing himself to stand, he began going through the stretches that Gold had shown them for loosening up their muscles. He grimaced with every new pose, but forced himself to hold them for a full count of sixty before switching to a different one.

By the time Sarah shuffled out of her room, looking disheveled and half asleep, Morgan was feeling a whole lot better.

"You should do those stretches Gold showed us this morning," Morgan said as she winced in discomfort. "It'll help with the pain."

Sarah didn't answer, but did as he suggested. She ran through the various poses that he'd just finished. By the time she was done, Gold had walked back into the room and was nodding in approval.

"Good. I see you're ready to go. You will be fighting, so if there is anything you need, now is the time to get it."

Morgan was about to say he didn't need anything, when he remembered the shin guards sitting in his room. He quickly dashed in and grabbed them, rolling up his pants to strap them on underneath. He then pulled on the fingerless gloves that would protect his hands and tightened them around his wrists.

Now he was ready.

"Do you need to get anything before we go Sarah?" Gold asked.

She shook her head and Gold nodded, pulling something from his pocket. It was only then that Morgan realized how differently the man was dressed. His usual garb normally consisted of a long robe that was split down the center and a loose fitting pair of pants.

Now he was dressed in a black leather breastplate, leather bracers and greaves and a pair of the same canvas pants that he and Sarah were wearing.

Gold noticed him appraising him and grinned.

"Didn't think I'd go into a *Beast Zone* wearing nothing but a robe did you?"

Morgan shrugged.

It made sense after all. Why would he wear a robe in a combat zone?

Gold finished fiddling with the item he'd pulled from his pocket, then shoved it into something and twisted. Morgan's eyes went wide and Sarah exclaimed in surprise, as a tear in space opened right in the center of the living room.

"What the hell is that?" Sarah yelled.

"That is our way into the *Beast Zone*," Gold answered. "This a portal and the only way to reach our destination. Now, after you." He motioned Sarah to go first, but she just shook her head.

"There is no way I'm going through first!"

Gold turned to Morgan and gestured to the portal. Morgan shrugged once more, then walked straight through the tear in space.

There was an odd feeling of vertigo and then he was standing on a path before a massive rocky plain. The sky was gray and cloudy, and the air smelled, oddly enough, of salt.

He heard the sound of boots scuffing over stone and turned to see Sarah emerging from the tear. She wobbled for a moment, then walked over to join him.

"Where are we?"

There was awe in her voice as she took in the surrounding landscape.

"No idea, but we're definitely not in the Central Kingdom."

"Right you are!"

They both turned as Gold materialized as well and walked over to join them.

It didn't escape Morgan's notice that the tear in space slammed shut behind him, leaving them effectively trapped.

"In fact, we aren't even in the five kingdoms. Right now, we have entered a *Beast Zone,* which is located in an entirely different space! No one is quite sure how they function, but that's just the way it is with some things."

"So what you're telling us, is that no else can enter while we are here?" Sarah asked.

"Exactly! I am the only one who currently holds the key to this *zone*. If someone else wishes to come here, I would first have to open the portal in their location."

"So what exactly will we be doing here?" Morgan asked.

He was eager to begin.

"You will be fighting and killing beasts. I am here to supervise and will only intervene if you are in mortal danger. However, seeing as this is a *rank 3 Beast Zone,* the only real challenge will come at the end."

"Would you mind explaining exactly how this place works before we begin?" Sarah asked. "And what do you mean by *'rank 3 Beast Zone?'* Does that mean that all the beasts are *rank 3*?"

"I'll be happy to explain the function of *Beast Zones* and how they work. These zones are rich with the energy of the world and therefore a very many beasts will be found here. They will also be reborn a fixed amount of time after they are killed. Even if you kill every single beast in here today, they will all be back tomorrow."

"All *Beast Zones* are given a *rank* to match the level of difficulty based on the highest *ranked beast.* That means that the most powerful beast you will encounter, will be at *rank 3*. All the beasts have cores, you will collect them and hand them over to me. At the end of your lesson, I will split the cores in half and hand each of you your share."

"I expect you to assign all the energy from your cores at night and tell me of your progress. I also expect you to hand in the remains of the cores once they have shattered. The academy has need of core dust and requires any student using a *Beast Zone* to hand it in once the cores have been used. One last thing before we go."

A warning note entered his voice. "There is one exception to the maximum *rank* of one beast in every zone. This beast is called the *Zone Patriarch* or *Matriarch.* That beast will be far more powerful than the others you'll be facing, so use caution when fighting it. I think that about sums it up. Any questions?"

Morgan and Sarah both opened up their mouths, but before they had a chance to ask, Gold cut them off.

"No questions? Great! Then off we go!"

He walked past them and entered the rock strewn plains, whistling as he did so.

"If he wasn't going to answer, then why bother asking?" Sarah muttered as the two of them followed.

It only took about five minutes of walking to come across their first beats. They stopped as they saw a small flock of sheep grazing in a small patch of open ground up ahead.

"Well, there's your first challenge," Gold said with a grin. "Go on and attack them."

"Those are beasts?" Sarah asked, incredulously. "They're just a bunch of sheep!"

Morgan on the other hand, just did as he was told. He ran forward, covering the distance between him and the animals and gearing up for an attack.

As he drew closer, he could see that these were no ordinary sheep. Their wool was thick, gray and wiry; almost as if it were made of some sort of metal, not at all like the white fluffy sheep back home. They were also slightly larger, coming up to about waist height.

He skidded to a halt in front of one of the sheep and lashed out with a kick to its side. The sheep let out an angry bleat and whirled around; its rear hooves coming up and smacking Morgan square in the chest.

It didn't hurt, as his canvas shirt absorbed most of the damage, but he was stunned at the lightening reactions of the seemingly harmless farm animal.

The sheep turned to glare at him and Morgan could see that it was completely unharmed. At first, he was confused at the lack of injury to the animal, but then it clicked.

Of course! The wool must have absorbed the force of his attack. Since it appeared to be made of some kind of metal and seemed to be quite springy, blunt attacks wouldn't do much to hurt them.

A grin touched Morgan's lips as all six sheep turned to glare at him.

This was going to be fun!

22

Morgan got into a fighting stance as the first of the sheep ran at him.

If he was going to use blunt attacks, he would have to aim for spots not covered by the wool. On the other hand, he could switch over to his mage abilities. His wind blade could probably tear through the wool with no problems, but he liked the challenge of meeting them head on.

He shifted his weight to one leg in preparation to pivot out of the way, when a spear of ice slammed into the creature from the side, killing it instantly.

Morgan turned and glared as Sarah dispatched another two of the sheep in short order.

"Hey!" he called out as she readied another *icicle spear.* "What are you doing"

Sarah turned to look him, a confused expression on her face. "What?"

"I was going to kill them! It's not okay to just butt in during someone else's fight!"

The other sheep had stopped at the sight of their downed brethren and were now looking back and forth between the two of them, as if deciding on who they should attack next.

"Fine," Sarah said, holding her hands up. "You can have those three."

Morgan nodded and turned back to the other sheep, who had by now decided that he was the easier of the two targets.

One of them launched themselves at him with an angry bleat, eyes rolling and baring its teeth. Morgan dodged quickly to the side, lashing out with one of his fists and hearing the satisfying crunch of bone as its head caved in. He stepped back as a pair of hooves flew at him and turned to lash out with a kick of his own.

The heel of his foot slammed into one of the sheep's legs and it went down with a bleat of pain. He quickly stomped down on its head, feeling the skull flatten under his boot. When he pulled it away, he grimaced as blood, bits of bone and brain matter clung to the bottom.

He turned just in time for the last sheep to land on top of him. He was so surprised, that he caught it by reflex, feeling the rough, metallic wool press into his fingers. He grunted with effort as the sheep began to gnash its teeth, trying to bite him.

It was much heavier than it looked.

With a surge of effort, he threw the sheep high into the air, hearing a bleat of panic as it soared high. He waited for it come down, then spun and kicked it in the side as hard as he could.

He smiled in grim satisfaction as the shin guards, along with the steel woven canvas pants absorbed the impact and watched as the sheep's body was slammed into a nearby boulder. Despite its dense coat of wool, the impact was too much for the sheep to handle. There was a loud splat and the sheep fell to the ground, leaving a bloody smear on the rock.

Morgan turned to see both Sarah and Gold staring at him; her in annoyance and him in amusement.

"Though I will give you points for creativity, that took way too long and required way too much effort," Gold said as he approached them.

"I got the job done, didn't I?" Morgan said, feeling a bit defensive.

"You did," Gold conceded. "But Sarah killed three in the time it took you to kill one. If you're going to fight, then you have to learn to use your skills. From what I just saw, you fought without using a single one. If you want to fight using your fists, that's fine by me, but I'd like you to keep at least one skill active the entire time we're here."

Morgan nodded, concluding that Gold was probably right. He thought over which skill would be the most useful and decided on using *tailwind.*

He liked the huge increase in agility and it would help him finish fights faster. He could, of course, have gone with his heavy handed skill, but he liked the idea of precision over brute force. That was not to knock it; brute force definitely had its place, but here he could afford to use other means of fighting.

"Alright, now go and get those cores," Gold said, handing each of them a slim metal rod with a small button on one end.

"What are these for?" Morgan asked, as he and Sarah each accepted one.

"These were designed for the sole purpose of fetching a core. After all, I'm sure that getting yourselves covered in gore isn't too fun, so this will do it for you. All you need to do is shove the pointy end into its chest and press the button. Go on, give it a try!"

He gave them both a shove toward the sheep corpses which almost knocked them off their feet.

Morgan bent down next to one of the sheep and did as Gold instructed. Shoving the rod deep into the beast's chest cavity, he pressed the button. There was a clicking sound and he felt a slight shudder go through it.

Pulling it free, Morgan saw that three tiny prongs had extended from the tip and were now wrapped around an acorn sized core.

Taking the core in his hand, Morgan opened his status to view the core's properties.

Name: Ironwool-sheep core
Rank - 0
Total available energy - 14/14

This core was taken from an Ironwool-sheep and has no special properties.

Only 14 energy?!

Morgan closed the screen and glared at Gold.

"You didn't tell us that the cores would give so little energy!"

"Well, what else did you expect from a sheep?" Gold said with a shrug.

Morgan sighed and walked over to retrieve the rest of the cores.

Sarah didn't look nearly as disappointed as he was. She'd probably known to expect that amount of energy from the sheep.

They handed the cores to over to Gold, who placed them in a pouch by his waist. He then showed them how to clip the core retrieval rods to their belts.

So that was why he'd insisted they buy belts despite their uniform's ability to do without one, Morgan realized.

"Don't look so disheartened," he said, patting Morgan on the shoulder. "The beasts will grow stronger the further in we go, and the *Patriarch* of this *Zone* will give you a nice sized core. But we'll only get it *if* we make it there in the next three hours, so let's hop to it."

This news cheered Morgan up somewhat and he hoped they would make it in time to fight this *Patriarch.*

They ran into a few more flocks of the ironwool-sheep as they moved through the plains and soon fell into a comfortable rhythm.

Morgan, using his *tailwind* skill, would rush in and attack the sheep head on. Sarah stood back and took out any that tried to circle him to attack from behind.

As they were handing over another batch of cores, Gold commented on something he'd been meaning to for a while.

"I've noticed that you're quite adept at hand to hand fighting. Care to tell me where you learned to handle yourself like that?"

Sarah's head perked up at this. She'd been curious about it as well and waited with baited breath for a reply.

"No," Morgan said, as his face hardened. Then he turned and walked away, making sure to get a good distance from them before slowing down.

Sarah stared after him as he went, more than a little surprised at his blatant refusal to answer the question. She turned to Gold, expecting him to be angry, but instead found him with a contemplative look on his face.

"Can you tell me why he's so guarded with everyone but you?" Gold asked her.

Sarah bit her lip for a moment, wondering if it would be alright to tell him.

"He's an orphan," she finally relented as they began following Morgan. "He grew up on the streets, so he didn't have an easy life."

She sighed sadly as she watched his back.

It was stiff as a board, which meant that he was upset, but trying to hide it.

"I see," Gold said, now understanding just a bit more about the boy who so intrigued him.

He would not to press the issue any further, at least not for today.

For the next two hours, they walked deeper into the *Beast Zone*. As they went, the ironwool-sheep grew slightly larger and began to hit a bit harder.

When Sarah commented on this, Gold nodded.

"We're getting close to the *Patriarch,* so the sheep around here are likely *rank 2* or *3*."

Morgan hadn't spoken since his earlier refusal to answer Gold's question, but now he broke his silence.

"How much farther is it?"

Gold shaded his eyes for a second, then pointed up to the top of a nearby hill, where a large boulder was obstructing their view.

"The *Zone Patriarch* is up there. That boulder marks the entrance to his territory."

As soon as Gold finished speaking, Morgan sped up and began running towards the top of the hill.

"Wait up!" he heard Sarah call out behind him, but he ignored her.

He was still feeling annoyed at Gold's earlier question as he couldn't remember who had taught him. In fact, there was an entire two years of memories that were just not there. It was almost as if someone had gone into his head and blocked him from accessing them.

Morgan reached the top of the hill and took a deep breath to calm himself.

This was no time to lose his composure. He would deal with this when the lesson was over and he had time to think.

The *Patriarch* came into view as he rounded the large boulder and Morgan felt his heart rate redouble with excitement and trepidation.

23

The beast stood at the center of a massive plateau strewn with rocks and small clumps of grass. A tall wall of stone rose around the edges of the plateau, forming a sort of closed in half circle.

The ram- because this was undoubtedly a ram- stood in the midst of a flock of sheep, its ears flicking back and forth as it lowered its head to graze.

It was half again as large as the surrounding sheep, and two massive horns curled around the sides of its head.

Morgan crouched as he prepared a strategy for taking them on.

There were currently eight sheep surrounding the Patriarch. If he moved fast enough and used his wind blade, he could probably kill half of them before they realized what was happening. He could then use his superior speed to finish off the rest and take on the ram.

His planning complete, Morgan used *wind blade* and felt the familiar rush of air as the spinning lance formed on his arm.

It was then that Sarah finally caught up to him.

"What's the big idea running off like that, you moron?!" she yelled, placing her hands on her knees and panting for breath.

Morgan winced at the volume of her voice and turned to see that all of the beasts were now looking directly at them.

"Damn it, Sarah!" he shouted, as the sheep let out a collective bleat and charged at them.

She looked up and seemed to notice, for the first time, the predicament they were in. Her mage shield flickered on around her as she straightened. Her arm shot out as she used her *frostbite* skill and the sheep all noticeably slowed.

"That should give you some time. I'll cover you!"

Morgan nodded and shot towards the oncoming sheep with lightning speed. The air swirled around him as he ran, aided by his *tailwind* skill.

He needed to be careful with how much he used it. His *regen* still wasn't fast enough to keep the skill going indefinitely and he was already down to only half his remaining MP.

He met the oncoming sheep with a grim smile, his arm shooting forward and skewering one of them through the eye.

There was an explosion of gore as the sheep's head was torn apart and he just managed to avoid being showered in it, by jumping to the side.

He whirled on the spot and his other hand whipped out as he used *wind blade* once more. Another lance of air appeared, just in time to shear one of the sheep nearly in half.

A spear of ice flew passed his face and buried itself into the skull of a sheep that was trying to sneak up on him and Morgan waved his arm in thanks. He rolled to the side, avoiding a pair of lashing hooves and came up on one knee; bringing his arm up and destroying the animal completely.

A sound like a thousand sheep bleating at once shook the plateau and Morgan's head whipped around to see that the ram; who'd been ignoring them up until this point, had turned its gaze on them.

The sheep surrounding him suddenly disengaged and ran back towards him, bleating in terror.

Morgan rose slowly to his feet as Sarah came up next to him, never taking his eyes off the ram. It shook its head, pawing at the ground and snorting. Then it let out another rage filled bleat and charged at them.

"Slow it down. I'll try to kill it, but I may not be able to do so alone. If you see the opportunity to strike, take it!"

Morgan didn't even wait to hear her reply before taking off towards the charging ram. He could feel the ground trembling as he approached the massive creature and wondered if he could really kill it.

The ram was only a few feet away when Morgan used *tailwind* and dodged to the side. The ram snorted in fury as he missed his mark. The roar turned to a bleat as he lashed out with one of his *wind blades* and cut a deep gash through its wool and into its side.

As the beast turned to face him once more, the telltale shimmer of Sarah's *frostbite* appeared around the ram. It shook its head and roared once more. Then it's horns began to glow a bright red.

Crap, it's using an ability!

Morgan readied himself as the ram charged once again, lowering its glowing horns and aiming right for him. There was a muffled thump as two *icicle spears* buried themselves in the ram's rear and it shrieked in pain, redoubling its speed as it ran towards him.

Morgan was easily able to dodge the incoming beast and watched in horror as its glowing horns impacted against a nearby rock. The rock exploded in a shower of stone fragments and the ram kept going for a few feet before turning around to glare at him once more.

It pawed at the ground and snorted, this time with seemingly more anger, bellowing out in rage and pain before charging once more.

"Challenge accepted, you wooly bastard!" Morgan yelled.

He ran at the beast, fully intending to end the fight.

He closed the distance between them in a matter of seconds and buried a *wind blade* right between the beast's eyes.

The ram died instantly, however the momentum of its charge couldn't be stopped. Morgan grunted as several hundred pounds of ram crashed into him at full speed. He was thrown several feet through the air and landed on his back with a whoosh as the wind was knocked out of him.

He could dimly hear Sarah laughing as he desperately gasped, trying to get in a lungful of air. He floundered for a few seconds, then finally managed to take a deep rasping breath.

The laughter grew louder as he gasped and spluttered, and soon Sarah's laughing face came into view.

"Ha ha ha ha! You should have seen it! The great and powerful supermage defeated by a farm animal!"

Morgan groaned in pain as he forced himself into a sitting position. Gold was standing off to one side, a look of amusement on his face as Sarah clutched her sides in mirth.

"I bet you wouldn't be laughing if you were the one down here," he said with a scowl, wincing as he got to his feet.

The clothes he was wearing definitely helped, but there was only so much they could do. He was sure he'd gotten a few bruises, but thankfully nothing was broken.

"I wouldn't have ended up down there! Only an idiot would take a charge like that head on!"

"At least I managed to kill it instead of just shooting it in the ass," he said, walking over to the dead ram and pulling the metal rod from his belt.

It only took a few seconds to retrieve the core. This one was much larger than the others and Morgan eagerly pulled up its stats.

Name: Ironwool-ram Patriarch core
Rank - 5
Total available energy - 524/524

This core was taken from an Ironwool-ram. As this ram was the Patriarch of a Beast Zone, the amount of available energy has been increased.

Now this was more like it. He could do a lot with this much energy; and if they killed it every day, it wouldn't take long to move to the next rank.

"Great job, you two."

Morgan closed the status screen as Gold approached the two of them. He rose to his feet and was about to hand the cover over, when a very noticeable problem presented itself to him.

"Who will get the ironwool-ram's core?"

"Well, seeing as you were the one who killed it and the beating you took; I believe you deserve it today Morgan," Gold said with a grin. "Sarah will get the next one and we will switch off by the day."

He nodded, feeling his growing excitement ebb slightly.

His growth was significantly slower than average, due to him needing energy for two abilities instead of one. If he got three cores like this a week, plus the regular cores of the ironwool-sheep, he should be able to rank up pretty soon. Though he had to wonder how long it would take to unlock the supermage ability.

Morgan looked up as Sarah slapped him on the back, still chuckling to herself.

"I agree, he's definitely earned that core."

"Thanks," he answered dryly.

"Alright, enough of that."

They turned to see Gold turning the key in midair. The next moment, a tear opened up in space and they all walked through to exit the *Beast Zone*.

They stepped into their living room and Gold closed the portal behind them.

"Lessons are over for the day. I would recommend you wash off before you eat," he said, gesturing to their mud and gore splattered clothing.

"I'll count up the cores and divide them. They'll be waiting for you in your rooms when you come back from dinner."

He grinned then and turned to leave the room.

"I'll see you at eight sharp tomorrow morning; and don't forget your badges."

Then he was gone.

Morgan stared at the closed door for a few seconds before he heard a loud exclamation from Sarah.

"You mean we'll have to do this all again tomorrow?!"

24

Morgan was sitting on his bed, examining the small pile of cores laid out before him. He had already bathed and eaten, making sure to leave his soiled clothes in the laundry bin near the door.

He and Sarah had debated going to the arena to check out some ranked matches, but almost immediately decided against it. They were both too exhausted and had no interest in further fighting.

Now he absent-mindedly rolled the cores around before him, as he contemplated where to put the energy.

There were sixteen cores including the one from the Patriarch, all together giving him an impressive 784 energy to assign.

He was having a hard time, though, deciding on whether to put it all into one ability or to keep a balance between the two. At first he'd been tempted to dump it all into his super ability as it was closer to ranking up, but something told him that he needed to keep his abilities balanced.

With a sigh, he opened the stats of each core in turn and began assigning the energy. Gold had provided a large felt cloth to spread out on his bed and when the cores shattered, the cloth caught all of the fragments.

When he was finally done, he gathered up the sides of the cloth and tied it together with a small piece of string. Then, he set it on his dresser and planned to hand it over to Gold in the morning. He laid down in his bed and turned down the lamp. He could already feel his eyes closing, but decided to take a look at his status before he did.

Name: Morgan
Super: Rank - 4
Energy to next rank - 700/2,300
Mage: Rank - 4
Energy to next rank - 719/2,300
Super ability - Gravity
Mage ability - Air
CP - 170/170 (Regen - 1.8 per second)
MP - 170/170 (Regen - 1.8 per Second)

Strength - 16
Agility - 21
Constitution - 16
Intelligence - 17
Wisdom - 18
Super skills - Fly, Heavy handed
Mage skills - Wind blade, Tailwind

He sighed as he closed his status and pulled his blankets up to his chin.
Not bad for a day's work.

***

"Run faster, you lazy good for nothing sacks of garbage! I've seen snails that could move faster than you! Pick up the pace!"

Morgan didn't even have the energy to groan, instead doing his best to run faster under the crushing weight of the chain. His muscles were screaming their protest and he felt like his lungs would soon be exiting his body, but he made sure to keep running.

"Drop to the ground and give me fifty pushups!"

He stumbled to a halt and dropped into the correct position and began loudly counting as he did them.

He'd made the mistake of counting in his head earlier and Gold had made him repeat the entire set, saying that if he couldn't hear him counting, he probably did it wrong.

Morgan finished counting his set and got shakily to his feet. His arms were so shot, that at this point they felt numb, but his legs had recovered just enough for him to start running again. He passed Sarah who didn't look any better off than he did.

She was wearing a chain as well, albeit a much lighter one than him. She'd made the mistake of asking why a mage needed physical training and Gold had punished her for it.

After another hour of pure torture, Gold finally called an end to their lesson. At this point, the two of them merely wobbled over to their respective showers without saying a word.

This was their fourth day training under him and the lessons seemed to be increasing in difficulty by the day.

Morgan gritted his teeth as the icy cold water washed over his tortured body. He didn't hear any sounds from the stall next to him. Gold had so thoroughly wrecked them that Sarah didn't even have the energy left to curse him.

When the two of them emerged from their showers, they were surprised to see Gold still standing there. He was accompanied by another man that Morgan vaguely recognized.

"Good, let's be quick about this. Come on you two, step up."

Wondering what fresh hell Gold had dreamt up, the two of the warily stepped forward until they were standing just a few feet in front of them.

"You really did a number on these two," the man said, turning to look at Gold. "It's almost as though you enjoy torturing them."

A wide smile stretched across their teacher's face and he raised his hands as if to say; *well, you caught me.*

The man stepped up to Sarah and placed his hand on her shoulder. She flinched back a little at his touch, but then stopped. She stood absolutely still for a second, then a cry of ecstasy escaped her lips and she slumped in obvious relief.

The man walked over to Morgan next and placed a hand on his shoulder. He felt a familiar cool feeling wash over him as his battered and abused body knit itself back together.

He groaned in relief as all his aches and pains were washed away, leaving him feeling healthy and refreshed.

"You're Eric, right?" he asked, as the man stepped back. "You're the one who healed me after my test to get in."

"It's nice to be remembered," Eric said with a kind smile, as he stepped back to stand next to Gold.

Morgan was almost afraid to ask, but he decided it was best to get this out of the way.

"Why have him heal us?" he asked, noticing that Sarah had suddenly tensed up.

Gold pretend to think for a second before answering.

"Well, since you haven't gone to the healers since we began our lessons, I figured I'd bring one to you."

Morgan gaped.

They could have gone to a healer this entire time?!

"You purposely left that out didn't you? You psychotic sadist!" Sarah practically exploded in outrage.

"Who me?" Gold asked, putting on an innocent look that didn't fool either of them for a second.

"Come on Morgan, we're leaving!" she said, grabbing his arm and dragging him towards the door.

"Don't forget, Sarah, our next lesson is at half past two," he called after her.

Her only response was to stick her arm up in the air, middle finger extending out in a very clear message of what she thought of his lesson.

"You really are a sick bastard, Gold," Eric said, patting him lightly on the back before following them out.

***

Morgan growled in annoyance as the mana slipped from his grasp and the blue light surrounding him went out.

"This is impossible!" he said, throwing his arms up in frustration.

He'd been trying to get his mage shield to stay up, but the mana kept slipping out of his control.

"It's not impossible, just difficult to get the hang of," Gold calmly replied. "Now, try again."

Morgan took a deep breath to calm himself, then tried once more to form the shield.

He reached inside himself for the sphere of mana sitting in his chest. Grabbing hold of it with his mind, he began slowly siphoning off a stream of it, flattening it out and coating the inside of his body.

Sweat beaded his brow as a weak blue glow began to emanate from his skin. He willed more mana to flow out and the light around him grew brighter. He tried to feed a bit more into the shield and once again, his control slipped.

He couldn't understand what he was doing wrong. He was following Gold's instructions to the letter, but no matter how much he tried, it just wouldn't stick! It was as though the mana was fighting him at every turn.

Gold sat in silence as Morgan fumed and tried to figure out what the problem might be.

He closed his eyes and began to run though the process.

First he would take his mana and stream it out, but it took forever that way. Sarah had her shield up in less than a second and she made it look easy.

An idea struck him then.

What if, instead of pulling it and shaping it, he tried to force his mana core to explode outward? It was worth at least a try.

Taking a deep breath, Morgan opened his eyes and tried to force the mana core to expand all at once. He felt a light tugging sensation, then a bright blue glow outlined his body. Morgan was so shocked, that he lost control and the shield disappeared.

He turned to Gold who had a pleased look on his face.

"I knew you could do it."

"I was doing it wrong the whole time because of you," Morgan exclaimed, having a hard time believing that a person could be so twisted.

"But you figured it out in the end didn't you?" Gold said with a raised eyebrow.

"No thanks to you. Why am I even taking this crap from you anyway?! I don't need you! I could have taught myself how to use a mage shield just by asking Sarah."

Morgan's fists were clenched and his heart was pounding by the time he was finished.

He didn't normally lose his temper like this, but Gold had been torturing them for days without any apparent reason. Whenever they'd asked, they were forced to do even harder exercise. Sure, the Beast Zone was great, but it hardly made up for the abuse this man was putting them through.

"Tell me why I shouldn't walk out of here right now and never look back?" he asked, muscles tense and ready to spring.

"How close are you to ranking up?"

Morgan was used to Gold's seemingly ridiculous questions, so he just answered without asking why.

"I need a total of *423* to rank both up."

"After we clear the *Beast Zone* today, you should have enough energy to make it to the next *rank*. If you are unhappy once you rank up, then you no longer have to learn from me. I will find you a new instructor and never speak to you again. Do we have a deal?"

Morgan thought about it for a moment, then reluctantly nodded.

"Good. Our lesson is over for today. I will see you at half past two."

With that, he walked around his desk and left the room.

25

Morgan stared down at the *Patriarch's* core.

All he had to do was assign the energy and he would rank up. Gold's words kept coming back to him and he wondered what he could have meant by them.

Only one way to find out.

Taking a deep breath, Morgan assigned the energy. He felt the telltale tingling run through his body and shivered at the sensation.

He felt amazing. Much better than any previous rank ups.

Opening his status, Morgan was stunned.

There was no way!

Name: Morgan
Super: Rank - 5
Energy to next rank - 155/3,500
Mage: Rank - 5
Energy to next rank - 102/3,500
Super ability - Gravity
Mage ability - Air
CP - 210/210 (Regen - 2.2 per second)
MP - 210/210 (Regen - 2.2 per Second)
Strength - 21
Agility - 26
Constitution - 21
Intelligence - 21
Wisdom - 22
Super skills - Fly, Heavy handed
Mage skills - Wind blade, Tailwind

Every single one of his attributes had jumped by a massive amount!

Morgan closed his status and his mind began racing.

That crafty bastard! Gold knew this would happen, but didn't tell either of them. The question was, why he didn't. Well, he couldn't ask him until tomorrow, but he could talk to Sarah about this. At least she should know why she was working so hard.

He slid out of his bed and left the room. Walking across to Sarah's room, he knocked on the door.

"I'm sleeping. Go away!"

"Well, wake up then. I've got something important to tell you!"

He heard muffled cursing and the sound of stomping feet, then the door flew open to reveal Sarah, dressed in a nightgown and not looking very happy.

"What?" she asked, her voice laced with annoyance.

Morgan looked her over, noticing the deep *V* down the front of her gown, which revealed a generous amount of cleavage.

"That doesn't look very warm," Morgan said, pointing to her gown.

"What are you...?" Sarah asked, before looking down.

Her face flushed a deep crimson, then she slammed the door in his face.

Morgan blinked, staring at the closed door in incomprehension.

Was it something he said?

He was raising his hand to knock again, when the door suddenly opened once more. Sarah stood there, her face still deep crimson in color. A blanket was draped over her shoulders, hiding the revealing nightgown.

He thought about asking what all that was about, but figured he'd just let it go. She'd been flushing and running away so many times now, that he just figured it was what she did.

"What did you want?" she asked.

"How close are you to *rank 8?*" Morgan asked.

"Pretty close."

"How much energy do you need?"

Her eyes focused on the air in front of her for a second, before they turned back to him.

"I need *48* energy to reach *rank 8.*"

She smiled here and Morgan could understand why.

That meant that she'd be able to rank up tomorrow.

"Here," Morgan said, fished around in his pockets and handed her three cores. "These are *rank 3* cores and should have enough energy to get you to the next *rank.*"

She took them hesitantly and looked between him and the cores.

"Not that I don't appreciate it, but why do you want me to rank up now?"

"Just do it, trust me."

"You don't have to tell me twice," she said with a smile.

The next instant, all the cores in her hand crumbled and fell to the floor as they shattered. Sarah shivered as she moved up to the next *rank* and a pleased looking smile touched her lips.

He saw her eyes focus on her status and she froze; her eyes going wide with shock. He remained silent as she looked through her attributes several times to make sure she wasn't dreaming. Finally, she closed her status and turned back to him.

"How did my attributes increase so much?"

"I think you already know," he answered.

She opened her mouth to ask what he meant, then snapped it shut.

"Oh, that sneaky bastard! Of course he wouldn't tell us this was going to happen!"

"Well, I'm going to sleep. I'll leave you to clean up the mess," Morgan said and headed back towards his room.

"Morgan, what the…!"

But he'd already closed his door.

***

"Since you're both still here, I will assume that you've already ranked up and see the benefits of my classes," Gold said as they walked into their morning lesson.

Neither of them bothered rising to his bait, instead waiting for him to begin their daily torture.

"No questions? Demands that I explain myself?"

He faked a look of surprise.

"We've already figured it out," Sarah said with a shrug. "No point in asking what we already know."

A genuine smile spread across his face this time.

"Excellent, you've figured out that the physical training has raised your *strength, agility* and *constitution*, but have you figured out why your *intelligence* and *wisdom* have gone up as well?"

"For me, it was the additional classes you recommended I take," Sarah answered for them. "And for Morgan, it was your misinformation about the correct way to use a mage shield."

Gold nodded his head enthusiastically.

"Yes, you figured it out! Now I can tell you why I'm pushing you so hard. At the earlier *ranks*, increasing your attributes by four or five per *rank* is completely possible. However, once you break the first threshold, your ability to increase your attributes will slowly begin to decline."

"What's a threshold?" Morgan asked.

If Gold was in a talkative mood, it wouldn't hurt to try and get some information out of him.

"A threshold is when someone moves into a new stage of power in their ability. For example; Sarah is now *rank 8*. When she moves up to the next *rank,* she will break through the threshold and thereby become more powerful."

"How do you mean?" Sarah asked.

No one had explained any of this to her yet. She was sure her father had known all about this, but of course had never mentioned it.

"As you both know, all people that have an ability will begin at *rank 0*. Every tenth *rank,* the person will experience a significant increase in power."

"How much of an increase are we talking about?" Morgan asked.

"Let's just say that if you come across someone at *rank 9,* you'd better run the other way."

"You don't think I can win?" Morgan asked with a raised eyebrow. "I killed a *rank 6* mage when I was still at *rank 1*."

"While that is impressive, you still wouldn't stand a chance. Take my word on that."

Morgan nodded again.

Gold may be a twisted bastard, but he was a knowledgeable one. If he said that someone at rank 9 was too strong for him, then he would believe it.

"Now, as I was saying. Every time a threshold is broken, the person will feel a significant increase in power. However, their ability to increase their attributes will decrease with each breakthrough.

"While the maximum amount of attribute points you can get between *0* and *8* is five, the maximum amount you can get between *9* and *18* is four. Between *19* and *28* is three and once you hit *rank 39,* the maximum is two.

"So, you can understand why increasing your attributes is so important at lower *ranks*. Now, are there any further questions?" he asked, the familiar wicked grin now replacing the scholarly enthusiasm.

Neither of them bothered to answer.

This was another thing he did. He would ask if there were questions; then when one of them tried to ask, he would cut them off.

"You two are no fun," he said, retrieving two chains from a pile against the wall.

Morgan was excited for this part.

His strength had gone up enough that the weight shouldn't bother him too much. He couldn't wait to see the look on Gold's face when he sprinted easily around the room.

He should have known better.

Morgan's eyes went wide as the chain wrapped around his shoulders. His legs already beginning to tremble under the weight as he stared at Gold in incomprehension.

"Did you really think I wouldn't use a heavier chain?" Gold asked in mock surprise. "I thought you knew me better than that."

He saw Sarah's legs buckle next as a new chain was tied to her and resigned himself to a miserable two hours.

26

"I've noticed that the two of you have yet to fight in any ranked matches," Gold said, as they exited the portal.

Morgan and Sarah both turned to glare at him as he tucked the key into his pocket. They were both exhausted and splattered from head to toe in mud and gore.

This run had been especially difficult. The ram had charged Sarah instead of Morgan this time and had managed to shatter her mage shield with its glowing horns.

They had both gotten pretty banged up in the process of killing it, as they had been forced to fight more recklessly than they usually did. Gold had, of course, done nothing to aid them; instead standing on the sidelines and egging on the ram to attack them harder. For some reason, the ram had seemed to take his advice and did his best to kill them both.

"Oh, don't give me those looks," he said dismissively. "If you don't fight and win, at least one ranked match a week, your class rankings will begin to fall. Do I need to remind you what will happen if you fall below 50th?"

"No," Morgan sighed.

While Sarah didn't technically need the scholarship, he definitely did. Which meant that after supper, he would have to visit the arena.

***

"Will you be coming with me?" Morgan asked, as they exited the dining room.

"Why not," Sarah answered resignedly. "May as well meet some of the people in our year; see who we're up against."

Morgan wholeheartedly agreed with her, so they stopped back at the house to get ready. While Sarah changed into a set of combat clothes, Morgan laced on his shin guards and tied his fingerless gloves to his waist. He then took the map out to find the arena's location. About ten minutes later, Sarah was ready and the two of them headed out.

It was about a ten minute walk from their block, which Morgan was quite grateful for.

He hadn't been looking forward to an hour long walk to the other side of the academy.

It didn't take long for the arena to come into view, a tall oval-shaped building that took up the space of several blocks.

When they approached, they could see a bunch of other students waiting near one of the entrances and headed over to wait along with them.

"What do you think it looks like on the inside?" Morgan asked, as the line moved forward quickly.

"I've never been in an arena before, so my guess is as good as yours," she answered.

It took another ten minutes to get to the entrance, where a woman sat behind a desk with a large stack of papers before her.

"Names and classes?" she asked as the two of them stepped up for their turn in line.

"Morgan, super class."

"Sarah, mage class."

The woman began rifling through her stack of papers, growing more and more aggravated as she couldn't seem to find them. Finally she looked up, a suspicious expression on her face.

"I don't see your names anywhere on the list. What are your class ranks?"

"I'm ranked 9th in mine and she's ranked 1st in hers," Morgan answered, becoming worried that they would be turned away.

The woman's expression changed in an instant. She went from open mistrust to all smiles.

"Why didn't you just say so?" she asked, rising from her seat and waving someone else to take over for her.

"Follow me," she said, walking through the small entrance and into the arena.

He and Sarah exchanged a confused look, but she just shrugged and followed the woman, Morgan trailing a few steps behind.

He openly gaped as they entered the massive structure, his head swiveling from side to side as he tried to take it all in. There was no ceiling overhead, leaving the arena open to the darkening sky. It was brightly lit despite the gloom and he didn't have a problem seeing anything.

Rows upon rows of seats sloped upward surrounding a large open area in the center. The area was huge and currently taken up by twenty or so fighting stages where people were battling for a higher ranking.

"We don't usually have students in the top fifty come in through the main entrance."

Morgan's attention snapped back to the woman as she began talking again.

"Where would we come in, then?" Sarah asked.

"Right over there," she said, stopping and pointing to a fenced off area.

While the rest of the arena was quite crowded, this area was practically free of people, with only one or two standing inside.

"Go speak to the person sitting behind that desk and they will tell you all you need to know."

"Thanks for your help," Sarah said, and the two of them headed to the gated area.

They walked in and saw a small group of people loitering around the entrance and Morgan thought that they looked quite unpleasant. From what he could hear, one of them was bragging about fighting prowess and how no one could even hope to match him.

As they approached the woman sitting behind the desk, the group containing the braggart moved in front them, spreading out in a semi-circle to block their path.

"Can I help you?" Morgan asked, not at all interested in dealing with these people.

"Yeah, there's something you can help me with," the boy in the front said, folding his arms and sneering down at him.

"You can buzz off. This area is for people ranked fifty or above in the class and since you're clearly a weakling, you don't belong here."

Morgan took a moment to size the boy up.

He was a few inches taller than him, maybe five foot eight; with short cropped brown hair, brown eyes and a slightly flabby face. He was clearly a weakling and felt the need to make himself appear stronger by belittling those around him. He knew how to handle these types.

"Get out of my way. If anyone doesn't belong here, it's you," Morgan said in a flat tone.

The boy's condescending sneer slipped and an angry red began to suffuse his face.

"We're ranked in the top fifty, now step aside and let us pass," Sarah said, stepping in front of Morgan and trying to diffuse the situation.

"Oh, and what might your name be, gorgeous?"

Another boy separated himself from the group and stepped up to join him. He was tall and lanky, with skin so pale it appeared to be green. Long strands of greasy hair hung down his face and when he smiled, Morgan could see a mouth full of very yellow looking teeth.

"None of your business, slime ball," she said, wrinkling her nose in disgust.

"Oh come on, don't be like that," the boy said, stepping forward and leering at her. "After all, I think you would quite enjoy my company."

"Get out of our way," Morgan said, stepping up beside her, a frown now touching his lips. "We're here to compete in a ranked fight so we can keep our spots. If you want to fight and are ranked in the top 50, then I'll be happy to take you on."

"Like I said, there's no way a couple of weaklings like you are in the top fifty," the other boy said, stepping right up to Morgan and grabbing the front of his shirt. "Now I suggest you beat it, before you make me angry."

Morgan sighed; then slammed a fist into the boy's solar plexus. The boy wheezed, letting go of him and bent double, clutching at his stomach.

"Come on, Sarah," Morgan said, stepping past the shocked group of people and walking up to the desk.

The woman sitting behind had looked up when the commotion had started and was now looking at the two of them with narrowed eyes.

"You do know that fighting outside an official match is against school rules, correct?" Her tone was icy and her gaze like steel.

"He attacked me first," Morgan said with a shrug, completely unapologetic.

"We're sorry for the trouble we caused," Sarah quickly put in. "They were refusing to let us pass."

"Why didn't you come in from this entrance if you're in the top fifty?"

"We didn't know there was a separate entrance," Sarah answered. "The woman at the main entrance guided us here as it is our first time in the arena."

"Well, we can sort this out easily enough. Tell me your names and current ranking in your respective class."

Sarah quickly gave her the information and the woman looked down to her desk, checking their names and corresponding ranks. After a few moments she looked up with a smile.

"Your names are on the list. I would caution you, however, to not be caught fighting outside of academy sanctioned matches, as there are severe consequences for any who do."

She waited for them both to nod their understanding before continuing.

"I can see here that neither of you has fought in the arena before. Would you like an explanation of how the rankings function, or has that already been explained to you?"

"It's already been explained," Morgan answered. "We're just here for our weekly match."

"It's on then, punk!"

Morgan turned to see the boy he'd punched approaching with his groupies once again. His face was beet red and he looked about ready to burst.

"My name is Grub, and I'm ranked 5th in the super class. I'll take him on!"

27

"Grub? You mean like those little white things that live in rotten trees?" Morgan asked.

"Not Grub, you stupid commoner, Grub! You need to roll the *R* on the tip of your tongue, not that some common trash like you could say it right!"

"I'll take on the redhead," the greasy boy said, walking over to the desk. "My name is Frush, and I'm ranked 3rd in the mage class."

Morgan noticed that he too pronounced his name with that weird *R* sound and wondered if they were related.

"You keep referring to me as a commoner. Does that make you a noble?" Morgan asked as the woman checked the other boy's names to verify their identities.

"Not yet, but I might as well be," Grub bragged. "Me and Frush here come from a very wealthy family and it's only a matter of time until Queen Beatrice gives us what we deserve."

So he was right, they were related.

"So you're from the South Kingdom," Sarah said, now looking a bit more interested.

"That's right, gorgeous," Frush said, clearly looking directly at her chest. "Maybe after I beat you and take the top spot, you'll come back to my room and I'll tell you some more about it."

Sarah's face flushed a deep red at the insinuation, but this time Morgan could tell why she was turning that color. She was angry; very angry.

He wasn't sure why an invitation to someone's bedroom would make her so upset.

"That's quite enough of that!" Everyone turned to see the woman glaring at them. "If you have any grievances, you can fight it out during a match."

She looked around, as if daring any of them to argue with her. When no one did, she continued speaking.

"I have confirmed your identities and have set up the matches accordingly. Please follow me to the fighting area."

She then walked out in front of them and headed back into the arena. Grub glared at Morgan, and Frush threw Sarah a wink before following her.

Morgan started to walk when he noticed that Sarah wasn't moving. She was glued to her spot, practically shaking with rage.

"Are you alright?" he asked, walking over to her and placing a hand on her shoulder.

She turned to him and Morgan felt his stomach drop at the look in her eyes. Then she seemed to come to herself and visibly relaxed.

"I'm fine," she said, brushing his hand away. "Just need to show that slimy little toad that he can't talk to me that way."

"Okay then," Morgan said, hurrying to catch up to her.

Why did girls have to be so confusing? One second she looked ready to burst and the next, she was so calm- it was almost scary!

They caught up to the others just as they entered the main fighting area filled with stages. Morgan could see that each stage had a number painted on the side, as well as two people standing next to each one as the competitors fought.

He watched a few fights as they wove their way through the throngs of people and found that he wasn't impressed. With very few exceptions, most people were just floundering around and hoping to get a lucky hit, rather than fighting with any real technique.

"Here we are… Stage twenty."

Morgan turned his attention back to the woman as they all walked into another fenced off area.

Here, there were only two stages, with four people standing alongside each. It didn't escape his notice that as soon as they walked in, everyone on the outside who wasn't fighting turned their attention towards them.

A man stepped up to the small group then and asked the woman for the names and ranks so he could record them once the fight was finished. When the woman was done, she left the area, giving them all a nod.

"My name is Percival and I am in charge of the ranked matches between students in the top fifty of their classes."

Morgan looked over the man who began talking. He was tall, maybe six and half feet, with dark coffee colored skin and coal black eyes. He was bald and very well built. Morgan could immediately tell that this man was to be respected. After all, they wouldn't put a weakling in charge of a place like this, especially seeing as he likely oversaw *all* ranked matches; including those of fifth year students.

"The rules for first year fights are simple. To win a match, you must either render your opponent unable to fight; or strike a hypothetical death blow."

He looked over the four students standing before him, making sure to make eye contact with each.

"While injuring your opponent is allowed, attempting to actually kill them is most definitely not. If it is deemed that you are about to strike a killing blow, the match will be stopped. Our referees are very good at spotting this, so when a match is called, you will immediately cease all fighting. Any continuation after a match is called will result in a warning."

His eyes bore into them and his voice took on a threatening tone.

"There will only be one warning. After that, your ranking in the class will be dropped by ten. If you continue fighting after that, I will intervene. If I am forced to stop a match, the offending student will be kicked out of the school indefinitely and banned from ever entering again. Do I make myself clear?"

They all nodded emphatically, none wishing to earn this man's ire.

"Good. Supers, you will be fighting there. Mages, stage twenty one."

"Good luck," Sarah said, as he headed towards the indicated stage.

Stepping onto the raised platform, Morgan saw a small man standing at the center. He heard Grub climbing up behind him, and saw the man motion them both over.

The stage was about twenty square feet, so it was large enough to fight, but still small enough to ensure that there would be no running away.

They both stopped in front of the man, who grabbed Morgan's wrist and pulled him around so he was facing across from Grub.

"I'm sure Percival explained the rules so I won't bother going over them. This match will be between Grub, who is ranked

5th in the class and Morgan, ranked 9th in the class. Since Grub holds the higher rank, it will not increase, should he win. Morgan's will only drop by one. Should Morgan win, however, his rank will increase by two while Grub's will fall by the same amount. Any further questions?"

He looked to both of them, but they shook their heads.

"Very well. Each of you, back up to your side and wait for my signal to begin."

Grub gave him one last glare before walking over to his side of the stage. Morgan walked to his as well, pulling the gloves onto his hands and tightening the straps to secure them. He noticed that quite a crowd had gathered behind the gate, all talking excitedly.

Maybe they'd already seen fights between students in the top fifty? Morgan didn't know, but he also didn't have time to think about it further.

Morgan took up a fighting stance as the referee held his arm up in the air. Across the stage, Grub just cracked his knuckles, looking confident.

"Begin!"

The referee swished his arm down through the air, then quickly left the stage.

Morgan shuffled forward slowly.

He wasn't sure what Grub's ability was, so he had to careful. He also couldn't use any of his mage skills while so many people were watching and, as he'd discovered during his fight with the golem, his fly skill wouldn't be useful in a fight with a quick opponent.

Grub, on the other hand, looked completely unconcerned. He swaggered right into the center of the stage, leaving himself wide open.

Morgan hesitated.

Was he really that dumb, or was it a trap to lure him in?

He shrugged to himself and decided on his favorite course of action: go for it and see what happens.

He launched himself towards the bigger boy, springing lightly on the balls of his feet. Grub didn't look at all surprised, instead slamming both of his fists together and activating a skill.

The ground shook for a moment, then chunks of rock began flaking off the ground and flying towards him.

Morgan stopped, watching in fascination as the boy was slowly covered in a rocky armor. He left his face uncovered for some reason and walked towards him a confident smile.

Morgan didn't move, staring at the approaching stone covered boy and wondering how much power he would have to use for it to be considered a death blow.

"Got nothing to say now, you cocky bastard?" he sneered, throwing a few punches in the air in front of him.

"Look at him, you guys!" he called to his groupies standing by the side of the stage. "He completely froze up when he saw my awesome power!"

"He looks like he's about to piss himself!" one of them called out, getting a round of laughter from the rest of them.

"What do you think, guys? Should I finish him off quick, or play with him a little?" he asked, holding his arms out to the sides.

"I bet if you hit him hard enough, he'll start crying for his mommy!"

"I bet he begs for mercy within ten seconds!"

"He'll probably shit himself, too!"

The others in his group began voicing their opinions, each growing more detailed and graphic as to what Morgan would do when Grub started fighting.

Morgan just stared as the boy strutted around basking in the attention of his followers and completely ignoring him.

He'd been wrong to think this boy was a threat. He was a complete moron!

"I bet he runs off the stage, after he's pissed and shit himself. Then he'll trip over himself in embarrassment and end up eating his own shit!"

"You guys are too much," Grub said, holding his sides and roaring with laughter.

This was the chance Morgan had been waiting for.

The idiot had dropped his guard so much that there was no chance to defend himself.

The air distorted around his body as he activated his *heavy handed* skill and threw a punch towards Grub's exposed head.

"Stop!"

Morgan stopped in his tracks, his fist extended straight out just a few inches from Grub's head. He stared at the boy not believing how someone could be this stupid.

The idiot hadn't even noticed he'd lost. He was still carrying on about all the ways he would make him soil himself.

His minions did notice, however, it was hard not to and went silent as Grub continued on.

"I think I'll tear his clothes off and make him run back to his room naked! Though I'd probably be doing him a favor. After all, who wants to walk around in shit stained pants?!"

He roared with laughter, but it soon died down when he realized he was the only one still laughing. His expression darkened and he glared at his silent groupies.

"Why aren't you laughing? That joke was funny!"

Instead of answering, one of them just pointed to his side, where Morgan still stood with his fist outstretched and an incredulous expression on his face.

Grub's head whipped around to see Morgan's fist just a few inches from his face. He held the pose for another few seconds before relaxing and backing away.

"The match is over, and Morgan is the winner by deathblow!"

The crowd was deathly silent at this and Grub stared; first in shock, then outrage.

"That doesn't count!" he yelled. "He attacked me when I wasn't looking!"

The referee gave him a disgusted look.

"The match had officially started and you were stupid enough to not only take your eyes off of your opponent, but completely drop your guard and start making fun of him. If he hadn't attacked you, I might have called the match on principle! Morgan will be raised to 7th in the class. Since you can't drop by two ranks, as Morgan currently holds that spot, you will be dropped to 8th! You're lucky I don't drop you by one hundred ranks for the utter stupidity you displayed just now!"

The referee was screaming by the end, spittle flying from his lips and flecking across the boy's face. He turned back to Morgan, his anger settling somewhat.

"You should be congratulated for pulling your punch when I called the match. Were I in your position, I don't think I would have had the self-restraint."

Morgan thanked the referee and turned to walk off the stage, glad that his fight had been so easy.

"This match shouldn't have counted! I demand a rematch!"

He stopped when Grub's voice rang out and turned to face the other boy, who hadn't released his skill and was still clad in rocky armor.

"I already competed in a match this week," Morgan said with a shrug. "If you want another fight, you'll have to wait until next week. Though, I'm not sure if I'll fight you again, seeing as you're ranked lower than me right now."

"No, we're going to fight right now!" he shrieked, nearly beside himself with rage. "You cheated and I'm going to make you pay!"

As he took a threatening step towards Morgan, the referee's voice sounded once more.

"Stop! This is your only warning. Take another step and you will be demoted by ten ranks!"

Grub froze in place and Morgan could see the struggle going on behind the boy's eyes. After a few tense moments, the stone armor began to fall, hitting the stage with a loud clatter.

"This isn't over, you piece of shit! You'll pay for this, be sure of that!"

Morgan shrugged once again and walked off the stage. He could see that Sarah's match hadn't started yet and walked over to the side of the stage to watch.

For some unknowable reason, Frush was thrusting his hips back and forth and making odd noises while staring at Sarah. Sarah, for her part, was standing absolutely still and waiting for the referee to begin the match.

"Don't worry sweetie, I promise I'll be gentle! Unless you like it rough, I'll be fine with that, too!" Frush called out to her.

Morgan looked to the referee, who had a disgusted look on her face and was standing by the side of the stage as if trying to decide whether to should start the match or not.

He quickly made his way over to the woman while Frush continued to do his weird dance and calling out things that made absolutely no sense to him.

Why would Sarah want him to 'go hard all night?' If she was up fighting all night, she wouldn't be able to function during Gold's torture sessions. Morgan was puzzled.

"Excuse me, referee," Morgan called out.

The woman turned to him and quickly walked over, looking relieved for some reason.

"Why aren't you starting the match?"

"Can't you hear what that boy is saying to her?" she asked, in shock.

"I can, but I don't understand why that should prevent Sarah from fighting," he said, looking confused.

The woman blinked, wondering how dense a person could be.

"Are you sure your friend is in the right state of mind to be fighting?" she finally asked.

"She looks fine to me. Just let her fight. She needs to, in order to keep her rank in the class."

The referee looked back once more at Frush's lewd display and at the girl's rigid body; and decided that it wouldn't be fair if she deprived her of the opportunity to take her revenge.

She knew she would have to keep a close eye on her to make sure she didn't kill him, however.

"Very well. We'll begin the fight right away," she said, motioning to the two healers on standby to be ready.

"Thanks," Morgan said, and moved back around the stage so he could have a better view.

He debated wishing Sarah good luck as he passed her, but decided against it. She looked really focused and he didn't want to ruin her concentration.

The referee walked out into the middle of the stage and raised her arm in the air before dropping it.

"Begin!" she called out, running anxiously to get clear of the stage.

Sarah's arm shot out in front of her and Morgan watched in awe as no fewer than eight *icicle spears* formed in the air at once.

"Take this, you sick minded piece of shit!" she screamed and sent all eight spears flying at him.

Frush, who was still in the middle of thrusting his hips, was suddenly impaled in eight different places. The force of all eight spears hitting him at once threw him off his feet and clean off the stage, where he lay writhing and shrieking in pain in a spreading pool of blood.

None of the spears had been lethal. Sarah had made sure of that. Instead, she had carefully placed each of the spears where they would inflict the most damage and pain.

Morgan stared in shock as she darted across the stage, condensing a large ball of water into ice as she did. She came to a stop at the edge of the stage, where the healers were already working on stopping the bleeding.

The referee, who was also crouched over the wounded boy, opened her mouth to give her a warning, when she saw where her attack was aimed.

She deserved this much, at least. She would issue his warning only after she acted.

Frush, who was now whimpering softly as the spears were being removed, suddenly jerked up. His body froze in a half upright position for a few seconds before crashing back down and howling in agony. His voice was pitched quite a bit higher than before and the healers looked up to see Sarah with a smug look on her face.

They didn't quite understand what had happened until the referee spoke up.

"This is your warning, Sarah. If you attack again, you will be dropped by ten ranks."

She was smiling while she said this, however, and Sarah bowed respectfully to her.

"My apologies. It won't happen again."

It was only once she left that the healers noticed a large ball of ice lying on the ground between their patient's legs.

28

Morgan stretched, feeling the wonderful relief of having his bruised and battered body fixed by a healer.

"It's been almost a month, but I still can't get used to this training!" he heard Sarah complaining as she was healed as well.

"He just makes it harder whenever I rank up. You're lucky it's taking you so long, otherwise you'd be getting the same treatment."

She just stuck out her tongue at him and the two of them headed to the dining room for breakfast.

What she said had been true. Over the last month, Gold had been methodically destroying them on a daily basis. And while he'd managed to rank up twice in both abilities, Sarah still hadn't reached *rank 9*.

Apparently, breakthrough *ranks* required triple the energy of the previous one, so it was taking her a while to get there.

Gold had also begun teaching Morgan how to work on gaining his supermage ability. Apparently, he would have to slowly combine his mana and chi inside of himself, until he'd converted it all into reiki.

It was a slow process, but he already had a small core of reiki in the center of his chest, between his mana sphere and chi-heart.

When he'd asked what would happen when his chi ran out, Gold explained that the process was less than pleasant. Apparently, when he was converting the last five percent, he would begin to feel unimaginable pain. He would only pass out once it was all converted and would remain that way while the reiki took over functioning as his heart.

Gold also explained that he would need to be at *rank 8* in both abilities for it to work and once he completed the merging of his mana and chi, he would wake up as a *rank 9* supermage.

"Do you think Gold will take us to a new *Beast Zone* soon? I'm getting tired of killing sheep," Sarah said, cutting into a very large stack of pancakes.

"Don't know," Morgan answered, his mouth full of the fluffy and syrup drenched breakfast treat.

Whoever had invented these should be raised on a pedestal and be crowned King of the world, Morgan thought as he chewed happily on his massive stack of pillowy goodness.

"He'd better! It's taking me forever to reach the next *rank*!"

"I don't know what you're complaining about. Before we left City Four, you were still *rank 6* and it took you three years just to reach it!"

"I know," she huffed. "Guess I've just become spoiled with how easy it's been to get energy."

Morgan grunted in reply, too busy with his food to give her his full attention.

Sarah, seeing that she wasn't going to be able to talk to him until he was done, sighed in resignation and concentrated on her own food.

***

Morgan reclined back on the plush couch in the living room of house *Q87*. Their lesson with Gold would be starting soon and he had a feeling that they would indeed be going to a new *Beast Zone* today.

Gold had been hinting at it for weeks and he'd let slip in their previous lesson that he and Sarah should wear a few extra layers, as they might be going somewhere cold later on.

He didn't have any clothes for cold weather, as it was still the summer when they'd left the North Kingdom. Since it was warm in the Central Kingdom year round, he hadn't bothered to buy any, either.

So after eating lunch with Sarah, the two of them paid a visit to their favorite shopkeeper, James; who had been more than happy to supply them with cold weather gear.

Since there wasn't a high demand for it, they got it at a great price as well. Not that they would have to pay for it, as their scholarship covered all clothing expenses.

Now he had a thick canvas coat lined with wool and threaded with steel mesh, a pair of thick pants of the same material and boots suited for colder climates. He also had a pair of gloves and a warm woolen cap.

Morgan looked over to where his clothes were lying in bags against the wall.

He really hoped they were going today. Just the thought of another Beast Zone was exciting enough; but one that required equipment like this...

Morgan decided to go through his status one last time before Gold arrived, just to check how much further he had to go until his next *rank*.

Name: Morgan
Super: Rank - 7
Energy to next rank - 534/5,700
Mage: Rank - 7
Energy to next rank - 497/5,700
Super ability - Gravity
Mage ability - Air
CP - 310/310 (Regen - 3.2 per second)
MP - 310/310 (Regen - 3.2 per Second)
Strength - 30
Agility - 36
Constitution - 31
Intelligence - 31
Wisdom - 32
Super skills - Fly, Heavy handed
Mage skills - Wind blade, Tailwind

His agility was still his highest attribute, easily outstripping the others, but he wouldn't be able to continue this increase for much longer. Once he reached rank 9, it would be slowed down. Not to mention that if the cost to rank up was tripled between 8 and 9, it would take a whole lot longer to reach each new rank after that.

He next checked his *skills* to see how they'd improved.

Fly: Manipulate gravity to make yourself lighter and move through the air
Cost - 1 CP per second
Maximum height - 37 Ft
Maximum speed - 20.7 Ft per second

Maximum carry weight - 57 pounds (carrying any more weight will decrease speed by 0.1 feet per second for every additional pound)

Heavy handed: Manipulate gravity to make your blows land harder (currently X2.07)
    Cost - 20 CP
    Duration - 17 seconds

Wind blade: Manipulate the air around you to create whirling blades sharper than steel
    Cost - 40 MP
    Duration - Until dismissed

Tailwind: Manipulate the air around you to increase speed (Currently X2.07)
    Cost - 20 MP
    Duration - 17 seconds

So, his skills were increasing in power and duration. He could now use heavy handed or tailwind pretty much non stop. With his regen and the duration of the skill increasing, he almost felt like he had too much CP and MP for his low cost skills.

Gold had told him that skills evolve over time, and that if a skill is used a certain way, it would eventually offer a change or upgrade.

Maybe when they upgraded or changed, his CP and MP wouldn't look as enormous as they did now.

He closed his status as he heard Sarah's door open. She was dressed in her usual combat clothes and had her hair in it's now customary single braid.

"So, what do you think?" she asked, flopping down next to him. "Will we be going to a new *Beast Zone* today?"

"We will indeed!"

They both turned as Gold walked into their living room. He was wearing a thick pair of pants, winter boots and had a coat slung over one arm.

"Really?" Morgan asked, shooting to his feet in excitement.

"Yes, really. Before you rush off to change into warmer clothing, I have a few things to tell you about this particular *Beast Zone.*"

Morgan, who was already pulling the winter clothes from the bags, stopped what he was doing and went back to sit on the couch.

"The place we're going is a *Beast Zone* ranked from *6* to *31*," Gold began, then held up a hand to forestall any questions. "I will explain and if you have any questions at the end, I will do my best to answer them."

"Yeah, right," Sarah muttered under her breath.

"This *Beast Zone* is very special, as it is only one of two under the academy's control that is *staged*. What this means, is that this *Zone* has several stages, with a different *Patriarch* or *Matriarch* in charge of each. Each *stage* will be more difficult than the last, with more dangerous and higher *ranked* beasts on each one. These *Zones* are also unique, in that exiting will be impossible until the end of the *stage* is reached."

"We will be going to the first *stage* which is ranked at *6*. We won't be going here every day as it is a popular *Beast Zone* and in very high demand, but I will try and get us in at least once a week."

"How exactly do the *stages* work?" Sarah asked as soon as he finished with the explanation.

"This *Beast Zone* is set on an arctic mountain. What that means, is that it will be very cold and have a lot of snow. There are nine *stages* in this *Zone*, the first of which is set at the base of the mountain. Once you defeat the *Matriarch* at the base, you will have the option to move further up or leave. The further up the mountain one goes, the higher *ranked* the beasts will be."

"Is it possible to go directly to the top?" Morgan asked, fascinated by all this new information.

"It is possible," Gold answered with a smile. "*Staged Beast Zones* are unique in more than one way. While a regular *Zone* only has one key, a *staged Zone* had multiple keys, each one leading to a different *stage*. They are also unique in another way. Once you defeat the *matriarch* on the final *stage,* a portal will automatically open, whether you have a key or not. This portal can take you pretty much anywhere, so powerful supers and mages have used it as a form of transportation in the past." He finished.

"I've been curious about something for a while now," Sarah said. "It doesn't have to do with this *Beast Zone* in particular, just something I wanted to ask."

Gold looked to the clock on the wall.

"We have time for one more question, then you will need to get ready."

"If *Beast Zones* are accessible, why does it take people so long to reach the *max rank* of *50*? I know that the energy from a *rank 1* beast isn't much, but the energy from a *rank 29* beast should be plenty."

"The answer is quite simple, really. Aside from the fact that high ranked *Beast Zones* are rare and that most people don't even have access to any *Zones* at all; once you reach *rank 19*, you will no longer be able to absorb energy from beasts below your *rank*. So even if someone reaches *rank 29* in a decade or so, they will be very hard pressed to find *beasts* of a higher *rank*.

"The South and East Kingdoms each control a very high *ranked Beast Zone*, but they charge an exorbitant fee for any wishing to enter. They do have high *ranked* cores for sale as well, but they charge even more for those than entry to the *Zone*."

"What's the highest *rank Beast Zone* you've been in?" Morgan asked, as the two of them stood up from the couch.

"The academy has one *rank 37 Beast Zone*. I've been to the *Zone* in the South Kingdom once, but that was many years ago."

He smiled ruefully as Morgan pulled the warm clothes from the bags on the floor.

"That was a *rank 39* to *49 staged Beast Zone*. It was one of the most terrifying experiences of my life. I nearly died on the first *stage* and was forced to call for help so I could leave. I didn't even get the chance to see the *stage Patriarch*, as the men who came to save me stopped me from entering the final room until they killed it."

"Seriously?" Sarah asked. "How much does it cost to get in?"

"Why?" Gold asked with a puzzled expression. "It's not like you would survive a place like that."

"No, but if I can afford to send you there, maybe the beasts will finish you off for us," she replied with a wicked grin.

29

The cold was the first thing that hit Morgan as he exited the portal. An icy blast of wind tore straight through his layers of clothing and chilled him to the bone. He shivered lightly as he took in the new landscape.

He was standing in the middle of a wide, open area. Snow blew across the area and collected in huge drifts, making visibility difficult at any distance.

He could see the shadow of a mountain some way off and figured that was where the *Matriarch* of this *stage* was located.

He turned as he heard the sound of crunching snow, and saw Sarah and Gold emerging from the tear in space.

"It's freezing!" was the first thing she said as she exited the portal, followed by, "what the hell, Gold!"

"I did warn you," was his only response. "Now come on, time is wasting and we've got a long ways to go before we can fight the *Matriarch.*"

With Sarah grumbling under her breath, they started walking towards the distant mountain, feet crunching through the hard packed snow underfoot.

"What kind of beast will we run into on this *stage*?" Morgan asked, stomping his feet to keep the blood flowing through his limbs.

"There's more than one type in this *Zone,*" Gold answered in a chipper tone. "The *Zone* we normally go to is meant for beginners. So there is only one type of beast. Here, you'll run into loads of them, though there are only three different types on this *stage.*"

"I think I see something up ahead!" Sarah called out.

Shading his eyes, Morgan could just make out something moving though the large snow drifts.

If all the beasts blended into the landscape, it would be a lot more difficult to fight them. He really hoped that this was the only one.

As they made it closer, he could begin to distinguish some type of four legged creature with white fur and a big fluffy tail.

Maybe a fox?

There was a loud growl and Morgan turned to see three of the creatures coming up behind him.

"There are more behind us!" he called out, eyeing the three beasts.

They weren't that big, maybe coming up to his knees, but they looked quite dangerous. They looked like foxes, but their fur was white instead of the usual red and brown. They had large glittering green eyes, long snouts and mouths full of razor sharp teeth.

Morgan took up a fighting stance and activated his mage shield.

He needed to be careful. He hadn't heard anything from Sarah, and Gold wouldn't intervene unless it looked like he would die.

These beasts looked fast, so his mage skills would likely be more useful here. He also had to keep in mind that they could be up to rank 6, so he would need to be very careful.

He tensed as one of the foxes let out a bark and launched itself at him. It didn't escape his notice however, that as soon as it leapt, the other two moved to flank him.

They weren't just stronger and faster than the sheep, they were smarter as well.

Morgan used *wind blade* twice in a row, hearing the familiar rush of air, as two lances formed on his arms. He then used *tailwind* and nimbly dodged to the side, avoiding the lunging beast and plunging a *wind blade* into one of the foxes that was trying to flank him.

He was surprised when the lance of air didn't immediately kill the fox. He felt actual resistance for a second or two, before the *blade* sunk in and killed the beast.

He jumped back, narrowly avoiding a mouth full of sharp teeth, then rolled to the side to avoid a set of wicked looking claws that sprouted from the other.

He came to his feet, quickly assessing his situation.

He could vaguely make out a humanoid shape off to his right; probably Sarah fighting some foxes of her own. One fox was down, but killing it hadn't been as easy as he'd thought it would be. Their fur was tough, so maybe they had some sort of resistance to mage abilities.

He quickly dismissed his *wind blades* and stood with his fists raised, waiting for his *tailwind* timer to run out. The foxes weren't about to wait for him, though, and they both lunged forward at once, each aiming for a different spot on his body.

He dodged one and brought his fist in a short hook, slamming it into its side. He heard the satisfying crack of bone as the beast's ribs buckled under the blow. Then he hissed in pain as he felt something sharp break the skin on his leg.

Looking down, he could see that the fox had bitten through his mage shield, all his protective layers of clothing, and right into his leg.

He could feel that the bite wasn't deep, but the fact that the fox had even made it through said more about the danger this Beast Zone posed than anything Gold may have told him before. It also meant that his mage shield and his armored clothes would do little to stop an injury here.

He used *wind blade* once again and brought it down on the back to the fox's head. He felt some resistance again, but after a second or two, the *blade* sunk into its skull and he felt the jaws clamped around his leg relax.

He then dismissed his *wind blade* and let his mage shield go out.

It would do him little good here, so he may as well.

Bending down, he pried the fox's jaws apart and examined the wound.

He could see a few tiny pinpricks of blood through the holes in the pants, but nothing that looked too serious.

He then straightened and rushed toward where he saw Sarah fighting, passing Gold as he ran.

The man was, as usual, doing nothing to help, just standing there with an impassive expression and watching the fight.

As she came into view, Morgan could see that Sarah wasn't fighting a group of foxes. Instead, she was fighting one large, furry creature with gray and white fur. It had a face shaped somewhere between a bear and a wolf, with small black eyes and a short snout.

While the foxes had come up to around knee height, this creature came up to around mid-thigh and looked a whole lot more intimidating. It had four pairs of very sharp looking claws and a blue glow was currently surrounding them.

Sarah was breathing very hard and Morgan could see several places where the animal had scored hits on her shield.

He was amazed that she'd lasted this long on her own, especially since her shield had held out, when his hadn't.

The creature wasn't undamaged, however. Two broken off *icicle spears* jutted out of one side, matting the fur red with its blood. One if its paws also looked as if it had been crushed and the creature was moving more slowly than he though it should be.

"Good to see you finally made it," she panted, forming another *icicle spear* and hurling it at the beast.

Morgan watched in amazement as the beast's front paw shot up and neatly sliced it out of the air.

"Any idea what it is?" he asked, as she launched another attack at it.

"No clue, but it's got some sort of mage ability."

She pointed to section of ground which had turned to solid ice.

"Those claws did that, so watch out for them."

The beast roared then and lumbered toward them at a fast trot, its teeth bared, and puffs of steam rising from is nostrils.

"Wish me luck," he said, running off to the side and allowing the beast to focus only on Sarah.

His *tailwind* timer had run out some time ago, so he used his *heavy handed* skill and rushed it from the side.

To its credit, the beast did manage to twist its body out of the way as Morgan threw a punch at its side. He wasn't sure how the beast had done it, seeing as he'd been coming in from a blind spot. However, that momentary distraction was all that Sarah needed to finish it off.

Now they both stood trying to catch their breaths as they stared at the dead beast. Sarah had aimed well and a long, jagged spear of ice protruded from one of its eyes.

"That wasn't half bad."

They both turned to see Gold walking up to them, slowly clapping his hands.

"I half expected to have to intervene during your first fight. You surprised me."

"You get the core from this one. I'll go back and get the other ones. Don't hand them over to Gold yet, I want to see what kind of beasts we'll be dealing with," Morgan said, completely ignoring him.

Sarah nodded and bent down near the beast, pulling out her slim rod to fetch the core.

Morgan turned and walked straight passed Gold, who looked both indignant and hurt at the same time.

He wasn't buying it.

Pulling a rod from his waist, Morgan quickly extracted the cores from the three foxes, noting that they were a good deal larger than those of the sheep. He decided not to check them there and instead walked back to Sarah, who had by now retrieved the other core.

"So, what kind of beast are those from?" she asked, nodding to the three cores clutched in his hand.

"Check for yourself," he said, tossing one of them to her and opening his status so he could see as well.

Name: Frost-fox core
Rank - 5
Total available energy - 192/192

This core was taken from a frost-fox and has no special properties.

He closed his status, happy that the amount of available energy was so much higher than that of the sheep.

The fight may have been harder, but if every beast gave just as much, or more, then it was well worth it.

He handed the core over to Gold, who pocketed it, grumbling about ungrateful students.

Then Sarah handed him the core from the beast she'd killed and he opened his status once more.

Name: Ice-clawed wolverine core
Rank - 6
Total available energy - 377/377

This core was taken from an ice-clawed wolverine and has no special properties.

So the beast was called a wolverine. He'd never heard of a creature like that before.

"Do you know what a wolverine is?" he asked Gold, as he handed over the core.

"I do," Gold said, taking the core and putting it away in a pouch. "We'd better keep moving. It's not getting any warmer and if you want a crack at the *Matriarch* we'll have to pick up the pace."

As he walked passed them, Morgan and Sarah shared a look.

Of course he wouldn't tell them!

30

They trekked on for another two and a half hours, running into a few more packs of foxes and two more wolverines. The silhouette of the mountain had grown larger all the while and now he could clearly make it out, though only a bit of the mountain was visible, as the rest was covered in clouds of whirling snow.

Morgan noticed that the longer they walked, the more worried Gold appeared to become. Finally, he just had to ask.

"Is something wrong?"

Gold started as he spoke and gestured to the surrounding landscape.

"We should be running into a lot more beasts than we have been. Something doesn't feel right."

"Do you think we should go back?" Sarah asked, moving closer to the two of them.

"No," Gold said after another moment of silence. "Besides, the portal will only open once we reach the end of the *stage*. Just be on guard. We'll be coming up on the *Matriarch's* territory in a few minutes."

"About time, too," Sarah said. "It's getting so cold, I can hardly feel my fingers! How is it that you look so comfortable?"

This question was directed at Gold, who had actually taken off his coat and had tied it around his waist.

"Benefits of a high *constitution*," he answered distractedly, not even trying to be vague and unhelpful.

This more than anything, highlighted just how serious the situation was.

"There's the *Matriarch's* territory," Gold said, pointing to a large tunnel made of ice at the base of the mountain.

The ground started to slowly slope upward as they approached, making the walk just a bit more difficult.

The air became noticeably warmer as they entered the shelter of the tunnel. The sound of the howling wind echoed off the walls as they walked, and he and Sarah looked around in wonder as they headed deeper in.

After another minute of walking, the tunnel abruptly ended and opened up into a massive icy cavern. Morgan heard a sigh of relief and turned to see Gold looking at the beast lying asleep in the center of the cavern.

It was a wolf, but a wolf unlike anything he'd ever seen before. It was massive.; larger even than the bear they'd fought on their way to the Central Kingdom, and was covered in bristly blue and white fur. Its paws were larger than his torso and he could see the gleam of long white fangs as it growled in its slumber.

"Is that thing the *Matriarch*?" Sarah asked in a lowered tone, not wanting to wake the beast.

"No, the *Matriarch* is a *rank 8* ice-clawed wolverine alpha. That is an ice-bristle wolf. They range from *rank 9* to *11* and normally roam in packs on *stage 3* of the *Zone*."

"So what's it doing down here? And where is the *Matriarch*?" Morgan asked.

"Every once in a while, beasts will wander down from higher *stages*. It's uncommon, but not completely unheard of. And as for the *Matriarch*…" Gold gestured to the far wall, where the corpse of some animal was just visible behind the tunnel exit.

"I'm just glad that it's only an ice-bristle wolf and not something worse," Gold said, reaching into his pocket and fetching the portal key.

"I'll report this to the *Beast Zone* management and they'll send someone in here to take care of this."

"So we're just going to leave without fighting that thing?" Sarah asked.

"Like I said; it's *ranked* between *9* and *11*. The two of you wouldn't stand a chance against it and it's not my job to kill beasts that wander down by accident," Gold answered, already fiddling with the key.

"It's only a *rank* or two above Sarah; three at the most," Morgan said, coming to her defense. "I bet we can take it without too much difficulty."

After all, the core from a rank 9 to 11 beast probably had a ton of energy and he didn't want it to go to waste.

"This is an evolved beast. Have you both completely forgotten what I told you about those *ranked 9* and above?" Gold asked with a raised eyebrow.

"You said we wouldn't stand a chance," Sarah said, now getting into it as well. "But that beast doesn't look much tougher than the bear we fought and we were both lower *ranked* back then."

Gold turned back to Morgan, a grave expression on his face.

"Do you think I'm over exaggerating as well?"

Morgan hesitated for a moment.

He knew that despite his quirks and tendencies towards sadism, Gold was a very good teacher. If he said this beast was out of their league, it most likely was. That wasn't going to stop him from trying, though.

"I do believe you, but I'd still like to try and take this thing on. I haven't had a real challenge in a *Beast Zone* yet, so I'd like to test myself to see how I've progressed."

Gold was silent for a moment as he contemplated this. He was silent for so long that they both began to fear he would shoot them down.

"Very well," he finally said. "I will let you fight the ice-bristle wolf, but on one condition. If I have to intervene, we'll be starting our morning sessions at six instead of eight for the next month. If you agree to this, then we have a deal."

Gold folded his arms and smiled smugly, sure that neither of them would be willing to take that sort of risk.

"You've got a deal," Morgan said excitedly.

"He does?!" Sarah asked, staring at him wide eyed. "I agree that fighting the beast would be a good challenge, but do you really want to take the risk of losing?"

Morgan nodded, grinning madly as he thought of the upcoming challenge.

Now he'd be able to test himself against a beast that had ready broken through rank 8 and evolved. This would be an excellent way to both gage how powerful he could become after a breakthrough, and how he currently stacked up.

"Alright," Sarah said, with a sigh of resignation. "But if we lose, I'm holding you responsible for all the extra pain I'll be enduring over the next month!"

They turned back to Gold, who was looking both astonished and pleased at the same time.

"Alright, but don't say I didn't warn you," he said with a wide smile. "I'll be looking forward to those extra two hours of training!"

Morgan was about to step into the cavern when Sarah placed a hand on his shoulder.

"Wait just a minute," she said.

She turned to look at Gold with a shrewd expression on her face. "What will you give us if we win?"

"Why should I give you anything?" he asked with a raised eyebrow. "I'm allowing you to fight the wolf. That is your reward."

"So if we fight and win, we get nothing; but if we fight and lose, we get a month of extra training? How is that a fair deal?"

Morgan was about to protest.

He thought fighting the wolf was a pretty good reward. Why did Sarah want more?

"Alright, fine. I can see your point," he conceded, after a moment of thought. "What do you want if you win? And before you ask, I won't give you time off of training," he quickly added in.

"That's fine," she said, with a wave of her hand. "We need the training anyway. What we want is to not have to go back to fighting sheep after today. We know that we can't come here every day, so on the other days, you will take us to a more challenging *Beast Zone*. Also, on the first run through that *Zone* you will be doing all the work, while we get to keep the cores."

"Fine," he replied after a few seconds. "But you only get ten minutes to beat the wolf; after that I will intervene!"

"Deal!" Sarah said quickly, and shook on it.

Morgan, who had been staring in shock the entire time this was going on, had to wonder if his friend had taken leave of her sanity.

"And I thought I was the crazy one," he said, as Sarah walked back to him with a smug grin on her face.

"Oh, you are," she said, patting him lightly on the back. "But I just got us a great deal."

"You did," he agreed, "but do you really think we can beat it in under ten minutes?"

She shrugged.

"The way I see it, is that if we can't beat it in ten minutes, we'll likely be either too wounded to fight; or too weak to hurt it."

"Alright. But if we lose now, you can't blame me for any extra hours of training."

"Agreed. Now let's go kill us a wolf!"

31

Morgan was amazed that the wolf hadn't so much as twitched the entire time they'd been standing there.

He wondered if they could sneak up on it and finish it off in its sleep.

The second they left the shelter of the tunnel, however, the wolf sat bolt upright and turned to look at them; it's muzzle bunched up in a snarl. It slowly uncurled itself from its position on the ground and rose to its full height.

Morgan felt his heart rate increase as he beheld the ice-bristle wolf in all its glory. Over six feet at the shoulder and at least fifteen feet from snout to tail, the beast was not something to be trifled with.

"So what's the plan?" Sarah asked, as her mage shield outlined her body in a bright blue glow.

"Same as always, I guess," he answered, using his *tailwind* skill and activating *wind blade* twice in a row.

"Slow it down using *frostbite*, then attack using your *icicle spear*. I'll test out its defenses and see if any of my mage attacks get through. If not, I'll have to switch to my super ability, so slowing it down will be even more crucial then."

She nodded her understanding and held her arm out to use her skill.

"Your time begins now." He heard Gold's voice from behind him.

He flashed Sarah a grin and dashed toward the massive wolf. The wolf, seeing him approach, threw back its head and let out a howl that shook the cavern. He stumbled for a moment, as he felt his adrenaline spike and a sudden rush of fear hit him.

Just what kind of attack had it used on him just now?!

He shook himself, making a mental effort to keep going, and not turn tail and run. There was around a hundred feet between him and the wolf, and he covered it in an instant.

With *tailwind* active, he had an effective agility of around 73, so there was no way the wolf could dodge his attack.

He leapt to the side as the wolf swiped at him and stabbed forward with his *wind blades,* throwing six strikes in a matter of seconds, into the wolf's unprotected side.

He groaned in frustration as every single attack bounced off the wolf's hide. without leaving so much as a scratch.

So much for that plan.

He jumped back as the wolf turned to snap at him and dismissed his blades. He then watched as four *icicle spears* slammed into the wolf's skull; and shattered, leaving the wolf unharmed, if not a little dazed.

"Oh, shit. That's not good," he heard Sarah say, from across the cavern.

No kidding! If they couldn't even manage to scratch it, there was no way they could win!

"Sarah, my *tailwind* is about to run out! Slow it down so I can use my super skills!" Morgan called out.

Even though his speed was more than doubled, he was still barely managing to avoid being hit and he didn't dare let his tailwind run out until Sarah slowed it down.

He felt an icy gust of wind wash over him and noticed the wolf slowing a bit, but not nearly as much as it should.

Maybe the higher rank meant that the effects would be weakened? Or since it was a creature of ice, the slowing effect wasn't as strong? Either way, it didn't look like he'd be coming out of this fight uninjured. *Oh well.*

Morgan felt his *tailwind* run out and jumped backwards just as it did. He sailed back a good thirty feet and landed in a crouch.

The wolf whipped its head toward him and snarled, its icy blue eyes seeming to glow with malevolence.

It ran at him and Morgan frantically used his *heavy handed* skill, taking up a fighting stance and preparing for a slugfest.

The wolf raked at him with its front claws and he wasn't fast enough to dodge it. Morgan winced as the claws tore through his armored clothes and scored deeply into the skin on his right side. He yelled, slamming a fist into the side of the wolf's head pivoting his hips for extra power.

The wolf's head was rocked to the side, but the sound of breaking bone that he'd been expecting didn't come. He cursed, shaking his hand in pain as the wolf turned back toward him, snarling in rage.

He took a step back as it swiped at him again and managed to avoid being hit this time. Seven *icicle spears* slammed into the beast's head as it took a step towards him, each one aimed at the same spot. Morgan turned and ran to Sarah, as the wolf staggered back under the barrage of attacks.

He stopped next to her, panting and clutching at his side, which was now bleeding heavily.

"Are you alright?" she asked, eyeing his side with concern.

"I'll live," he said in answer, keeping his eyes on the wolf, who was shaking its head and staggering slightly as if dizzy.

"No luck on getting through its skin then?" she asked, also watching the wolf who was now steadying itself.

"No, but I think I've got an idea after what you just did. If we hit it in the head hard enough, we may be able to crack its skull. The problem is that I'll need to be close enough to hit it; which means that it'll be able to do the same to me."

He winced again as his side throbbed with renewed pain and he began to feel a bit lightheaded.

"If you can pin it down for a minute, I may be able to get through. Can you do it?"

"Only if you can keep it in one spot for at least ten seconds. I'll need the time to condense water in so many places at once. I'll also need to freeze its mouth shut so it can't bite you while you're attacking."

Morgan nodded, as the wolf righted itself and glared over at the two of them. Then it raised its head once more and howled.

Morgan felt his skin crawl as the wolf's fur stood on end and ice crackled over the surface. When it finally stopped howling, its fur stood out from its body in a mass of icy bristles, that looked sharp enough to cut steel.

This fight had just gotten a whole lot more dangerous.

"You better do your part," he yelled, as he ran towards the ice-bristle wolf. It now appeared to be even larger than before, due to its fur standing on end. He used *fly,* feeling his feet leave the ground as he slowly picked up speed.

The problem with using fly in a fight, was that it took him a few seconds to build up speed. He didn't have the same reflexes in the air as he did on the ground, either, and it was therefore much harder to dodge attacks, if he stopped moving for even a second.

"Over here you overgrown mutt!" he yelled, launching a kick at the wolf's head. Instead of dodging as he'd been expecting, the wolf lowered it's head and Morgan cried out in pain as his shin collided with the icy spines on its back.

He quickly pulled back from the wolf, feeling hot blood running down his leg as the icy spikes tore free.

He chanced a glance at the leg and was relived to see that it wasn't bleeding too badly, which meant that an artery hadn't been hit.

He was sure that he had the extra protection of his shin guards to thank for that.

He flew forward once more as the wolf raised its head, and screamed, launching another kick at it. As he'd expected, the wolf lowered its head once more, but this time he pulled his strike, stopping a few inches from the bristly fur and backing off.

He was sure that Sarah had had enough time by now, so where was her attack?

The wolf raised its head, baring it's teeth and growling at him.

He wasn't sure why the wolf was so angry; so far, they hadn't even managed to scratch it, while he'd had his side laid open and managed to impale his leg on its fur.

He flew forward, intent on keeping the beast in place when it finally happened. The wolf froze as four massive blocks of ice formed around its legs. It snarled, opening its mouth to howl, when a fifth block of ice froze its jaws shut.

Thank you, Sarah!

Morgan stopped in front of the wolf and landed, testing his leg to see if it would still hold his weight.

Now it was all up to him.

He used *heavy handed* and slammed his fist into the side of the wolf's head. It tried to lower it again, but he brought his knee up and caught it under the chin. It's head whipped up under the force of the attack and Morgan began throwing a flurry of blows, aiming each for the same spot between its eyes.

He winced in pain.

He felt as though he were punching solid stone, not a living animal.

But he didn't stop. A loud crack signaled that the wolf was beginning to break free of its icy restraints and Morgan redoubled his efforts, hitting the wolf as hard and as fast as he could.

Blow after blow landed on the same spot, leaving bloody smears on the fur from where his knuckles had split. He was heaving for air, as he attacked over and over again, but still the bone would not give. There was another crack and Morgan flinched as one of the back paws came loose.

"Morgan, hurry up and kill it already!" Sarah yelled from behind him.

"I'm trying, but the stupid beast just won't die!" he yelled back.

There was another crack and Morgan screamed in pain as the wolf's teeth sank deep into his left arm. He didn't stop attacking however, slamming his fist between its eyes over and over again; even as he felt his arm being savaged by the wolf.

There was a crack and he yelled in pain once again; as the bone is his arm gave way.

"I will not lose!" he roared, moving closer to the wolf, despite the additional pain it caused.

He pulled his good arm high into the air, then brought the point of his elbow down between its eyes, dropping his entire body as did so. There was a loud snap as his elbow impacted with the wolf's skull and his arm went limp, the bone broken from the impact; but his arm wasn't the only thing that broke.

With a loud whine of pain, the wolf released his savaged arm and staggered back from him, lowering its head and shaking it back and forth. Morgan straightened shakily, his vision going fuzzy with blood loss and shock.

The wolf wasn't dead yet. He had a job to finish.

With a howl of rage, Morgan staggered towards the injured wolf.

He couldn't hit the beast, as both his arms were broken, but one of his legs was still whole and uninjured.

The wolf had lowered its head to the ground and was pawing at the spot where its skull had fractured when Morgan reached it. With a yell, he swung his good leg up in an arc, ignoring the lance of pain from his other leg; then brought it crashing down onto the wolf's skull.

The ax-kick landed with all the force of his *heavy handed* skill and the momentum of his leg at the end of its trajectory.

There was one last loud crack, and the wolf finally went still.

Morgan stared at the dead beast for a few seconds, blinking rapidly to try and clear his vision. Then he spun around, staggering a bit as the room swam around him.

"Told you I could do it!" he yelled with a mad grin.

Then he fell forward, hitting the ground in a dead faint.

32

Morgan was laying in his bed, rolling the ice-bristle wolf's core between his fingers when there was a knock at his door.

He sighed and sat up, placing the core down on his dresser and walking to open it.

Sarah stood there, hand raised and ready to knock again. "What?"

"Don't 'what' me," she said, placing her hands on her hips. "What are your plans for the day?"

Morgan shrugged. "Probably sleep."

"We have the entire day off and you're going to spend it sleeping?" she asked with a raised eyebrow.

Morgan had come to the previous day, after he'd killed the ice-bristle wolf, to find Eric crouched over him. The man had done an excellent job of healing him and aside from a line of silvery scars on his arm, his body was good as new.

Morgan had felt exhausted when the healing was finished and Eric had told him that it would take at least a day for his body to replenish all the blood he'd lost.

Gold; after clapping him on the shoulder and congratulating him, had proceed to give him and Sarah the next day off to do as they pleased, despite his earlier insistence that he wouldn't.

"Well, yeah," he said, yawning widely. "I'm supposed to take the day and rest."

"I'm not going to have you moping around all day," Sarah declared. "Now go put your boots on; we're going out."

Morgan considered closing the door in her face, but decided that his best option would be to just go along with it.

There were a few things he needed to take care of anyway, and she wouldn't leave him alone until he joined her. His new winter clothes had been completely destroyed, as well as his shin guards and one of his armored uniforms.

"Fine, what did you have in mind?" he asked, closing the door behind him and going to pull on his boots.

"Well, I thought we could go explore the academy," Sarah began, a wide smile now on her face. "We can go eat at a restaurant, explore the shopping district, maybe even watch a play! I heard that CAMS even has a massive area for swimming!"

Morgan just nodded as she spoke.

None of that really sounded that exciting to him. If he had a day to himself, he would rather spend it sleeping and training, maybe go look at some of the cool weapons in the shopping district, or go watch the older students fight in the arena.

"Did you listen to a word I just said?"

Morgan was snapped out of his wandering thoughts and saw Sarah once again glaring at him.

Her mood changed way too often. Why couldn't she just be calm all the time?

"Yes, you want to eat somewhere that will cost us money, when we have free food in the dining rooms. You want to wander around the shopping district for a few hours and then go splash around in some water for a bit. Oh, and see a play - whatever that is."

Sarah glared at him for a few seconds, before sighing in resignation.

"I'll pay."

Those were the magic words.

"I'm in!" Morgan said with a smile. "Where to first?"

***

Arnold did his best to keep the annoyance off his face as he spoke to the guards at the border of the Central Kingdom.

What should have been a two week trip on horseback, had taken them over a month. They'd had such a run of bad luck on this trip that he was almost ready to believe that some higher power did not want him here.

Now they were being held up at the border because he didn't have the requisite paperwork to be allowed into the kingdom.

"As I said before," Arnold said, keeping his tone neutral. "We are on a very important assignment from Lord Simon of City Four. This has been a very long trip and if you could just let us pass, we'd be very grateful." He patted the coin purse at his belt and gave the man a meaningful look.

"And like I said before, sir, you will need the proper permit from your Lord with his signet stamp of approval, along with a letter proclaiming you to be an official envoy," the guard answered, in the same official tone he'd been using thus far.

Arnold inwardly seethed at the man for not being a crooked, thieving and manipulative bastard.

It was just his luck to run into the only straight official in the world and this hiccup further emphasized just how badly this mission had been going.

Breaking into the kingdom was not an option, as he would be killed if caught. This was not the North Kingdom where he could get out of anything by just having Lord Simon send a message. There was also the academy to consider; he might be strong, but he wasn't stupid enough to believe that he couldn't be killed.

"Very well," Arnold said, still keeping his expression neutral despite the overwhelming urge to reach over and throttle the man. "Would you perhaps have a way for me to contact my Lord so we can get this straightened out?"

The man nodded over to a booth set up by the side of the gate where a long line of people stood waiting their turn.

"You can talk to the mage over there. It'll cost you a pretty penny, but if you really do work for a Lord, you can have all the papers you need within a week."

Another whole week?!

Arnold wanted to howl in frustration, but instead he nodded to the man and walked over to the back of the line.

Weasel joined him then, slinking up to him and giving him a questioning look.

"We don't have the right paperwork to get in, so now we have to pay someone a ridiculous amount of money to get them here quickly."

"Ah, bureaucracy. What would we do without it?" Weasel said, sneering over at the gate guards who were letting people pass without issue.

"We're already running behind schedule as it is. Lord Simon will not be happy about this, especially since it's taking so long."

"I wouldn't want to be you right now," Weasel said with a nasty smile. "Bet ol' Simy is fuming away in that fancy manor of his, waiting for news."

"I'd keep my comments to myself. That is, unless you want 'ol' Simy' to pull your intestines out through your asshole."

Weasel did shut his mouth then.

Arnold wasn't one to make idle threats, and in the mood he was currently in, he might just do it himself.

***

It was nearly dark out by the time Morgan and Sarah began heading back towards their block.

The two of them had gone to eat at a fancy restaurant, then to the shopping district, where Morgan had ordered a bunch of new clothes from his favorite shopkeeper.

He'd been dismayed to hear that James didn't have any more of the canvas uniforms in his size, nor did he have any more winter attire. So he'd had to place an order for it with the shopkeeper, who had taken down his house number and promised to have it delivered as soon as he had it back in stock.

He'd been forced to buy a woolen substitute for the outfit that had been destroyed, just in case he needed a third pair of combat clothes. He'd made sure to order four more sets of the canvas uniform. He liked them so much that he was almost unwilling to wear anything else.

He was able to get a new pair of shin guards, this one made of leather as well, but reinforced throughout with a metal weave.

After that, he'd been forced to sit and wait as Sarah went shopping for a swimsuit. She'd made him sit down outside the shop and refused to let him enter, though he wasn't sure why.

When she'd finally come out nearly an hour later, she immediately dragged him halfway across the campus to the swimming area.

When he got his first look at the place, he was glad that Sarah had brought him along. It was magnificent! A huge lake filled with clear and sparkling blue water, was set in the middle of an ocean of sand.

Sarah had dug around in her bags for a second before handing him a pair of pants that were cut off at the knees. Then she'd pointed to a low wooden building and told him to change into them.

When he'd asked why, she'd shaken her head and told him he was free to swim in his combat uniform if he wanted. Then she'd gone off to change herself.

After he'd changed, he just stood around waiting for her to show up. He saw tons of other people walking around the sandy area. The men were wearing similar cut off pants and nothing else, while the women's seemed to vary. Some had a suit covering them from their chests to their waists, while others had two pieces of fabric instead.

There were others still who were wearing so little that he had to wonder if they actually wanted to run around without anything on.

After all, those clothes didn't do a very good job of covering them. Maybe they were all poor and less fabric meant spending less money?

He'd nodded to himself, happy that he'd figured it out without having to ask someone else.

Sarah had come out then, wearing the one piece suit he'd seen some of the women wearing and this just affirmed his earlier suspicion.

Sarah was rich, after all, so she could afford a suit with more fabric.

She'd asked him how she looked for some reason and her face had turned red again. He just shrugged and said she looked fine. This had annoyed her and she spent the next hour in a bad mood.

Maybe he should have said more about the expensive bathing suit she'd bought?

She did calm down eventually and they'd spent the rest of the day splashing around in the water. Despite his earlier misgivings, he'd had a good time and decided that they would have to come back again.

"Did you enjoy yourself today?" Sarah asked, wrapping her arms around one of his and leaning into him.

"Yes, I actually did," he said, smiling at her.

Why was she grabbing his arm like that? Maybe she was tired and needed someone to lean on? Swimming had made him tired and very hungry.

He shrugged to himself, once more resigned to not knowing anything about the way girls worked.

"I bet you're glad I dragged you out, then," she said, pulling his arm tighter to herself.

"Yes, especially since you paid for everything," he answered, pulling the map from his pocket and checking where they were right now.

"If we cut through those buildings there, we'll save twenty minutes," he said, folding up the map and putting it back into his pocket.

"Aww, but don't you want to take the long way back?" Sarah asked, pouting at him.

"Why would I want to do that?" Morgan asked, genuinely confused.

"Never mind," she said with a sigh, as they turned into the block of darkened buildings.

They walked on in silence for the next few minutes. As the noise from the main road began to fade, it soon became apparent that this area was not a place where people hung out at night. Sarah clung a bit tighter to Morgan the longer they walked, her head swiveling from side to side at every little noise.

Morgan on the other hand, felt right at home. After all, this was no different than the alleys back in City Four.

After another minute of walking, Morgan suddenly stopped. Sarah, who had been clutching his arm, stopped right along with him.

"What's wrong?" she asked in a hushed voice, looking fearfully around.

"I know you're there, come on out," Morgan said, turning to the open mouth of an alley to their right.

"So, you spotted us," a voice echoed out of the darkness. "Don't think you'll be getting away just because you did!"

As they watched the mouth of the alley, six figures materialized out of the darkness.

"I told you that it wasn't over, you commoner piece of trash. I'm here to make good on my promise!" Grub said, as five of his cronies moved to surround them and Frush swaggered up next to him.

33

Morgan blinked in surprise.

He'd known someone was following them and had even been expecting a fight. Dark alleys like these seemed to attract those kinds of people; but he'd been expecting a cutpurse, not this moron.

Grub sneered down at the two of them, as his greasy relative Frush moved in front of him.

"I haven't forgotten what you did to me either, gorgeous," the greasy boy said, blowing Sarah a kiss.

"But I'm not mad," he said, walking around until he was standing behind her. "All I want is an apology, and then I'll be happy to give you the ride of your life!"

Sarah let go of Morgan's arm and had begun to turn in Frush's direction, when the boy's arm dropped on her shoulder.

She tried to cry out, but her body completely locked up, leaving her unable to utter so much as a sound. Her anger began to turn to fear as she fought in vain to break whatever skill he was using to hold her in place.

"That's a good girl. You can try to struggle, but it won't work," he giggled, a high pitched sound full of lust and a bit of madness.

Sarah had never been more afraid in her life. She was completely at his mercy as he pressed his back into hers and allowed his hands begin to glide down her shoulders.

Revulsion gripped her as Frush slid his hands down towards her breasts, stopping just a few inches away and giggling in her ear.

"Do you like my mage ability? I like it quite a bit," he whispered, sticking his nose in her hair and inhaling very loudly. "It comes in very handy when girls need a little extra persuading."

Sarah was practically shaking in rage and disgust at this point.

This sick piece of shit had done this before! He'd used his abilities, the one thing that made them special, to take advantage of others. Well, she wasn't nearly as helpless as they were and she would make sure he paid for what he'd done.

Gritting her teeth and doing her best to ignore Frush's fingers inching ever downward, she concentrated with all her might on moving her hand just a few inches.

Morgan felt Sarah let go of his arm, but didn't think much of it, as his attention was focused on the idiot in front of him.

"Now I'll have my revenge for the way you cheated me out of my rightful victory in the arena," Grub snarled, cracking his knuckles and glaring at him.

"You lost, fair and square," he answered with a shrug. "It isn't my fault that you're so stupid."

Grub's already angry expression morphed into one of rage.

"No! You cheated and I'm going to beat you senseless here and now to show you who's really stronger!"

Morgan was about to reply, when the sound of something shattering next to him made him stop. He quickly turned and saw that Sarah had been captured by Frush and she wasn't moving. His mind went into overdrive as he tried to process the situation before him and how best to handle it.

Sarah was more powerful than Frush, which meant that he must be using a skill to keep her from moving. But since she was stronger, she'd been able to get his attention by dropping that small block of ice lying near her feet.

He could also see that Frush was pressed up against her and was about to touch her in a way that he knew women didn't like.

Morgan may have been completely ignorant of social norms, but this was something he was all too familiar with.

He didn't know exactly what this was, but the guards back in City Four would do this all the time. The women would always scream and cry out for help, but who would dare fight against the city guards? Well, this wasn't City Four and Sarah was his friend. No one would get away with touching her like that!

Morgan felt his blood begin to boil as his fists tightened.

He didn't need to think twice about what he was going to do next.

Sarah grinned as her body unfroze a mere five seconds after the ice block had hit the ground. She heard a thump, and then screech of pain, and turned to see Frush, pinned to the ground face first, with Morgan's foot planted on his back.

He'd pulled one of Frush's arms up and was slowly pushing it farther and farther up as the boy under him screamed in agony.

Her friend might be dense, but he was as reliable as they came!

She felt a sick sense of pleasure to see the boy lying on the ground as his arm was slowly being bent the wrong way.

But that wasn't enough. A sick bastard like this had to be stopped. Otherwise, he'd just do this to some other poor girl.

She took a step towards the two of them, heart pounding with adrenaline as an *icicle spear* began to form in her hand.

She didn't like the idea of killing in cold blood, but this was a necessary evil.

"Get him! I want the bastard dead!" Grub yelled, his face livid with rage and hatred. He'd been standing there in shock ever since Morgan had acted, but now rage had broken him out of his stupor and he wanted revenge.

Sarah turned, just in time to see the others gearing up to rush them.

"Damn it all!" she snarled, turning to face the oncoming threat.

She held her arms up and six *icicle spears* formed in the air before her. Grub's minions, who'd been expecting an easy fight, froze in place as the icy spears hovered before them.

"I'm not in a very good mood, since that toad tried to have his way with me and all of you were just going to watch," Sarah said with a wicked grin.

"So I'll give you an ultimatum. Either you leave by the time I've counted to five, or die. Your choice."

The cronies hesitated for a moment, looking between her and Grub. They'd seen what she'd done to Frush back in the arena and were not eager to receive the same treatment. But at the same time, Grub was from a powerful family and going against him could mean future trouble.

"One!" Sarah said loudly, and that was all it took.

Screaming in terror, the group of boys took off, abandoning their leader and his cousin to their fate. They might get in trouble later, but right now, they were more afraid of her than they were of them.

"Bunch of cowards," Sarah muttered, allowing her *icicle spears* to vanish and turning back to Morgan. He had already broken Frush's arm and had now moved onto the fingers, snapping them one by one. She winced at the loud cracking sound, followed by the wail of pain, every time one of them snapped.

She'd known he was ruthless in a fight, but this was something else. *Did he really care about her that much? Maybe there was hope for her yet.*

Then she spotted something shifting in the shadows behind him and felt her heart skip a beat.

"Morgan, behind you!" she yelled, arms already coming up in preparation to use *icicle spear*.

Morgan turned just in time to see a stone clad fist flying at his face. Only his high *agility*, and Sarah's timely warning, saved him from what would have undoubtedly been a very unpleasant experience.

Morgan jerked his head to the side, causing the fist to just barely brush his cheek as it flew by.

Grub, who'd been expecting to hit him, stumbled forward, completely off balance. Morgan took the opportunity to use *heavy handed* and slammed an open palm into the center of his chest.

It wasn't a very powerful blow, as he didn't have much room to maneuver, but the attack had the intended effect. Grub stumbled back, giving him more room to move and Morgan spun on the spot, letting go of Frush's arm and lashing out in a sideways kick.

The kick impacted with such force that it completely shattered the larger boy's armor, snapped several ribs underneath, and sent him flying back to crash into the opposite wall of the alley, where he lay groaning and barely conscious.

He then turned back to see that Frush had gotten to his feet as was trying to slink away. He ran after the boy and caught him by his broken arm. He screamed once more as Morgan threw him to the ground then stomped down hard on the back of his knee. There was a loud snap, and Frush's screams doubled in volume as he writhed on the ground.

That should keep him from running away.

Morgan turned back to see Sarah relaxing her posture. All of the others were gone, presumably chased off by her, and he was grateful for that.

He didn't really think that the others had any real issue with him. They were just weak and followed Grub, either out of fear or hopes of greater power. Not that he really knew what Grub could offer.

"Are you alright?" Morgan asked, as Sarah walked up to him. "He didn't…?" Morgan trailed off here, not sure exactly how to phrase the question.

Frush had clearly touched her, so asking her that wouldn't get to the heart of the matter.

Thankfully, Sarah knew what he meant and gave him a smile. "No, you stopped him before he could do anything."

Morgan nodded, glad she understood what he'd meant to ask.

For some reason she was red again, likely still angry about what happened.

They heard a loud whimpering sound, and both turned to see Frush, leaning up against the alley wall and clutching at his broken limbs with trembling fingers.

"Sarah, what are you doing?" Morgan asked.

As soon as she'd laid eyes on him, her expression had darkened and a spear of ice had formed in the air before her.

"You might have stopped him this time, but this sick piece of crap has done this before. I need to kill him so he won't be able to do it ever again!"

Frush's eyes widened when he heard this and he let out a whimper of fear as Sarah stopped just a few inches from him.

"You can't," Morgan said, placing a hand on her shoulder.

"And why not?" she asked, whirling to him. "Since when have you cared about sparing the lives of your enemies!?"

"I don't," Morgan said, keeping his expression calm. "But use your head for a moment. Even if we kill these two, there are still six others who witnessed this attack. In the best case, we'll be expelled and in the worst, executed."

Sarah seemed to hesitate for a moment, then sighed in resignation.

"Then what would you have me do?"

Morgan shrugged.

"Send a message. I've already sent mine," he said, and gestured to the boy's broken limbs and then to Grub's unconscious form.

Sarah thought on that for a moment, then a truly evil smile lit up her face.

"Thank you Morgan. That is an excellent idea!"

Frush, who'd been watching along the entire time, sagged in relief as he heard his life would be spared. Sarah gestured then, and the spear thunked into the ground between his legs. Then he screamed; but this scream was unlike any he'd previously uttered.

"Oh, quit your whining," Sarah said, rolling her eyes. "I'm sure the healers can reattach it if you go quickly enough."

"Was that really necessary?" Morgan asked with a pained look on his face. "It seems overly excessive."

It wasn't that he felt sorry for the boy, but any man who saw that would feel a twinge of sympathetic pain.

Sarah quirked a brow at him, ignoring the howling boy by her feet.

"This, coming from the person who broke his arm, leg and all the fingers on one hand?"

She placed her hands on her hips as her face hardened.

"This was my message and hopefully it'll stick with him. Now let's get going, we still need to tell Gold what happened here."

Morgan nodded in agreement, taking one last look at the howling Frush; before shuddering and turning away. He scooped Sarah up in his arms and used *fly*, moving as fast as he could to escape the cries of pain, from the now member-less Frush.

34

Morgan was twirling the ice-bristle wolf core between his fingers once more; admiring the way the red and blue colors swirled around inside.

They had knocked on Gold's door once they'd gotten back the previous night and had told him everything. Once they were done with their story, he'd told them to go to bed and that he would talk with them the following day. He'd then rushed out of the house, leaving the two of them alone.

Sarah had thanked Morgan then, for saving her from Frush and for stopping her from killing him. She had then done something completely unexpected. She'd leaned forward and kissed him on the cheek, then her face had gone completely red and she ran back to her room.

Morgan dropped the core onto his stomach and sighed.

He still wasn't sure how he felt about that. No one had ever kissed him before, so how was he supposed to feel after getting one? He'd seen people kissing back in City Four, though he wasn't really sure why they did it.

He couldn't decide either way, so he instead opened up his status and viewed the core in his hands once more.

He'd already seen it several times and it troubled him to no end.

Name: Ice-bristle wolf core
Rank - 9
Total available energy - 2,154/2,154

This core was taken from an ice-bristle wolf and has no special properties.

He sighed once again and dropped the core on his dresser.

What bothered him wasn't the fact that it had so little energy compared to the bear; what bothered him was the fact that he'd nearly died while fighting a beast just two ranks higher than he.

He'd fought and killed people that we're four, or even five, ranks above him. He'd even killed the bear while taking minimal injuries; but this *rank 9* wolf had nearly done him in.

He needed to unlock his supermage ability and reach *rank 9*. That was the only way for him to gain that sort of power. If the difference between rank 8 and 9 was really so huge, then he needed to reach it.

Gold should be coming back within the next hour or so, but until then, he could work on combing his mana and chi.

So, closing his eyes, he did just that.

***

There was a knock at his door sometime later and Morgan slowly opened his eyes.

He'd made good progress on growing his *reiki* and had now channeled over half his mana and chi into it. The purple orb was now larger than both the red and blue. Now all he needed to do was continue working on it and reach his next rank.

He slowly unfolded his cramped legs and went to open the door.

Sarah stood there, looking quite chipper; which he though was odd considering what'd happened the previous night.

"Gold is waiting for us in the main room and he asked me to come get you."

Morgan nodded, closing his door behind him, and followed her out of their living room and into the kitchen.

Gold was seated by the table and looked up from his bowl of porridge when they entered, motioning them to take a seat.

The two of them sat and waited for him to finish eating before he began to speak.

"You made a real mess of things," he said, placing his spoon down and looking at the two of them. His tone was deadly serious and not even a glint of his usual humor shone through.

"The boys who attacked you last night were taken into the infirmary and thankfully, they were all treated in time. That includes the boy you took the liberty of... dis-membering."

He said this last bit to Sarah, who just snickered at the bad pun.

"In light of what happened, the academy has decided that they will not expel you for the way you acted, but they will be keeping a closer eye on you."

"Wait, what?!" Sarah exploded. "They attacked us! Why are we the ones who are being scrutinized over this?"

She was on her feet now, hands clenched at her sides in indignation.

"The only reason you're still here, and not in prison, is because they attacked you first. The way you handled it, on the other hand, is why you're under scrutiny. If you had just beaten them up and left it at that, they would most likely be out of the academy.

"Since you decided to take it a step further and send some sort of message, the academy has decided to let both parties off with a warning. If either of you steps out of line again, you will be thrown out."

Morgan winced when he heard that and shot Sarah an apologetic look.

It had, after all, been his idea to send a message.

Sarah just ignored him though and continued yelling.

"So what you're telling me, is that after what those pieces of shit tried to do; they're just going to be let off?"

"What I'm saying, is that the next time something like this happens, you make sure to finish the job!"

Sarah was so shocked by Gold's sudden outburst that she jumped. The normally calm man had such an expression of anger on his face that she was actually afraid.

"To be perfectly clear, I am not okay with what happened to you! To either of you! I wanted that boy strung up by his scrawny throat and the rest of them expelled. But someone is blocking me from seeing the board about this. Someone with real influence and power."

He leaned forward, eyes blazing as he looked at the two of them.

"Do you understand?"

They both nodded; his message very clear. Frush and Grub were from a very wealthy family and had likely bribed more than a few people to look the other way. And although Sarah was from a noble family, she would have to keep quiet, unless she wanted to blow her cover.

"Good," Gold said, allowing the anger to slip from his face.

"Now that that's out of the way, we can move on to more exciting things. Morgan, I know that you're at *rank 7* right now, how close are you to the next *rank?*"

Morgan quickly glanced at his status before answering.

"I need a total of *1,273* energy to move up to *rank 8* in both."

Gold nodded at that and directed the same question towards Sarah.

"I need *1,328* energy to reach *rank 9.*" She answered.

"Good. Morgan, we'll work on getting you to *rank 8* in the next few days. Then we can begin the real work of unlocking your supermage ability. Sarah. I want you to hold off on moving up to the next rank for now."

"Why?"

"That's the other thing I wanted to talk to you about today," he said, leaning back in his chair as his usual smile spread across his face.

"The end of term fights will begin in three weeks from now; after which, the tournament will be held for the top eight students of each class."

Morgan felt his heart speed up in excitement.

He'd been looking forward to this ever since he'd first heard about it. Gold hadn't really given them any details, so hopefully they'd be finding out more now.

"I can see from the expressions on your faces that you're interested. To answer your question, Sarah; the main reason I don't want you ranking up, is that it would attract way too much attention. No one your age should have such a high *rank*. I've been able to falsify your *ranks* in the school records, but the moment either of you reach *rank 9* it'll be impossible to hide it."

"Wait, so what you're saying is that we can't go past *rank 8* for as long as we're here?" Morgan asked.

"That's not what I'm saying. What I'm saying is that you should hold off on ranking up until after the tournament. If you win, and I don't doubt for a second that you can, you will each receive a very potent, *rank 39* core and one platinum coin."

He waited for a moment to allow what he'd just said to sink in.

"A platinum coin and a *rank 39* core!"

Morgan had very nearly jumped out of his seat when he heard that.

A platinum coin was worth a thousand gold. With that much money, even if he lost his scholarship, he'd be able to continue on for at least another year. And with a rank 39 core, he could probably boost himself several ranks all at once, especially once he merged his two abilities into one.

"Quite the prize, I know," Gold said mildly. "So you can see now why it wouldn't be suspicious if you ranked up after the tournament; but it would be if you did so before?"

Both Morgan and Sarah nodded emphatically.

Sarah was less excited about the money than Morgan was. After all, she had over eighty platinum sitting in a hidden compartment in her room. The core, on the other hand, was something that was definitely worth winning.

"So how do we get into the tournament? You said only the top eight students of each class would be competing," Morgan asked.

"As I mentioned earlier in the year; the top ranked student of each class will have an automatic entry into the tournament. Sarah, if you can hold your spot for the next three weeks, your entry into the tournament will be secured."

"Morgan, I believe you currently hold the 5th rank in your class, which means that you most likely won't move into the number one spot in time. In three weeks, you will go to the arena with all the other students of your year. There, you will be fighting once a day until you either lose a fight, or make it to the end.

"This entire process can take up to two weeks; then once only seven are left, there will be a week long reprieve for the fighters to get ready and for the people wishing to watch the tournament to make it here."

"Who will be watching us fight?" Sarah asked.

She was understandably nervous of being recognized by someone outside the academy. If word got out to her father that she was here, he would demand she be returned to him and the Central Kingdom would be obliged to comply, or risk losing their neutrality.

"Aside from parents wishing to watch their children fight; only citizens of the Central Kingdom will be allowed in."

Sarah breathed a sigh of relief when she heard that and smiled over at Morgan.

"You think you can fight your way into the tournament?"

He smiled back at her, the same slightly crazed smile he'd had before going to fight the ice-bristle wolf.

"For a platinum coin and a *rank 39* core? You better believe I will!"

35

The next few weeks were not easy for either of them. Clearly, news of the upcoming tournament had become general knowledge and both of them were constantly challenged to fights in the arena.

People wanted to beat Sarah, in hopes of getting to the top spot and beat Morgan, in hopes of holding a higher class rank by the end of the semester.

At first, they'd tried to turn down the fights, stating that they'd fought in their official match that week. Then they'd both been told that if they didn't fight at least one challenger a day, they would risk losing their spots.

When they'd asked Gold about this, he'd put on his usual innocent look and said he must have forgotten to mention that specific rule. So in the last two weeks before the official fights began, they were each forced to defend their spots at least once a day.

This didn't stop Gold from their daily torture sessions; if anything, he was pushing them even harder than he normally did. By the end of the day, both of them would collapse exhausted onto their beds and go straight to sleep.

Grub and Frush didn't approach them in the weeks leading up to the tournament, but every once in a while, Morgan would spot them lurking out of the corner of his eye. He didn't think that Sarah spotted them and decided not to tell her for her own peace of mind.

The time passed by in a flash for Morgan and soon it was the night before the official fights were set to begin. He lay on his bed, once again playing with the ice-bristle wolf core. He'd already decided against using the energy in the core, instead opting to keep it as a memento of their fight.

He sighed, placing the core down on his dresser and staring up at the ceiling. Sarah, despite all the fighting, had managed to keep the top spot in the mage class and would therefore not have to fight tomorrow.

He, on the other hand, had only managed to make it to third in the class and would have to fight his way into the tournament. He was now very glad that his new uniforms had arrived that day, as he was sure that the sturdy outfits would be taking quite a beating over the next few days.

He sat up then, mind too restless to sleep and opened his status instead.

Name: Morgan
Super: Rank - 8 (Max.)
Energy to next rank - N/A
Mage: Rank - 8 (Max.)
Energy to next rank - N/A
Super ability - Gravity
Mage ability - Air
CP - 350/350 (Regen - 3.7 per second)
MP - 350/350 (Regen - 3.7 per Second)
Strength - 35
Agility - 41
Constitution - 36
Intelligence - 35
Wisdom - 37
Super skills - Fly, Heavy handed
Mage skills - Wind blade, Tailwind

When Morgan had first seen that he had no way to reach *rank 9*, he'd nearly lost it. He knew that Sarah's status wasn't experiencing the same issue, as he'd made sure to ask. All she had was a greatly increased energy cost to the next *rank*.

When he'd told Gold about this, he was surprised as well. He'd never come across this in his all his studies of supermages. He'd then told Morgan to calm down and said that he likely couldn't progress further until he unlocked his supermage ability; and for that, Morgan would first need to finish combining all of his remaining mana and chi into reiki. He'd run off after that, muttering to himself in an excited fashion about new discoveries and mysteries of the world.

Morgan closed his status; on the one hand, he was happy that he wouldn't need to waste a ton of energy unlocking his new ability, but on the other, he was afraid that Gold was wrong and he would be stuck at rank 8 forever.

By now, he'd already managed to convert over three quarters of his mana. The purple orb sitting at the center of his chest was growing larger each day and he could feel something inside himself changing. But the more he depleted his spheres of energy, the harder it became. At this point, it was a struggle just to grab ahold of both at once and he could only maintain the flow for short bursts before the strain became too much for him.

He snorted and turned his attention inward, finding the two energy sources and examining them once more.

He was too nervous to sleep at the moment, so instead of worrying, why not take the time to continue combining his mana and chi.

He grasped a tendril of each with his mind. It was really difficult to do this now and he had to struggle to keep ahold of it as he slowly pushed them both towards the sphere of reiki. They finally connected and both his mana and chi spheres began slowly shrinking once more. They were now only about a tenth the size of his reiki and shrinking with each passing minute as he funneled more and more into it.

Gold had warned him that once only five percent of each sphere remained, he should hold off on continuing until he was ready to unlock the supermage ability. Because once he passed that point, they would begin trying to pull the reiki apart back into their separate components and he would then need to fight to force the last bit to combine.

After an hour of painstaking work, Morgan was well and truly exhausted. He'd managed to convert nearly all of it, but was too tired to do the last bit. He lay down in his bed and pulled the blanket up to his chin.

At this rate, he'd definitely reach his ninety-five percent goal before the tournament. Of that, he was certain.

**

Arnold stood at the top of the hill overlooking the academy.

It was a truly magnificent sight and one that he'd been sure he would never see again. It had been nearly a hundred years since he'd been thrown out for killing someone and he knew that if anyone here recognized him, he would be hunted down and killed.

Weasel had assured him that his quarry was in the academy. He was no longer with him, as he'd gone off to begin enacting the first part of King Edmund's plan and he was glad to have a break from the smug man. Now all he had to do was get Sarah out of there before the plan came into full effect.

He frowned.

That was easier said than done. CAMS was massive, boasting over a hundred thousand students, instructors and merchants. At this point, there was no longer any doubt that this trip was cursed.

Snorting to himself at his bad luck, Arnold began his trek down the hill and towards the entrance of the academy.

**

Morgan stood across from a nervous looking girl on one of the many fighting stages in the arena.

This was the fourth day of the tournament qualifying rounds and over three quarters of the students had already been eliminated.

At first, Morgan had been nervous as well, but after the third fight in a row, in which his opponent had posed no challenge whatsoever, he became more relaxed.

He watched as the referee walked onto the stage and announced the rules. He asked both of them if they understood and when they both nodded, began the fight.

Morgan took up a fighting stance as the girl rushed him.

She was clearly hoping for a swift victory and thought that attacking straight away was the best course of action.

Morgan easily dodged her first few attacks, then lashed out with a kick. He'd needed to be careful to hold back in his previous fights, so as not kill his opponents. Gold had warned him that since his *rank* had been falsified, the referee wouldn't call the fight unless his blows were aimed at a vital area.

Since his *strength* attribute was so high, he could easily kill someone if he hit them with all his might, even if the area he was aiming for wouldn't normally be considered fatal.

The girl winced as she was thrown back and clutched at the side where his kick had landed. Her rush attack was likely the only reason she was still in the running and she looked surprised that her attack hadn't had its intended effect.

She poked at her side to make sure nothing was broken before turning back to him with a cocky grin.

"You're a tough one, I'll give you that. Guess I'll have to start using my ability if I want to win."

Then her skin shifted in color and took on a scaled appearance. Morgan looked on in interest as her features warped, becoming more reptilian.

He'd never seen an ability like this before. He hadn't even know that transformation was a possibility. He had to revise his opinion of the girl, maybe she had earned her place here after all.

"I see you're impressed by my power," the girl said, flexing her arms and grinning. "How about I give you an up close and personal look at it?"

Morgan didn't understand why so many people felt the need to prattle on in the middle of a fight. They boasted of their amazing power and how he didn't stand a chance. At first he'd just been amused, watching one idiot after the next put on a show before he pummeled them into the ground. Now he was just annoyed.

All this wasted time and for what?

Morgan easily dodged the girl's attack and brought his knee up into her stomach. There was a loud whoosh of air as the girl bent almost double; then Morgan brought his arm up into the air and pulled his elbow down toward the back of her head.

"Stop!"

Morgan froze with his elbow just a few inches from the girl's skull. Then he relaxed and took a few quick steps back.

He'd learned to do this soon after his daily challenges had begun. Not everyone was happy after losing and more than one person didn't care about their class ranking dropping.

"The winner is Morgan, by deathblow," the referee said, coming into the center of the stage.

The girl straightened and allowed her features to shift back to normal. She winced a bit as she felt at her stomach, but Morgan hadn't hit her hard enough to cause anything more than a nasty bruise.

"Guess I deserved that for all the bragging I did," she said with a rueful smile, holding her hand out for him to shake.

Morgan was a little surprised, as no one he'd beaten before had taken it this well.

"Next time, focus more on your opponent rather than yourself," he said, shaking the girl's hand.

"So your name is Morgan; that's quite some ability you've got to be able to dish out so much damage," she smiled, moving a little closer to him. "My name is Cassy by the way."

Morgan, feeling distinctly uncomfortable at her proximity, took a step back.

"I didn't use my ability; just my knowledge of hand to hand combat."

"Really? Well, that makes you even more interesting, in my book."

She now had a predatory gleam in her eye that made Morgan even more nervous. He looked frantically around for an excuse to leave, when he spotted Sarah.

"Oh look, my friend is waiting for me. It was nice talking to you." And with that, he hopped off the stage and practically ran from the girl. Looking back over his shoulder, he could see Cassy standing there with a slightly hurt expression on her face.

He did feel bad about being so rude, but she was making him uncomfortable. If he ever ran into her again, he would apologize.

"Great job on the fight," Sarah said as he approached her.

"Wasn't much of a fight," he answered as they began walking towards the exit.

They stopped by the large archway and looked up at the large board full of the competitor's names. According to the board, he would have to win three more fights to get into the tournament.

He sighed in frustration, wishing he could just get them all over with today, rather than over the next three days.

He also couldn't forget that once the super fights were over, he would have to wait for the mage class to finish theirs. That would take another whole week. Then he would need to wait another week after that for the tournament to begin. Why did it all have to take so long?

It was as they were leaving the arena when he once again spotted Grub and Frush lurking out of the corner of his eyes. They both looked surly and were staring at them with such looks of hatred, that he was surprised that on one else seemed to notice.

"What's got you so down?" Sarah asked, as the two boys were lost from view.

"It's all the waiting. It's driving me crazy!"

She laughed and lightly punched him in the arm. "Since when are you the impatient type?"

"Since there was a platinum coin and a *rank 39* core up for grabs," he muttered, as they turned towards their block.

"Well, why don't we stop by a restaurant before we go home? My treat!"

Morgan grinned when he heard that.

A free meal at a place that served good food?

Sarah really did know him better than anyone else.

36

This was it.

All he had to do to secure a spot in the tournament was win this fight; but that was easier said than done.

Morgan stared out across the stage, where Shul, the number two in the super class stood. He'd never had the opportunity to face him in a ranked match before, but from what he'd heard, he was pretty tough.

The referee came out onto the center of the stage and repeated the rules once more. He then asked if they were ready and announced the start of the match.

Morgan took up a defensive stance as Shul approached cautiously.

"I've heard a lot about you, Morgan," he called out, keeping his fists raised as he shuffled forward.

Morgan ignored him, keeping a close eye on his opponent's movements.

He was trying to distract him with conversation, but he could clearly see Shul's muscles tensing, which meant he was about to attack.

Sure enough, Shul launched toward him and threw a hard cross right at his face. Morgan stepped to the side and deflected the blow, then came back with a short uppercut aimed for his solar plexus.

Surprisingly enough, Shul turned his body to side; causing what would have been a crippling blow to miss altogether. He then returned with an attack of his own, stepping forward and driving a stiff punch into Morgan's unprotected side.

Morgan winced as the punch connected, but luckily his *constitution* was high enough to stop any bones from breaking. He wasn't about to let Shul get away with a clean blow, though. His back leg snapped up in a modified roundhouse kick and Shul winced this time, as Morgan's shin connected with his side.

They both took a few steps back, each re-evaluating their opponent's threat level.

"It's a shame you had to end up facing me, Morgan," Shul called out after a few more seconds of silence. "I would have liked to face you in the tournament. There aren't many in our year that actually took the time to learn how to fight, so out of respect for you; I'll end this quickly."

Morgan wasn't normally one to banter in the middle of a fight, but Shul had done what no one else in the school had managed to do so far. *He'd managed to impress him.* He felt a smile spread across his face despite himself.

Here was someone he could finally test himself against. Not a beast, or a stone golem, but an actual person who knew how to fight!

"I don't plan on losing. You are the one who is going to lose," Morgan answered back.

He winced inwardly at the horrible line.

Banter really wasn't his strong suit.

Shul simply laughed at this, shaking his head in amusement.

"You're a strange one. I'll give you that."

The smile soon died off and he changed his stance, turning more to the side and lowering both fists to chest level.

Morgan studied his new stance, baffled by it.

He was leaving himself wide open! Why would he switch to such an obviously terrible stance?

His question was answered a moment later as something sparked across Shul's skin. Then he was engulfed in crackling yellow energy, which leapt off him in arcs every few seconds.

Morgan widened his stance a bit at this and used his own *heavy handed* skill.

He didn't know much about Shul's ability, but if it enhanced his strength the way his did, then he wouldn't be holding back.

They stood still for several seconds, the only sounds being the light crackling coming off Shul's body. Then he dashed forward once again, but this time it was much different.

Shul seemed to fly over the distance between them, covering it in less than a second and threw a punch into Morgan's stomach. To his complete shock, Morgan wasn't fast enough to even react. The air whooshed out of him as the blow connected and he took a step back, trying to recover.

Shul wasn't about to give him the chance and began raining down blows from all sides. His speed was incredible! Even with *agility* being his highest attribute, Morgan couldn't keep up at all. He tried throwing a few punches of his own, hoping the referee would call the fight on a deathblow; but each time, Shul moved out of the way leaving his attacks to go wide.

Morgan winced as a blow struck him in the right side, then his left, and then his right once more. He tried putting up a defense, managing to block a few blows, but Shul was simply too fast for him to avoid all of them.

Despite the beating he was taking, Morgan could feel a wide smile on his face.

He hadn't felt this way since facing the wolf; a wild rush of adrenaline and the thrill of fighting a strong opponent.

Shul noticed him smiling and disengaged, leaping back a full ten feet and landing gracefully in a ready stance.

"Why are you smiling? You clearly don't stand a chance. You haven't managed to hit me even once. I don't know why the referee hasn't called the match yet."

"That's quite simple really," Morgan said, straightening and rolling his shoulders. "I'm having fun. And as for the match not being called, you haven't managed a deathblow yet."

He grinned, hunching his shoulders and tucking his chin.

If he were to stand a chance of winning this match, he would need to get his hands on him somehow. Landing a lucky punch was still possible, but he wasn't one to leave things to chance.

Shul just shook his head, then crouched and threw himself forward once more. If at all possible, he was even faster now and seemed to appear in front of Morgan rather than covering the distance through normal means.

Morgan winced as the fist connected with his upraised arm, actually feeling the bone grind through his heavy clothes.

He would need to be fast, because if this kept up for much longer, he might actually lose and Sarah would never let him live that down.

He weathered a new onslaught of attacks, only blocking those aimed for a vital areas. His ribs, legs and arms took a serious beating for this and he could feel the attacks starting to take their toll. He stumbled back, breathing hard and rolling his shoulders to relieve some of the built up tension.

Now came the most dangerous part of his plan. If he was off by even one second, the match would be called and he would lose.

Shul took a minute to catch his breath as he stumbled back.

So apparently his stamina wasn't limitless. Perhaps his skill was more taxing than it had first appeared.

Morgan straightened a bit, allowing his fists to lower by an almost imperceptible amount.

"Looks like that ability of yours doesn't come without a cost. By my guess, you'll be forced to slow down in another minute or so," he said, allowing his fists to drop another fraction of an inch.

He knew that movement, however slight, would not escape his notice and he had to hide a grin as Shul's eyes flickered between his face and hands.

Shul didn't rise to the bait, as Morgan knew he wouldn't. He just came at him again and began throwing a barrage of punches, designed to wear him out rather than causing any real damage.

As the seconds ticked by, Morgan allowed his defense to slip inch by inch, pretending to be more exhausted than he actually was. The moment to act came when Morgan moved his arm outward to back a hook punch aimed for his face. Morgan blocked the blow, but when he brought it back into his guard position, his arm was just a little too low.

With a cry of triumph, Shul's fist shot forward on a collision course for Morgan's face, and victory. It was only when Shul noticed his wide grin, that he realized his mistake.

Morgan pivoted on his back leg, one arm trapping Shul's arm to his chest and the other hooking under his armpit. He then slammed his hip into Shul's, then swept his leg up as he completed the turn.

Shul sailed neatly over Morgan's hip and landed with gasp of pain on the stone stage. Morgan had kept ahold of Shul's arm as he fell and now pulled it straight, locking it against his inner thigh. He then dropped his knee into Shul's side, hearing the crackling sound of breaking bones; then twisted his hip, driving a punch toward his face.

"Stop!"

Morgan froze as the referee's voice rang out and quickly backed away, giving the healers room to tend to his downed opponent. Morgan then felt a hand on his shoulder and looked back to see another healer standing with a look of concentration on his face.

After a few moments, he sagged in relief as all the pain in his battered body was washed away. He thanked the healer once he was done and turned back to see Shul already on his feet and approaching him.

Despite losing the fight, Shul didn't look at all upset. Instead, a wide smile was plastered on his face.

"That was an excellent feint you pulled on me," he said, clapping him heartily on the shoulder. "Not many people would have taken that kind of beating and still prevailed. I have no doubt that you are the one deserving of the spot in the tournament."

"There was a moment there when I wasn't sure I could win," Morgan admitted, smiling as well. "But I know one thing for sure; we should definitely fight again some time."

Shul grinned even wider at that and the two of them shook hands, each knowing that a rematch would definitely take place.

"You won! That means you've made it in!"

Morgan stumbled a bit as Sarah barreled into him the moment he left the stage and wrapped her arms around him in a hug.

"Yeah, thanks," he answered, patting her awkwardly.

He didn't think he'd ever get used to all this hugging that she seemed so fond of lately. She hadn't been nearly this touchy back in City Four, so why the change?

He didn't voice these thoughts out loud though, just waiting for Sarah to let go before turning to the entrance of the arena.

Today was a bit different than the others, as there were only fourteen people left standing after six days of fighting. The arena was still packed, even though almost everyone had already been eliminated.

Morgan could see that most of the people were congregated before a raised platform that had only appeared there today. The headmistress stood up there with several instructors and a large covered board stood behind her.

"Was I the last one to finish my fight?" he asked Sarah, as they pushed their way through the crowd.

"Yes," she answered, sticking close so as not to get separated from him.

"So what happens now?"

"I think that they're going to announce everyone who made it into the super tournament. I can see Gold up on the stage, so they probably called all the instructors of the students who made it in."

Looking up to the stage, Morgan could count seven people, aside from Gold and the headmistress.

"Yeah, you're probably right," he said, as they finally managed to get near the front of the crowd. It was so densely packed near the stage that they couldn't move forward any further.

"Did you happen to see who else made it in?"

Sarah shook her head. "I was too busy watching your fight."

He was about to ask her something else, when Headmistress Loquin's voice rang out over the noise of the crowd.

"Quiet down, everyone, and gather in front of the stage!"

Loquin waited patiently for a few more moments as all the students turned to face her, hushed.

"First of all, I would like to congratulate all those who fought to make it into the tournament. Over half of the first year students didn't even try to compete, so to all those that fought, you have my respect."

There was a polite smattering of applause as she said this and she waited for it to die down before continuing.

"Since I'm sure that there isn't much my respect can do for you; all those who competed will be getting a reward. Sometime in the next semester, you will all be getting a run through one of our *Beast Zones*. For those that don't know what that is, a *Beast Zone* is somewhere where you can gather a large amount of energy. If you have any further questions, ask your instructors."

The applause was noticeably louder this time and Morgan was once again reminded how lucky he was to be able to visit a *Beast Zone* on a daily basis.

"Now, without further ado, I will announce the competitors in this year's first tournament. Gold, if you will."

At this, Gold reached up and yanked the cloth covering the board. It came off with a loud whoosh and everyone leaned forward to get a better look. A bracket system was laid out on the board with eight boxes on the bottom, then four, two and finally one. As Morgan watched, eight names showed up in the bottom boxes. The names of those who had successfully fought their way into the tournament.

His name was the third from the left, but his eyes were glued on the last name to appear, all the way on the right.

He turned away, scanning the crowd until his eyes fell on the boy who's name was displayed. A boy who shouldn't have made it in at all.

Grub stood off to the side of the stage. His usual groupies were standing around him and Frush was clapping him on the back.

How that moron had managed to get into the tournament, he had no idea, but he knew if he faced Grub in the arena, he would show no mercy!

37

"You'll have to be lighter on your feet if you want to win!" Gold's voice rang out as Morgan caught a stony fist with the side of his face.

He cried out in pain and his hand shot up to feel at what was undoubtedly a broken jaw; that was a mistake. The stone golem's fist slammed directly into his nose and he was laid out flat, groaning as stars swam before his eyes.

A warm sensation ran through his body a moment later and the fog of unconsciousness retreated, along with the agonizing pain in his face.

"Thanks, Eric," Morgan said, sitting up and rubbing at his nose and jaw.

It was a week to the tournament and Gold had taken it upon himself to make sure that both his and Sarah's skills were up to snuff.

Off to his right, he could see Sarah hurling *icicle spears* and using *condense water* on a similar golem. Just like his, this golem was agile and powerful, not allowing a single attack to land. Even as he watched, the golem rushed Sarah, shattering her mage shield and sending her sprawling.

He heard Eric sigh and run over to heal her. Getting slowly to his feet, Morgan kept an eye on his own golem.

Gold had told him that this was the same golem he'd faced, back when he was taking his test to get into CAMS. He wasn't stupid enough to believe that for even a second.

He was a good deal stronger, faster, and a whole lot more durable than he was back then. Yet he hadn't managed to land a single blow and every time he was hit, the golem would break bones.

"I don't see the point of this exercise," Morgan called out, as the golem once again moved in to pound him into the ground. "How will constantly getting beat up help us in the tournament?"

He managed to duck a blow and tried to return with a palm strike, but all he managed to do was catch a rib cracking blow from the golem's knee.

"Ow!" he yelled, as he was sent sprawling, yet again. His eyes were watery with pain and he could see Eric rushing over to heal him once more.

He didn't bother getting to his feet this time, instead glaring at Gold as he heard the sound of Sarah's shield shattering and the muffled thud of an impact.

After Sarah had been healed- this time she'd been knocked out cold from a blow to the head - she, too, glared at Gold, refusing to get up.

Gold folded his arms and shook his head in mock disappointment.

"You two don't seem to be getting the point of this exercise at all."

"Then how about you tell us, instead of having your stone monstrosities beat us half to death?!" Sarah yelled.

She was in an understandably foul mood. On top of having several bones broken and healed in quick succession; the qualifiers for the mage tournament had ended the previous day and Frush had managed to get in. So it was pretty safe to say that she wasn't having the best day today.

"I can tell you, but neither of you will be getting an *intelligence* or *wisdom* boost if I do. So it's up to you."

Sarah was about to answer for both of them, when Morgan stopped her.

"Can we have a few minutes to think about it before we make our decision?"

Gold nodded, a smile coming to his face. "Good. You're using your head, for once. I'll give the two of you five minutes; after that, you either go back to fighting, or I tell you the point of the exercise."

Morgan nodded, then rose slowly to his feet, keeping an eye on the golem the entire time. When it didn't immediately move to attack, he made his way over to Sarah and sat down next to her. Like him, she was covered in sweat and looked exhausted from the previous two hours of beatings they'd been taking.

When they'd come in this morning, Gold had announced a schedule change for the week leading up to the tournament. Their first training session would last four hours; after which they have a two hour break. After the break, there would be another two hour lesson. Then they'd be free for the day. The entire week would be focused on combat training; so they would not be going into any *beast zones*, or have other classes until after the tournament.

"We have five minutes, so let's try and figure out what we've been doing wrong. After all, we don't want to give Gold the satisfaction of having to ask."

Sarah snapped her mouth shut. She was going to argue that they should just ask, but just the thought of Gold's smug face was enough to temper her mood.

"I can't seem to figure out what I've been doing wrong, so how about this: you tell me what mistakes I've been making and I tell you yours. That sound fair?"

"Yeah, that's actually a pretty good idea," Sarah said, actually cracking a smile for the first time that day.

Morgan nodded, then began sharing his thoughts.

"I've noticed that you tend to throw a lot of attacks at once. While this isn't an issue with a stationary target, you'll have issues hitting anything that can move out of the way fast enough."

"So what would you recommend I do? I can always throw my attacks one after the other, but the thing is too damn fast to hit. Also, from how hard that thing hits, it'll probably be impossible to take it down even if I do."

"Not necessarily…" Morgan said thoughtfully.

"Gold told me that these golems were the same as the one I faced when I tested to get into the academy. Until now I didn't believe him at all, since that golem was a whole lot weaker and slower. At first I thought that since I couldn't use *tailwind* like I did last time, I was just too slow to hit it, but then I remembered my growth since I've been here. Even without the skill active, I'm nearly as fast as I was back then, so the golem is clearly faster."

"That's all well and good, but what does any of this have to do with our current predicament?" Sarah asked.

"It's actually quite simple. If I'm right, then you shouldn't have any problem destroying the golem with a single attack."

Sarah looked thoughtful for a few seconds as she digested all the new information.

"So what you're saying, is that the golem isn't any more powerful than it was previously, but that it's attributes are skewed towards *strength* and *agility*. It's *constitution* has been drastically lowered as a result, meaning that a single hit would finish it."

"Exactly!" Morgan said, nodding excitedly.

"What I think you should do is watch how the golem moves. Everyone has a pattern, so watch it carefully, then aim your attacks for where it's going to be rather than where it is right now."

"That's a great idea," she said with a grin.

"I'm sure I'll be able to nail that thing this time!"

Morgan looked up to the wall, noting the time on the clock.

"We've only got two minutes left, so tell me what I've been doing wrong. I know now that the golems can be destroyed if hit; but that doesn't stop the fact that I'm just not fast enough to hit it."

"Well, I've noticed that you've been moving a lot less during your most recent fights," Sarah began. "You used to move around a lot more rather than stand still and attacking head on. I think I heard Gold mention something about staying light on your feet, so that may have been a hint that you're not moving around enough. Another thing that I noticed is that you don't really use your skills, or at least not your super skills anyway."

"You seem to prefer using your *tailwind* skill over your *heavy handed* and you almost never use *fly* during a fight. Since Gold forbade you from using any mage skills at all, that leaves you at a severe disadvantage when facing opponents who do."

Morgan though about what she said.

He always used tailwind because out of the two skills, it had always seemed more useful. He had used heavy handed during fights where power was required, but since he was limited to using either one or the other, he always picked speed over power.

He also never used *fly* in a fight, since it took him a few seconds to build up speed and he didn't have the fast twitch reflexes he did on the ground; but maybe there was a way to utilize both in a fight.

"Thank you for that," he said, getting to his feet and offering her a hand up. "You've definitely given me a lot to think about."

"What are friends for?" she replied, taking his proffered hand and getting to her feet.

"Time's up!" Gold's voice rang out. "Have you made your decision?"

"Yes," Morgan answered for the both of them.

"We'll fight the golems without taking any of your advice."

"Very well then. Better get back into position, because they'll be attacking in ten seconds."

Morgan rushed back to face his opponent, his mind alight with new ideas and possibilities.

As the countdown ended, the golem rushed him, almost as if it were eager to break something new, but Morgan was already on the move. As the golem ran at him, he began moving to the side, forcing it to change direction and slowing it down a bit. The golem closed in on him and threw a kick designed to crack his shin, but he threw himself to the side and used *fly*.

This was an idea he'd come up with, after Sarah had mentioned his lack of movement in a fight, as well as his lack of skill usage. He might not be able to move very quickly in the air, but that didn't mean he couldn't us his skill in short bursts while staying low to the ground. If anything, using it this way would actually aid his movement rather than impede it. That was assuming that it would function in the way he hoped it would.

As soon as his feet left the ground, Morgan knew that his idea had worked. He rocketed to the side as his feet glided a few inches off the ground; the force of his momentum, along with the decreased gravity more than enough to outmaneuver the golem.

He laughed as he deactivated *fly* feeling his feet touch the ground; then dashed forward and used *fly* again to launch himself at the golem. The golem, to its credit, actually managed to get mostly out of the way, but it was just a hair too slow to completely avoid the attack. Morgan's fist clipped it in the side and the construct shattered into a thousand pieces.

He let out a whoop of triumph, turning just in time to watch Sarah send an accurately aimed ball of ice right into the path of her charging golem. He saw Sarah pump her fist in the air, making a very rude gesture to the now inanimate pile of rubble and laughing hysterically.

"That was well done."

They both stopped their cheering as Gold approached along with Eric, the former clapping slowly and the latter looking amazed.

"You managed to figure out how to beat the golems all on your own; excellent work," Gold said, continuing his clapping.

They both glared at his mocking applause, but even he couldn't dampen their good mood.

"Did you see the way we destroyed those things, Eric?" Sarah asked excitedly.

"I did indeed," the healer replied with a grin. "That was most impressive."

"Makes you wonder if we even need an instructor like Gold. All he does is beat us bloody, then takes all the credit when we figure out his latest lesson," Sarah said, making air quotes when she said the word 'lesson'.

"I'm hurt!" Gold said, placing a hand on his chest and adopting a wounded look.

"And then he does this," Morgan said with a sigh.

Gold's expression then changed to indignation and the three of them just nodded sagely.

"Yes, he does seem to go through the same process each time," Eric said, rubbing his chin. "You'd think he would come up with something new, after all this time."

"Alright, enough of that," Gold said, this time with a little heat in his voice. "None of you appreciate all the hard work that goes into teaching a bunch of upstart brats. Maybe the golems weren't challenging enough; I think we aught to remedy that, don't you?"

He smiled now, an evil grin that both Sarah and Morgan knew quite well.

The next two hours were not going to be pleasant.

38

It was finally the day of the tournament and Morgan could not remember ever feeling so nervous in his entire life. He was currently sitting next to Sarah in a private booth on the ground level of the arena.

Apparently all competitors got their own booths, but since the two of them shared an instructor, they decided to share a booth as well.

"How many people do you think are out there?" Morgan asked, tugging at the straps on the side of his new shirt.

"My best guess is around eighty thousand," Gold replied cheerily, as he entered.

Morgan visibly paled at that number.

Eighty thousand people would be watching him fight?!

"How is there even room for that many people?"

"In case you haven't noticed, the area at the center of the arena had shrunk by quite a bit," Gold said, sitting down in one of the plush chairs. "Care to guess where all that extra room went?"

Morgan sighed as the truth sank in.

They must have sunk a good portion of the seats into the ground when the arena was being used during the semester. Now they'd raised it so people could watch the fights.

He voiced his thoughts out loud and Gold grinned.

"Good to see that you can still think clearly, despite your nerves."

Morgan just scowled and surveyed the open area in front of them once more. They, along with all the other competitors, had seats right near the fighting area.

It had been drastically reduced and was now only fifty feet across. The ground underfoot had been changed to sand in place of the usual stone and a white line had been painted across the center.

Three figures were currently out on the arena grounds; the headmistress, the referee and Eric, their healer. There were also two large transparent boards floating above their heads; one red and one blue; each displaying the competitor's names.

"How will this work?" Sarah asked. "Will all the students in one class fight, then all the students from the other; or will they switch in between matches?"

"It will go by round," Gold replied, seemingly distracted. "The super class will have their first round, then the mage class will have theirs. It'll keep going like that until the tournament is over. This will give all the competitors a chance to rest in between matches."

"What about tournaments for the other years?" Morgan asked.

"The second year tournament will be held two days from now and the third year's will be next week. All the others will be held in two weeks from now, as foreign dignitaries will want to come watch the top students compete."

"Why would they want to do that?" Morgan asked.

"To try and make them offers to come work for them," Sarah answered before Gold could. "You have to remember that the students who made it into the tournament are the best of the best, which means that they get scholarships. Consequently, their kingdoms don't have to pay their tuition, which means that they don't have to fight in their military."

"That was very well put, Sarah," Gold said, patting her on the shoulder.

"When will the first fight begin?" Sarah asked, looking out at the open space where they would soon be fighting.

"Probably in around thirty or so minutes. Until then, why don't you just sit back and relax." Gold replied.

***

Arnold entered the packed arena looking around at the massive gathering of people. He'd been in a foul mood over the last week, as he'd had absolutely no luck in locating either Sarah or Morgan.

Weasel had contacted him the previous night to let him know that the preparations were complete and that their plan would be carried out shortly. That gave him only twenty four hours to find Sarah and get her out of the academy.

Someone bumped him from behind and he very nearly turned to attack the person out of reflex, but managed to stop himself just in time.

He was way too jumpy, but that was perfectly understandable, considering what they were about to do.

He glanced at his wrist where his timepiece displayed that it was just past noon. He really didn't have a lot of time at all, but if there was any chance of finding those two, it would be here.

Walking further in, he looked around for a place to sit, that would also give him the best vantage point. His eyes traveled up to the seats near the top of the bleachers.

Perfect. Some of those seats were still open.

It took him nearly five minutes of climbing and shoving to make it to the top and find a seat. Slumping down on the stone bench, he allowed his eyes to roam over the gathered crowd, taking note of the various entrances and exits throughout the arena.

As he was looking, his eyes inevitably fell upon the two floating boards displaying the names of the competitors. His eyes widened in disbelief and he rubbed them a few times to make sure he wasn't imagining things; then a wide smile spread across his face and he had to restrain himself from leaping out of his seat right then and there.

It looked like lady luck had finally shined down upon him; and not a moment too soon. He could of course be wrong, but what were the chances that the Sarah and Morgan competing were not the two he was after?

Arnold slumped back in his seat and let a content sigh escape his lips.

There was no way he could get to either of them right now, because he didn't know where they were. Plus, they were also likely to be surrounded by a whole lot of people. Once the tournament began, he would see from where they emerged, and once he was given the signal, he could easily make it down to them in the confusion and he would finally be able to complete this damn mission.

***

Morgan, who had been concentrating on combining the last bit of his mana and chi, opened his eyes as Sarah shook him. He allowed his hold over the two spheres to slip and felt the two energies retract into their separate spheres.

He'd done it. All but five percent of both had been converted into reiki, and soon as the tournament was over, he would combine the last bit and finally become a supermage.

"Why do you have that creepy smile on your face?"

Morgan, who had been off in his own world, realized that he was indeed smiling.

"I did it," he said in an excited tone.

He was careful to keep his voice lowered, as they were out in public and he didn't want anyone to overhear them.

"Did what?" Sarah asked.

"I managed to combine all but the last bit!"

"That is excellent news," Gold cut in; "but now is not the time to discuss this. The Headmistress is about to begin the tournament."

Sarah, who'd wanted to ask him more, glared at Gold for interrupting her.

It was then that Loquin's voice rang out over the arena.

"Welcome all, to the first year quarterly tournament!"

Morgan was shocked at how loud her voice was and how well it carried.

It could be clearly heard, even above the voices of eighty thousand people.

"Now I don't want to make you wait any further, so allow me to explain the rules and how the bracket system will work. The rules are simple; to win you must render your opponent unconscious, or unable to continue fighting. Hypothetical deathblows will not count as a victory here. Killing an opponent is allowed, as stated in *chapter 24; section 6,* under the laws of an official, kingdom sponsored tournament."

"People can be killed?!" Morgan and Sarah said at the same time, turning to stare at Gold.

"It's not against the rules," Gold said with a shrug. "But it's only happened a handful of times in all the years I've been here, so you have nothing to worry about."

Morgan was about to ask who had been killed, but stopped himself as Loquin continued her speech.

"We will however, strongly discourage you from taking that course of action. The referee can and will stop a fight if he believes that a competitor is no longer able to fight. If the fighter believes they still can fight, the matter will be brought to our panel of judges."

Here she gestured behind her to a booth where four people sat behind a stone desk. Morgan noticed that more than a few academy guards were standing there as well.

With a crowd this large, that was hardly a surprise.

"The tournament will be as follows," Loquin continued. "The first fight will be a bout between two students in the super class. The next one will be from the mage class and we'll continue switching off between the two."

She stopped for a moment as the referee walked toward her and whispered in her ear, then walked back to the side of the arena.

Morgan didn't like the look of the man. He was tall, dressed in fine clothes and had an impetuous look about him.

"I almost forgot to mention," Loquin said after the man had walked back to his post. "That we have a special guest who will be acting as the referee in place of our Deputy Headmaster Gold this semester. As Gold has two students who are competing, we believed that it wouldn't be fair to have him oversee the tournament."

"In his place, we have the esteemed Keldor, second in command of the merchant guild in the South Kingdom. He has graciously come all the way from the city of Dunmere to oversee this tournament."

There was a smattering of polite applause as the man bowed, looking very smug for some reason.

Something about what Loquin had just said tickled the back of Morgan's mind, but he couldn't quite place what. It was only when Sarah started yelling that he finally understood who this man was.

"How can a man from the merchant guild in the South Kingdom be allowed to referee this match?" she practically exploded.

"Both Grub and that toad Frush are from the South Kingdom and from a wealthy merchant family. If they're not letting you referee the tournament, they shouldn't allow this man to either!"

Gold just sighed and placed a calming hand on her shoulder, guiding her gently back down into her seat.

"I didn't have a say in this, so there's no need to yell at me. Yes, the man is most likely going to be playing favorites, but he can't be too obvious about it; otherwise the judges will overrule him. Eric is also going to be down there and he will call Keldor out if he doesn't make the correct decisions."

This seemed to mollify Sarah somewhat, but Morgan felt distinctly uneasy.

If killing was allowed and Keldor was the one in charge, then this could only be one thing- a setup.

"Now, there is one last thing before we announce our first fighters," Loquin's voice rang out once more. "Unfortunately, our esteemed ruler, King Herald was unable to make it to the first tournament of the year, as he is currently away on a diplomatic mission. His Majesty apologizes to the competitors for his absence and hopes to see them all in the next tournament. Now, without further ado, let's get this tournament started. All fights will be chosen at random, so please look up at the screen for our first two fighters!"

The names on the boards disappeared and a bunch of names started scrolling quickly in the first two open brackets of the red one.

Morgan felt his heart thumping as the names began slowing down. He groaned, placing his head into his hands as the names stopped, revealing the first two lucky fighters.

"Guess you're up first," Gold said with a grin, as he patted Morgan on the back. "Best of luck out there!"

39

Morgan felt his heart practically beating out of his chest as he slowly walked out onto the arena sands. He could hear the roar of the crowd as he approached the white line in the center, where the referee, Keldor, stood waiting for him.

On the other side, he could see a girl approaching. She was tall and slim, with tan skin, bright golden eyes and long brown hair tied in a braid down her back. She was dressed similarly to him; in a tight fitting canvas uniform, and walked with the confidence of a trained combatant.

Morgan knew this girl's name even without it being written on the board. Hilda, the only person aside from Sarah who hadn't had to fight her way into the tournament. The number one in the super class.

How had he gotten so lucky?

Morgan could feel his nervousness evaporate as excitement for the upcoming fight took its place.

If Shul, the number two, had nearly beaten him, how strong would the number one be? He couldn't wait to find out.

Morgan came to a stop once he reached the white line, facing across from his first opponent, as Keldor began to speak.

"You both heard the rules, now shake hands and walk back to your respective ends of the arena."

Morgan and Hilda shook, each sizing the other up; then walked back to the opposite ends of the arena. Once they'd both reached their designated spots, Keldor held a small device up to his lips.

"Ladies, gentlemen and nobles of all kingdoms, the rules have been stated and our combatants are ready. For those of you sitting higher up, please turn your eyes to the screen for a better view of the fight."

Looking up, Morgan could see that the two screens that had been displaying the fighter's names had now been replaced by a single massive screen showing a live view of the arena. He could see himself looking up and quickly turned his attention back to his opponent.

"Now, without further ado, let the fight begin!"

There was a loud roar as the crowd cheered their enthusiasm, but Morgan tuned them all out, focusing in on Hilda. As soon the referee began the fight, she began moving forward at an incredible speed.

Not nearly as fast as Shul, but definitely close to matching his own.

Morgan grinned and launched himself forward as well, using *fly* as soon as his foot left the ground. He shot toward his opponent; feet just a few inches off the ground and spun in the air, using his momentum to enhance the power of his kick.

His foot collided with the side of Hilda's head and sent her flying. Not to give up on his advantage, Morgan landed, then launched himself through the air, skimming low to the ground as he closed in.

Hilda was already on her feet by the time he reached her and surprisingly, looked to be completely unharmed. Morgan landed, then pivoted his back leg and threw a punch aimed straight at her face.

She wasn't fast enough to dodge, yet his fist didn't connect with its intended target. Instead, it impacted an invisible something just a few inches from her skin.

She grinned at the surprised look of his face and threw a punch of her own. Morgan moved his head to the side to avoid the blow, but as the fist passed, something slammed into his face and sent him staggering back.

Hilda moved in and followed up with a kick. He threw his arms up in a block, but when he caught the foot, he felt a heavy blow land on his side. He gritted his teeth and shoved back, sending Hilda stumbling and off balance; then he reached out to grab her collar for a throw, but his hands were stopped once again by the invisible barrier.

Hilda regained her balance and threw another punch at him, but Morgan had already begun moving as soon as his grab had failed. He threw himself backwards, using *fly* and landed a good twenty feet away.

Just what kind of ability did this girl have? When he threw an attack, it was blocked by some kind of barrier. When she'd retaliated, he'd been hit, both when he dodged and when he blocked!

Morgan took up a defensive posture as Hilda approached once more. He grimaced inwardly as he felt his face and side throbbing in pain.

Hilda wasn't just a skilled fighter; she had an ability that seemed to be able to cause damage no matter what he did. He couldn't let this fight drag on and look for an opening, the way he'd done with Shul. Hilda hit way too hard for that to be an option.

A few more hits like that and he'd be out of the fight. He wasn't sure how her ability worked, but he thought he had an idea on how to counter it, now he just needed to test it out and hope it worked.

"What's the matter there, Morgan?" Hilda called out, as she slowly closed the distance between them.

"You look worried. Is it because you can't seem to hurt me?"

Morgan was surprised by Hilda's light and airy voice.

He wasn't sure why, but he'd been expecting something a little deeper.

"I'll take your silence as confirmation," she shouted, suddenly lunging at him and covering the ten foot gap in the span of a second.

Morgan watched her movements carefully. He saw the punch aimed at his face, moving as though in slow motion. He moved his face to the side as the fist passed, then threw his arm up; not to block the punch, but to block the second blow he knew was coming.

He felt a blow slam into his upraised arm, wincing at the power of the strike, but glad that he hadn't caught it with his face. A punch like that would have dazed him, at the very least.

Morgan grinned at the shocked look that was now on Hilda's face, then used *heavy handed* and threw a strike of his own. Hilda was standing too close to throw a punch, so he tucked his fist against his chest and pivoted on his back leg; bringing his elbow across in a powerful strike aimed at her jaw.

His elbow slammed into the barrier and Morgan heard a distinct cracking sound; then the strike slipped through. The power of his attack was greatly reduced because of the shield absorbing most of it, but Hilda still staggered back, clutching at her face.

"How did you do that?" Hilda looked both shocked and impressed. "No one's ever managed to break through my shield. Just what kind of ability do you have?"

"I could ask you the same thing," Morgan answered, using the same tactic she had before and lunging in as soon as he finished speaking.

She got her hands up just in time to deflect two of his blows, but the third one landed; a knee to her stomach. Morgan, who'd been expecting to hit the shield, put all the force he could into the blow; but he'd been mistaken. There was no shield.

His knee impacted against her stomach and Morgan felt it give way before him. He tried to pull the blow, but by then it was too late. The air whooshed out of her lungs and she let out a gasp of pain as her internal organs ruptured. She was thrown backwards under the force of the attack, bouncing several times before coming to a bone jarring halt. She didn't get up.

Morgan ran towards her, already feeling a twinge of fear as he approached her prone form. The crowd had gone deathly silent and he could hear the distinct crunch of the sand under his feet.

He'd still been using his heavy handed skill when he'd hit her and without the shield in the way, his attack could very well have killed her!

As he approached the downed girl, he could see both Eric and Keldor running over as well. They reached her first and Keldor held up a hand, stopping him from coming any closer. He watched as Eric bent down over the girl, placing a hand on her stomach; which Morgan could now see, contained a nasty indent in the shape of a knee.

He waited with baited breath as Eric worked over Hilda, feeling a mounting sense of panic that he'd accidentally killed someone for no reason.

Sure, he'd killed before and felt absolutely no remorse, but this girl didn't deserve to die! All she'd been doing was trying to win a fight.

He could hear the crowd begin muttering behind him as Keldor left Hilda and walked over to talk to Loquin. Eric was still leaning over the girl and with Keldor out of the way, he had a better view of her prone form.

Her eyes were wide open and staring up at the sky. Blood flecked her lips and her chest wasn't moving.

Morgan could feel his heart sink even more as he saw this.

He'd seen plenty of dead bodies before. Hilda was most definitely no longer among the living. So why was Eric still trying to heal her?

Morgan took a step forward, thinking to pull the healer away and at least save the girl's dignity, when a shudder seemed to move through her. Then she blinked, coughed a few times, then turned her head to the side and began vomiting up a fountain of blood.

Eric was covered in the stuff, but to his credit, didn't even flinch, keeping his hand on Hilda the entire time. After another minute of this, she finally stopped and began taking in huge heaving lungful's of air.

"Back away, boy! I think you've caused enough damage to the poor girl."

Morgan looked up to see Keldor approaching. He didn't look at all upset and a nasty half sneer covered his face.

"I was told that you had a vicious temper, but I never could have guessed that you would try and kill someone during your first match."

Morgan wasn't about to rise to the man's bait.

He may have severely injured Hilda, but she was alive, which meant that he had nothing to feel guilty about. He would apologize for nearly killing her, but to feel guilty about it would just be stupid.

Keldor's smirk vanished when Morgan didn't reply and was instead replaced an angry glare.

"Did you hear what I just said, boy?"

"I heard you," Morgan said, turning to meet the angry man's stare with an impassive one of his own. "It was an accident. I thought she still had her shield up and, as a result, hit her much harder than I normally would have. She isn't dead, thanks to Eric, so you have no reason to be angry with me. Now if you don't mind, I would appreciate it if you would announce my victory, so I can go rest before my next match."

Keldor stared at him for a moment in disbelief. Then his face contorted in rage and went from a light pink, to a deep crimson in a matter of seconds.

"Listen here, boy! I am the referee here, not you; and I say that you're disqualified for the attempted murder of another student!"

Morgan folded his arms and stared back, not allowing even a hint of emotion to touch his face.

"Last I checked, killing wasn't against the rules. Now, you can either announce my victory, or I can go to the judges and ask them to do it."

Keldor seemed to blanch at that and after taking a look back at the judges table, he finally conceded defeat. He raised the small metal device to his lips and made the announcement.

"For rendering Hilda unable to continue, the victory goes to Morgan!"

The crowd burst into cheers and Morgan began to move past him to speak with Hilda. He was stopped however, when Keldor's hand dropped on his shoulder.

"Don't forget who makes the calls in this tournament, boy," he hissed so only he could hear. Then he let go and walked away.

The message was perfectly clear. If he went up against Grub, Keldor would make sure to do all in his power to sabotage him.

He knelt down next to Hilda, who was drinking something from a cup that Eric was holding up to her lips.

"I'm sorry," he said, as soon as Eric removed the cup. "I was expecting to hit your shield and didn't hold back."

Hilda stared at him for a few seconds, her mouth a hard line. Then she smiled and Morgan felt instantly relieved.

"I can't blame you for getting hurt during a fight. I have to know though, what kind of ability do you have? No one's ever managed to break through my shield before. I've never been hit that hard in my entire life! Just how high is your *strength* attribute?"

Morgan smiled back as she became more animated with each question.

He liked this girl; she reminded him of Sarah somehow.

"I'll answer one of your questions, since I did almost kill you. I won't tell you my *strength* attribute, but I'll tell you what the skill I used does. It doubles my *strength* for a set amount of time, that's how I managed to bust through your shield."

Her eyebrows shot up at this.

"That skill sounds amazing! Why aren't you the number one with a skill like that?"

Morgan shrugged.

"I don't really use it in fights where I'm not trying to kill my opponents. I tend to rely more on my hand to hand skill than any chi related ones. If anyone's amazing, it's you. I couldn't figure out what kind of ability you have and you hit harder than just about anyone I've come up against so far," he said, patting his side and wincing.

He felt a hand on his shoulder, then he felt the throbbing pain from where Hilda's blows had landed recede and then vanish.

"The two of you better get off the ring before they kick you off," Eric said with a weary smile.

Morgan rose, holding out a hand to help Hilda to her feet.

"Thanks, Eric. You always do an amazing job."

"Yeah, thanks," Hilda said, taking his proffered hand and getting to her feet. "Without you I likely would have died."

"Just doing my job," Eric said humbly, but he had a wide smile on his face all the same.

It was then that Morgan realized that Hilda hadn't let go of his hand yet. He tried to do so, but she pulled him in close to her, bumping her shoulder into his and patting him on the back before letting go.

"I expect we'll fight again," she said, giving him a dazzling smile. "And I look forward to the day we do." Then she turned and exited the ring.

Morgan stared after her for a few seconds, trying to figure out what had just happened. Then he turned and headed for his own booth, wondering at the strange behavior of people from other kingdoms.

Morgan entered the booth to see Gold standing there with a smile and Sarah looking distinctly unhappy.

"Congrats on winning your first match, though you did have a pretty close call there," his teacher said, clapping him on the shoulder.

"Yeah. Guess I'll need to be a little more careful in my next match," Morgan replied.

"What did that girl want from you?"

He turned away from Gold, to see Sarah glaring at him.

He had no idea what could possibly have made her so angry. Shouldn't she be happy that he'd won his fight?

"I apologized for nearly killing her," he said carefully, not sure if this would make her even angrier.

"Did you talk about anything else?"

"Um, no," he answered, feeling that this would be the best course of action.

He wasn't sure why she was acting this way.

Maybe her upcoming fight had her on edge.

This seemed to be the correct answer though, as she instantly brightened.

"Well, then. Congrats on winning your first fight."

Just then, Keldor announced the next fight, this one for the mage class. They all turned their attention towards the board and watched as the names rotated through the open brackets. As they came to a stop, Morgan felt his heart begin to race once more.

This had to be rigged! There was no other way this could have happened on the first fight!

Keldor had an almost malicious smile on his face as he announced the two fighters.

"For the first fight of the mage class, give it up for Frush and Sarah!"

40

Morgan and Gold both turned to look at Sarah as the fight was announced, expecting to hear another outburst. She didn't look bothered in the slightest, however, and had a contemplative look on her face.

"This is such an obvious setup, it's ludicrous," Gold said, turning to exit the booth. "I'm going to have a talk with the judges about this!"

"No."

Gold stopped and turned to look at Sarah, who now had a smile on her face.

"This is perfect! I'm sure that little toad is still smarting from what I did to him last time. So long as I don't let him touch me, I'll be able to take him out without a problem."

"Are you sure?" Gold asked, giving her a questioning look. "After all, you can't forget who's going to be overseeing this fight. It was most likely set up this way so that Frush can kill you."

"I know," she replied with a shrug. "But I don't plan on losing. That slime ball won't even last five seconds."

She turned to Morgan then and flashed him a grin. "Wish me luck."

"Why? You won't need luck to beat him, only skill, and you have plenty of that."

"Just do it," she replied in exasperation.

"You know that you make no sense at all sometimes ,right?" he grumbled.

Sarah just folded her arms and began tapping a foot impatiently.

"Good luck. Are you happy now?" he finally relented.

"Yes; very," she replied with a cheeky grin, then she turned and walked out of the booth.

***

Arnold had already seen Morgan fight, so he'd been fairly certain that Sarah would be here too. Regardless of that, he felt a massive sense of relief when he saw Lord Simon's daughter walking out onto the ring below.

Now all he had to do was wait for the signal, then he could go down and retrieve her. It was about time, too; he was sick of this mission and would definitely be taking a long vacation once it was over. But for now, he may as well enjoy the fight.

***

Sarah stopped on her side of the line, not three feet from her would be rapist. She stared him down as Keldor made his pre-fight speech, but when he asked them to shake hands, she abruptly turned her back on him and walked to her side of the arena.

Keldor glared at her once she'd turned back around, but she simply ignored him. After all, he was working with that toad, so she didn't owe him anything.

After seeing that Sarah was completely ignoring him, he just motioned Frush to his side of the arena and began the fight.

Sarah's mage shield flared around her as soon as the fight began. Even as she was putting up her defenses, she used *frostbite* to make sure Frush's movements would be slowed.

Frush was much slower in getting his mage shield up and as a result, was blasted full force by the skill, lowering his speed by thirty percent.

Sarah smiled grimly as she saw her attack land, then both her arms snapped up as she began using *icicle spear*. Within a few seconds, ten icy spears were on their way to Frush, spread out in a wide pattern so she couldn't miss.

Frush was surprisingly nimble and managed to dodge all but two of the incoming spears. One of them glanced off his mage shield, but the other punched straight through his stomach and out his back.

Sarah ran forward as soon as she saw this, conjuring a few more spears as she went.

He was defenseless!

She made it halfway there, then stumbled, suddenly feeling very weak. Her spears dropped to the ground and her vision began to grow blurry.

What was going on? Was this another one of Frush's skills?

Frush slowly walked towards her, pulling the spear out of his stomach with a cry of pain. She could see blood staining the front of his uniform, but the wound apparently wasn't bad enough to stop him.

She tried to take another step forward, but she just felt so tired.

Maybe she should just lie down and take a nap. She could always continue fighting afterward.

She dropped to her knees as her vision began to go fuzzy, then she was instantly awake as a fist crashed into the side of her face. She screamed as she was sent sprawling by the blow, clutching at her cheek as she looked around for the source of the attack.

Frush stood there with a wicked grin on his face and Sarah could see that he looked different than he had before. His skin had turned a dark blue color and was flecked with black splotches. His eyes had turned red and his pupils were vertical, like those of a frog.

Just what the hell was he? And how had he gotten through her shield?

It was only then, that she realized that her shield had somehow gone out.

When had that happened? Come to think of it, how had she gotten on the ground? Wasn't she just about to end the fight?

She got shakily to her feet, once again activating her mage shield, and used *icicle spear*.

"I don't know what you just did to me, but I'll make sure to finish you off quickly so you can't do it again," she growled through gritted teeth.

She began lifting her arm to send the spears at the offending boy, when the overwhelming exhaustion hit her again. Her arm dropped and Frush rushed in, slamming a slimy fist into her face once more.

Sarah went down with a cry of pain, but this time Frush pounced on top of her and began raining blows down on her, one after the next. She tried to fight back, but every time she tried to use her skills, she was suddenly too weak to do anything at all.

She cried out as Frush's fist connected with her nose, with a loud snap. Her nose broke and blood spurted out, once again waking her from her sleepy haze.

What the hell was going on?

Her head was rocked to the side as Frush cracked her across the jaw and her vision swam once again. She tried lifting her arm to ward off the blows, but it dropped as soon as she tried.

She was just too tired, and going to sleep sounded so nice. She should definitely go to sleep, after all, she was in so much pain. If she went to sleep now, she wouldn't be in pain anymore.

Sarah felt one more vicious blow to her temple, then she blacked out.

***

"What the hell is going on out there?"

Morgan was pacing back and forth in the booth, as Sarah once again failed to do anything.

This wasn't right! She stopped her attack when that idiot was wide open. Then she dropped her mage shield and just let him attack her.

"I don't know what's going on, but something smells rotten," Gold said, getting to his feet as well.

Morgan's eyes flicked quickly to Keldor, who was standing to the side as Frush pounced on top of Sarah and began pummeling her face. He had an oddly pleased look, as though he were in on some sort of secret that on one else knew.

By this point, he should have stepped in and ended the fight, but it looked as though they couldn't count on him doing that. Then the true horror of what was going on hit him like a ton of bricks.

It was Keldor! He was interfering in the fight. There was no other reason why Sarah would be acting this way. Sure, Frush could freeze someone with a touch, but Sarah was at least twenty feet away from him the first time she dropped.

"It's Keldor, isn't it?" Morgan asked, turning quickly to Gold. "He's doing something to her."

Gold nodded, already rolling up the sleeves on his robes and tying his belt more firmly.

"What are you going to do?" Morgan asked, preparing to move out as well.

"I'm going to kill him," Gold stated calmly. "Interfering in an official tournament is a crime punishable by death."

"Should I come with you?"

He was eager to fight; to pound the ugly bastards into a bloody pulp, then have Eric heal them and do it all over again.

"No!" Gold said sharply. "You stay here. This is a messy situation and the fewer people who are involved, the better."

Morgan nodded as Gold finished tying off his robe and headed out of the booth.

He hated sitting on the sidelines while his friend was being beaten to death, but Gold was more than capable of handling the situation. He just wished there was something more he could do.

He silently fumed as he watched Frush continuing to pummel a clearly unconscious Sarah and all the while, Keldor just watched. He could hear the crowd becoming uneasy as this went on. They were likely wondering why the match wasn't being ended, as well.

Morgan clenched his fists as his sides, raging inwardly at his inability to help right now.

He just hoped that Gold knew what he was doing.

41

Arnold watched in mounting horror as Lord Simon's daughter was being beaten to death.

How could this be happening? Why was this happening? And why wasn't the referee stepping in to stop the fight? He knew the rules, and while killing wasn't illegal, the fight should have been called as soon as it became clear that Sarah was unable to continue.

Arnold rose from his seat and began shoving his way through the other spectators, many of which had risen from their seats to get a better view.

He had to make it down there, no matter the consequence. If Lord Simon's daughter was killed, his life would be forfeit; and he didn't feel like dying over what was likely some sort of childish grudge.

He finally broke free of the crowd and emerged onto the stairs. He took one step down when a booming voice shook the entire stadium.

"Keldor! You have interfered in this fight long enough!"

Arnold staggered under the force of that voice and more than a few people fell to the ground in a dead faint.

What kind of person could produce that much power with only their voice?

His question was answered a moment later, as Deputy Headmaster Gold walked out onto the fighting grounds.

Arnold felt a shiver go down his spine when he saw him. There were very few people that he was truly afraid of; and that man down there was near the top of his list. He took another step forward, then stopped.

If Gold was down there, then Sarah was most likely going to be fine, but if he went down there now, the entire plan could be in jeopardy.

Arnold clenched his fists as he scanned the crowd for any sign of the signal.

Nothing yet; but it couldn't be long now. He just needed to be patient.

***

Keldor's head whipped up the moment Gold's voice rang out. He grimaced as his concentration was shattered and he was forced to release his grip on the girl's mind.

"How dare you interfere in the middle of a tournament match?" Keldor yelled back. "This is a crime punishable by death! Loquin, get this man out of here."

Loquin dropped in to the ring from where she'd been seated and approached Gold, face set in an angry expression.

"Just what do you think you're doing, Gold? You know interfering in a match is against the law!"

"Then you won't mind executing Keldor for attacking my student," he replied, motioning over to where Frush lay prone on the ground next to Sarah.

As soon as Gold had entered the ring, he'd made sure to knock the boy out. There was now a stone golem standing between him and Sarah, who was already being attended to by Eric.

"How dare you accuse someone of his status of such a serious crime," Loquin yelled. "You overstep your station, Deputy Headmaster." She made sure to stress the word 'deputy', reminding Gold of his position under her.

"I see," Gold said, folding his arms and frowning. "Now things are starting to become clear to me. I've been wondering who kept blocking me from speaking to the board about expelling those two boys. Or whose idea it was to let Keldor, a man who is clearly biased against my students, referee this tournament! I can see why a boy who attempted rape and another who attempted murder weren't immediately expelled. I expected a lot of people to be corrupt, but I never suspected you would be one of them, Loquin."

The Headmistress' face went pale for a moment. Gold was speaking with enough force that the entire arena could hear their conversation and he was throwing around some pretty serious accusations. Then she seemed to regain her confidence and laughed condescendingly.

"I've known that you've been after my job for years, Gold, but this a low even for you. Guards! Arrest this man; if he tries to resist, do not hesitate to kill him!"

"I wouldn't recommend that if I were you," he casually said as a group of guards emerged onto the arena sands.

"You all know that I'm too powerful to be killed by the likes of you."

The guards froze in place, looking to Loquin uncertainly.

"I have a proposal to make," Gold continued, this time turning to face the judges, who were now on their feet and staring down at the spectacle below.

"Honorable judges; I propose that you allow a diviner to come down and figure out how truthful my statements are. If Loquin is innocent, as she claims, and Keldor didn't interfere with the fight, then they should have nothing to fear. If I am right; then I demand you allow me to kill them both, under the law of non-interference in a kingdom sanctioned tournament."

This was a gamble on his part. The judges were given the same power as the king when it came to making decisions during a tournament. They could, technically, give him the power to meet out instant justice to both guilty parties. The risk with this was that one or more of the judges could be in Keldor's pocket, in which case, he'd be forced to flee.

The judges convened for a moment as Gold stared impassively at Keldor and Loquin; both of whom were glaring daggers at him. After another minute of debate, the judges finally convened their meeting and turned to deliver their verdict.

"After some deliberation, we have decided that Deputy Headmaster Gold is not making an unreasonable request. After all, if Keldor was interfering during the match and Headmistress Loquin was aware of this, then this would merit further investigation. We will have a diviner sort this issue out and make our decision based on the outcome."

"Very well," Loquin was quick to speak up. "Instructor Blue, come down here and verify that I and the esteemed Keldor are innocent."

"Not so fast," Gold immediately cut in. "Honorable judges, I believe that in a situation like this, Instructor Blue may be biased in his judgment. I propose that you allow an outside party to divine the truth in this matter."

The judges immediately agreed with his decision.

"If we are not mistaken, Duchess Helga of the East Kingdom is here to watch her daughter compete. We believe that she is a neutral enough party to sort this mess out. Is that agreeable to you?"

Gold nodded; then the judges turned their attention on Loquin and Keldor. They had both gone very still, the confident looks they'd had a moment ago now gone.

Clearly, they'd been counting on Blue to falsify the verdict in their favor.

"No! It's not agreeable to us!" Loquin shouted. "This in a grievous affront to our positions and I demand this ridiculous judgment be rescinded!"

The judge's eyes all hardened and the one who had been speaking for all of them took a step forward.

"Either you submit to a diviner, or we will pass our ruling now. You claim to be innocent, but you act as though you are guilty. So tell me, Headmistress, which will it be?"

Loquin looked back and a forth between Gold and the judges, then a nasty smile spread across her face.

"I will do neither," she yelled. "I've worked too hard and too long to be stopped here! I'll get you all back for this; mark my words!" Then, she abruptly vanished.

Keldor stared at the space she'd just been occupying with a horrified expression. Loquin's actions were basically a confession of guilt, meaning that he was now all alone. He turned back to the judges and tried one last time to bluff his way out of the situation.

"The Headmistress was clearly distraught by this grievous offense, as am I! Now drop this ridiculous charge against me, or you will have the wrath of the merchant's guild to deal with!"

The merchant's guild were extremely wealthy and had several nobles in their pockets. Keldor thought this threat alone should be enough to have them dismiss the case entirely.

"Then we will make our judgment," the lead judge announced. "We find Referee Keldor guilty of interfering in a kingdom sanctioned tournament. Furthermore, we find him guilty of colluding with the former Headmistress, Loquin, to try and kill a student during said tournament. The sentence for both parties is death; Keldor's sentence will be meted out immediately by acting Headmaster Gold. Loquin will be hunted down by the military and executed for her crimes. We will also be reporting to the king and launching an investigation to see how many of the staff have been corrupted by the merchant's guild."

Gold nodded respectfully to the judges, then turned to face Keldor, whose face had gone a sickly pale.

"Well, you heard the judgment," he said with a grin. "I'd be lying if I said I wasn't going to enjoy this."

"This isn't over you, pompous bastard!" Keldor yelled, then spun in place and made a dash for the exit.

"Oh, I think it is," Gold replied.

Keldor didn't even make it five feet. A massive stone spike shot out of the ground; impaling him right through his back and hoisting him into the air. He let out a piercing scream as the spike emerged from his chest, completely destroying his mana-heart. His body convulsed a few times as a massive amount of blood pumped from the wound. Then his head slumped forward and he went limp.

***

Morgan looked on as Gold impaled the man who had attempted to kill Sarah. He could feel a distinct sense of satisfaction, as he watched the man in his death throes.

It served him right for what he did.

He only wished that he could have killed the man himself.

"I've meted out the punishment for Keldor's crime, but what about Frush and his cousin Grub? They were definitely in on this plan and Grub had probably planned on killing my other student in a similar fashion."

Morgan turned his attention back to the arena as Gold began to speak once more. He saw one of the judges open their mouths to give a response, when the entire section they were standing in exploded outward in a shower of dust and debris, leaving a gaping hole in the arena wall.

42

Arnold looked on as the once smug referee twitched one last time before going still.

He'd been worried when the Headmistress had entered the arena, but Gold had handled the situation quite well. He could see Sarah now, sitting against one wall of the arena with a healer tending to her wounds.

He was turning his eyes to the judges when he caught a flash of something to his right. Looking over, he saw a man dressed in red flashing a small hand mirror in a pre-prepared code. The man wasn't looking at him of course, as he wouldn't know where he was, but Arnold got the message all the same.

A grim smile touched his lips as he turned his eyes to where the judges were now standing.

It was unfortunate that they would have to die. After all, they had allowed Gold to end the man who had tried to kill Sarah. But they were located the furthest from the girl and he couldn't risk killing her.

He pulled his arm back activating his *concave* skill.

He didn't get a chance to use this particular skill very often, so he was more than happy for the opportunity to do so now.

Then he thrust his arm outward, sending the force of his blow to the designated area. There was a loud crack as the air was displaced around his arm, then the section of the arena he'd been aiming for exploded outward.

He stood still for a moment to admire his work.

He'd easily killed at least a thousand people with that attack, a new personal record. He just wished he could get an exact count, just so he'd know how many he'd need to kill in order to break it.

Then, as the first panicked screams began to ring out, he dashed down the stadium stairs.

He could just make out Sarah's form through the rising cloud of dust. He would have to move quickly if he didn't want to lose her.

***

Morgan reacted, even as the screams began. He dove through the open window of his booth, dropping the few feet to the arena floor, and dashed across it to where Sarah sat against the wall. Dust billowed around him as he ran and he covered his face to avoid breathing it in.

"Are you alright?" he asked, coming to a skidding halt and crouching down near her.

"Yeah, I'm fine," she said, giving him a weak smile.

"I've patched her up as best I could," Eric said, getting to his feet. "Her body is all healed up, but her mind may need a bit more time to recover. Now, if you will excuse me, there are likely a lot of injured people that will be needing my help." And with that, Eric jogged off into the dust cloud.

"We've got to get out of here," Morgan said, pulling one of Sarah's arms over his shoulders and hoisting her to her feet.

"Yeah, probably a good idea," she replied, leaning on him for support. "Can you see Gold? He was pretty close to the wall when that explosion went off."

Morgan shook his head, casting around for a clear way out of the arena.

"He's pretty tough, so I doubt something as small as an explosion could do much to hurt him."

"You're probably right, but I'd feel a whole lot better if he was with us now. What do you think caused that explosion, anyway?" she asked as Morgan began walking toward the exit that looked to be the least clogged up.

"No idea. But whatever it was, I doubt it was an accident."

Sarah looked over to the open gap in the arena wall and shivered.

How many people had just died because they were sitting in the wrong place?

She was about to ask Morgan what he thought when a loud crack sounded over the panicked cries of the people around them.

Morgan recognized that sound and immediately threw both himself and Sarah to the ground. A moment later, the exit that they'd been heading toward exploded outward in a similar fashion to earlier attack.

He winced as he saw torn bodies being hurled through the air, their lives snuffed out in an instant.

Who on Earth had this kind of power?

He didn't waste any time pulling Sarah back to her feet.

"We need to get out of this death trap, and we need to get out *now!*"

There was no time to have Sarah climb onto his back, so he just scooped her up in his arms and ran for the open section of wall left by the explosion.

Sarah let out a little shriek as he did this, then clung tightly to him as he ran; face going white as she saw the devastation that the attack had caused.

They had only made it halfway to the opening, when a group of men wearing red and white uniforms began streaming in. They were all cloaked in mage shields and began hurling their various attacks into the fleeing masses, killing indiscriminately.

Morgan reversed his course as soon as he saw the men and bolted for the opposite exit. He could see that this one was congested as well, as panicked people tried to force their way out. Another section of the arena wall exploded, making Morgan turn yet again.

If he didn't know better, he would think that someone was deliberately stopping them from leaving. He'd debated using fly to get out, but knew they'd be too easy a target in the air.

He saw a bolt of something green heading right for him and quickly ducked, barely managing to avoid the attack. One of the men broke off from his group to come after them and Morgan cursed under his breath.

He couldn't keep running while holding Sarah like this. She was too exposed and it made avoiding attacks much more difficult.

"Can you move on your own yet?" he asked, ducking yet another attack.

"I think so," she replied, still clinging tightly to him as he dodged through the rubble strewn ground.

Morgan skidded to a halt and quickly set her down, then turned on the spot and ran back towards their attacker. His arm snapped out as he used *wind blade*, the air swirling around his arm to create the two foot lance. He used *tailwind* at the same time and rocketed toward the mage.

Morgan's drastic increase in speed and sudden change in direction completely threw the mage off. He tried to use his skill again, but Morgan was already on him. He thrust forward with the *wind blade* and the tip connected with his mage shield.

The shield shattered under the blow and Morgan's blade sank deep into the mage's eye, emerging from the back of his skull. The blade spun viciously, tearing the man's skull to pieces and by the time he pulled it back, there was little left of his head.

He dismissed his *wind blade* just as Sarah made it over to him. She looked pale and very afraid. He'd expect her to be scared in a situation like this, but not this afraid; she was practically shaking.

"What's wrong?"

"I recognize these uniforms," she said in a quiet voice. "They are the uniforms of King Edmund's elites. The most powerful supers and mages in the North Kingdom."

"Wait, so what you're saying, is that the North Kingdom is responsible for this?" Morgan asked.

This was supposed to be a neutral kingdom. What could the North possibly gain from starting a war?

"Yes, there's no doubt that King Edmund is the one behind this, though I'm not sure what he stands to gain by attacking the academy."

"That's really quite simple; the King has grown tired of neutrality and has decided to stake his claim as the rightful ruler of all the five kingdoms."

They both spun at the sound of that voice and Sarah went even paler than she already was.

A man emerged from the billowing clouds of dust. He was wearing black painted armor and had a massive sword strapped across his back. His head was bare, leaving his short cropped black hair and hard features free to the wind.

"Arnold?!" Sarah exclaimed.

"It's good to see you, Lady Sarah. You've led me on quite the merry chase," Arnold replied with a wicked smile.

Morgan wasn't sure who this man was, but judging by Sarah's reaction, this was not good.

A man came screaming out of the billowing dust, welding a mace made out of some sort of energy. Morgan recognized the uniform as belonging to the academy guard and breathed a sigh of relief.

Academy guards were highly trained and not a single one was under *rank 24*. He should be able to handle whoever this man was without too much difficulty.

Arnold didn't even break his stride. Turning on the spot, he used some sort of skill and lashed out at the guard's face with a gauntleted fist. The fist connected with an audible crunch and the guard's head exploded into a fine, bloody mist.

Morgan felt his heart rate redouble when he saw this and, for the first time, truly understood what the two of them were facing.

A monster. A monster with power that he couldn't even come close to matching.

"Should we make a run for it?" Morgan asked quietly as Arnold turned back to them; but Sarah was already shaking her head.

"There wouldn't be any point in running. He'd catch us before we made it more than a few steps."

She sounded utterly defeated and Morgan could understand those feelings well. When facing down a power like this, who wouldn't be terrified?

Someone with equal power, Morgan thought, as another academy guard came charging at Arnold.

At the moment, he didn't have nearly enough power, but maybe if he unlocked his supermage ability he'd have enough.

He grimaced as the guard's chest cavity was blown out of his back and Arnold turned to face them once more.

Probably not, but what did he have to lose at this point?

He concentrated inward and grabbed ahold of both his mana and chi.

This was going to be unpleasant, but dying would suck a lot more than feeling a little pain. This man knew Sarah, which meant that he'd most likely been sent after them by Lord Simon.

What this also meant was that this man likely had orders to kill him, or bring him back to Simon for an execution. Neither scenario sounded particularly appealing to him at the moment, as dying wasn't high on his to-do list.

"Sarah, I'm going to try and unlock my supermage ability. I know that it probably won't do us much good, but it's the best I can come up with."

"Are you sure it's a good idea to do it now?" she asked, keeping her eyes on Arnold, who was busy fighting against a group of guards who had rushed him.

"No," he replied with a wry chuckle. "But it's the best I've got."

"I'll try and keep him talking, then. I assume you know why he's here?"

"He's here to get you and kill me; that about sum it up?"

"Just about," she said, giving him a weak smile. "Now hurry up, I don't think those guards will keep him busy for long."

Morgan nodded, then turned his attention inward. He grimaced as the two streams of energy began to slowly funnel into his reiki core. The pain started just a few moments after that. It began as a dull throbbing in his chest, as his chi-heart shrank further and further; then the pain drastically increased as his chest began tightening.

He turned his eyes back towards the approaching man, to try and distract himself from the pain, just in time to see the last of the guards who'd been assaulting him, fall to the ground. Arnold smiled as he turned back to the two of them.

"I see that you were at least smart enough to not attempt an escape," he said, continuing his approach and stopping just a few feet from them.

"What the hell are you doing here, Arnold?" Sarah demanded, stepping in front of Morgan and placing her hands on her hips.

"I thought that was quite obvious. I'm here to retrieve you on your father's orders, of course, and bring him the head of that boy you're trying to hide."

"I'm perfectly content staying here, thank you very much, so you can leave!"

"I don't take orders from you," Arnold said, folding his arms over his chest and staring down at her impassively. "Now step aside, so I can kill the boy."

"Who the hell do you think you are?" she yelled at him, her voice rising in anger.

Arnold smiled a wide toothy smile, that looked more like one of a predator than a man.

"Right now, just a mercenary following orders; but once this attack is over and the Central Kingdom is ours, I'll be promoted by the king, himself!"

His smile faded then and hardened into a line.

"Now for the last time; get out of my way!"

The very air trembled under the force of those words and Sarah staggered back, bumping into Morgan, who placed a steadying hand on her shoulder.

She looked back at him, her face white and tears threatening to break out.

"Don't cry; for me," he said through clenched teeth.

The pain was horrible. His entire body was on fire and breathing had become so difficult that he could barely get any air into his lungs.

"I'll hold him off for as long as I can. Now run," he wheezed, shoving her back and stepping out in front of her to face Arnold alone.

He'd never backed down from a fight before and he wasn't about to start now.

"Morgan, you can't! He'll kill you!" Sarah begged, tears falling freely down her cheeks.

"Probably, but he'll kill me anyway. Now go," he tried to yell, but it came out as more of a croak.

Sarah tried to grab his arm, but he shrugged her off and staggered out to face Arnold; gritting his teeth against the agonizing pain wracking his entire body.

Arnold grinned when he saw this and held his arms out to the sides in a mocking gesture.

"How very noble of you. Holding off the villain, while the girl makes her escape. I must applaud your sense of dramatic flare, though I'm not sure why you look to be in so much pain; I haven't even touched you yet."

Morgan just grimaced and used one of Sarah's favorite gestures to let the man know what he thought of him.

Arnold's expression hardened and his fists clenched at his sides.

"You led me on a wild goose chase that lasted nearly three months! I'm going to enjoy killing you!" He let out a roar of anger, then ran at him.

Morgan grimaced as he took up a fighting stance.

He knew he didn't stand a chance, but he had to do his best to buy Sarah time to escape.

Arnold covered the distance in a flash and took a massive swing at his head.

From the moment Arnold began his attack, Morgan knew that he wouldn't be fast enough to dodge. He tried desperately to use *tailwind,* but for the first time ever, the skill refused to activate. He chuckled grimly as the metal-clad fist flew toward his head.

At least he'd die on his feet, facing an opponent in open battle, rather than some dark alley in City Four.

He kept his eyes wide open; refusing to close them until the very end. That was why he was able to see when a massive hammer, made out of stone, slammed into the man and sent him flying across the arena.

Morgan watched in astonishment as Arnold collided with the arena wall; creating a crater with the force of his impact.

"Oooof. That's gotta hurt!"

Morgan's head whipped around when he heard that voice and grinned as Gold emerged from the billowing clouds of dust, looking completely unharmed; with a relieved looking Sarah standing a foot or so behind him.

"About time you got here," Morgan exclaimed.

Then a massive pain wracked his entire body and he fell to the ground, as darkness washed over him.

43

Sarah ran over as Morgan hit the ground, afraid that Arnold had managed to land an attack before Gold had arrived.

"Morgan, wake up," she said, shaking him roughly, and starting to panic when he didn't respond. She felt for a pulse, placed her hand by his mouth and even pressed an ear to his chest.

There was nothing there. He was dead.

She looked up at Gold, already feeling her chest beginning to tighten as panic threatened to overtake her.

"Do calm down, Sarah," Gold said, crouching down next to her and placing his hand on Morgan's chest. His palm glowed blue for a second and then he removed it, shaking his head in bemusement.

"Of all the times to unlock his supermage ability, this is probably the worst."

"So he's not dead?" Sarah asked, in a voice full of hope.

"Well, technically speaking, he doesn't have a heart; so yes, he is dead."

Sarah's felt her heart sink yet again, as the news hit her.

"But he won't be for long," Gold continued after a few more seconds. "Give him a few minutes and he'll be up on his feet again, stronger and more powerful than ever."

"You're such an asshole!" Sarah yelled, as her face went red with anger.

This was too much for one person to handle! If she had one more scare like this today, she might seriously lose it.

"Looks like your friend is getting back up."

Sarah turned quickly to see Arnold extracting himself from the wall and shoving away the men in red uniforms who had come to help him.

"What should we do?" she asked fearfully.

She knew Gold was strong, but Arnold was a *rank 36* super. Worse still, she'd never seen him lose a fight.

"*We* won't be doing anything," Gold said. "*I* will take care of him while *you* look after Morgan. I'll try to finish this quickly; the arena may almost have emptied out, but the main fighting is happening outside these walls."

Sarah nodded, rising to her feet and activating her mage shield.

If Gold was confident he could beat Arnold, then she would make sure to do her part and keep Morgan safe.

She watched Arnold finish tearing himself free of the wall and land on the ground with a clank of rattling armor. She could see that a few of the plates were horribly mangled where Gold's attack had struck, but the man himself appeared to be unhurt.

Sarah heard the distinct slither of metal on leather, as Arnold drew the huge sword from his back and held it in a two handed grip. There was a loud whooshing sound and the blade was suddenly engulfed in bright red flames.

This wasn't the red-orange color fire usually had, but a bright crimson that painted his features in an otherworldly cast. He swished the blade through the air a few times, leaving bright red trails in its wake. Then he let out a bellow of rage that shook the entire arena, and charged.

Sarah had thought she'd known power, but the fight that unfolded before her made her rethink her entire notion of what true power really was.

As soon as Arnold had charged, Gold's mage shield surrounded him in a brilliant blue flash; but it was unlike any mage shield she'd seen before. Normally, when a mage shield was used, it would only outline a person's body and seem almost insubstantial. It would leave the user's clothes and other features uncovered.

Gold's mage shield was like a suit of armor; a solid mass of blue energy that covered every part of his body. The only part that remained uncovered was his face, which was coated in the mage shield she was used to seeing.

Gold raised his hand and massive chunks of stone tore themselves free of the surrounding walls. He gestured and they rocketed towards Arnold, converging on him with more speed than should physically be possible.

Arnold wasn't about to be outdone and, with a yell, he brought his flaming sword across to intercept them. The blade cut through the stone as easily as a hot knife through butter, leaving the areas he'd cut glowing a bright red. Gold clucked his tongue in annoyance, then the larger stones shattered and the fragments began pelting Arnold from all directions, but he managed to parry them all.

"Is that the best you can do, mage?" Arnold snarled, as he cleaved another massive boulder in two, then brought the blade up in a sweep, sending a massive column of red fire at him.

Gold flicked his wrist and a wall of stone materialized between them, blocking the flames; then he gestured outward and the wall exploded into thousands of tiny fragments.

Arnold snarled and brought his fist up, using the same skill he'd used to bust open the arena wall. The fragments of stone all turned to dust before they reached him and he grinned, pulling his fist back to use the attack again.

Suddenly, a boulder the size of a small horse landed on his head. Arnold let out a cry of pain as he was driven to the ground, losing his grip on the flaming sword. He was quick to recover and shoved the boulder off with a heave, springing back to his feet.

Sarah was shocked to see actual blood leaking from the corner of his scalp.

Gold flicked his wrist once more and another boulder flew at him. Arnold turned and punched it as hard as he could; the stone exploding into fragments as it flew passed him. Gold smiled then and the thousands of stone fragments suddenly reversed direction, flying back so quickly, that they actually broke the sound barrier.

There was a massive, sonic boom as the stone shrapnel pounded into Arnold's unprotected back. Most of it was repelled by the armor and his tough skin, but several fragments broke through; tearing muscle and breaking bone, before emerging out the other side.

The scream of pain that left Arnold's throat was so loud that Sarah was sure the entire academy had heard it.

"Well, I think that about did it," Gold said, as his mage shield disappeared.

He looked no worse for wear and was staring at the other man with an impassive expression.

Arnold took a few more staggering steps, then collapsed to his knees trying to reach around and feel for the damage that had been done. He turned bloodshot eyes on the two of them and Sarah could see blood gathering at the corners of his mouth.

"I think it's safe to come subdue him now, men," Gold called out.

A troupe of academy guards emerged from one of booths at his order and jogged over to the kneeling man.

"This isn't over, mage!" Arnold yelled. "The North will prevail and the Central Kingdom will fall!"

"From where I'm standing," Gold said, "it looks like you've lost. With their commander out of the fight, the soldiers will soon break and be routed. Then we'll send word to King Herald that the treaty has been broken and he will call upon the other kingdoms to crush Edmund and his ilk."

Arnold glared at him for another few moments; then he began to laugh.

It was a sound that chilled Sarah down to her very bones. This didn't sound like the laugh of a man who'd been defeated.

"You think that I'm the one in command of this invasion?" he cackled, as blood flecked spittle flew from his lips.

"Do you really think that King Edmund would entrust his entire military to a hired mercenary? You really have begun slipping in your old age, Gold!" His laughter continued, but soon devolved into a coughing fit. His palms hit the ground as he heaved for air, then began vomiting up blood.

"If you are not the one in charge; then who is?" Gold demanded, taking a step forward and raising his hand.

"That would be me."

Everyone turned at the sound of that voice and Sarah's eyes widened, as the most beautiful woman she'd ever seen entered the arena.

She was tall, nearly six feet and was dressed in flanged armor pained a deep red. The armor hugged her body in a way that suggested everything, yet showed nothing. She had long golden hair, which billowed out around her as she walked and bright violet eyes that seemed to glow in the light of the mid-afternoon sun. She had flawless, lightly tanned skin and when she smiled; revealed a mouth full of perfect white teeth.

Sarah instantly hated this woman.

She didn't know who she was, but anyone that perfect deserved it.

"Stop, you idiots!" Gold yelled.

Sarah turned back, just in time to see the group of guards who'd been surrounding Arnold, turned to run at the woman. Her smile didn't diminish in the slightest, as she raised an open palm towards the oncoming men. Then she swished it downward in a chopping motion and the very air tore apart.

There was a loud crack, like the sound of shattering glass, and the guards exploded into a fountain of blood; except for their heads, which landed one by one, with wet thumps on the blood soaked ground.

Sarah screamed, feeling bile coat her mouth. Then she leaned to the side and threw up, retching and heaving as she emptied the contents of her stomach.

When she straightened, the woman had already made it to Arnold and was looking down at him disapprovingly.

"My father will be quite disappointed with your performance, Arnold. Just look at you, allowing yourself to be beaten this badly. Though I suppose I can't really blame you; you were facing one of the most powerful mages this academy has to offer. Well, don't just lie there! Get up!"

Arnold got slowly to his feet; face pale from pain and blood loss.

"Sarah; I want you to take Morgan and run."

Sarah turned away from the woman as Gold began speaking. "Why? Who is she?"

"That is Princess Katherine."

Sarah felt her stomach drop.

She knew that name. Princess Katherine was King Edmund's oldest daughter and one of the most powerful supers alive. She'd once overheard her father talking to someone about her and he'd estimated her rank to be close to the maximum.

Although there weren't any wars in the last few centuries, there were always territorial disputes between the kingdoms, especially by the borders. That was where Katherine had made her name; mercilessly butchering thousands of soldiers and ending disputes within hours of her arrival.

"I see that you understand our current predicament, then," Gold said when he saw her expression. His eyes flicked back to the princess, but she was still busy chastising Arnold.

"Take this."

He pulled a small leather bag from his pocket and handed it to her. She took it, giving him a puzzled look as he bent down and lifted Morgan, who was still out cold.

"Do you think you can carry him?" he asked, as she pocketed the small pouch.

"He's not any heavier than those chains you made me carry," she tried to joke, but it fell flat.

Gold moved behind her and put Morgan onto her back.

She got a good grip under his knees and took his full weight as Gold let go.

He was surprisingly light, though she shouldn't really be surprised by that. He may have been eating regular meals over the last three months, but that couldn't erase years of malnutrition.

Gold looked them over one last time, then issued his instructions.

"CAMS is no longer safe. If Katherine is here, then I must assume that the academy has already fallen and the kingdom isn't far behind."

"What about King Herald? Surely he could stop her," Sarah asked.

"Unfortunately, the king is far away at the moment on a diplomatic mission, along with his most powerful soldiers. That's probably why the North felt secure enough to attack. By the time the king makes it back, they'll already be securely dug in and it'll be a challenge to get them out."

"So, what do we do? My father won't stop looking for me and if anyone finds out about Morgan, he'll be hunted down and killed!"

"No, not everyone will kill him. Go to the East Kingdom; once there, head for the duchy of Duke Ingram and Duchess Helga. They're old friends of mine and will be more than happy to take you in. They can be trusted to keep Morgan's secret, and can help both you and him further your abilities. Everything you'll need for the journey is in that bag I gave you. Now go; I'll hold them off while you make your escape."

Sarah stared wide eyed as the man smiled at her and patted her shoulder.

"Wait. Can you win against her?"

"Oh, most definitely not," he replied with a wide grin.

"You can't stay here, you'll die!"

"Yes, but if I can save my students, then I'll gladly sacrifice myself," he said solemnly.

Sarah felt her bottom lip begin to tremble, but Gold continued speaking.

"Then again, I do have a way to escape once you've made it far enough away, so maybe I'll use that instead of dying," he said, with a thoughtful expression.

"You're a real asshole, you know that?" Sarah yelled.

"Yup! Now you better get going. I think the Princess is gearing up for a fight."

Sarah turned her head and sure enough, Katherine was now approaching them; Arnold staggering along behind her and looking thoroughly miserable.

44

Sarah dug in her heels and ran, clutching tighter to Morgan's legs as she felt him shifting around on her back. She heard a shout from behind her and looked back to see Gold raising a massive wall of stone between himself and Katherine.

There was no way that would stop her, but it might slow her down.

There was a loud, echoing boom and Sarah heard the distinct sound of cracking stone. She didn't look back this time, instead focusing on running even faster. She exited the arena and swung her head back and forth, looking for her best path out of the academy.

She knew that there were many ways to get in and out, but the streets were swarming with soldiers and she didn't want to run into any.

Finally making a decision, she turned east and dashed down the cobbled path.

She'd decided it would be best to take the most direct route and hope she didn't run into anyone.

As she ran, she could see the damage that had been done to the academy. Over half of the structures she passed were either on fire, completely destroyed, or were in the process of being looted. Soldiers were moving around in small groups and attacking anyone in sight; so whenever she spotted a soldier in red, she would duck behind a building and wait for them to pass.

The dead were also a prevalent sight as she wound her way through the ruined grounds. Bodies littered streets; some still breathing, while others lay ominously still. Sarah thought she preferred the dead; every time she passed a living person, they would cry out for help. Their piteous pleas were enough to make her sick; and had she not already emptied the contents of her stomach, she would be doing so now.

She came to the end of a block and, lost in her thoughts, dashed carelessly out between two buildings, and right into a group of soldiers. Both groups stared at each other for a few moments; then the lead soldier raised his hand and blasted something at her.

Sarah's mage shield flared to life around her and the attack bounced off. The other soldiers began to take aim, but she wasn't about to wait around and let them kill her. She dashed past them and into the mouth of an alley.

Maybe they wouldn't bother following her.

"After her!" She heard one of them cry out.

Of course they wouldn't let her go.

There were six of them in all and, with Sarah encumbered as she was, she knew they would catch up with her soon. She took a sharp corner and her foot skidded on a patch of blood. She was lucky she had; as the corner of the building near her head was blown clean off.

She grimaced, flinching away from the wall and trying to run faster.

"We're gaining on her! She can't keep it up for much longer!"

Sarah chanced a glance over her shoulder and cursed once more.

They were only thirty or so feet back and would catch her within a matter of seconds.

She burst out from the alley and found herself running through an open courtyard. There was a huge water fountain right in the middle of the cobbled space; and just beyond she could see an exit heading into the city.

The courtyard was completely deserted; meaning that none of the soldiers had made it here yet. If she could somehow manage to stop them, then she and Morgan could escape.

Dashing around the fountain, she lowered Morgan gently to the ground. *The lip of the fountain should protect him from any stray attacks,* she thought.

"I hope you wake up soon, Morgan. I could really use your help!" she said, rising quickly to her feet.

She'd just managed to make it to the front of the fountain when the soldiers emerged into the courtyard.

"Finally decided to give up?" the lead soldier asked with a smirk, as the others quickly spread out into a semi-circle before the fountain.

"Not even close, asshole!" Sarah yelled, then used her *condense water* skill.

Her skill was unique, in that she could use it on as large a scale as she wanted; albeit at a massive increase in mana consumption. She somehow had a feeling that this was not a time to be conserving mana.

Sarah gritted her teeth as her *MP* began plummeting at an alarming rate. The lead soldier had taken another step forward when the fountain behind her exploded and over a thousand gallons of water rose into the air.

What she was doing right now was only possible, due to the presence of the fountain. It would have been impossible to conjure this much water otherwise.

The lead soldier's cocky look vanished in an instant and he opened his mouth to issue a command, but never got the chance.

Sarah screamed as the water moved around her in a swirling vortex; then she thrust her arms outward, sending the water in a wide arc at the soldiers. Two of them managed to fire off attacks before the water hit. One completely missed her, but the other slammed into her shoulder.

Her shield just managed to absorb the attack before shattering under the pressure, but she didn't let up on her attack for a moment. As soon as the water hit all of her targets, she triggered the secondary effect of the skill. There was a loud cracking sound as the water froze solid and she slumped to the ground as her *MP* hit zero.

Despite her exhaustion and her mounting headache, Sarah couldn't help but marvel at what she'd just done.

All of the soldiers were frozen solid inside a three foot thick wall of ice. Even if they did manage to survive, they wouldn't be giving chase anytime soon. All she needed was a minute or two to recover, then she and Morgan could be on their way.

She got to her feet, swaying a bit with the fatigue and made her way back around the now ruined fountain. Morgan was still lying unconscious and she began to worry at how long it was taking him to wake up.

It had been nearly twenty minutes since he'd passed out and she didn't have any idea of what amount of time was normal for this. Then she noticed something that she hadn't before. It was very slight and she would have missed it, had she not been looking very carefully. He was breathing again.

Sarah quickly placed her ear to his chest and after a few seconds, she heard a very faint heartbeat.

He'd done it! The reiki core had successfully shifted over and was now acting as his heart, which meant that he should be waking up any second now.

Sarah straightened from her kneeling position over him and felt herself smiling, even though what was happening around them was horrible. The academy had been sacked and thousands were most likely dead, but she just couldn't bring herself to care about that at the moment. Morgan was alive and that was all that mattered to her.

"There they are! I told you I saw the bitch heading this way!"

Sarah felt her blood run cold as she heard that voice. It belonged to the last person she'd wanted to run into at the moment.

Looking up from her kneeling position, she saw Grub and Frush emerging from the alley and they were both grinning from ear to ear.

***

Morgan's eyes opened and he took a deep, shuddering breath. He blinked a few times as bright sunlight filtered down through the foliage overhead. He was sitting in a clearing surrounded on all sides by massive trees that towered hundreds of feet above his head.

Where was he?

Getting slowly to his feet, Morgan began to look around the clearing, until his eyes focused on a small cottage near the opposite end. A table was set out in front and a man sat there, sipping tea and reading a book.

How strange. The last thing he remembered was the arena. *How had he gotten here? He decided that his best option would be to ask the stranger. Maybe he could help him.*

"Excuse me," he called out as he approached the man. "Can you tell me where I am?"

The man looked up from his book as Morgan called out, and he smiled, closing it and placing it down on the table.

"That is a difficult question to answer, young supermage, but have a seat and I will do my best to explain."

The man had a deep and mellow voice which Morgan found very relaxing.

He knew he should have been surprised that the man knew what he was, but for some reason he just wasn't. The man seemed to exude an aura of peace and he felt better just standing near him.

Morgan took a seat across from the man and got his first good look at him. The man had very plain features. Short black hair, dark colored eyes and a dark complexion.

He felt as though he knew this man, but at the same time he'd never seen him before.

Then the man smiled once again; his white teeth contrasting with his dark skin and Morgan felt all his worries simply melt away.

It didn't matter who this man was. So long as he could sit here and bask in his aura, he would be content.

"It's good to finally meet you, Morgan. I would have liked to meet you sooner, but circumstances beyond my control have made that difficult until now."

"Who are you? Where are we? How do you know who I am? And why would you want to meet me?" Morgan asked

The man laughed at this; a deep resounding sound that made Morgan smile for some reason.

"Please, do excuse me," the man said as his laughter died down. "It has been so long since I have experienced the exuberance of youth." He chuckled again, then settled back into his chair.

"To answer your first question; my name is Dabu and I am a supermage who has reached omniscience. As to where we are; let's just say that we are in a world between worlds, neither in the realm of mortals, nor in the realm of gods. Though it has been quite some time since I have walked in the realms of mortals, I cannot help checking in from time to time; and that, young Morgan, is how I came to know of you. As to why I wanted to meet you… Well you are a special one, even among supermages. Your aura stands out like a bonfire in a ring of candles. I know you must have many questions, but staying here for too long is perilous for those who have not yet broken the bonds of mortality. You are also desperately needed back on your world, so I will allow you to ask three questions; after which you will have five minutes to look over your new status. I am sorry that I can't do more, but for now this is all I can do."

Morgan slumped back into his chair as the deluge of new information washed over him.

He had a thousand questions, but he could only ask three? Why was it, that everyone he met who had answers, always had to be so cryptic?!

"You said that you were a supermage who had reached omniscience; what did you mean by that?"

This was the first question he'd decided to ask, as it pertained directly to his new ability.

"Omniscient is the highest *rank* a supermage can achieve. Unlike regular supers and mages, supermages do not stop growing after *50 ranks*. Supermages will grow until they reach *rank 99* and only after that will they become omniscient."

Morgan gritted his teeth in frustration.

He really wished he hadn't asked that question. The answer had only given him more questions.

"You implied that you are immortal, how is that possible?"

This was another question that he needed answered. If he could somehow find a way to avoid dying, fighting powerful enemies would become a whole lot easier.

"Once a supermage reaches their final *rank*, the path to immortality becomes clear. I'm sorry that I can't give you a straight answer, but even if I explained it to you, your mind would not be able to comprehend it."

Of course the answer would have to be some cryptic mumbo jumbo like that.

Morgan thought carefully about his last question.

He was about to ask if he knew who his parents were, when a memory of his first lesson with Gold popped into his mind. He wasn't sure why it had, but now that it was there, he just had to know.

"Who stopped the Tyrant King's war all those years ago?"

He knew right away that this had been the correct question to ask. The figure who'd stopped the war had also been the one who shaped the world into what it was today. Even though the question of his parentage had bothered him his entire life, he felt that it was of the utmost importance, to know who this being was.

Dabu started when he asked this question and a shocked expression came to his face.

"How is it that you know about the Tyrant King's war? I thought that all knowledge of that time had been erased."

"My instructor at the academy founded by King Herald told me about this in my first lesson. He told me that it was important to know where out abilities came from and why they work the way they do."

Dabu looked lost in though for a few moments, then sat up straighter.

"Then perhaps I have not been keeping as close of an eye on the mortal realms as I thought. To answer your question, the one who ended the war and created the power structure you are familiar with, is a being as old as time itself. I have never personally met him, but I know that he likes to wander the mortal realms in the guise of a traveler. He likes to go by a certain name while there. Now what was it…"

Dabu tapped his fingers on the table for a few moments as he tried to recall. Then he snapped his fingers and smiled.

"Samuel. That's what he likes to call himself."

Morgan froze, feeling his stomach drop out from under him.

"Is something the matter?" Dabu asked, when he saw the look on Morgan's face.

"I met a traveler by that name when I was running from a city lord," he answered dumbly. "I had been terribly injured during a fight, but he healed me back to perfect health. Then he told me to be careful how I used my abilities and vanished into thin air."

"That does sound like him," Dabu said with a thoughtful expression. "Guess he must have taken a liking to you ,if he was willing to help."

Morgan opened his mouth to say something when a horrible pain shot though his head. It was gone in a second, but Dabu didn't miss his grimace of pain.

"I'm afraid that our time together is up. You must look through you status now, otherwise you won't know how to use your new abilities when you get back."

"How will I be getting back?" Morgan asked.

"Your physical body is still in the mortal world; only your mind has traveled here. Now no more questions, your friend is in peril and you will be, too, if you stay too much longer."

That put an end to all of his questions.

If Sarah was in danger, then he had to get back to her as soon as he could.

He nodded once to Dabu, then reached inside himself for his new source of power.

45

"What do you assholes want?" Sarah asked, grimacing as she rose back to her feet.

This was not good. Her mana was regenerating slowly, but she wouldn't be able to use her skills more than a couple of times before it ran out again. Plus, Morgan was still unconscious and she didn't think these two would wait for him to wake up before attacking him.

"I think you know what we want," Frush said with a snarl. "You were supposed to die back in the arena, but because of you, our cousin Keldor was killed instead!"

"And don't think we forgot about that other asshole, either," Grub put in. "I was supposed to finish him off, but because of your interfering teacher, I didn't get the chance."

He grinned as cracks appeared in the ground beneath his feet and chunks of stone floated up to begin coating his body.

"My interfering teacher?!" Sarah yelled, her face turning red. "The only reason you even stood a chance against me in the arena, is because your bastard of a cousin cheated! Without him here, neither of you stand a chance. And, since no one is watching, there's nothing to stop me from killing you."

Her fists clenched and three *icicle spears* appeared in front of her.

It was a bluff, of course, as the three spears she'd conjured had completely depleted her mana once again. All she could do was hope that they would back down. They hadn't seen Morgan yet, because he was hidden by the lip of the fountain, but she knew that if they came any closer, they would spot him.

Frush took a step back as the spears appeared in the air, but Grub only laughed.

"You're bluffing!" he said, as his stone armor finished covering him. "It's pretty hard to miss the wall of ice covering those soldiers; and seeing as you haven't moved on yet, the fight ended no more than a few minutes ago. Even if you weren't exhausted, which I'm sure you are, you couldn't hurt me with those little icicles."

"Are you sure about this?" Frush asked.

"Yeah, I'm sure. If she had any *MP* don't you think she'd have attacked us right away?"

Sarah cursed as Frush's expression changed from one of fear to one of arrogance.

Little coward.

He'd been terrified a moment ago, when he'd thought she could put up a fight, but now he was ready to go at it.

"I always knew it would come to this, you bitch!" Frush screeched in an excited tone.

His skin began to shift in color until it was the same blue and black that it had been in the arena. His features also became distinctively more froglike and he cackled loudly.

"Now, I'll be able to get you back for the humiliation and pain you caused me. Even though the healers managed to fix it, it just hasn't felt quite the same, no matter how many girls I've persuaded to test it for me!"

He calmed a bit and began walking towards her with a noticeable bounce in his step.

"But don't worry; I'm sure you'll help me test it one last time, before you die!"

Sarah felt her blood boil at those words.

So this sadistic bastard had raped a whole bunch of girls since, and was again planning to do the same to her? Not a chance!

Without any warning, she sent all three *icicle spears* flying at him, intending to end the fight, and worry about Grub next.

Frush flinched back as the spears approached, but Grub was unbelievably fast and moved to shield his cousin. The three spears smashed into his rocky armor; one shattered on impact, but the other two managed to punch through cracks in his defenses.

Unfortunately for Sarah, neither had gone deep enough to cause any real injury.

"That the best you got, bitch?" Grub roared.

Sarah cursed, taking one last look down at Morgan.

There was only one thing she could do now. She would have to lead them away from him and hope he wasn't spotted.

She dashed out from behind the fountain and made a rush for one of the alleys to her right.

"Oh, no you don't!" Frush screamed, leaping after her and catching up within a matter of seconds. He reached out to put an arm on her shoulder, but Sarah twisted out of the way and kicked him in the shin.

He staggered back, cursing in pain as Sarah attempted to make a break for it.

"Take one more step and your boyfriend gets it!"

Sarah spun around and had her worst fears confirmed. Grub had spotted Morgan and was leaning over him with a wicked smile on his face.

"Now, you're going to be a good girl and not resist what's about to happen. Otherwise…" Grub pulled his thumb across his throat in a very clear message.

Frush, now recovered from the attack, flashed his cousin a grin. Then he turned his attention on Sarah. He licked his lips and Sarah shivered as she saw a long slimy tongue instead of a human one.

"You bastards won't get away with this!" she yelled as Frush came closer.

She wanted to run, but knew if she tried to resist, Morgan would be killed. They were likely both going to die anyway, but if she could buy him enough time to wake up, they might be able to get out of this.

"Oh, I think we will," Frush said, laying a hand on her shoulder.

Sarah had been expecting her body to freeze, but was surprised when it didn't.

"I'm not going to freeze you," Frush said as he trailed his fingers up to her chin. "How will I hear your screams if you can't move?"

His hand moved away from her face and he slapped her; hard. She winced as her head was rocked to the side, but she otherwise didn't move.

When Frush saw her defiant expression, it just made his smile grow wider.

"Good. I like it when they're all tough. It'll make it all the more pleasurable when you crack and start begging me to stop!"

He slapped her again, even as his other hand moved down and started undoing the strap holding her pants in place.

Sarah winced again as the slap rocked her head to the side, but she didn't give him the satisfaction of crying out. She could feel

Frush tugging at her pants, but her eyes were locked on Morgan. Despite her outward calm, she felt her heart thundering in her chest, as her pants buckle came loose.

Morgan! I really need you right now!

She could hear Frush panting in excitement, as his thumbs hooked into the waistband of her pants and she closed her eyes, waiting for the inevitable.

* * *

Morgan felt the power flow up from his new reiki-heart, as he accessed it for the first time.

This felt nothing like combining mana and chi to open his status. Compared to what he was feeling now, that had only been a cheap imitation.

The status screen that opened before his eyes was a deep, rich and vibrant purple; not at all like the pale color he'd seen previously.

His eyes began moving rapidly over the status to see what changes had been made.

Name: Morgan
Supermage: Rank - 9
Energy to next rank - 0/18,000
Ability - Divine Gravity & Air
RP - 580/580 (Regen - 5.6 per second)
Strength - 53
Agility - 64
Constitution - 57
Intelligence - 58
Wisdom - 56
Skills - Enhanced flight, Heavy impact, Gale force, Condensed wind blade
Traits - Gravity field, Recovery
Extra - Gravity storm

Whoa!

Those were some serious changes. Gold hadn't been kidding about the increase in energy cost, either. It was more than triple than his last rank up. His attributes had also gotten a major boost. No wonder the difference between 8 and 9 was so big.

His mage and super abilities were gone now, replaced by the supermage ability. His CP and MP were also gone, replaced by RP, which he guessed to be reiki points. But what on earth did 'Divine Gravity & Air' mean?

He tried to select the ability tab, but it refused to open.

That was odd. Last time both his mage and super ability had opened without any issue.

What was also new, were the changes to his skills and the addition of two new tabs in his status. He wondered if they were exclusive to supermages, or of they were added after the first breakthrough rank. He would have to ask Sarah after she ranked up to be sure.

He directed his attention to his skills tab and opened it up to view the changes. Thankfully, these opened without any problems and he stared in amazement at the new descriptions.

Enhanced flight - Manipulate gravity and air to reduce your weight and move quickly through the air.
Cost - 10 RP per second
Max. height - 60 Ft
Max. speed - 40 Ft per second
Max. carry weight - 200 pounds (Adding any more weight will reduce speed by 1 foot per second for each additional pound).

Heavy impact - Manipulate gravity and air to make your blows land significantly harder (Currently X2.25).
Cost - 15 RP per second

Condensed wind blade - Manipulate gravity and air to create a dense whirling blade in the shape of your choice. The type of weapon you create will determine additional effects.
Piercing weapon - Double damage is dealt to mages, or beasts with mage abilities.
Slashing weapon - Double damage is dealt to supers, or beasts with super abilities.
Cost - 350 RP
Duration - Until dismissed

Gale force - Manipulate gravity and air to significantly increase your speed (Currently X2.25).
Cost - 15 RP per second

Morgan wasn't sure whether to be ecstatic, or scream in rage.

His new skills were amazing, but the cost of each had gone up by so much that he would have to massively increase his intelligence, if he wanted to use them for any prolonged period of time. Not to mention that if he used several skills simultaneously, his RP would be depleted within a few minutes.

He sighed and closed the tab, deciding that he would only judge his new skills once he got to test them out. Next he opened the traits tab and read the description.

Traits: Traits are a special skill unique to supermages. They are skills that are always active and do not cost any RP to use.

Well that answered his question about whether it was unique to supermages. It was nice that his status was helpful for once.

Gravity field - Your body is surrounded by a dense field of gravity, making all attacks; both physical and magical, 10% less damaging.

Recovery - The spirits of the air have blessed you with the power of healing. If you can survive for 24 hours after being wounded; no matter the injury, your body will be completely healed.

Holy crap! Now this was something that he could get behind. Less damage from all attacks and his body would heal itself?!

He felt like jumping up from his seat and cheering.

"You have sixty seconds."

Dabu's quiet voice reminded Morgan that he was short on time, so he closed the traits tab and opened the last one.

Extra: Extra skills are skills unique to supermages. While both supers and mages get access to a new skill after a breakthrough rank; supermages get access to an extra powerful skill, that is a unique combination of their abilities.

> *Gravity storm - Create a storm of intense gravity, damaging winds and lighting strikes in a targeted area.*
> *Cost - 600 RP*
> *AOE - 30 Ft*
> *Duration - 30 seconds*
> *Cooldown - 8 hours*

Now that was one hell of a skill! It cost so much that he couldn't even use it yet and even when he could, he would only be able to use it once every 8 hours. Still, he could attack an area that was 30 feet in diameter and wouldn't need to worry about getting in close.

He'd really been missing ranged attacks from his arsenal, so this would really be helpful if he found himself in a pinch.

He closed his status and looked up at Dabu. The man was smiling and Morgan found himself relaxing once again.

What was it about this man? He'd never felt so at ease in front of a stranger in his entire life, but Dabu seemed to exude such an aura of peace that he just couldn't help himself.

"Your time here is nearly up and it will be quite some time before we can speak again; so allow me to give you one last piece of advice before you go. Keep your friends close and be wary of strangers you meet in the night. You have now entered into a new world and those that hold power here do not take kindly to new arrivals."

Morgan was about to ask the man what he was talking about, when the forest glade disappeared and he found himself lying on his back, with Grub's knee pressed against his chest.

46

Sarah clenched her jaw as she felt Frush's fingers begin to tug her pants down.

Morgan, where are you?!

She bit her lip as she felt her pants move down another inch. Then she felt the fingers in her waistband go inexplicably slack. She trembled, wondering what new twisted idea Frush had come up with, when she heard him screech in pain. Her eyes snapped open in an instant and she took in the new scene unfolding before her.

Frush had staggered back from her and was screaming in pain as he stared at the two stumps where his hands used to be. His skin had shifted back to it's normal sickly pale color as blood pumped out of the severed limbs at a prodigious rate.

"What the hell?" Sarah exclaimed, staring in disbelief at the screaming boy.

"I'm sorry it took me so long."

Those words were enough to make her heart skip a beat and she whirled to face Morgan, a huge smile already spreading across her face.

***

The air was knocked out of his lungs as Sarah crashed into him and he hugged her back, despite his discomfort with the gesture.

He wouldn't complain about it this time. From the looks of it, Frush had been about to do something terrible to her; though he couldn't really see what, as his vision had been obscured.

Once she let go of him, Morgan looked down at her with an odd expression.

"Your pants are unbuttoned."

"No shit!" Sarah yelled, as her smile melted away to be replaced by a grimace.

"It's thanks to that asshole over there." She gestured to Frush, who had tucked the stumps of his arms into his armpits to try and staunch the bleeding.

"Why would he want to unbutton your pants?" Morgan asked, becoming even more confused.

The guards back in City Four had enjoyed grabbing women through their clothes. Wouldn't removing them defeat the whole purpose?

Sarah just stared at him for a few seconds, before shaking her head.

"Your social skills need a lot of work. When we get to the East Kingdom Duchy where Gold sent us, I'll make sure that you get a tutor! Now give me a second while I take care of some unfinished business!" She growled, then stalked over to Frush.

Gold was sending them to the East Kingdom? When had that been decided? And what on earth was a Duchy?

Sarah formed a large, needle sharp, icicle as she approached, using her *condense water* skill. Frush whimpered in pain as Sarah grabbed him by the collar and yanked him forward until he was looking into her eyes.

"I told you that you wouldn't get away with this," Sarah growled, as terror flashed in the boy's eyes. "This isn't just for me, but for all the women you've raped during your miserable life!"

"No, don't," was all he managed to get out, before Sarah rammed the icicle up under his chin and deep into his brain.

She let go of his body and let it drop to the ground; where he twitched a few times before growing still. She fastened the straps on her pants, then spit on the boy's corpse.

He deserved a lot worse than a quick death, but a least he'd suffered for a bit after Morgan had lopped his hands off. *Come to think of it, how had he done that; and what had happened to Grub?*

Turning back to Morgan, she could see him standing still with a thoughtful expression on his face. Looking past him, she could see Grub, getting slowly to his feet near the fountain. He looked to be badly injured; one of his arms was bent the wrong way and he was bleeding from several gashes along his legs.

"Uh, Morgan," Sarah said, as Grub used his skill and stone began forming over his body again. "I think you should look behind you."

Morgan started, then looked over his shoulder and an expression of annoyance crossed his features, as Grub began running at them.

He really didn't have anything against the idiot. The only one that he hated was Frush; and that was because he'd hurt Sarah. But for some inexplicable reason, this boy hated him. Well, he'd given him enough chances to back down. If this moron wanted to die that badly, then he would oblige.

Sarah stared as Morgan seemed to disappear from where he'd been standing, only to reappear right in front of the shocked Grub. There was a loud howling sound as a lance of purple and black energy formed around his arm. Then he brought it up and plunged it straight through his chest.

Morgan tore the *blade* free as he watched Grub fall back and hit the ground; blood already pooling around him as he stared up at the sky. After a few moments, his body went still.

Morgan dismissed his new *condensed wind blade* and walked back over to Sarah, who was staring at him in awe.

"That was amazing!" she exclaimed. "Guess the whole supermage thing wasn't all made up then."

"Yeah. It's real, alright. Now what's been going on since I passed out? The last thing I remember is Gold showing up in the arena."

"I'll tell you about it on the way; for now we really need to go."

"Alright, then. Hop onto my back. My skills have been upgraded, so now I can move pretty quickly through the air; not to mention that I can use my other skills at the same time. So if I use my upgraded *gale force* skill, I can move through the air two and a half times faster than normal."

"Wow! If your skills got that much of a boost, I can't wait to rank up!" she answered excitedly.

She was about to get on Morgan's back when she caught something glimmering out of the corner of her eye. Turning back to Frush's body, she could see something shiny sticking out of one of his pockets.

"What's wrong?" Morgan asked, when she didn't immediately get on.

"There's something sticking out of Frush's pocket," she said, squinting and trying to get a better look.

She was curious as to what it was, but not enough that she'd go loot his corpse.

Morgan had no such qualms. He walked right over to the dead boy and leaned down to rummage through his pockets. After a few moments, he stood back up and let out a bark of laughter.

"What's so funny?" Sarah asked, not able to see what he was holding.

Morgan turned around and she could see two large cores in one hand and two shining platinum coins in the other.

"That sneaky bastard stole the tournament prizes?!" Sarah yelled

Morgan continued laughing, walking back over and handing her one of the cores.

"The way I see it, you would have won if they hadn't cheated; so one of these is rightfully yours."

Sarah stared at the swirling red and blue core in her palm for a few seconds; then looked back up at Morgan, her eyes shining.

"Better check yours to make sure they didn't take any energy from it," she said.

"Good thinking."

Morgan concentrated for a moment, then brought up the core's status.

Name: Azure-crystal wyvern core
Rank - 39
Total available energy - 68,376/68,376

This core was taken from an azure-crystal wyvern. As this core is from an advanced beast, the amount of available energy has been massively increased.

The amount of available energy was staggering! There was likely enough here to boost him four or five ranks. He had no idea what a wyvern was, or what an advanced beast was either, but he knew one thing for sure; he needed to find more beasts like these!

"Mine hasn't been touched and the amount of energy is massive!" Sarah said as Morgan closed the status of the core.

"Neither has mine. What beast did your core come from?" Morgan asked as he stashed his core away in one of his pockets.

"An azure-crystal wyvern; yours?"

"Same," Morgan replied, a little disappointed that she hadn't had a different one. "Oh, one of these are yours too," he said, flipping her one of the platinum coins.

Sarah deftly caught it, then pocketed the coin with a nod of thanks.

"Should we be stopping back at our house to get our stuff?"

Sarah shook her head.

"Gold said it would be too dangerous, but he gave me a small bag and said that it had everything we'd need."

She stuck her hand into one of her pockets and fished out the small leather bag.

"How would everything we need fit into that tiny thing?" he asked, moving closer to her and trying to peek in.

Sarah pulled apart the drawstring and upended the bag, but nothing came out. She shook it a few times, expecting that whatever was in there must be stuck, but still nothing happened.

"Do you think this is one of his sick jokes?" Morgan asked.

"Could be," she said with a sigh, sticking her hand into the bag to see if she'd somehow missed something. After a few seconds, her eyes widened; then her entire forearm disappeared up to the elbow. She let out a loud laugh as she pulled her arm out, clutching a large brown bag that turned out to be her money pouch.

Morgan stared, not understanding how such a large pouch could have fit into such a small one; then it hit him.

"This bag must have the same enchantment as the buildings we trained in!" he exclaimed excitedly. "Quick, check to see what else he's packed for us."

After a few more minutes of rummaging, Sarah came up with all of their clothes; including new gear for cold weather, a month's supply of trail rations and all the cores they'd managed to collect since they stopped using them.

Morgan quickly spotted his money pouch as well and found all the gold still there. His platinum coin soon joined them and he stuck the pouch in his pocket; not trusting anyone else to handle his money. He also found the ice-bristle wolf core among the others and was quick to pocket that as well.

The last thing Sarah pulled from the bag was a small leather sack containing four small circular devices and a note.

"What are these?" Sarah asked, spilling the small circles of metal onto the ground.

They were all marked with numbers; one a *9,* another *12* and a third *18.* The last one was marked with two numbers separated by a line *6 - 31.* It took Morgan a few moments to figure out what they were, but when he did, a wide grin split his face.

"They're *Beast Zone* keys and it looks like he's even included a *staged zone* key as well!" Morgan exclaimed.

Sarah stared at them for a few moments as well, then opened up the note and read it out loud.

Now you can't say that I've never done anything for you.

-Gold

"Of course he'd have to be an asshole about it," Sarah said, folding up the note; but she was smiling as she did so.

They packed everything back into the bag and Sarah pulled the drawstring shut, tucking it back into her pocket.

"I guess we should get going then," she said, stretching her arms over her head and arching her back.

"Yeah. We've got a long trip ahead of us if we're heading into the East Kingdom," Morgan said as she climbed onto his back.

"I forgot to mention the best past about my *fly* skill being upgraded," he said as Sarah settled in behind him.

"Oh, yeah?" Sarah asked, placing her cheek against Morgan's back as he floated up off the ground. "And what would that be?"

Morgan snickered as he began to build up speed.

"Your weight will no longer give me a penalty to speed!"

A loud, ringing slap echoed out across the empty courtyard; then there was silence.

Epilogue

Arnold tromped through the destroyed academy grounds with a scowl on his face.

Nothing had turned out right from the moment the attack started. Sure, they'd won the day and the city was theirs, but he'd failed in his mission. Not only had Sarah and Morgan escaped, but that damned Gold had somehow managed to slip out right from under their fingers!

He slammed his fist against the side of a building, sending cracks across the solid stone. A few passing soldiers eyed him nervously and walked just a little faster.

The attack was a success, so he was going to be promoted by the king himself; but Lord Simon wasn't the type to forget about failure and he wasn't delusional enough to think that the king's protection would save him if Simon decided he should die.

"Damn it!" he yelled, slamming a fist into another building, this time reducing the wall to rubble.

"Something troubling you, Arnold?"

Arnold sighed and turned to see Weasel emerging from an alleyway, his ever present smirk fixed firmly in place.

This was the first time he'd seen him since before the battle and he'd secretly been hoping that he wouldn't survive. Weasel might be the best tracker he knew, but he absolutely hated working with him.

"Figures you'd manage to survive," Arnold said, regaining his composure.

"I'm hurt," Weasel said with a mock frown. "Aren't you glad that your favorite tracker managed to stay alive?"

"No," Arnold answered bluntly.

Weasel laughed; a high pitched sound that grated on his nerves.

"You might be a bastard, but at least you're an honest one," Weasel said as his smirk fixed itself in place once again.

"Just tell me what you want or leave," Arnold snarled, folding his arms across his chest. "I have no patience to deal with you right now."

"My, my; aren't we impatient today. Fine, I just thought you'd like to know that I found the last place your quarry was before they left the academy grounds. Unfortunately, I was unable to pick up their trail. They must have wised up and found a way to foil my ability."

"Is that all?" Arnold asked with a snort. "All you're telling me, is that you know where they were and nothing else."

"Oh, there was one other thing," Weasel said as his smirk grew even more self satisfied. "There were several people in that particular area. I thought they were all dead, but just when I was about to leave, I noticed that one of them was still moving."

Now this got Arnold's interest.

"Where is he?" he asked excitedly.

"In the temporary headquarters set up by the main square," Weasel said, turning his back to him and staring to walk away.

"You'd better hurry, though. I hear that the Princess will be interviewing him soon and I'm guessing you'll want to be there when she does."

Arnold gritted his teeth and took off running toward the main square; Weasel's echoing laughter following as he did so.

He would kill that bastard one day, but Princess Katherine was known to kill people on a whim. If he made it there too late, the boy could already be dead and any lead on Sarah would be lost.

Arnold burst into the main building and grabbed the first soldier he saw.

"Where is the witness?" he yelled.

The soldier, who was obviously terrified of the intimidating man, began stuttering out an answer.

"First door down the hall!"

The soldier screamed as Arnold hurled him away with enough force to crack the wall behind him.

He'd better still be alive!

Arnold grabbed the door handle and practically tore the door off its hinges, looking wildly around the room.

The boy, who had been lying down, sat bolt upright as the door flew open, a look of terror on his face.

"My apologies for barging in," Arnold said, when he saw they were alone.

He closed the door behind him and walked over to sit in an empty chair.

The boy didn't say anything, simply kept his eyes on him as he sat.

"I hear that you have some information on two people that I'm very interested in finding. Their names are Sarah and Morgan."

As soon as he mentioned the two names, the boy's face twisted in hatred.

"Why do you want to know about that smug bastard and his murdering bitch of a girlfriend?"

Arnold blinked.

This wasn't at all the response he'd been expecting. Why did this boy hate them both so much?

"I've been ordered to retrieve Lady Sarah, as she is a noblewoman of the North; as for Morgan, I've been ordered to kill him. Now, will you help me find them?"

The boy looked a little surprised by that answer and his face scrunched up as he tried to make up his mind.

Arnold waited patiently while the boy decided, all the while keeping an eye on the door.

He didn't need Katherine to come in and ruin everything at the last moment.

"I don't really care about the bitch one way or the other," the boy finally spoke up. "The only reason I wanted her dead is because she killed my cousin; but he was a twisted bastard, so I really don't care either way."

His face darkened and rage burned behind his eyes as he continued.

"Morgan, on the other hand; I want him dead! I want to kill that bastard with my bare hands. I'll help you, but only on the condition that you take me with you and let me kill him myself!"

He was breathing hard by the time he was finished. Fists, clenched at his sides and face, an unhealthy shade of red.

Arnold laughed; a deep menacing chuckle that reverberated around the room, chilling its other occupant to the bone and making him wonder if he'd gone too far.

"I like your style, kid!" Arnold said with a grin. "You've got a deal; now tell me what you know."

The boy visibly relaxed when Arnold agreed to his demands and began telling his story.

"I'm not sure exactly where they were headed, as I was going in and out of consciousness; but I know for sure that they're headed to a Duchy in the East Kingdom."

Arnold looked thoughtful at this.

There were several Duchies in the East Kingdom, all of them quite large; but this was definitely more than Weasel had been able to give him. He would have to check in with some of his contacts there to see if they'd been spotted, but this was a start.

"Very well, boy," Arnold said, rising to his feet. "We're expecting a message from King Edmund in a few days. Once we receive it, the two of us will be going after them."

He was heading to the door when the boy spoke up once more.

"One last thing before you go."

Arnold turned back and raised an eyebrow. The boy looked hesitant for a moment, as if not sure whether to say something or not, but then his expression firmed and he spoke up.

"There's something very wrong with Morgan."

"Oh? How do you mean?" Arnold asked.

"I mean that I've fought him before. I'm not too proud to admit that he's stronger than me, but this last time I fought him, he was in a whole other league."

"How so?"

Arnold's head whipped around as Princess Katherine walked into the room. She looked perfect, as always, and he noticed that the boy's eyes were taking in every ounce of her figure.

Katherine smirked as the boy's eyes roamed over her. She was perfectly aware of how well endowed she was and used her looks nearly as often as her fists, to get what she wanted.

"How so?" she prodded again and the boy's eyes snapped up to hers, his face reddening at being caught staring.

He cleared his throat nervously and Arnold had to suppress the urge to scowl.

Of course she would have to come here now.

"He was unconscious when we came across the two of them. I had him pinned down while my cousin was taking care of Sarah."

He noticed Katherine's lips tighten a bit at that and he remembered that Sarah was supposed to be a noble.

"He didn't get a chance to do anything," he said quickly, putting his hands up in surrender and breathed a sigh of relief when the woman's frown vanished.

"One second he was unconscious and the next he was on his feet. I tried to attack him, but he used some kind of skill that I'd never seen before. He completely shattered my armor and broke several bones with a single strike; then he suddenly appeared next to my cousin, who was standing over thirty feet away and lopped his hands clean off.

"I had a hard time getting to my feet after his first attack and, by the time I did, Sarah had already killed my cousin. I challenged that bastard then, gathering my strength and preparing to take him down for what he'd done…"

He trailed off here and shuddered at the memory of that horrible fight.

"He moved so quickly that I didn't even see the attack coming. I felt a horrible pain in my chest and then I was lying on my back. The last thing I saw before I passed out, were his eyes. The sclera were a solid black and his irises were a deep purple, shot through with silver. I don't know why I picked up on that specific detail," he said with an embarrassed laugh, "it was just so different from his usual colored eyes that, I just latched onto it."

He stopped talking as he saw both Katherine and Arnold staring at him with shocked expressions.

"What?" he asked, wondering if he'd said something wrong.

Katherine was the first to compose herself and flashed him a dazzling smile, that made his mouth go dry and all coherent thoughts vanish in an instant.

"It's nothing, dear boy; just give me a moment to confer with my man over here."

He nodded dumbly as Katherine grabbed Arnold by the arm and pulled him to a corner of the room.

"Did you hear what that boy just said?!" she hissed, all traces of her smile now gone.

Arnold nodded.

He'd heard the legends and knew well what the implications were, if what this boy said was true.

"Did you know about this?!" she hissed again.

Arnold shook his head in the negative.

"All I know is that Lord Simon ordered me to hunt him down after he killed some city guards and fled with his daughter."

"Damn that Simon! Of course, he would be so short sighted!" She tapped a manicured fingernail against her lip for a few moments before making her decision.

"I want that boy alive! I don't care how many men you have to take. Do you understand!"

Arnold swallowed hard, but nodded once again.

"If I may be so bold as to ask, Princess; what exactly do you want him for?"

Katherine smiled then, a brilliant flashing of perfect white teeth.

"I thought that would be quite obvious. I don't have a husband yet and I can't think of anyone more suited to the role than a supermage. My father has been sitting on his throne for over four hundred years and I think it's high time to get rid of him. He's constantly sending us to the front lines, while he cowers back in City One! Then takes all the glory for himself when we succeed. My brothers have grown sick of him as well, but none have dared to oppose him so far. If, however, I had a legendary supermage as my husband, they would gladly back me in overthrowing him."

Her smile widened and she almost vibrated with suppressed glee.

"I was against this pointless war, but this presents the perfect opportunity! No one will think it suspicious if he dies now. This couldn't have worked out better!"

Arnold was completely dumbfounded; and at the same time; terrified for his very life.

He had just overheard the king's daughter planning treason; which meant that he would now be stuck going along with what she said, or she would kill him. He could always try approaching the king with this, but that was too big a risk to take. How the hell did he keep getting himself into these situations?

Katherine's excited expression melted away an instant later and she grabbed him by the collar; yanking him off balance.

"You will go after him. Tonight! I don't want any delays! And if you harm so much as a hair on my future husband's head; I'll tear your manhood off and shove it down your throat. Do I make myself clear?"

Arnold nodded vigorously; and Katherine's smile returned as she released him.

Crazy bitch!

"Great news," she said, turning to face the boy, who was sitting quietly while they'd had their hushed conversation. "You'll be heading out after Morgan tonight. Arnold will fill you in on the details." She gave him a wink, then turned and walked out the room.

The boy's eyes were glued to her shapely backside as she left and only after the door closed behind her, did he look up at Arnold.

"Don't let her fool you, kid," Arnold said with a snort, as he also headed for the door. "She's like a snake; pretty to look at but deadly if you get within striking distance. We'll be leaving in five hours; I'll send someone for your things."

The boy nodded and Arnold opened the door to leave, when he seemed to remember something.

"Oh yeah; forgot to ask your name."

He didn't really care to know this boy's name. The Princess didn't have to say it, but she'd spelled it out clearly enough- this boy was a witness and they didn't need any loose ends.

The boy seemed to perk up at this and grinned at him, the first smile he'd shown since Arnold had walked in.

"The pronunciation is a little tricky; but I'm sure you won't mess it up the way Morgan did."

He hopped out of bed and offered Arnold his hand.

"My name is Grub, and I'm looking forward to working with you."

Hey, this is Aaron; for making it all the way here, you get 5 points of *intelligence*!
If you like GameLit, or LitRPG, check out this cool page. It's a great way to keep up with all the latest news on your favorite genre of books!

LitRPGsociety

Coming Soon

Somerset: The Rules (Book One) June 2019
Rise To Omniscience (Book Three) Summer 2019

Out Now

Supermage: Rise to Omniscience (Book One)
Starbreak: Rise to Omniscience (Book Two)